THE
ASSASSIN
GAME

KIRSTY McKAY

sourcebooks
fire

Published by Sourcebooks Fire, an imprint of Sourcebooks, Inc.
P.O. Box 4410, Naperville, Illinois 60567-4410
(630) 961-3900
Fax: (630) 961-2168
www.sourcebooks.com

Originally published as Killer Game in 2015 in the United Kingdom by Chicken House.

Library of Congress Cataloging-in-Publication Data

Names: McKay, Kirsty.
Title: The assassin game / Kirsty McKay.
Other titles: Killer game
Description: Naperville, Illinois : Sourcebooks Fire, [2016] | Originally
published in the United Kingdom by Chicken House in 2015 under title:
Killer game. | Summary: "At Cate's isolated boarding school, Killer Game
is a tradition. Only a select few are invited to play. They must avoid
being killed by a series of thrilling pranks, and identify the murderer.
But this time, it's different: the game stops feeling fake and starts
getting dangerous and Cate's the next target. Can they find the culprit
... before it's too late?"-- Provided by publisher.
Identifiers: LCCN 2015027625 | (13 : alk. paper)
Subjects: | CYAC: Boarding schools--Fiction. | Schools--Fiction. | Secret
societies--Fiction. | Games--Fiction. | Assassins--Fiction.
Classification: LCC PZ7.M47865748 As 2016 | DDC [Fic]--dc23
LC record available at http://lccn.loc.gov/2015027625

Printed and bound in the United States of America.
VP 10 9 8 7 6 5 4 3 2 1

For Emma Sear;
she's killer, and she's game.

CHAPTER 1

It is about 4:00 a.m. when they come for me. I am already awake, strung out on the fear that they will come and the fear that they won't. When I finally hear the click of the latch on the dormitory door, I have only a second to brace myself before they're on me.

"Do as we say!"

A rasping voice, sudden and violent, in my ear.

I swallow my scream as a hood—a pillowcase?—is shoved over my head. A large hand clamps across my mouth and nose, mashing my lip against my upper teeth, and I taste blood. Weight presses down on my pajamaed chest, and panic rises as I wriggle a little to clear my nostrils to breathe. Silently, I'm lifted from my bed. Efficiently. They've done this before.

They bundle me to the floor and flip me on my stomach, yanking my hands behind my back. My gut lurches with panic. A pinch of plastic, and my hands are trussed so tight that I can feel the blood thudding out a frantic heartbeat back and forth from wrist to wrist.

"One noise from you, Cate, and this is over."

I want to puke. I try to nod, but my neck is twisted at an awkward angle, and that hand is still clamped over my hooded face. But they must understand my compliance, as the hand is removed; I'm forced to my feet and pushed forward, one bare foot stumbling after the other. The urge to pee is extreme, but I have to fight it with everything because, hey, if I wet myself, I'm dead for sure.

We walk; there's the shove of shoulders to either side of me, and the hands are there again, on my arms this time, pulling me to one side then another. Light seeps into the pillowcase from somewhere, but I still can't see anything other than shadows. My feet tell me we have exited the dormitory as the carpet briefly gives way to a strip of bare boards before they find the hall runner and turn left, left toward the short staircase down to the ground floor. The staircase! Will they push me? Will I fall? My fears are unfounded as suddenly my legs are swept up from under me and, with a grunt, someone carries me downstairs.

I know that grunt. He remembered to disguise his voice when he spoke but not the grunt. Does the fact that it's him carrying me make me feel better or worse?

Dark again. The cool September night air hits me; we must have left the building by the side door. And then I'm lowered, surprisingly gently, and I feel cold, damp metal beneath my PJs. A hard rim under my shoulders and knees. A box? Some kind of coffin? Would they go that far? The panic comes back. I'm tilted, and I draw my feet inside to brace myself against the rim. There's a wobble, a crunch of stone, and then a squeak.

OK, a wheelbarrow. The squeak gave it away. I breathe again. I'm being pushed in a wheelbarrow, my bum rubbing in earthworms and soil. This is their idea of funny.

Slowly we travel over the gravel, silently except for that tiny, little squeak every rotation. I'm sure someone was tasked to oil it, but not well enough. They'll get into trouble for that.

There's a slight bump as the terrain gets softer. I sink and wobble again, and then we take off, much faster than before, a wild ride. The squeak becomes a constant whine. I wish I could hold on to the sides, but all I can do is push down on my feet to wedge myself in there as we bump along, my abs burning in a half crunch. I hope the ride will be short. Which way are we heading? North to the woods or east to the causeway? Please, please, not south to the cliff path; surely they wouldn't risk that? I don't have much idea, no sense of direction, but as we jog on, I hear a few muted giggles and pants, even a whisper that is quickly shushed. Three of them with me? Four? One pushing, the others running alongside.

We stop. I strain to hear the sea, but all I can hear is the blood in my ears. And then:

"Woo-woo!" goes the world's least convincing owl.

"Twit-twoo!" No, strike that. The second one is worse.

"Coooo-oo!" The third sounds like a drunken dove, and suddenly the first two seem very realistic.

Muted giggles. We're off again, faster this time, and I hear a rumble to my left, a rumble to my right. More wheelbarrows? Yes, without doubt, and we're racing. I'm not the only one who has been taken, and that's reassuring. The race is almost fun at first—apart from the sheer terror, of course—but it's exhilarating at least. Just when I'm thinking I can no longer hold on, my knees are burning and my feet are turning to ice, I sense my kidnappers are tiring as well, and we slow. There's more panting, unabashed and unconcealed this time. Someone mutters, but I can't hear what's said. Almost there. The fear comes back.

We stop again, this time for good. I'm lowered with a thud, pulled out of the wheelbarrow and on to my cold, bare feet. Blood wells up into my face, and I sway a little. I squeeze my toes, trying to find my balance.

I'm standing on sand. Cool but not damp. And yet, no sound of the waves hitting the rocks...where are we? There's a smell too, but it's not of salty air—at least, no more than this whole island smells of the sea. It's an acrid, oily smell. Something is burning.

I dare to open my eyes, and through the pillowcase, there's light out there. Orange, glowing balls of light, suspended off the ground. Of course. Suddenly, I know exactly where we are.

My hood is whipped off. Shadows slink away into shadow. I squint and try to stop the ground from spinning.

An amphitheater, carved into the side of a hill, and I am onstage. Oil lanterns hang from stands, lighting the scene. There's also the full blood moon—but it only winks at us as blue-gray clouds blow across it, obscuring its light. My kidnappers gone. I turn around to see my fellow captives, blinking and swiveling their heads, all of us nodding dogs, taking it in.

Martin Parish is next to me, bent over, panting and grinning his goofy, gap-toothed grin. He's just stoked to be selected; he doesn't care what they might do to us. Tesha Quinn stands to his right, eyes wide and also swaying on her bare feet, her dark-blond corkscrew curls standing out in shock from her head. She doesn't look at me—trying to hold the panic down—because if she does, she might break. Both kids have tied hands, both in night attire. I thank luck and good judgment that I'm wearing modest pajamas; Martin is shivering in boxers and Tesha's not much better off in underwear and a cami. They're cold and vulnerable. At least I have flannel to hide behind.

Only three of us harvested tonight? The final selection for this year. The Game can begin.

I rub my chin on my shoulder and try to see the shadows moving on the tiered seats, but I can't focus that far yet. Two kids were harvested on Monday, or so it was rumored. Two kids were taken on Tuesday, and then none on Wednesday and Thursday, so we thought that tonight would be big. But only us three?

A figure moves into view above us on the steps of the auditorium. He's wearing a long cloak, which ripples in the night breeze. The hood is pulled low over his face, revealing only a square jaw and a hint of thin lips with a Cupid's bow.

"Fresh meat!"

He raises his face, and he is wearing a black half mask. There was never any doubt it was him. The grunt, the voice in my ear. Alexander Morgan, alpha male of the senior class, and the one who is running this show.

"Welcome to the Game, apprentices." Alex walks down the steps and onto the sand, smiling at us. "Be happy. You are the chosen few."

I allow myself to relax slightly. We have this weird dynamic, Alex and I. He's nice enough to me when he remembers to be—basically because of my family owning this island—but I'm not inner-circle cool, so most of the time he ignores me. Well, apart from that one time we kissed, but few people know about that. It certainly wouldn't improve my popularity here; most of the girls and a handful of the boys go gooey for Alex. He's blond and tall and good-looking in a screwed-up Hitler Youth kind of way, and that's obviously not my type on a typical day. It just wouldn't fit in with my admittedly half-baked idea of who I am. But...for all the smooth breeding and athlete OCD neatness about Alex, there's something feral there too. He's like a wolf: he likes to run, and he likes the smell of fear.

"Tesha!" Alex kisses his fingertips and touches them gently to her lips. "Welcome!"

She jerks her head back and scowls at him, her curls bouncing, Medusa-like. He moves down the line. "Martin, my friend!" He scruffs Martin's spiky, brown hair, and Martin grins up at him like the little boy he is.

And then he walks to me. "Cate." I wait for the touch, but

there is none. "Fully dressed, unlike the rest." He makes it sound rude, his eyes burning through the mask. I hate it that he can switch on that power, like he won something from me just because we kissed that one time. And now it's some horrible in-joke between the two of us. He laughs, walking backward, away from us. I'm glad it's too dark for anyone to see my red face. "All kneel before your Grand Master!"

I glance at Martin, who is already down on the sand. He's so pathetically grateful to be here, he'd kneel before Alex under any circumstances. Tesha is slower, but at least the command annoys her even more, and that seems to give her courage. She catches my eye this time, and we both reluctantly sink to our knees.

"Cower before the Assassins' Guild!" Alex cries. Somewhere, someone hits a button on an MP3 player and music plays, not quite loud enough to let anyone know we're here. It's the Doors, "Riders on the Storm." I suppose this was an edgy choice back in the days of yesteryear when the Game began, but it's simultaneously unnerving and slightly silly, and it makes me feel like I'm in someone's dodgy straight-to-video.

The Assassins' Guild walks out in front of us, all wearing masks. Four are in cloaks like Alex's; they are the Elders, the veterans, the movers and shakers of the Game. Then come the two Journeymen: two boys who have played the Game once before. Finally, the four apprentices who were harvested earlier in the week.

Faced with them all like this, I realize that I'm terrified. I have friends behind those masks—well, two of them—but even so, the weight of What Comes Next is frightening. Marcia, my best friend and an Elder, stands next to Alex, wisps of long, languid hair escaping her hood and blowing across her face in the breeze. A couple days ago, I was moaning to her that I wasn't going to get harvested, and she must have known all along. And then there's Daniel, a skinny Journeyman standing at the back, and my only other real friend at this school. I wish I could read his expression.

I take a breath. This part will be over soon. And after all, isn't this what I've been looking forward to? The Game?

We call it "Killer."

Every autumn term, it begins, for a few short, crazy, wonderful weeks. The Assassins' Guild harvests new members to play, and the rest of the school holds on tight and watches the fallout. We call it Killer, but you might know it by another name— Gotcha, Assassin, Battle Royal. And if you don't? Well, it's the twisted love child of Secret Santa and Wink Murder, but even then you're only halfway there to understanding it all. The Assassins' Guild makes the rules, and they are this:

One Killer is chosen, and he or she has to Kill. Not actually, you understand; this school is tough, but the Game needs some boundaries. The Killer has to think of wacky-but-child-friendly ways to off their victims. Death by rubber snake in the desk during double geography. Death by gassing with a stink bomb in the common room. Death by "suffocation" with a duct-taped duvet in the dorm room. It's funny; it's thrilling and silly-scary.

One by one, the Guild is picked off, and every week the remaining players can take a guess at who the murderer is. If you guess right, you're the glorious victor. If you guess wrong, you're dead.

And nobody wants to be dead, because then it's back to life, back to reality—the reality of school days at Umfraville Hall, Skola Island, Arse-End-Of-Nowhere, Wales.

"Tie them!" Alex shouts, and I'm jolted back into the present. Tie us more? How? I'm about to find out. Masked bods run forward. We're pushed from our knees to our stomachs, and more plastic ties are tightened around our ankles. I brace my feet so I'll have some slack when I relax my muscles, but my assailants know what I'm doing and pull the ties tighter. They hurt like hell.

A long rope is clipped around the plastic tie; I feel a pull. I twist to look behind me. Two masked Guild members are pulling on the rope and it is stretching. It's a bungee cord. The Masks clip the other end into some kind of stake that is protruding from the ground a couple feet away, and I'm tethered like an animal.

Alex claps his hands, and a Mask brings something forward on a velvet cushion. Alex picks the thing up and waggles it at us, and a glint of blade flashes in the light. Two blades? Pruning shears. Bitterness rises in my throat.

"Freedom through the blade," Alex says, walking a few paces away from us and drawing an X in the sand with his foot. He drops the pruning shears on the ground.

Before I have time to consider the implications of this, I feel the hit of freezing water on my back from above. I gasp in shock; someone has tipped a bucket of seawater over me. Martin and Tesha yell beside me as they get their own showers.

"Be cleansed by the spirits of assassins past!" cries Alex. "Wash in the souls of those who have gone before you!"

Another bucket. This one feels almost warm after the shock of the first. But now I'm utterly drenched, dripping hair and freezing face. I gulp to get my breath.

"No!" Tesha cries out.

At first I think she's protesting another wetting, but from my place in the sand, I see someone walk forward holding the pillowcases again.

"Please!" she begs. "I'm claustrophobic. I can't stand it anymore!"

A ripple of laughter goes around.

"Bag her!" someone shouts.

"Bag her! Bag her!" A cluster of Guild members—some, I think, are actually Tesha's best friends—begin a chant.

"Yeah, bag the bitch!" a voice shouts.

"Silence!" Alex is genuinely peeved. Oh dear. A recent initiate has gone too far.

"No need to get overexcited," Alex says, kicking sand expertly into the initiate's masked face. "Tesha"—he shakes his head and the hood waggles a bit, making him look even more ridiculous—"you've persuaded me."

"Boo!" the Guild cry.

"But..." He puts a foot on the center of her back and rolls her a little, back and forth. Sand sticks to her ample curves as she rolls, she looks sugar-coated. "Make no mistake, Tesh. You owe me one."

More laughter. A couple boyish jeers. Yuck.

"I'm freezing, Alex—" Tesha begins.

"Quiet!" he shouts. "What? You expected this to be easy?" He shakes his head again, relishing his power over her. "It cannot be easy."

The cold wetness is making me shake involuntarily, but I'm grateful to Tesha for stopping the pillowcases. And then I see what's coming next, and I wonder why I felt glad a second ago.

"Bring out the Dumper!" Alex cries.

A Mask steps forward, and I recognize him immediately; it's my dear friend, Daniel. He's carrying a bucket, clutching it with those freakishly long, white fingers, holding it at arm's length. I don't think this bucket is full of seawater. Alex points to the place on the sand where he dropped the pruning shears.

Daniel reluctantly walks over to the spot and slops something dark and viscous from the bucket on to the ground, covering the pruning shears.

"All of it," Alex says. Daniel sighs then jerks the bucket downward, slapping its bottom like you would a glass ketchup bottle. But the slop is stubborn. "Use your hands," says Alex, like it's the most obvious thing in the world. Daniel's face hardens, but he puts a hand in anyway and scoops the remainder of the stuff onto the ground, the gloop dripping delicately from his slender digits. The smell has reached me now: cow. This is not going to end well.

"Now," says Alex. "As you know, entry into the Guild is subject to passing a test. You have received the cleansing waters, but an assassin must also be prepared to get his or her hands dirty." Laughter. "You have until sunrise to free yourselves and return to your beds, making sure to clean up this mess so all trace of us is removed. Failure to complete this task in its entirety will render your attempted entry into this Guild unsuccessful." He smiles. "Good luck."

On cue, minions extinguish the oil lamps, and we are plunged into the damp semidarkness. A second later, and they are all gone.

"Alex!" screams Tesha. "Come back!"

"You shouldn't call him Alex," hisses Martin, lying on his back and jerking his feet into the air in an attempt to dislodge the peg tethering him to the ground. "He's the Grand Master."

"Yeah, and doesn't he know it?" Tesha mutters. "Alex!" She clearly feels like she can break rank. There was that rumor about them tussling tongues last term, not long after we did, so maybe she has something on him. Didn't help me much, and it doesn't seem to be helping her either.

Martin has given up on trying to pull up the peg and is now moving away from it in a kind of breakdance body-roll style. He's not your natural athlete, but he gets a gold star for effort.

Tesha looks at him scornfully. "What the hell are you doing, Martin? Ack!" She gives a cry of frustration. "You're so bloody keen it's unnatural!" She turns to me. "What are we supposed to do?"

I shrug. I absolutely know, but I'll give her the bliss of a few more seconds of ignorance.

I wiggle forward on my belly. Sand sticks to me. It's quite tempting to burrow into the sand for warmth, but I have no intention of burying myself so early on in the Game. No, I'm in this for the long haul.

Martin's ahead of me, with the same idea in mind. "The pruning shears," he grunts. "We can cut ourselves free."

"But they're covered in something. What is that crap on the ground?" Tesha calls.

"Crap, on the ground," Martin deadpans. His bungee rope is now taught. He stretches his upper body forward, then flops like a charging walrus, but the bungee pulls him back, tauntingly dragging him in the sand. "Too short!" He strains forward again, groaning, but he can't move any farther.

So this is our test: snake our way over to the crap on the ground, retrieve the pruning shears, cut ourselves free.

I feel the tightness on my ankles too. I inch toward the cow poo, digging toes into the sand to give me a foothold, but I'm still a good body length away. This is impossible.

Behind me, Tesha is getting with the program. She's trying to bring her tied hands under her feet; yes, tied hands in front are much more useful than tied hands behind. Tesha might be fleshy, but she's certainly supple. I try to copy her, but neither of us is successful. I'm not sure I'm willing to break my wrists, even for the Game.

Martin's waggling his tether again, but he can't shift it. He moves to mine. "Help me pull my peg!" he says to both of us.

"First time for everything." Tesha rolls her eyes at me and falls onto her side, knickered bum in the air.

I wiggle over to Martin.

"It's stuck fast," he says, trying to pull it up with his hands behind him. "Dig around the bottom, maybe we can get them out of the ground that way."

"Dig with what?" I answer my own question by sitting on the sand with my back to the peg and scrabbling ineffectually with my cupped hands. Tesha joins me, and we all dig. After a minute, we've made a pathetically shallow hole.

"It's no good." Martin grimaces as he reaches down. "It's attached to some kind of steel ring." He reaches farther. "Set in concrete. I think they have them here to anchor scenery to the stage."

Tesha swears. I don't blame her. I'd be even more miffed if I were in my drawers. An idea hits. "Teamwork." I sigh. "Right idea, just wrong place." I push myself up to my feet and jump toward the cowpat until my bungee is taut. I crouch down and begin to dig a little trench. "OK. Now, Martin, come toward me and pull my rope behind you as much as you can to give me some slack. Tesha, here." I nod to the ground.

She looks at me, not moving. "You scare me, girl."

"Come on!" I say. "We have to do this. We can't be the only initiates to fail the test; it would be so embarrassing. Plus, I'm flippin' freezing."

Tesha jumps over and flops down beside me. "What do I do?"

"Feet in this trench," I show her. "Then stretch out on the ground on your back."

She plants herself on the sand reluctantly. "Now what?"

"Now I climb up you." I lean against the extent of my bungee. "Martin, more slack!"

He hefts my rope and I feel the bungee slacken a little. I kneel and lean forward until I'm lying lengthways on Tesha. She's tall and meaty. A good launching pad.

"Hey!" she shouts from under me. "What the hell?"

Despite her protestations, I squirm up her using her body for traction. We must look like two slugs bumping bellies. I manage to get all the way up her and put my feet against one of her shoulders, pushing myself the rest of the way across the sand to the pile of poo.

"Ow-ee!" Tesha shouts. "You're killing me!"

"I'll swap with you if you like," I say, straining my head over the ominous pat. "In a heartbeat." There's a lump in the middle of the crap. The pruning shears.

"Actually, you're all right." Tesha is looking at the cowpat too. Suddenly she's realizing she has the better deal in all this. I give myself one more push and, hands stuck behind my back, I'm cobra-ing over the pile of stinking mess. Oh God.

"Hurry up!" Martin shouts. "My arms are burning."

"Sometimes you've just got to suck it up," I mutter.

"What did you just say?" he shouts.

"Suck it up." I shudder. And then before I can stop myself, I plunge face-first into the dark-green gloop. I screw my eyes up and push the horrible stuff out of the way with my face, like a kitten with a ball of wool. Except this isn't wool. The smell is horrendous, but the worst part is that it is warm. It actually steams. It covers my mouth, goes up my nostrils, gets in my eyes. I splutter, blowing the stuff off my lips as best I can. I want to scream, but I have to go down again. I nuzzle the plop until I can feel something hard and cool against my cheek. I shove at it, and the handles stand up a little. There's a loop of metal between the handles. I try to hook it with my nose, but my nose is not pointy enough. There's only one thing attached to my head that is. My tongue.

"No!" I splutter, but then I go for it. It's only grass, it's only grass, cows just eat grass and it's only grass and festering bacteria from four stomachs and flies' eggs and heaven knows what else oh help oh help oh help.

I snag the loop. A handle falls toward me, and I bite it, and jackknife the hell out of there. Martin's muscles must give way, or maybe Tesha's shoulder dislocates, but I am catapulted out of hell and scraped along the sand, all the way back to my peg. I spit out the pruning shears at Martin's feet. And spit and spit and spit. And suddenly with a snip my wrists are free, and my ankles too, and I can stagger off to the front row of the amphitheater and throw my guts up, tearing at my mouth with my wet pajama top to try and rid myself of the warm, stinky goo.

Job done.

The Game is afoot.

CHAPTER 2

I have a very long shower the next morning.

Too much of a risk to shower in the dead of night. In the morning, however, I scrub at my body like I'm Little Miss OCD. You can bet that I wash my hair more than once, thanking my stars that it's short and shaggy but wishing it was not the kind of dishwater blond that picks up a hint o' green from being dunked in dung. And yes, I brush my teeth three times, trying to erase the remnants of taste and the memories of texture. Mouthwash, floss, the works. Once done and dressed in my usual outfit of don't-care jeans and oversized checked shirt, I don't think I've entirely shifted the smell. So what? I'll wear it like a badge. I'm extraordinarily happy because I'm in the Game.

New term, new me. On the way to breakfast, I strut, feeling enlightened and shiny with the guilty thrill of being in the Game. I'm walking down the oak-paneled corridor of Main House on my way to breakfast in the dining hall, and

I'm convinced that everyone can see my halo of initiation...
or maybe they just smell me coming. It's as if everyone in the
know is absolutely aware of last night and how it changed me.
Except everyone is not. Only Martin and Tesha truly know
what depths I sank to. As far as the Guild is concerned, one of
us somehow retrieved those pruning shears from the cowpat,
but they don't know which of us, and they don't know how. And
Martin, Tesha, and I have sworn a solemn oath on our appren-
ticed behinds not to tell the details. Honor is everything; they
will not break our bond.

After we cut ourselves free in the early hours, part of the
deal was that we had to clean up and sneak back to school
undetected. This was as important—in some ways, more
so—than the initiation itself. Stealth is everything in the
Game. Although the staff here know about the Game, we have
to be very careful about how much we shove in their faces. They
expect some disruption, and most of the teachers who actually
possess a personality find it quite amusing. It's tradition.

However, the tolerance only extends so far, and it's a sign
of the times that certain methods of Killing have been banned
outright. Laxatives—for a death by "poison"—are out. Bombs
have to be extremely metaphorical. And for anyone in posses-
sion of a firearm more realistic than a fluorescent-yellow water
pistol, it's instant expulsion. We play along. As weird as this
place is, nobody wants to be kicked out. Least of all me.

I've been at Umfraville for three years now, since I was
thirteen, and it has taken me that long to find my feet. For the

first year, I spent most of my time with my stomach in perpetual knots of anxiety. Imagine it: a huge, gargoyley, mental hospital of a school, set on a remote and windswept island, and largely populated by superkids. My parents own the island, but I'm the most normal here by far.

Umfraville Hall is the only thing of significance on the little island of Skola, off the Welsh coast. The school has been here for a hundred years, in one form or another. It was a lunatic asylum until the sixties, and then a visionary by the name of Ezra Pendleton decided to turn it into a "center of excellence" for gifted kids. Now Umfraville educates over a hundred teenagers, luminous with specialness. We have mathematicians, track-and-field athletes, world-class musicians, and master chess players. It's an intense mixture of ego, hormones, and Geekosity In Extremis. Ezra's still here today, old, wheelchair bound, and mad as a bundle of sticks, but he loves the school, sure enough.

Not everyone here is genius level; some just have überwealthy folks. And my story? Like I said, my family owns the island. When I was eight, my great-uncle died and left my parents a little bit of money and a little bit of Wales. If asked, I'm sure my parents would have preferred an island in the Caribbean or maybe the Med, but four hundred acres of moorland in the Irish Sea is what they got. There are some nice beaches here, but the sea is cold and the tides ferocious. We have cows and sheep for neighbors, and that's it. Lonely? You can wave to the Liverpool-Dublin ferry, and when the weather is clear, you can see the nuclear power station on the mainland. When we got rich, my beloved parentals decided to stay in London but moved to a nicer postcode. Due to some kink in the deeds, they couldn't kick Ezra and Umfraville off Skola, so what did they do? They sent their only child to school here.

When I first arrived at Umfraville, I felt like I was drowning. I'm certainly no clever clogs, and my talents are few and modest. This is no humblebrag; it's just the truth. I'm OK at art, and luckily I like my art teacher, Mr. Flynn. He was the first person here I felt I could talk to. Yeah, well done, Cate; befriend a teacher. But after a while, I managed to chisel out precisely two friendships with people my own age: Marcia, who is the school newspaper editor and one of the cloaked Elders from last night. She has an IQ of 156 and no idea what to do with it. She'll probably end up running a tabloid.

And then there's Daniel, again Guild, the "Dumper." Poor, lovely Daniel. Alex gets off on tormenting him, but Daniel rarely complains about much. That's one of the reasons I love him. He plays the violin, wonderfully, but is terminally shy. He finds it almost impossible to hold a conversation with anyone apart from me or Marcia. He was at the Lausanne Conservatory, but he's killing a couple years here because his parents want him to get straight As and a sense of proportion.

I get along with most of the people here now, you know? Many of them are loners anyway. Hothouse kids who never got to learn how not to chuck sand in the playground. Apart from the athletes, of course. They band together. Go team! It's like elves and orcs around here, the geeks and the jocks. And me in the middle. Invisible.

But not today, finally. Today, I am Guild. Today, I am in the Game. Today, I am part of Killer.

As I turn the corner, a lively hubbub emanates from the dining room. It's louder than usual, because it's a Saturday, and the kind of Saturday that only happens around here a handful of times a term. People are excited about escaping to the mainland. There's a causeway to this island, and today the tide is right.

Twice a day a window opens up when it is safe to cross the causeway. On Saturdays we have lessons until midday, and all pupils have to be back on the island by 9 p.m. at the latest. So if the tide is out for a decent chunk of time, a bus is scheduled to take us to the mainland at lunchtime and back again in the evening. This timing only works out about once a month, and sometimes not even that, as there are fairly ridiculous safety margins in place to account for wind and foul weather and the inevitable naughty folks who are late for the return journey. There's nothing much on the mainland—a few shops, a café, a pub that doesn't always check IDs—but at least it's not school.

So yes, the dining hall is humming, and there's the smell of toast, which always makes my mouth water—except on the mornings when I've spent the night apple bobbing in excrement.

As I enter the hall, I see the tables at the far end have been commandeered by the Guild. Most of them see me walk in, and those that don't have soon been elbowed. Alex is center;

he flicks sandy hair out of his eyes with a toss of his head and beckons me over, slowly. As I approach the open spot on the end of the last table, I see Martin and Tesha sitting there, both with a steaming bowl of oatmeal in front of them. My stomach lurches. Oh, I have so exhausted my tolerance for things that steam. But everyone at my table has the same gruel. I scan down the line of faces. I'm last. I sit, and someone places a bowl in front of me. I grit my teeth.

"Dig in!" Alex shouts. Every pair of eyes in the dining hall is on us as I lift the spoon out of the bowl. There's something other than oatmeal on it. I gingerly pick it out of the oats.

A wristband of black, plaited leather, with a neat silver clasp at one end.

I look around me; everyone has the same surprise.

A cheer goes up from the Guild, which prompts some cheering and clapping from the rest of the school, eventually dissolving into laughter and whooping.

"Have a happy death!" someone cries.

"Aaaaargh!" a fake yell sounds out. More laughter.

"All right, all right!" Mr. Flynn—I mentioned, he's my art teacher—drew the short straw and is on dining hall duty today. He's one of the good ones though. He pretends he thinks the Game is ridiculous, but you know that if he was seventeen again, he'd totally be running the gig.

I can't help the smile from spreading over my face. I suck the oatmeal off my band, wipe it down, and clip it around my left wrist. All down the table, kids—apprentices—are doing the same. I marvel at the inky-black of the leather, and the clean silver glistening against the brown of my summer tan. There's plenty of space for it there, because I think I lost my watch last night. That sucks, and I'm not in any particular hurry to retrace my steps and dig around in the sand for it. For now I'm more than happy to replace it with the black band. Game rules state that if I get Killed, the band will be cut off and nailed to the common room bulletin board. Some other members of the Guild have a bloodred knotted thread from last year. Alex has a very faded multicolored ribbon from the year before. Apprentices picked from lower down the school are few and far between; only Alex, my friend Marcia, and another boy called Carl are on to their third Game, but Alex is the only one who's never been Killed, hence he has all the bracelets. I like this year's trinket. There it will stay, hopefully, for the duration of the Game.

I can't eat my oatmeal; I'm too hyped. I get coffee, playing with that thing around my wrist, the outward mark that they like me now, at least enough to be included, enough to be Killed. Around me, nobody is eating the oatmeal. The overexcitement is manifesting in an oaty war, and Mr. Flynn is threatening to lose his cool, which is considerable.

A small, neat book bound in the same shiny black leather as the bands is pushed in front of me. I look up. Marcia is standing behind me, doling out the books to the apprentices.

"Read this; it's the rule book." She's all business. Then she bends down, her long, brown hair nearly dipping into my oatmeal, and whispers, "Come and find me before class. Usual place."

I nod, a little too frantically.

"We have plans for later this afternoon," she says.

"Wait a minute," I say. "Aren't you going on the bus to the mainland?"

She shakes her head. "None of us are. Too good an opportunity to get everyone together here."

There's a crash to my right; a yellowed skull has been slammed down on the table. Alex and the rest of the Guild leave, in a flurry of laughter, toast crumbs, and clattering plates.

"Quietly!" booms Mr. Flynn. "And don't think you're too good to clean up after yourselves!"

"We have people to do that for us, Mr. Flynn, you know that!" Alex shouts back, and there's more laughter.

Mr. Flynn shoots him a look, but then the Elders and the Journeymen have gone and it's too late for a retort. We apprentices are left alone at our table, along with our horrific new friend, the skull.

"Here it is!" Martin cries, holding up the black book, then remembering the rest of the school around him, he leans in and whispers dramatically, reading from the book. "It says here, a skull means a Summoning is called. All Guild members are required to meet for the Summoning in the Place Most Holy."

Tesha picks up the skull with her fingertips and puckers her full lips. "Mmm, date night. Where and when?" she asks the skull.

"Here!" Whitney, one of the other girls in my year, plucks a rolled up piece of paper from one of the skull's eye sockets. She turns the paper around to us with a flourish. There's a number four on it in black ink.

"4:00 p.m.?" I guess.

Whitney blinks her big baby blues at me from underneath an artfully ragged fringe of black hair. She has a brother in a rock band and a not-so-secret tattoo, and she thinks she's hella edgy. "You're going to go far with that detective work, Cate."

"The first Summoning," thrills Martin. "The Killer will be selected! I cannot wait."

"Where's the Place Most Holy?" I say. "The amphitheater?"

"Way too public," says Whitney. "And during the day it's overrun by the drama crowd, shouting or whatever they do."

"Hey, there's a map!" It's Emily, a long-limbed, sporty girl who was harvested first, earlier this week. She's found something at the back of the black book. A very basic map of Skola is inked on the inside cover. "PMH, it says." She taps a short, teal fingernail. "Hazarding a guess that's Place Most Holy. Here on West Beach."

"The beach?" Tesha says. "Brrrr!"

"No, the caves." Martin's eyes gleam, pupils dark and wide with pleasure.

"Really?" I say. "OK…"

"Dangerous," says Tesha. "But I guess that's what we signed up for."

The bell rings for the end of breakfast. We pocket our books and clean up the Guild's mess, as Alex predicted. I glance at the clock on the wall—twenty minutes before lessons start, joy of joys. But just enough time.

I duck out into the corridor and hurry toward the side door, crossing the courtyard of the school's Main House at pace. Then it's a quick sprint down by the side of the art studios to the small prefab building that houses the Loathsome Toad— the school's newspaper. There's a cluster of pine trees to the rear and a small wooden shed. I walk around to the back, and there, on a big, flat boulder looking out to sea is Marcia. She's smoking a cigarette.

"You were the lucky one last night, then?" She doesn't bother turning around, just runs a hand through her heavy, brown hair. She has the longest hair, and it's utterly gorgeous, a thick sheet hanging down her back.

"I was?" I perch beside her on the rock, the smoke piercing my nostrils and making my eyes water. She proffers the cigarette in my direction, and I shake my head as I invariably do. She looks at me, her down-turned hazel eyes smiling, an amused dimple twitching in her olive cheek.

"You got to go face down in the doo-doo."

I huff. "Martin and Tesha swore they wouldn't tell!"

"Relax," Marcia says. "They didn't say a word."

I frown at her. "So how—"

"Guild knows everything, darling," she purrs, her voice rich and low, with only the slightest hint of her Spanish homeland. "Soon as you accept that, the happier you'll be, young apprentice." She winks one heavy-lidded eye, trying not to smile. "But what a trial!" She takes my hand and squeezes it. "You must forgive us. It was very tough."

I clench my jaw, remembering the taste. "It was crappy, Marcia."

She nods, serious. We look at each other. We scream. She hugs me.

"I'm in!" I yell, rocking her from side to side. Her long hair covers my face, smelling sweet and spicy.

"Of course you are!" she says, giggling. "My lovely, we are going to have a ball!"

We tip and roll off the rock, screaming some more, then picking ourselves up, still laughing.

"Oh!" I fling my head back to the sky, letting the relief run through my body. "I really didn't believe it was going to happen. I am so stoked!" I can be truthful with Marcia. She's probably the only one. With everyone else there's an element of cool that has to be maintained. I beam at her. "And there's a Summoning this afternoon! The Killer will be selected, right?" I delve for the book and flash it at her. "Is this your work?" I ask.

She tilts her head. "Some of it. Rules don't change that much year to year, but you've got to write them down in a new and exciting way. And sometimes there are little twists."

"Hmm." I flick through the book. "I bet there are. Nice font, by the way."

She laughs. "Thanks, sweetie. Thriller was getting so predictable, come on..." Her mouth forms a pretty pout.

"So, the Summoning is in the caves?" I shake my head in wonder. "That's where you've been hanging out every autumn term?"

"No." She stubs out the cigarette and flicks it to the grass, exhaling a dragon blow of smoke from her red lips. "This is new for us too. The oldies always used to meet there, back in the beginning, but then Ezra declared it out of bounds."

I nod. "Because it's too dangerous? Because of the tides?"

"Tides and tunnels and sinking sand." She shrugs. "Plus they used to drink and play dumb games."

"Oh, I see," I say, smiling. "And there'll be absolutely none of that with us."

She raises an eyebrow. "It's a place we won't be discovered, won't be disturbed. That's the main thing." She frowns at me. "Speaking about fun and games, have you had a chance to talk to Daniel yet? Properly."

Instantly my excitement is dulled.

"No."

Marcia sighs. "Did you see him over summer break?"

I say nothing.

"Message him?" She rolls her eyes. "Anything at all?"

"Don't start!" I groan at her. "He hasn't talked to me either. It takes two to tango."

"Hmm. I don't think that's what you two were doing at the pool last term..." She tuts at me.

"It was just a stupid kiss!"

"Maybe." Marcia shrugs. "But it's up to you to tell him you're not interested."

"Why?" I moan.

She looks at me closely. "Because he is." She puts a hand on my arm. "Interested. In you. Like that." I look down, embarrassed, but she goes on. "You owe him the talk at least. He's a good friend, Cate. And let's face it, you don't have that many."

"Thanks!" I snap. But I can't exactly argue. She's right on both counts.

She gets up. "Come on, we're going to be late." She grabs her huge tote bag. "Ah! I cannot wait for you to see the cave. It looks so spooky! Spooky!" She elongates the Os as she swings the bag over her shoulder and heads up the path back to relative civilization again. "See you later."

"Any tips?" I shout after her.

She turns around, frowns. "For Daniel?"

"No!" I shake my head. "For the Game."

She laughs and sets off again. "Don't get Killed!"

I stay on the rock. "But what if it turns out I get to be the Killer, Marcia? Ever think what would happen then?"

This stops her sure enough. She turns around and blinks at me, face suddenly serious. "Then I would be afraid. Very afraid." She does a little salute, laughs, and then turns, her hair swaying after her.

"You and me both," I mutter.

CHAPTER 3

Big things on my mind and none of them are Daniel.

It's not like I don't feel for Daniel. I know what it's like to lust and lose someone; it sucks. I had that scene with Alex. Well, same but different. With Alex, we had that one make-out sesh, and then he expected me to come back for more, and remarkably, I didn't. I wanted to, I'll admit it, but he's messy with exes and way more in love with himself than with anyone else. He's also Popular, Hot, and A Great Kisser, but I just knew I shouldn't go there, not again.

To my terrified delight, Alex actually chased me a little afterward, which was a first for him, as far as I know. He turned the charm on again, and guess what: I didn't bite. He tried to act casual, but I think it rocked his world that I said no. Not something he's used to hearing.

And me? I was shaken up by the whole thing so much I ended up kissing one of my best friends on the rebound. Daniel.

Ever accommodating. Now I'm terrified he might think we're something other than friends. Since we've been back at school, Daniel and I have only said hi, smiled, done the pleasantries. I hope he doesn't expect that we'll soon be whispering sweet nothings.

We won't. I like him as a friend, but I don't really fancy him. He's not bad to look at in a wiry, hipster kind of way. Scruffed-up hair, chocolate eyes. What's more, he's funny, he's clever and quixotic, and he keeps my brain ticking over. On the flipside, he's just too intense, and let's face it, he has issues.

If I was a social pariah when I was first at Umfraville, Daniel was the bug on my boot. Actually, he was probably the bug in the field in another county, he was so absent. It's your classic story of musical genius, I suppose. Crazy parents, prodigious kiddo, hours locked away raking a bow over strings. Zero socialization. School happened, and bullying came with it. His parents weren't rich and he went to some inner-city place with hundreds of kids. He was picked on, beaten up, humiliated, the full works. He says music got him through, and it certainly got him out. He won a scholarship to a private school, but the bullying didn't go away; his tormentors just had posher accents this time. I suppose some people are always victims. The way he tells it, this stuff follows him around. The truth is, when he was at the Lausanne, he had a mini-breakdown, and one of his teachers gave his parents a good talking-to. They pulled him out and sent him to Umfraville, in the hope it would give him some normal. Yeah, well.

He'd been here a term or two and Marcia interviewed him for the Loathsome Toad. The two struck up a friendship. She likes collecting loners and losers; she collected me, after all. And through her, Daniel and I became friends. Last term at the summer party, with end-of-term recklessness and the ache of rejecting Alex, Daniel and I became more.

Anyway…Marcia flits between different social groups, and last year, she dragged Daniel into the Game. I was sore at the time, because she didn't get me in too. But she said they'd only give her one choice of new member, and it had to be Daniel, because he needed it more. Now I'm in the Game, we'll all be in each other's pockets whether I like it or not.

Oh, hell. I have to speak to him. Soon.

But today, there is only the Game.

It is usually the law of the universe that when you have something to look forward to, time moves abominably slowly. It's always tough having school on a Saturday; it seems to go against the natural order of things. Saturday mornings should be for kicking back with several bowls of cereal and crappy kids' TV, lazily texting your mates to sort out the wheres and whens for meeting later in the day. But for the last three years here at Umfraville, I haven't been able to have the lie-in. I haven't been able to have the texting either, but I'll get to that later.

I can't really complain too much. Last year I had math and double French on a Saturday, which licked the sweat off a dead man, but this year I have it cushy: triple art. I love art; I get lost in it. Three hours always rushes by. Full immersion. There'll be no thinking about Danielgate or how my parents haven't called or wondering if I'll eat a proper tea tonight or sacrifice it for a guilty chocolate bar and a flatter stomach. With art, I just exist in the work, and it feels good.

And my art crew is pretty easygoing. Sure, we have some full-on prodigies here—like, kids who have exhibited in London and New York, and not just on their parents' fridges—but they're cool. Loony but chill. And Mr. Flynn is our teacher, which is most wonderful.

OK, I'm going to just preempt the Mr. Flynn thing with you, because I know what you're probably thinking. Rest easy, folks. Before you go having those thoughts that something inappropriate is going on in my head about Mr. Flynn—or, yuck, something is going on in his head about me—don't even. We have a strictly platonic relationship. Granted, it's a little more than student-teacher, and we're both fine with that. I think Ezra and some of the other staff might have something to say about it, and I know my parents would freak if they knew that we're friends, because adults have filthy minds about these things. Actually, kids do too. My friends have given me grief about it, it's true. Marcia teases me more than anything. Daniel is more hard-line, but I think that's because he's jealous. Face it, I'm too boring to be major news within the general populace. And Mr. Flynn would back off wholesale if he thought we were seriously being gossiped about.

So, this is it: we hang out with each other sometimes. As I said before, he was the first person I felt any kind of connection with here, the only person who talked to me like I was someone. It started with me stopping by the studio to work in my spare time, but then there was nothing unusual with that. Most of the kids who are serious about art practically live there. But then I was working on a project with driftwood, and so Mr. Flynn would take me to where the best stuff washes up and help me lug it back from the beach to the studio in his bucket-of-bolts car. We talked about art and music and movies and London. We found out that we both laugh at the same things and are randomly freaked out by pomegranates. But mostly I bonded with him because he listened to my nonsense and insecure babble and because he kind of got me in a way that nobody here does. Oh, I know it sounds utterly boyfriend/girlfriend-y, and as if I have some loser-type of crush on him, so you'll just have to trust me. He's old anyway. Eighties kid. Thirty-five or forty, I don't know. Yes, he's fit. But in that way your mum would like. When I started being friends with Marcia and Daniel, Flynny and I kind of dialed it down, but he's still my favorite teacher, no doubt.

According to the clock, I get to the lesson five minutes late, which is skillful, considering I was loitering with Marcia just down the path from the studio. Mr. Flynn is in full flow when I enter, outlining the things we'll be covering in the upcoming term. He has an air of agitation about him. He arrived back to school a week late this term for reasons unknown. The rumors were varied—a split with his girlfriend, the death of a parent, or most juicily, an arrest. The kids are nothing if not imaginative here. I'll get the truth from him at some point probably.

He doesn't comment on my tardiness to class as I slip into my place in the studio and quietly begin unpacking my stuff. I'm glad to be home. And this is home.

The next three hours fly by, and when the bell for the end of school sounds, I'm floating so high above myself that it's a real effort to come back down to earth. But then I do, and I get that lovely excited feeling of having something even better to look forward to. The Summoning! As I gather up my belongings and glance out of the window for Marcia, Mr. Flynn walks by my table. He nods to the Guild's band on my wrist.

"You're involved with those shenanigans this term."

I smile pleasantly as kids file out past us. "Do I detect a hint of jealousy?" I say, sotto voce.

He eyes me, face set. "Would I jump at the chance to be in your shoes? Er, no, Cate, I would not. Whatever devilry unfolds over the next few weeks is sure to be nothing but hard work for everyone else." Then something in him relaxes a little. "But I hope you enjoy it."

I fling my remaining things into my bag and stand up. Much as I like the chat, I have places to be. Everyone else has left by now, mostly to catch the bus back to the mainland.

Mr. Flynn puts a hand on my shoulder. My stomach jumps and I look at him, surprised. Physical contact between us is unprecedented, probably because he knows how it might seem to others.

"Just be careful, OK?" His eyes are gray, cool. "They throw some seriously stupid stunts sometimes. Don't get overinvolved."

Ha, if only you knew what I was doing last night.

He removes the hand. "All I'm saying is, don't lose focus. It's an important couple of years for you, and you need to channel your energy." The cool grays dart around the studio. "This is where you belong. We're going to get you into art school, aren't we?"

I nod, smile, but inside, my heart is flipping. Blimey. How about putting the pressure on first day you're back, Flynny? I've got two full years before I have to quit this joint and figure out what I'm actually going to do with my actual life. Unlike most people here, I don't have my every move planned out for me.

"Sure." I nod, tight-lipped, and make a run for the door. I glance back and see him still watching me. Something's off. Maybe he was late back because of some hideous trauma during summer break? I'd kind of thought it was just a music festival.

As I jog past the Main House courtyard, I see crowds boarding the two buses bound for the mainland.

I head toward the clock tower quad, which comprises the library building and the upperclassmen common room. Just off the common room there's also a long hallway lined with doors leading to the much-envied "study rooms." Major upperclassmen perk. I'm so stoked to finally have a study. It doesn't look like much—a basic, teeny-tiny office shared by two students. But my study is central to my life here at Umfraville, it's where I work, but it's also my bolt-hole and a place to hang away from the masses.

A few people are still milling about, but the small study I

share with Marcia is empty. I dump my art stuff on my desk and take a glance at my laptop to see if I have any new IMs on the Umfraville intranet.

Yes, intranet. Umfraville is weird and trying in many ways because it's on an island and it's an island that we only get off once every few weeks. What's even worse, however, is that we are cut off from the real world in a much more significant way. We have no phones, no Internet.

I know. Can you imagine teenage life without them?

I'm exaggerating slightly. There is phone reception here—patchy, in the north of the island, almost two miles away from the school buildings—but use of mobiles is strictly forbidden anywhere. We have to hand our phones in when we get here, and we're only allowed them back for the rare Saturday exeats off-island. There is a coin pay phone in the dorms and one more in a cold porch off the common room.

Of course, we have computers…and laptops, tablets, e-readers. It's not the Middle Ages here, and with the kind of special kids we have, it's not like you can deny people access to the World Wide Web. However, Ezra is completely against ninety-five percent of the Internet. His view is that Umfraville is an academy of excellence, and his prodigies have no business being distracted by the junkyard of the web. We have a school intranet, set up and policed by the technology teacher, Ms. Lasillo. Through this we have instant messaging, the Loathsome Toad newspaper site, and access to timetables and shared files. And once a day during evening study time, you can get online to the rest of the world for a whole sixty minutes—send emails home and visit approved (read: educational) sites. But no social networking, no gossip pages. It would probably be easier to find information on how to build a homemade bomb than watch a movie trailer or look at shoes. Of course, if there's something that you particularly want to peruse that is behind the firewall, you can make your case to Ezra and maybe he'll let you have a peep. Supervised, usually. Because Ezra knows that once there's a chink in the armor, a leak in the dam, before we know it, the whole world will come crashing down on our shoulders. And what are we, here, if not protected from the world?

Of course, one does not run a school full of geeks and freaks and expect that someone won't try a hack or two. Oh yes, there have been many. But Ms. Lasillo is extremely good at her job and takes a personal pride in staying two steps ahead of her pupils. According to what Marcia picks up (or what I pry out of Mr. Flynn), most of the time she's successful, and when she's not, it's mainly because she wants to see just where the hacker will go. She tracks them because that's all useful information to make the security tighter and, crucially, knowing what makes that kid tick.

Yeuch. I think it's all rather creepy, and even if I were clever enough to do it, I'm happy to stay put in my cage. The drug of aimless surfing is a hard habit to break, but you certainly have a lot of time on your hands for worthwhile stuff.

No messages for me. I'll wait until this evening and see if either of the parentals has fired off an email to me. I doubt it.

What with Art Coma and the prospect of the Summoning, I'm too buzzed to be hungry for lunch. But I'll show my face. Pushing some pasta around a plate is one way to kill time before I have to head down to the caves. I shut the door to my study and head back toward Main House.

The sun is out, but there's a chill in the air, and the smell of salt hangs heavy. I breathe it in deeply. I ease earphones in and crank up the volume. This feels great. So very great to wander around this place and actually have something happening.

The buses depart just as I pass through the courtyard, and there's not another soul around. But I know my fellow assassins are here—somewhere. I watch the last bus disappear down the road that leads to the causeway. A bubble of excitement fizzes up inside me, and I quiver with nerves and delicious anticipation. I turn and head for the Main House—

—and walk into someone standing directly behind me.

He yells; I yell, partly from shock, partly with embarrassment. I drop my bag and actually fall forward on to my hands on the gravel, bum in the air, earphones popping out.

I crouch, brush the grit off my palms, scrabble to collect my stuff.

A hand appears. I look up, and see a stranger's face staring at me.

"Cate." The face smiles. "Bet you thought you'd never see me again."

CHAPTER 4

I stare at the face.

Familiar and strange at the same time; I like this face. It's slim but not gaunt, just too long to be cutesy, with high cheekbones and a straight nose that has a boyish tilt at the end. The skin is a warm brown and hair a glossy almost black, hacked short at the sides and back, but with longer waves on top that move slightly as the boy laughs at me softly.

"Hello." He speaks again. That mouth...full lips are stretched across white teeth in a friendly, open smile. But it's his eyes that are unmistakable: greeny hazel with flecks of gold; they dance at me, delighted.

"You remember me, don't you?" His pale eyes—so startling against his brown skin—twinkle with barely disguised amusement.

I smile back shyly before I really know what my face is doing, but inside I'm frowning, confused. Looking at him is like looking at an old photograph that has warped in the sun or a puzzle that I've completed…but still can't quite make out the picture. Familiar and yet strange.

Oh God. The picture refocuses, the pieces of the puzzle finally make sense.

Bet I thought I'd never see him again?

That's an understatement.

The shock subsides, and as it does, a different emotion seeps in, something uncomfortable, something I can't quite identify.

"Vaughan?" His name comes out as a gasp; it almost feels forbidden. I haven't said that name in such a long time.

"Phew." He sighs, relieved. Then the soft laugh again. "That could have been extremely awkward." His outstretched hand reaches lower, toward me. "Help you up?"

Before I can think better of it, I'm grasping the hand with the smooth, brown skin and letting it pull me to my feet. The hand is so much bigger, so much stronger than I remember. I stand in front of him, uncomfortably close. He is taller—well, he would be, he's not a little kid anymore, but he's seriously tall—and the face, the face is still weirding me out. I can't think why, and then I realize it's because there is a shadow of stubble. Oh fudge. I'm not sure I can process this. How long has it been? Seven, eight years?

"You were a skinny eight-year-old, the last time I saw you," he says, reading my mind. He looks me up and down. "There have been some changes…"

It doesn't sound creepy, just pure statement of fact, but that doesn't stop me from being doused in hotness, not knowing how to respond.

"And with you too," I say, and it almost sounds like an accusation.

"We've both changed for the better." He leans forward, conspiratorially. "Hormones, eh?"

I concentrate really hard on not dying from embarrassment. It's partly that voice he has now: deep and earthy. I remember his preteen whiny tone that was always telling me he knew better or laying out the craziest plots and plans, and now the voice is...it's a man's voice. It's...nice. But it sure as bananas freaks me out.

"I suppose so." I get it together, trying to shake off the awkward. It has started to rain—that fine, unthreatening drizzle that has the power to soak if you underestimate it. "So, um, Vaughan...what—what on earth are you doing here?"

"Aha!" he booms overly loud, and I find myself looking from left to right to see if anyone's around to witness this. "That's the million-dollar question, isn't it?" He points to the woods. "Still like climbing trees?"

"What?" I glance behind me, at the woods up the path beyond the courtyard. "Those ones?" I say stupidly, like it makes a difference and I'm picky about which trees I scale.

"Hmm." He looks me up and down again. I really wish he'd stop doing that. "I'm not so sure you can climb anymore. Let's see. Race you!" And then he takes off, full speed, toward the woods.

What? I look around again, for a second feeling very silly and worrying that someone is watching us—Alex? Daniel? And then, ridiculously, my feet are stirring up the gravel, and I'm pounding the ground chasing him, trying to catch up, wanting to beat him just like I did when we were eight. Only this time it doesn't look like I'm going to. He reaches the grass before me. It used to be I was the faster one. It used to be him following me, at least when it came to physical stuff, but like he said, it looks like we've changed. I go flat-out, I really try, and it feels better to be moving—legs pump, mind ceases to spin, banishing that uncomfortable feeling that I can't put my finger on, and I cannot shake. He's almost at the woods, this random visitor from my past, this complication I didn't need, back in my life… and I'm chasing him.

He darts off path, dodging around the trees like he knows where he's going, like he's come this way before. Still he's faster, and after a minute I guess where he's headed. He slows down as he reaches the big oak and jumps at it like a mountain goat, using his long arms to pull himself up on the pieces of half plank that still stick out of the thick trunk at intervals. Four, five yards up into the tree there are branches, sturdy and easily climbed. As I reach the bottom of the tree, Vaughan has eased himself onto the dilapidated tree house in the oak's boughs above.

I follow. I try to make it look like I'm climbing easily, but the branches are slick with rain, which slows me down. When I reach the broken-down tree house, I try not to puff and pant or give away that I don't love the height up here, no longer the fearless eight-year-old. This used to be a meeting place for the Guild, many moons ago, but now only the floor is solid; the walls are mainly gone and only a small section of roof remains. Vaughan is not looking at me anyway, stretched out on his back on the planks in the middle of the floor, one knee bent, chest heaving.

I sit down, as far away as I can get from him, my legs dangling over the edge like I don't care, which I profoundly do. I look down; we're pretty high up. It's a little creaky up here, but at least we're sheltered from the drizzle.

"A 'pleased to see you' would have been nice." Vaughan's voice floats toward me.

"What?" We're swaying gently, but it looks like the ground below is moving.

"You know, after all of this time," he says fake casually. "A 'how have you been?' I didn't expect a hug—we're practically adults, after all. It would be awkward—but I did expect a more enthusiastic welcome."

Now the adrenaline of the chase is dissipating, his words bring back the feeling I've been trying to suppress. The feeling comes back with a thud, a kick in the stomach, and this time I know exactly what it is.

Guilt.

"It's fine, you know, Cate," Vaughan continues. "It's not like I'm expecting you to apologize for abandoning me."

And there it is. The reason why this is not the wonderful reunion of childhood best friends. Guilt turns to anger, so strong and sudden it shocks me. This is not fair, just not fair of him. I swivel around and look at him, still lying there, gazing up into space.

"What did you say?"

"An apology is not needed." Vaughan sits up and gives me an almost sympathetic half smile, as if I've accidentally spilled his cup of tea. "Although an explanation of some variety at some point would be appreciated. But all in your own time."

I breathe heavily, looking down at the rough planks and spreading my hands over them, trying to push the anger down. And the guilt too. The guilt is the tricky part. Everything always stems from the guilt.

"Or let's do it now. Get the hard-core emotional stuff out of the way." He pauses. "You can just give me the bullet points, if you'd rather."

I laugh, a single, strangled burst that's gone instantly. Deep breath. OK, let's try this again.

"Vaughan, I was a kid. I never abandoned—" I can't quite say it. "Look, this is so weird! Why are you here? You still haven't answered my question. What the hell are you doing here on Skola? Did you come to find me?"

There's a pause. He's thinking about it.

"I am enrolled as a student here, of course." He gets up, tests a wall plank with his boot, reaches up to tag a branch above us, the platform shaking as he lands. "Well, I won't exactly be in all of your classes, as I finished with all the normal exams some time ago—but I will be studying here for the time being.

Cambridge said grow up and come back in a year." He jumps for a higher branch.

"Cambridge? As in Cambridge University?" I stare at him. "Studying what?"

He shakes his head. "Not a degree, been there done that. I'm doing research now. But Cambridge wanted me to have...a little break. Hey-ho. I might tell them toodle-oo and take myself off to do my PhD at the AI lab at MIT. See how they like that."

"PhD, AI, MIT?" I shake my head. "Is any of what you just said English?"

He chuckles. "I do computer science, Cate. I'm researching cognitive architecture, particularly looking at hybrid systems—"

"Sounds great." I cut him off. "Truthfully, you lost me at 'computer.' And you still haven't told me why you're at Umfraville."

He chuckles. My head is whirling, and he just sits there, chuckling to himself. Damn, he's annoying. Damn, he's good-looking too. There's something about him—somehow it all works together, that face and those eyes, and that stupid mop of hair. Vaughan's like an advertisement for something wholesome and happy. Not how I remember him at all.

The last time I saw Vaughan, he was crying. The removal van full of our modest possessions was in the driveway of our semidetached home, and my mother was making a big show of locking the front door for the final time.

"Good luck and good riddance!" I remember her saying.

Well, I don't really know what she said for sure, because, come on, I was eight, but I do remember the sentiment behind it. The curtains were a-twitching; they'd all heard the rumors about us coming into money. But at 4 Burnfield Avenue, there was a face at the window. A boy's wan face. Hands pressed to the glass. Streaks of tears.

I was in my father's car. The first thing he did when he got the money was buy this hideous red sports car and drive it up and down our old neighborhood with the windows rolled down. What an idiot. He wouldn't do that nowadays, so I suppose the money has finally bought him a little class. Anyway, this car—there wasn't even a proper-sized backseat, so I was kind of hanging out of the window.

"I'll see you soon!" I waved to Vaughan. I do remember saying those words because I never forget telling a lie. I knew then he was out of my life. My mother had made it abundantly clear that our lives—and our friends—were going to be very different now we had money. Vaughan had a Jamaican mother and an Irish dad, so in my mother's eyes, that was a perfect recipe for lazy and stupid. Now I have a sudden urge to call her and tell her about the Cambridge stuff. That would blow her racist mind.

Vaughan and I were best friends, brother and sister from the time we were bashing each other over the head with blocks at playgroup. We cut teeth together, went to school together, built dens in the back garden, and played practical jokes on the neighbors. It was like Halloween all year round. Vaughan was clever, scarily so. He designed the pulley system to lower the ghost from the big sycamore tree on unsuspecting passersby; I shinned up said sycamore to nail the thing into the branch. Whatever it was, Vaughan invented; I instigated. He set 'em up; I knocked 'em down.

But then my family inherited the money, and I left.

That day in the car, I cried so hard that my father was worried about his leather seats. I meant to keep in touch, meant to have Vaughan around for playdates at the new, palatial house in the posh end of town. But I was eight. Without my mother on my side, I had no way of keeping in contact.

Vaughan tried. He wrote; he called. The first time my mother cut the phone conversation short, I threw a tantrum. But pretty quickly there were lots of new things filling up my life—new toys, new school, riding, and ballet. Basically all the stuff you think you're missing as a kid, and then you get it and it's wonderful for a few weeks, and then it becomes normal and boring and you're already ruined.

I missed Vaughan madly at first, furiously, with night terrors and hives and just a whole lot of sadness. That gradually diminished into a dull sense of feeling like I'd left my favorite old teddy behind somewhere or forgotten to put on an item of clothing. Then I got used to it, which was worse.

And now here he is before me in a tree house, jumping around like a confusingly attractive dork. How does he fit into my life now? With my friends, such as they are? Why exactly did he come here? I sense I'm not going to get the answers now.

But I have to say something.

"It's nice to see you." It's woefully inadequate and not entirely true. But he stops jumping and beams at me.

"Thank you. I've been looking forward to seeing you. So much." The smile looks relieved and genuine, but I'm not going to assume he's let me off the hook yet; the old Vaughan wouldn't.

"You just got here on the bus?" I say.

"Yup." He grins. "Trunk was sent ahead. I was supposed to be here last week at the start of the term, but Dad took me on a field trip to Honduras and we got lost in the jungle."

Oh yeah. His dad did these crazy no-budget trips to the back end of nowhere, so there probably is some truth in that.

"Well, I'm sure you'll settle in quickly," I totally lie. I glance at the place on my wrist where my watch should be, then remember it is lost, and feel in my pocket for my phone, but remember I'm at school. Whatever. It's time to get a move on if I'm not going to totally miss putting in an appearance at lunch. "Everyone's pretty friendly," I lie once more. "Anyway, I should be heading back to the Main House." I shuffle to the edge of the tree house and try not to look too awkward and careful as I make my descent. At the bottom, I cheat a glance up; he's sitting where I was, swinging his legs and staring up at the leaves, and it doesn't look like he's planning on following me. It feels odd to just leave him there, but he found his way to this tree, so he'll find his way back. I start back on the path through the woods. Shadows are playing on the ground, and the wind is beginning to whip up some of the first leaves of autumn. I need to get a coat on.

"See you later," Vaughan finally calls after me. "I'm not too late to play the Game, I hope?"

I stop in my tracks and stare back at him.

"You know, Killer." He throws himself down the tree at breakneck speed and runs up the path toward me, smiling. "Not too late to join the Guild, I assume."

"You assume wrong." My stomach is in my mouth. "How do you know about it anyway? You've just got here."

He jogs right past me.

"How do you know about the Game, Vaughan?" I repeat, but annoyingly, he doesn't slow down, not even looking back at me. "Well, you can't just randomly join in," I shout after him, hurrying myself up to try to catch up with him, sounding more panicked than I mean to. "It doesn't work like that."

He stops now, finally, turning back to look at me. "How does it work, Cate?" The wind gusts, whirling orange leaves down around us as I catch up with him.

"It's secret." Wow, that sounds stupid. But it's all I can come up with. It's almost like I don't trust myself to speak.

"Hmm, let me guess." Vaughan rubs his stubbly chin. "You get chosen? Dragged from your beds at night? There's some kind of unpleasant test you have to pass before you are taken into the fold. Kind of...smelly?" He holds his hands out. "How close am I?"

"How on earth do you know about all of this?" My voice is shaking.

He walks around me, circling slowly. "And this afternoon

there's a meeting." He smiles, his voice low and velvety. "Because you're itching to get away. You want to reapply your smudged mascara and don your sexiest ninja outfit before meeting your fellow assassins. Am I right, Catey-Cate?"

I push past him, feeling ridiculed and ridiculous, sure he'll follow, sure I'll never be able to shake him, and with a gnawing feeling that he'll mess up everything for me now that he's here. I break into a run, and I hear him laugh. Once I've got a little distance I look over my shoulder and see him standing there, the orange-and-yellow leaves falling all around him, tall and handsome like he's in some awful sweater catalog. I run on, glance back another time, and he's gone.

It's almost as if I imagined him.

CHAPTER 5

I'm running down the cliff path, and it's raining, which is a really difficult combination. The path is chalky here, tufts of thick-knit grass holding the earth together. One slip or twist of the ankle and I could be tumbling to my death on the beaten rocks below. I'm irritated to death that I'm late—I had all the time in the world to get down here, but somehow after lunch, I lost an hour or more pacing up and down in my dorm and fretting about Vaughan. Why is he here? How does he know about the Game? Why do I even care? I glance behind me, absolutely expecting him to suddenly pop up behind a gorse bush, having followed me. I have no idea how I'm going to keep him away from the Game. I have no idea how I'm going to keep him away period.

But that's a headache for another time, and I won't let him spoil this for me. I've been looking forward to it for too long to let that happen.

The path is exposed at first, but as it winds down the cliff, the gorse and general fuzzy beach bushes get taller and the path twistier, and I can't tell who might be following me or who might be around the corner. I've been this way before a handful of times, but it's not exactly a commonly walked trail. There's nothing much down here apart from seabirds, just a thin strip of sand and shale–scattered beach, a long promontory of rock sticking out into the ocean, and some caves. All forbidden. This is a reckless move on the Guild's part, because if the school discovered where we were operating out of, they'd come down on us like a ton of bricks. But I know the reasoning behind the choice: secrecy. For a while, the Guild was held in awe by the rest of the school, but in recent years the uninitiated have ventured to crash the party. Kids either wanted to eavesdrop or join in or even play tricks on the Guild, sabotage them. Guild members were sworn to secrecy about the location of the Summonings, of course, but stuff always slipped out. And there were only so many locations on the island that were suitable.

A gust of wind takes me by surprise. I pull my parka around me tightly and suddenly question my attire. Do I look suitably assassin-y? Should I have fashioned a cloak from my bedsheets? Worn makeup and accessories? Was this a dressy occasion? I do not want to look sloppy, especially in front of Alex. I instantly berate myself for having the thought. I still want him to want me, is that it?

I reach the beach. There are footprints in the sand, and I feel a shiver go up my spine. I had wondered exactly how to find the caves, because the map is vague, and I've never actively looked for them before, just known they were down here somewhere. I'd wondered if there would be a sign or a pattern of sticks forming an arrow. But now I can follow the trail. I look up behind me, but no, there's no one later than me. I'll have to hurry. The wind is whipping a wicked spray up off the slate-gray sea, and it clings to the exposed skin on my face. So much for an Indian summer; I hope this cold patch passes and we go back to the mists and mellow fruitfulness.

I follow the footsteps hugging the base of the cliff, taking me along the stretch of sand toward the promontory. There doesn't look to be anything like an obvious entrance to a cave along here—no oil lamps hanging, no hooded figure beckoning. But I have little doubt that once inside, it will be a different matter. The Guild will surely be in full ceremonial garb, and there are probably a whole bunch of formalities to the Summoning. I really, really hope I haven't missed the beginning, and I hope they don't kick me out because of it. I scurry, head down, following the scuffs in the sand.

The footsteps stop. They are the footsteps of the whole Guild, I presume, so I'm not exactly following one trail. They stop at the beginning of the strip of tufted grass that lines the cliff face. I look at the rocks, which are covered in part by longer, hanging grass, with an occasional small tree or gorse bush clinging to the side of the cliff. It's steep but not sheer. And I can't see any kind of entrance from here. I walk over the tufted grass in the most direct way to the cliff, figuring that everyone would take the shortest route to the caves. But there is nothing in front of me apart from cliff. I look up, rain falling on my face. Seeing the drops gives me vertigo. Don't tell me I'm supposed to climb.

As I have the thought, I notice that there are signs that someone has done just that. Fresh soil has been turned over where clumps of grass have been pulled out; there are stones at my feet that don't look like they have been there long. A little ball of dread forms in my stomach as I find a foothold and pull myself up a little. I reach up and grasp a rock that comes away in my hand. I jump down. This is seriously dodgy. I look closer and see that the trail stops only a little higher up than I'd reached. Ah, Cate. This is all part of the fun. They wanted you to think this was where the cave was, but it's not.

I turn and stride off in the direction of the promontory. Those footprints in the sand are obviously a ruse to confuse us apprentices, or indeed, any outsider who is skulking around. The entrance to the caves will be farther along the grass. I hurry, scanning the cliff face as I go. It becomes sheerer, until the cliff turns a corner and the grass ends, and only rock remains between me and the sea, and me and the cliff face. Now I'm really scratching my head. The water is merely lapping at the rocks now, because the tide is out, but I'm sure that things get really wild around here at other times. There's an arch in the rock, big enough to allow a rowing boat underneath the promontory, but there's no boat to be seen. I'm sure they don't expect me to swim. Is there a ledge or some way of clinging to the cliff face to go underneath the arch? No, nothing. I look up again. Scaling this wall would take serious skill and equipment, and there is no indication of anything. I know this isn't the right way; I cannot for the life of me imagine Marcia being persuaded to turn the Summoning meetings into some kind of extreme sports exercise.

I lean my back against the rock, looking back across the little bay, and I feel panic rising. They don't want me after all. Maybe this was just a meeting place on the beach, and they went on somewhere else. They didn't wait for me because I was late, and I've been dropped from the Guild already. I get my little black book out of my pocket, sheltering it from the rain with one hand while I flick to the map with the other. Could this be a test that only I have failed? Maybe the real Summoning is somewhere completely different? Could the information on this map be in code—angles of locations or invisible ink or a play on words—or something I'm too ordinary and stupid to work out? I curse, shutting the book and staring out across the bay the way I came. I'm doomed.

And then I see them. The washed-out indentations peeking out of the surf. Right by the water's edge, more footsteps—not following the cliff this time, but cutting straight across the bay in a direct line back to the cliff path. There, where I descended, is a huge clump of gorse, but from this vantage point, I can now see that there's a rock behind the bushes and what looks like it might be an entranceway.

Ha-ha-ha, Guild. You sent us on a wild-goose chase.

I pick my way over the rocks, heading for the sand once more, following the footsteps of all my fellow apprentices who had the same realization before me. I feel relieved that the Game might not be over for me before it has begun but stung that everyone else probably figured this out together, not alone and late.

Sure enough, once I reach the bottom of the cliff path and walk around the big bush, there is a dark arch of an entrance, facing out to sea. There's a thick, oiled rope across the entrance with a small wooden sign hanging from it.

Strictly Out of Bounds

Ezra Pendleton

Jackpot. I step over the rope and into the cave.

The entrance is almost narrow enough for me to touch both sides, but the cave quickly opens up into a large chamber. The sand sticks to my shoes as I walk; it's dry in here, which at least gives me some confidence that we won't get careless and have to swim for it. I walk in carefully, out of the bright light and into the unknown. There's nobody here, but there are a couple shadowy alcoves on the far wall, indications of possible tunnels into other chambers. I walk carefully across the sand and reach the first one. It is a tunnel, a skinny one—I follow it. It narrows farther then hangs a sudden left. The light doesn't follow. It is dark here, thickly, chokingly dark. There is a low hum, something mechanical—a generator? I edge forward, feeling along both walls, and then suddenly, I've lost the right wall. Ack. OK, just keep going. I can't help but wonder how Tesha with her claustrophobia is dealing with this. The walls are smooth and slimy. Probably dripping with bat droppings. Yup, totally batty, the lot of us... Oh lordy, there must be a way out of here—

I stop in my tracks. I can hear it. Music. The ceremony must be in full swing. I head toward the sound, bolder now.

A faint glow off to my right. The hum is louder too. I take a chance and let go of the wall.

Ahead, a sickly yellow pool of light, spilling out from behind an edge of rock. The source of the hum is a low, square object, with a thick cable running out of it. I was right; it is a generator. I take a breath and step into the light.

And there they all are. I'm in awe.

It looks like a pirate's lair, lit with candles and oil lamps set into indentations in the rock. This chamber is smaller than I expected, only big enough to allow a little more than a dozen kids to sit around reasonably comfortably on an assortment of boxes, old rugs, and cushions. How did they get all this stuff down here? There are a couple wooden tables at the back of the chamber. A pecking order is apparent by everyone's position. The somber Elders are at the tables: Marcia sits at the smaller of the two, twirling a strand of liquid hair around a pencil. She has a velvet bag, a laptop, and an old-fashioned desk lamp in front of her. At the second, larger table, there's Carl, all serious cheekbones and dark-red hair, and Cynthia, whip-thin pretty with sharp eyes, compulsively playing with a bag of chips and not opening it. Alex and his best bud, beefcake Rick, lounge between the tables, on big beanbags. Rick's almost as wide as he is tall, with short legs, furrowed brow, and inch-long black hair, which he scrubs at with both hands, like it itches him. The Journeymen have bagged the best boxes to sit on: my very own Daniel and Roger, an amiable chubster with glasses. I feel Daniel's eyes boring into me through the scruff of hair falling over his face, but I avoid his glance.

Fairy lights are strung from the low ceiling. On the left at the back is a curtain covering an archway, glittering strings of beads hanging in front of a velvet backdrop. Faces look up at me as I come in; there are no masks here, no ceremonial robes or hoods pulled low. Just a bunch of kids sitting around listening to Jimi Hendrix. My fellow apprentices are all here: there's Martin and Tesha—reunited with her initiate mates: Anvi and "edgy" Whitney. Lastly, there's Becky, not really part of the circle, but officially the hottest girl in the school, so no surprise the Elder boys wanted her in the Guild. Thirteen players, one Grand Master.

"Bloody hell, Cate!" Marcia's voice rings out. "*Muy tarde, mi amiga.*"

Before I can say anything, a missile is launched in my direction. Instinctively, I fling out a hand and catch it. A can of drink, cold and fizzing ominously in my hand.

Well, I wasn't expecting this. The overall effect is that I've just wandered into somebody's boho chic study room. The atmosphere is not one of reverence, pomp, and circumstance; it's chilled in here and rather cozy. I'm simultaneously disappointed and relieved.

Alex glances at me, deliberately disinterested. He's semi-reclined on the huge beanbag, but it's an overexaggerated cool. I'll bet my life in this Game that he's psyched to kick things off.

"OK, Cate, pull up a rock," he quips. "Folks, we're finally all here. I'm glad you all found this place. It's not like it took too much brainpower to figure it out." He shoots me a look. "At least for most."

I open my mouth to explain that I wasn't really late because I couldn't figure it out but more because I've just been handed a nuclear blast from the past. But I don't, because it's only partly true. I find a corner of rug to sit on and plonk myself down between fellow apprentices Tesha and Emily.

"Marcia put together our little rule book." Alex leans over to grab one. "Hope you've all learned it by heart?" He looks around, amused. "For those who haven't, Rick will explain all the big stuff."

Rick stands, half leaning against a rock, one foot on a box of drinks. I always think of him as Alex's henchman. Another athlete—a rugby player—but the real reason he's part of this school is that he has a photographic memory and pretty much excels in anything that involves recalling any kind of data. Pity he doesn't have the intelligence to go with. You can bet that he remembers every last sentence in the rule book, but he might not understand all the words.

The music is turned down, and all eyes are on Rick. He straightens up. He's not as easy in the spotlight as Alex, and he shifts his huge weight from foot to gigantic foot. But he is an Elder, and he is an alpha, and so he's not going to die of nerves.

"Welcome to the Game," he says gruffly.

I shuffle a little on the rug, the cold can in my hands making my fingers ache, not wanting to open it and risk interrupting.

"Get this straight, Guild members." Rick glowers in the flickering light, looking like some mythical creature, half-boy, half-minotaur. "This is not D&D. This is not Vampires or Assassin or any of those lesser games." He rubs his meaty hands together, hunching huge shoulders forward and staring at us beneath his huge brow. His tiny eyes sparkle, and a seldom-seen smile creeps across his round face. "This is Killer, and you have all been invited to play. And you should play like your life depends on it."

CHAPTER 6

There's a nervous titter. Someone cracks open a can; obviously not everyone shares my reverence.

"Yeah, get comfortable now," Rick says gruffly. "Kick back while you still can. Because in a few moments the Game begins, and when it does, nobody is safe. You." He sticks out a stubby finger at the girl—new recruit Whitney—who flicked the ring pull. "You'll never open a drink the same way again, at least not for the next few weeks. Because all the stuff you just took for granted—eating, drinking, walking into a classroom or taking a dump, turning on a radio or opening a book—all that changes in a few moments. You're never safe, and you can trust nothing and no one. There will be booby traps, things lying in wait. The Killer will be active and after us. Every last one."

Rick is warming up. Alex looks on from his beanbag approvingly. Rick continues, "Apprentices, you have been chosen because: (a) we like you—enough to want to see you die humiliatingly, and (b) you can be trusted. This is a Game, but it's not for little kids. If you are a little kid, leave now."

Rick actually waits to see if anyone's going to vamoose. We're all frozen to the spot, barely daring to move. The candles flicker in the slight breeze coming in from the outside, but it feels as if we are tucked away, deep in the earth.

"Here's how it works." Alex leans forward, his sandy hair falling into his eyes, keen eyes that flick from one person to the next, transfixing us all with his gaze. "I'm the Grand Master. I run the Game."

As if we were in any doubt. I know he's been longing to be Grand Master for years, he even told me as much when we briefly got close last term. His big brother—some bona fide engineering genius—ran the Game a few years ago, and it was a legendary year. Little brother has a lot to live up to, and now his moment has come. Alex is no brainiac, no ace sports star or super-creative prodigy. He's kind of normal, like me. He's popular and quick-witted and more than averagely good at a whole bunch of things, but he's not special. He needs this Game to etch his name into the Umfraville history books.

So far, so good, Alex. He takes a moment to enjoy the suspense. "Later, everyone picks a card." He points to a large velvet bag on the table beside Marcia. "On each card there's one word, and if you're the Killer, you'll know." His laugh is low and soft—and short-lived. "Hear this!" He spreads his hands wide for emphasis. "Tell no one what is on your card. Do you understand?" He stares us down. "Nobody knows who the Killer is, except me, and I only know because the Killer tells me. That's his or her first job."

"What, here, tonight?" Tesha says. "How does that work?"

"No, not tonight, doughnut." Alex shakes his head as everyone laughs. "As soon as you can without your cover being blown. Don't be an idiot and tell me by Killing me either. As Grand Master I can't be the Killer or be Killed." He flashes those white teeth, but it's more of a snarl than a smile. "Just slip me a note, IM me, whisper in my ear, whatever. Only make sure I know who you are before you go on your Killing spree, or the Kills don't count."

"The rest of us are potential victims," Rick says. "And only us. Don't touch non-Guild."

Beside me, Martin shoots up a hand. Alex rolls his eyes. "We're not in the Cub Scouts, Martin. What is it?"

Martin beams, the gappy grin in full effect. "What if I don't want to be Killed?"

There's laughter.

"Sure, you can fight back to some extent." Marcia scoops the sheet of hair back from her face and nods at him, encouragingly. "If a masked attacker is chasing you with a rubber machete, yes, you can run away." She waves the book at us. "It says so in here. But look, it's really important that we all play fair. You get whacked, you stay whacked. Honor system."

"That's right, Marcia." Rick nods. "And remember, everyone, dead men don't talk. You know who did you, you keep mum on pain of excommunication from the Guild."

Alex smiles again. "You manage to stay alive? Different matter. It's all about finding the Killer. We meet here every weekend for a Summoning. We hang out. We talk—"

"We par-tay!" Roger, one of the Journeymen, shouts, and everyone cheers.

"We vote." Alex's words cut through the revelry. "Every weekend, everyone still in the Game casts a vote. If you know who the Killer is, write the name down. If you don't, write something else down—Mickey Mouse, Ezra, or 'I don't know.'" He claps a hand to his chest. "I read the votes. I'm the only one who gets to see. If you guess right, the Killer is exposed, you win. You guess wrong, you're dead and out of the game."

Rick picks up the ball again. "The Killer can Kill as often or as little as they want, but don't be a mug and bore us to death. Make your Kills entertaining. Give us something to talk about." He looks down at us, struggling to cross his muscled arms over his broad chest. "Yes, if you can get your victim on their own, you can do anything you want—shoot 'em with a water pistol, stab them with a rubber knife, whatever. But it's much more fun to do stuff in public. I know—I know we're not supposed to let the Game be 'disruptive to school life'"—he flicks his stubby fingers as quotation marks—"but give us all a show, won't you? It's what we deserve."

The Elders and Journeymen all laugh in agreement.

"Don't go slapping little red skull stickers on people!"

"Don't be that doof that puts a note on someone's desk saying 'Boom!'"

"If the Killer IMs me with 'You're Dead,' I'm totally giving them up."

"Oh no, that's been done and doner!"

Marcia cuts in, "We outlawed that one officially. It's a yawn. Check your book."

"Yeah, read it thoroughly," Alex intones. "No-nos are all in the book—paint guns, no; fireworks, no. No computer viruses and nothing that's going to hurt anyone or give Ezra cause to call the antiterrorist squad. Keep it classy. Put an alarm clock in a hollowed-out book or pop a friggin' balloon, but don't get our Game stopped, or you lose, big time." He waggles a finger at us.

Marcia winds her hair into a thick rope with one hand. "The only major rule we haven't mentioned is that Killing more than one person at a time is not allowed; you're a serial Killer, not a mass murderer. Other than that, go crazy."

I'm beginning to get serious anxiety that I'll be the Killer. What pressure.

Alex continues, "So be safe, be clever, and be exclusive. And remember, although your victim is sworn to secrecy, the best Killers are secret. It's so much more satisfying if you can be the ninja you were born to be and get in and out without being seen."

Rick glares at us. "Questions?"

"Nope. Crystal clear, m'dear." Becky smiles at Rick. I almost laugh out loud as he struggles not to melt under her gaze.

"What if no one guesses the Killer?" Beside me, Emily stretches her long legs out on the rug.

Alex checks out her legs, then answers her. "The Game goes on until there are only three people left, Killer included. A final Summoning and vote is scheduled at the earliest opportunity. The Killer then has to choose to try and Kill the others quickly before the Summoning or take their chances—go to the final vote and hope nobody guesses it's them."

We all take this in. I make a promise to myself that I'll be in the final three, Killer or not.

"Enough talk!" Alex says. He stands, holding the large, dark velvet bag tied at the top with a ratty gold cord. "Time to choose your destiny."

Everyone straightens up a little. I'm holding my breath. Alex unravels the golden cord and opens the bag just wide enough to put a hand in.

"No reading your card until everyone has one." He offers the bag to the Elders first. Each solemnly takes out a folded matte black card. Then he moves into the group, everyone taking turns to cautiously dip in a hand. I'm one of the last to get the bag. Before I reach in, I wonder if this puts me at an advantage or a disadvantage, but not being a math genius, I can't work out the odds. I stretch out my hand toward the bag, feeling like it might be bitten off by something hidden in there. I feel around for the cards; just two or three remain. I toy with them for a second then choose one, pulling it out and in close to my chest, as if it will jump out of my hand and reveal itself unless I hold it tight.

The last few take their cards. Alex moves back to his place

and sits, looking at us, smiling. He doesn't speak. We wait. We wait a little longer.

"Delicious, isn't it?" Alex's voice is hoarse and thick with pleasure. "The anticipation? This is one of the best moments, the moment before, the moment when no one is the Killer and all of us are."

No one giggles. The generator hums in the background. The lights flicker a little, prompting a ripple of noise, half-muffled screams, and nervous laughter.

"Yes." Alex nods, smiling. "The spirits of assassins past are with us! On my count, open your cards. Three, two, one..."

I hardly dare to. I'm not only afraid of what is written there, but also of how I will react when I see it. I mustn't give the Game away. I cup the card in my hands and slowly—oh, so slowly— unfold the stiff card. The inside of the card is bloodred, and there is black writing. I see the large capital *K* and feel a rush of adrenaline shoot up my spine into my head. As the lights flicker again, I squint at the card:

Kitten

Disappointment, then huge relief, then fear.

I look again, just in case I've read it wrong. But no, I'm a baby cat, not a murderer. Funny, Alex. I wonder how many different *K* words he could think of that would give everyone the same heart attack. I suppose I should be thankful I'm not "Kisser" or "Kipper."

Of course, as soon as I've looked at my own card, I'm looking around at everyone else to try to read reactions. And that's exactly what everyone else is doing too. Alex is chuckling away to himself. How very amusing we must look to him. I wonder if he can tell who got the Killer card, because whoever did won't be looking around at everyone else to see who got it. Probably only a split second, but Alex would have been looking for it. One of the myriad ways he makes this all entertaining for himself.

"OK folks, cards away," Alex says. "You need to keep your card so I can check the Killer is for real. But don't keep it anywhere anyone else can find it."

"It's getting late," Marcia says, leaning over onto a rock ledge and blowing out some candles. "We need to show up for high tea, or they might send out the search parties."

I shove my card, burning hot, into the inner pocket of my parka.

"OK, we'll move out," Alex says. "Staggered, not everyone at once."

"Yeah, girls," Rick sneers, looking at Tesha, Whit, and Anvi. "You do know you don't have to do everything together."

Alex and Carl snicker. The girls sneer back at Rick. More candles are blown out. Martin and Anvi start to extinguish the oil lamps, and Martin knocks one down, smashing it on a rock.

"Think stealthy, people!" Alex moans, and looks at Carl, who shakes his auburn head. "Give me strength. If the Killer's worth his or her salt, I give these intakes a week, no more." He gets up. "I'm around this evening if anyone wants to talk to me." He winks. "Read your book, and remember to watch the board in the common room for news."

Suddenly, the room plunges into darkness.

Several yells, and beside me, Emily screams.

"Nice one, Rick," says Carl. "Did you not fill the generator up again?"

"I did!"

I hear Alex chuckle. "Seriously, Killer. Tasting blood already?"

Silence. Someone has grabbed me on the arm; I think it's Tesha. I hope it's Tesha.

Nothing happens.

"OK, Rick." Alex sighs. "It is the generator. Where did you put the flashlights?"

A flashlight flicks on, but it's not one of Alex's. A huge figure is standing in the doorway, cloak billowing, flashlight pointed, and in its other hand, a dagger. The figure roars and slashes the air.

"What the—?" Alex says.

Someone barrels past me, heading for the door. There's a scuffle, the flashlight dances on the wall, and then suddenly the generator is humming and the lights are back on.

Rick is on the floor, panting. The figure is still there, standing above him, laughing at the assembled Guild. It flings the hood of the cloak back and screams, "Time to die!"

It's Vaughan. Time to die, indeed.

"Who the hell are you?" Alex is as purple as a beet. I've never seen him look so rattled.

"I'm Vaughan," says Vaughan, smiling. He waves a hand. "Hello."

"You're not Guild!" says Rick, struggling to his feet. "Bloody hell, Alex, he's not even Umfraville!"

Alex moves toward Vaughan, and my stomach hits the floor. But he stops short, and I see something I've never seen before: Alex is scared.

"Oh, I am Umfraville, I assure you!" Vaughan says brightly. "I'm new; I admit it. Missed the first week of school—just got here today, in fact—but I'll be in the classroom with you all on Monday, I promise." He squints at everyone. "Well, with the clever ones anyway."

Alex, Rick, and Carl all kind of surge toward Vaughan, but he's quick. He leaps back.

"How long have you been here?" Alex demands.

"Long enough," Vaughan says. "You're playing a game. It's secret. Someone's a killer." He tuts. "And you really shouldn't be in this cave." He shakes his head. "Breaking all the rules..."

"You tell anyone, and I'll—"

"Oh, I don't want to tell anyone!" Vaughan says. "All I want is to join in."

Alex barks out a laugh. Everyone in the room relaxes slightly. Some of the others begin to laugh too, except Rick, who looks like he's going to explode, his cheeks red with boiled-up rage.

"Dude," Alex says. "You've got balls, I'll give you that. But do yourself a favor and walk out before we kick you out."

Vaughan looks hurt. "But why can't I join in?"

"Because, you loser," Rick spits at him, "you don't just join the Guild. You get invited."

"Oh, I know," Vaughan sings, "Initiation, blah-blah, cowpats, whatever. But you'll let me in, because I have something you want."

"Right," Alex says. "I'm going to be nice for a couple seconds more, Vaughan, but then we're really going to mess you up unless you get out of here. If you don't want to be even more of an outcast than you already are, then I suggest you move it."

Vaughan frowns. "Hmm. Cate said you wouldn't let me in, but I didn't believe her."

Oh, just no. Thanks so much, friend.

Everyone looks at me. Alex is shooting me daggers almost as real as the one in Vaughan's hand—where the flob did he get a frigging dagger at school?! I cringe into myself. Don't, don't drag me into this, Vaughan. But I don't say anything, because I've already betrayed him once in this lifetime and I won't do it again, even if he just shoved me under the biggest bus in Toy Town.

"Now, don't blame Cate," Vaughan says. "We were besties in a previous life, but she has no part in this. Anyway, as I was saying, I have something you need, and that is why you'll let me into the Game."

"What could you possibly have that we want?" Rick scoffs.

"I can build you a social network," Vaughan says. "Wouldn't that be wonderful fun? The bulletin board in the common room is terribly old-school—if you'll excuse the pun—but wouldn't it be rather more millennial of you to have your own social network? Profiles, IM, posts, and threads? Think of the possibilities. Updates, news, strategy, theories? Pictures too.

Selfies with the Killer? You're a little deprived of Internet here, no? A social network all of your own, just think of it."

"Been done, friend," Carl says. "More than once someone's tried to put a student network up. Staff find it; staff take it down."

"They won't find this," Vaughan says. "Imagine. Space to post whatever you like. Clues, hit lists, the possibilities are endless. Plus, tracking individual users, the ability to see who is online and where at any time. How cool would that be? It would bring a whole new element to the Game."

"Sure it would," Rick says sarcastically. "What, the library, the studies, and a handful of classrooms? The only places in the school where we can pick up Wi-Fi?"

"Oh, there are other places. Aren't there, Marcia?" Vaughan looks at my friend. "The ones no one thinks about." He points to the laptop on the table. "The newspaper office has Wi-Fi, if I'm not mistaken. You can even get online at the art studio. And the PC in the secretary's office in Main House. Staff members' machines in their private quarters—encrypted Wi-Fi there." Vaughan shrugs. "Even so, even discounting those other opportunities…a murder is carried out while half the users are logged on in the library? You instantly know where those users are. Could be interesting."

"It would be great, no doubt," Marcia says. "But they would find it within a week and take it down. Probably shut the Game down too, because our headmaster is so paranoid about us actually being able to get online that he'd think he had a mutiny on his hands."

"They won't find it," Vaughan repeats.

"OK, OK," Alex says. "You have the guts to come here and throw your cards on the table? Let's talk. But first"—he looks around the cave—"you droogs need to get back to civilization. Only Elders for this."

Everyone groans, reluctantly beginning to leave. I cannot wait to get out, but I'm terrified of what Vaughan is going to lay on them when I go. In any case, I don't get the chance to escape.

"Cate!" Alex says. "This nut job is your friend. You can stay."

Great.

Everyone looks at me as they leave. Especially Daniel.

When they have all cleared out, Alex sits, and the rest of us—Carl, Rick, Marcia, Cynthia, and lil' old me—follow suit. Except Vaughan. He stands in the middle of the cave, still wearing the cape, looking a little like a disheveled crow that got left out in the storm. But he has a glint in his eye and the air of one who tastes victory. That's a little premature of him, I think.

"I know you all have trust issues." Vaughan grins at Alex. "That's only sensible. But I'm good at this. Ask her." He looks at me again.

Marcia looks at me too. I don't like her expression.

"He is good at this," I say. "Well, I think so anyway; I haven't seen him since we were eight. But even then he used to take computers apart and put them back together, program games for us to play, and that kind of thing. Then we…moved apart… and I heard he was a whiz kid. He was at Cambridge, I think?" I look at Vaughan. He nods encouragingly. "He probably knows a bit about computers."

Vaughan snorts at this. "A bit?" He thinks about it, smiles. "Oh, a bit! I get it. Quite good!"

Alex looks him up and down. "We're not lacking in talent at Umfraville, if you haven't already noticed. Don't you think that if anyone had the skills to effectively hide something like that, they would have done it already? What makes you so certain your site could stay hidden?"

"Because it already is." Vaughan points his dagger at the laptop. "Wi-Fi. Are we capable here?"

"Only just," Marcia says. "We put signal boosters on the cliff, directing the signal down from Main House, but it's patchy."

"Well done you," Vaughan says, moving to the laptop. "May I?" he asks no one in particular and brings up the Umfraville home page. He taps away with his slim, quick fingers. "*Et voila*. A portal."

A piece of art pops up on the screen. Seeing as art is the only thing I know anything about, I recognize it. It's by William Blake. My tastes are pretty modern, but this guy I like; he knows his spooky all right. And this picture doesn't disappoint. It's of a wood, with two people walking through it, and three weird owl creatures sitting in the trees. And on first glance you don't necessarily see it, but the trees are made of people. There are faces and body parts in the trunks, as if they are trapped there. It's heavy stuff. I can't remember the title, but is it something to do with murders?

"Excuse the obviousness. I couldn't resist." Vaughan moves his mouse in a pattern over the owl creatures, then clicks on something and a password prompt shows up over the signature at the bottom. He types something quickly, and the picture explodes in a thousand pixels. It is replaced by a faded-red background with a watermarked image of a skull and the header, CRYPT, at the top. Below there is what looks like a news feed, with pictures down the side.

"When I knew I'd be coming here, I hacked the Umfraville intranet and built this. I've been updating regularly. Rather a strange business, posting while no one's watching. If a tree falls in the forest and nobody is there to hear it, does it make a sound?" He grins. "This site went live four months ago. Plenty of time to have shown up on the radar by now."

"Some of that was break." Alex is reading the screen, shaking his head. "Nobody would be looking."

"Wrong," Vaughan said. "The school intranet had a lot of tinkering over the summer. They had someone do some serious coding to keep the likes of me out. Nobody noticed I was already there."

Marcia guffaws. "I have a couple kids on the newspaper who always have their heads in the intranet, trying to hack out into the net or, er, into school records." She shrugs at us, semi-apologetically. "'Crypt' has been live four months, you say?" She raises a thick eyebrow at Vaughan, and he nods at her. "That's more than enough time for my guys to have found it." Her dark-brown eyes flick to Alex. "He must be very good indeed to hide it for so long." She leans in and starts scrolling through the feed, clicking on links to other pages. "This is incredible. There're so many possibilities, Alex!"

"It won't last." Rick is showing his disapproval by not looking at the laptop, at Vaughan, or at anyone. "Even the fact you just shot your mouth off to the Guild. They'll talk, the staff will hear, and they'll kill it."

"The Guild will talk? Tsk." Vaughan shakes his head. "I thought this was a secret society? No matter. If anyone outside does get wind of it, they still won't find it." He stands up and flourishes a hand at the screen. "Say bye-bye!" He hits a couple keys and the screen flickers back to the Umfraville intranet home page. He turns his back and begins to walk away. As he reaches the way out, he turns and looks at us, dramatically.

"You take the next twenty-four hours and look for the network. Get your best minds on it. If you find any trace, any trace whatsoever—if you even find the portal, the William Blake page—fine, I won't join. But if you don't—and you won't—then I'm in. Do we have a deal?"

Alex's jaw clenches, his chest puffs out ever so slightly. He's still faking the laid-back 'tude, but if you know where to look, you can read his indecision. "It's sad, Vaughan, because I almost like your swagger. You've got stones, I'll give you that. But that's all I'll give you, because we will find the site. You think you're some computer hotshot? You're at Umfraville now. You're not special; you're just the norm. So better get used to it."

Vaughan blinks. "Er. OK." He laughs. "So nice to find a place where I fit in." He looks at me. "Especially among old friends." He chucks the dagger in the sand at my feet. "Have fun looking, Alex." He winks at him. "Because I know you will."

And he's gone.

CHAPTER 7

I spend Sunday hiding. Hiding from the Killer, hiding from Daniel, hiding from Vaughan and questions about Vaughan that inevitably will come my way from Marcia and Alex. I camp out in the art studio and get a lot done. Mr. Flynn will be delighted with me.

On Sunday night I dream of being stuck up a tree in the garden where I used to live, before we moved away. I'm shouting for Vaughan to come and help me, which is stupid because, in reality, it never worked that way. He was always the one who was stuck. That's not the case anymore. And in my dream, he doesn't come. Daniel appears at the foot of the tree, but he doesn't see me. He just sits at the bottom and weeps and weeps. I feel awful. Bad about being stuck and bad that I don't want Daniel to see me there.

Yeah. The alarm screeches, and I wake up in a super mood.

But not as bad as Marcia. Marcia and I share a dorm, and

she is not a morning person. There are days when I literally have to drag her out of bed before our housemistress comes in and gives her a detention for lateness. For a progressive school, we still have some pretty archaic ideas about scheduling. Genius does not keep ordinary hours, but for the most part, Umfraville does. I don't like getting up any more than the next healthy teenager, but mostly I'm grateful for the normality of routine.

This week though, Marcia and I are on wake-up duty. Each dormitory rotates, and lucky us, it's our turn. Our dorm is on the corner of the east corridor and the south corridor of the girls' wing, and we divide and conquer by 7:15 a.m., then shed our jammies and head for the shower room.

"I hate Mondays. And it's so cold." Marcia shivers as we walk down the hall; she's naked under her tightly wrapped camel-colored towel, and is wearing fluffy pink bunny slippers on her feet. "And it's only September! I will never get used to it."

It's a little chilly, she's right; I pull my dressing gown collar in a little. The school's radiators are probably originals. They are scorching to the touch but do little to heat the rooms. The plumbing is ancient too. If our showers are anything other than lukewarm this morning, then that will be a win.

"Are you awake enough to tell me what the Elders decided about Vaughan?" I whisper. I have been dying to ask her. She didn't get into the dorm until close to lights out and didn't say a word to me last night. "Did you find the site? Was that what you were doing all yesterday?"

Marcia rolls her big browns at me. "Have you talked to Vaughan?"

I shake my head. "I haven't seen him since Saturday night in the cave."

"And you guys were friends at home?"

"We were eight." I keep looking straight ahead. "I haven't seen him since we moved away."

"I know you haven't, lady," Marcia singsongs. "Otherwise I would have heard about him. Talk about fine. Crazy, but *muy hermoso*." She whistles.

For some reason, this makes me blush, but luckily we reach the bathroom, so I can turn away from her. Already there's activity. There are only seven shower cubicles, and all are occupied. The trick is to try to get one as close to the window side of the room as possible. That's the start of the line, and that's where the water is hottest. By the time the water makes its way to the last cubicle, it's goose bumps and icy nips all around.

"OK, do not say anything, but I'll tell you this." Marcia drops her sponge bag on the tiled floor beside me as we stand in line for the showers. "We couldn't find the site." Her voice is so low I almost can't hear it over the noise of the water running. "Everyone was on it all weekend. Alex and I even broke into Ms. Lasillo's office to access her machine and the main server. No trace. Vaughan has got skills."

"So is he in?"

Marcia looks at me sharply. "You want him to be?" When I don't reply, she continues. "We'll see. Alex is keen as hell on the site, but it's how to break protocol and ask Vaughan in without losing face. Some of the others are dead against it. Rick, mainly."

I don't know whether to be pleased or afraid. A big part of me is very uncomfortable with Vaughan being at Umfraville, because he's a part of the old me, and his very presence reminds me of how I once failed him. But as long as he is here, maybe it would be good to have him in the Guild.

Marcia looks at the cubicles, frowning. "What's taking everyone so long?"

Monday morning reluctance to get into cold water, that's what.

Becky—one of my fellow apprentices—has the prime cubicle, as always. Up early, hitting the track, working those already-perfect muscles. Her reward is the hottest shower, and it's only fitting. She's altogether a hot kind of girl. She speaks six languages fluently, has a banging figure and the shiniest black hair you ever did see, and she plays the flippin' harp. She was a shoo-in at the Guild's harvest—first to be selected, I'm sure. I think she'll probably end up Secretary-General of the UN, but for now she's every straight Umfraville boy's dream girl.

And what they wouldn't give to see what I can see. She casually discards her bright-yellow towel over the hook by the cubicle, and I marvel at the perfect caramel skin, long limbs, and gentle curves. She sets the water running and steps tentatively into the shower. The door shuts and the steam rises and fogs the glass.

"Aargh!"

A dripping head sticks out of the cubicle at the other end of the line. Tesha.

"It's running cold!" she screams, water bouncing off her curls, eyes glaring down the line in the direction of Becky's shower.

There's no response. Tesha ducks inside again, knowing how futile it would be to protest further. Becky can't help that her shower sucks the heat out of everyone else's any more than she can help that her cleverness and her beauty cast everyone else in the shade. It's true, she makes sure she bags that shower every single morning, she lingers over undressing, often spending several minutes twisting her licorice hair into a shiny knot on the top of her head before peeling off her towel and stepping in. And then once showering, she makes sure she spends just enough time in there to wind everyone up, but not enough time for anyone to call her on it. I glance at the cubicle, seeing her hands moving behind the steamed glass, massaging shampoo into that lovely hair, the suds appearing in the drain outside the cubicle. One of the hands reaches out to the glass door to steady herself. Her palm bleaches on the glass, and then...I see the red.

Red.

Becky's palm on the glass squishes the red, and it runs down the inside of the door. Red drips down the glass in long, graceful drips. The suds in the drain have turned deep pink. I gasp and take a small step toward the cubicle. Behind the steam, I can see the red better now, running down her body, dripping off her hair. Has she cut herself? She doesn't even realize it. Should I tell her—?

"*¡Dios mío!* What's that?" Marcia has seen it too.

The other girls in the line look, and there's a buzz of noise.

Becky's scream cuts through everything. The door flies open, and she stumbles out, holding her hands in front of her in horror, blood and shampoo suds running down her glistening body.

"What is happening?" she howls, blood pooling on the white tiles.

Someone—Whitney—runs up to her, grabbing the yellow towel and throwing it around her shoulders, someone else holds her arms, searching for the wound.

"My hair! Is it coming from my head?" Becky wails.

"No, it's not," Marcia says quietly, beside me. I follow her gaze; she's looking at the shower cubicle. The door is still open, the water still on. And it is red. Blood flowing from the showerhead.

More people notice—those who were still in their showers abandoning them, gathering to look at the blood shower. I glance down the line of showers. The rest of the water runs clear.

"Killer," Marcia mutters to me. She pushes through the crowd, walks up to the shower, and turns it off, all business. "Becky, you've been Killed."

"What?!"

The showerhead is removed, red powder paint turned to goo is discovered. Becky's fear turns to rage, then to laughter, and finally to disappointment. She's out of the Game, and what's worse, she was first.

Showers are hurriedly finished, and we all head back to our dorms to dress. The halls are alive with the news.

"You should see her face. She's all stained!"

"Is she ever going to get that stuff out of her hair?"

"How did the Killer know she'd be in that shower?"

"Becky's always in that one!"

"Still, the Killer must be a girl! Who else could know it would be a Guild member in that shower?"

I close our door behind Marcia and, my heart beating fast, we start to get dressed.

"Thus it begins." I can't help the excitement I feel. "You think it is a girl? Kind of specialized knowledge."

Marcia raises an eyebrow at me. "Not necessarily. Remember after sports day last term, when we all went to the cliffs for a smoke? Bunch of kids joking with Becky about how she always grabs that shower? It was this whole big laugh. Most of the Guild would have been there; anyone could have heard."

"Wow. You have a good memory." I blink at her. "Unless you're trying to deceive me, of course. You could be the Killer."

"Or you could be." She smiles at me. "And you're faking not remembering the conversation."

"I couldn't have got my act together so quickly." I shake my head. "It's only Monday! No way was I expecting things to kick off just yet."

"Sometimes it's like that."

"But the preparation!" I say. "This Killer had stuff up their sleeve, just in case they were chosen."

"Meh." Marcia shrugs. "Red powder paint in the shower? Easy. Done a couple times in the nineties. The kid just had to duck into the art studio and voila!" She looks at me, fake realizing. "Oooh! Art studio!"

I laugh. "No, it'd be too obvious!" I wish I could tell her I'm not the Killer. I wish she could reassure me that she isn't.

Later that day, Becky's black wristband is found nailed to the common room bulletin board. First Kill. First player down and out, and the place is jumping. Becky is a minor celebrity; at first she is embarrassed, but as the news spreads through the school, it's obvious she starts to like the attention. By the time the day is through, I reckon she's lapping it up.

After lessons are over for the day, I get my first real chance to do some sleuthing, solo style. I go to the dormitories; there's never anyone around at this time of day. I make a beeline for the showers.

I open the door to the bathroom, and he is standing there. Vaughan. Hands on hips, looking at the row of showers. I shut the door quietly behind us.

"Becky always chooses the same shower?" He doesn't turn around.

"You are going to get into so much trouble if you're found here," I say quietly, walking up behind him. "You're lucky it was me. How did you know it was me anyway?"

He turns, looks me up and down in that way again, smiles. "I dunno. Pheromones?" Before I can respond, he turns and goes to the windows. "All but the tiniest of windows are locked down and painted over. Probably some major flouting of fire regulations, but Ezra doesn't strike me as someone who gives a flying fairy about that kind of thing." He feels along all the window ledges. "At least we know the Killer didn't enter here."

"Er, no." I join him. "But then, why would she have to if she could just walk through the door?"

"Ah!" Vaughan says. "But that's assuming it is a she!"

"And you're assuming not?" I say. "The probability is that the Killer is female. This Kill was set up at night, and that means no easy access for anyone with a Y chromosome. Plus, us gals all know Bec's routine. And look at the numbers: thirteen Guild members—not counting Alex, who can't be the Killer—eight are girls, only five are boys."

Vaughan pulls a face. "I don't consider those odds significant. No, a shower death equals male Killer, I have no doubt." He walks over to the cubicle and screws off the showerhead. "You saw the whole thing?"

I move closer to him, nodding, looking at the showerhead. There's only the slightest trace of red in there now.

"But the question of access is a problem. You're girls with body odor paranoia; most of you have showers at night too, am I right?"

I roll my eyes at him but don't disagree.

He continues, "In that case, the Killer must have been here in the early hours, filling the showerhead up with paint." He looks at me. "Where's your room?"

"What?"

"Can I look at the windows in there?" He opens the door and starts off down the corridor.

"Vaughan!" I hiss at him. "We can't just walk around up here! Why my room anyway?"

Some weird sixth sense is guiding him in the right direction. He gets to the corner of the corridor, right by the door to my dorm, and turns around, looking at me. "In here?" Before I can answer, he goes inside. I follow, shutting the door quickly.

"Oh." He beams. "This is your room. Hello, Wuffy, old mate."

Argh. My ancient stuffed puppy is perching on my pillow. Hideosity.

Vaughan walks up to the bed and sits, reaching out for Wuffy. "How have you been, Wuff? Long time no see."

"Vaughan." I try to muster some kind of dignity. "You need to go. You're not even in the Game. There's no point in getting into trouble over this."

"Yet." He looks at Wuffy, places him carefully back on the pillow.

"What do you mean?"

"I'm not in the Game yet." He sniffs, still sitting on my bed. "You haven't answered my question. How easy is it for boys to sneak in here at night?" One hand strokes the top of my duvet. I try not to flinch. I think it's subconscious on his part, but it's skeeving me out.

I bite my lip. "Well, you just did. How easy was it for you?"

He shakes his head. "This is the middle of the day. Different story." He lies down on my bed, feet up. "Comfy."

"Hey!" I walk over to him, grab his hand, and try to pull him up. But he doesn't move, holding my hand, staring up at me.

"Are you telling me that boys never come up here at night, Cate?"

I pause. It's almost like he knows about Alex, but there is no way in hell that he can.

There was a night last term when Marcia had food poisoning and slept in the sick bay. Alex and I hung out in his study because we were partnered up for a joint psychology class project. We were doing these psyche quizzes, and it was kind of awkward but also kind of a laugh. I'm still not sure how it happened, but after a while, we slipped into some pretty heavy convos. We talked mainly about our families, and I got to see another side of Alexander Morgan, stuff about how he feels he'll never live up to his genius brother, how underneath it all he is struggling just like the rest of us. It made me feel special that he'd told me, he'd chosen me—of all people—to unload, to share that with.

At curfew he walked me back here via the woods, and by that time it was obvious there was something in the cards. He held my hand underneath that big oak with the tree house, and he kissed me. I kissed back, totally, in spite of the fact that I was rapidly realizing that "sensitive Alex" back in the study was probably a big fat line designed to play me like a fiddle. It all felt dangerous, and I let it happen because—well, Alex. Alpha male. The one everyone wants. Ultimate acceptance of me by the leader of the gang.

After the oak tree I turned in for the night, feeling kind of giggly, switched off the light…and just as I was going to sleep, crazy Alex slipped into my room, nearly gave me a heart attack. Don't worry. I kicked him out. Nicely but very definitely. As he left my room he acted so cool, like it was no big deal, but his eyes in the weak light of my bedside lamp gave him away. He looked angry, a bit embarrassed…but there was something else too. I think it was panic. Probably the first time in his life someone told him no.

The memory of that night, and now Vaughan's hand in mine, is making me flush so hot, and I hope it's not showing on my face.

Suddenly, there's the sound of a door slamming somewhere down the corridor. I swear, Vaughan leaps to his feet, and as one we move to the door, listening for footsteps, side by side, our ears pressed to the wood. No footsteps come. Vaughan looks at me after a minute.

"Just like old times," he whispers. "Having fun?"

"You should go." Being close to him like this is having a weird effect on me that I don't want to think about. Plus, I really don't want detention.

He nods. We wait a minute more, and then I slowly open the door, looking up and down the corridor for anyone who might be lingering.

"Stay here. I'll check the side staircase," I say to him.

I run down the corridor and skibble down the stairs lightly. No one. I run back up and back into the dorm. "Coast is clear," I say.

He smiles. "Thanks, Catey-Cate."

I mock frown at his use of my nickname, and he giggles and the eight-year-old comes back. It breaks my heart. Suddenly I want to tell him I'm sorry for getting into that car all those years ago and never looking back. And I want to tell him that I like this weird, funny person my best friend turned into. But of course, I don't tell him that. I give him a brief, tight grin and tap his shoulder lightly like I'm patting a dog.

And he's off. I follow him down the corridor and then partially down the stairs and let him go.

On my way back, I get the urge to duck into the shower room again—but not to do anything more useful than check out my reflection. Do I look all right? Hair OK? Face OK? I redden. Like it matters. Like I care what Vaughan thinks.

We left my dorm door open. I leave the bathroom and walk back up the corridor to shut it. When I get there, there's something off, and I stop at the door. What's wrong here? I can't place what it is exactly—is the door open a little more than we left it? The air feels different, fresher, like someone opened a window and closed it again. I walk in slowly, eyeing my window. It is shut, and there are no indications that it has been open anytime recently. I'm about to leave when something catches my eye on the pillow next to Wuffy.

My watch.

I walk up to it slowly, as if it's going to explode. Was that there before? Surely not. I would have seen it while I was dying of embarrassment over my furry friend.

Who put the watch there?

I swing around, looking behind me, back at the door. I'm alone. I glance over to Marcia's bed. Has she been in after Vaughan and I were here? I lean over to pick the watch up. There's some sand in the rubber strap, but it's not scratched, and still ticking. I see something half sticking out from underneath Wuffy: a small white strip of paper. I drop the watch down onto the crumpled duvet and pick up the paper. There are words in bloodred ink:

YOU ARE RUNNING OUT OF TIME.

Blood rushes to my head, making me dizzy. I sink onto the bed, reading the piece of paper again, as if it's going to suddenly change. Whose handwriting? None that I recognize.

I force myself to stand and run to check the window again, run to the door and check the corridor, even crouch down on the floor and look under the bed. But no one is there.

"Hello?" I call out, my heart beating.

But of course, no one answers. Finally, I scrunch the paper up and shove it in my pocket and run all the way to high tea.

CHAPTER 8

The days pass, and in spite of the fact that I am "running out of time," Thursday dawns and I'm still alive. I hide the note in my study, in a psychology textbook. No chance of anyone finding it there.

Thursday means games, rather than the Game, unfortunately, and even worse, it means swimming. Umfraville has a wonderful outdoor pool. At least, it would be wonderful if the school was on an island somewhere hot, but as we're in the middle of the Irish Sea, it's a frigid nightmare.

Ezra decided we needed an Olympic-size pool, just in case we ever got ourselves an Olympic swimmer. The water's heated, so on any given day between the months of April and October, we can find ourselves being ushered into the wet. What they forget, of course, is that the air is not heated. The pool is high on the cliffs, the perfect place for maximum exposure to the cruel wind. Ezra didn't think too hard about that when he told the pool people where he wanted it built. It's probably the world's coldest infinity pool, as one side blends in perfectly with the sea below. Very picturesque. There's a full-on grandstand for observers and built-in locker rooms below, where we scurry after the lesson, dripping, indignant, and freezing to death.

Marcia has somehow managed to wangle her way out of this ordeal. Newspaper deadline probably—it affords her many privileges. I shuffle out of the locker room in my flip-flops and baggy hoodie, towel wrapped around my waist. The keen swimmers are warming up around the pool; no one is allowed in until a responsible adult arrives, obviously. A group of kids—mainly Guild—are sitting on the grandstand, almost at the top. I start the climb toward them.

We have this petty routine to keep us out of the water for the longest time possible. It goes like this: the gym teacher, Mr. Churley, will pop up out of some underground tunnel or wherever they keep him and call us all down to get into the pool. We'll plod down, drawing it out as long as we possibly can. It might shave a minute off actual swimming, but mostly it's about control in a place where we have none. As I climb up, I see that most of the boys are balancing on the benches, Rick telling some joke and beating his bare chest in the wind. The girls and the rest of the boys are a little ways off, huddled and whispering. I notice that Becky has her lovely, long hair in a swimming cap—probably not risking exposure to any more chemicals.

Daniel is up there on his own, looking miserable. Violinists really shouldn't be made to endure any kind of physical exercise;

it's just cruel. He's Goofy-tall, wearing a long, green-and-red robe, thin, hairy legs stretched out. He doesn't see me as I climb but gazes out to sea and taps an intricate rhythm, his long index fingers beating like drumsticks on his knees. Maybe he does see me, but he doesn't want to engage. There's that conversation we have to have at some point, and I'm dreading it even more as time goes by. I wonder if he's already buried it and replaced it with low-level disinterest. Boys can be very good at that.

OK, so in lieu of Daniel, let us talk about the awkward. I might be holding out on him, but I'll give it up for you.

Every year at Umfraville there's a summer party. It started off as a senior-class thing—a way to find a release after exams, legitimizing the partying that would find a way to surface regardless of whether the staff actually allowed it. However, after a few years, there were some complaints from lower down the school, and in the spirit of equality, Ezra decided to extend the party to everyone.

Last term's shindig was a classic. It was a rare hot night, and there was a tent on the lawn so that any teen not totally self-preoccupied could enjoy the sun setting over the water. School bands played; there was food and even swimming in the pool. Someone spiked the fruit punch, and I felt woozy. I was feeling lonely and full of self-doubt after the Alex hookup, and Daniel was there, and something was done that could not be undone. We kissed, right here, on this grandstand. At the time, I felt careless; now, it bothers me greatly.

Like I've said, I don't fancy Daniel. I've tried to, because it would be easier, but he's a friend. He makes me laugh, and we have the most ridiculous, tangential conversations that blow my mind because he's so clever and random and off the wall. We like the same sad music (apart from the violin stuff, which I'm not so big on), and we both get a kick out of anime and sci-fi movies. We are dweebs together, and it's comfortable. But normally I don't want to kiss him, and unfortunately for both of us, that is not mutual.

Oh, I don't know what I was thinking on the grandstand. Summer madness, yucky punch, and a stupid attempt to get rid of Alex Aftertaste, that's all. Daniel and I didn't talk about it the next day, and we haven't said much to each other since, which is phenomenally sad. As Marcia so kindly pointed out, he knows I don't want to boyfriend/girlfriend-up, and he also knows that I know he does. That's awkward to say but even more awkward to live.

So I park my behind on the benches a few rows down from him, on my own. It's getting to the point where all this ignoring is just stupid. Which of us is going to be the bigger person and get this friendship up and rolling again? I look out at the cold, slate-gray sea, then down into the warmer, pale-blue pool. Not either of us today.

"My, this is bracing!"

I jump. Vaughan has plonked himself down beside me. He's just wearing a Speedo, the teeny-tiny kind, not even the bike short one. Oh, bloody hell.

"Although, when I saw swimming on the timetable, I

thought we'd all be greasing ourselves up and heading for Ireland. Disappointingly tame, really. I hear the jellyfish are invigorating."

"Wait till you get out of the water," I quip. "It's cold enough. And we'll probably be doing this until midterms."

Vaughan slaps his thighs. "Hoorah for that!"

I'm trying not to look at him. Considering the last time I saw him semi-naked we were probably running under a hose in somebody's garden, it makes me nervous to see him in all his Speedo-ed glory. But out of the corner of my eye, I'm absolutely checking him out. In spite of his height and slender build, he doesn't have the unappealing lankiness of most tall teenage boys. Daniel leaps into my mind, and I hate myself for making the comparison. Vaughan's no muscleman freak like Rick, but there's certainly...tone. As we sit, I'm becoming aware of the attention he's getting from above—a ripple of approval from the girls. Wait till the boys spot him. He's going to get annihilated.

Mr. Churley appears below.

"Get your lazy arses down here!" he yells up at us. I think he likes it. If he ever appeared and there was no one sitting on the grandstand, I'm sure he'd be disappointed. Shouting at us is his idea of a warm-up.

"Duty calls." Vaughan smiles, standing up. I look at him—eyes strictly on his face—and he blinks at me. "Chop, chop!" he barks at me, sternly, just like Mr. Churley. "Hurry up and take your clothes off!"

I gulp, not knowing if that little glint in his eye means that he's making fun of me or flirting...or if it's all in my horrible little head.

At this precise moment, Daniel troops down the steps past our row. He obviously overhears. He looks at me, as doleful as Droopy, but behind the sad is fury. It shocks me just as much as what Vaughan just said. I think about organizing my features into a picture of innocence, but it's too late. He's gone.

"I promise I won't splash you."

Snap back to Vaughan, smiling that weird smile. Does he think he's flirting? Do I think he is? Blimey, this was never a problem when we were eight. As I pick my jaw up off the floor, the girls schlep down the stairs slowly, and as they pass, they are sure as hell checking out Vaughan with none of my subtlety.

"Move it!" Mr. Churley yells from below.

The Guild boys bound down the benches on the other side from us. Vaughan glances at them, and his eyes twinkle.

"Want to know a secret? They let me in!"

"What?" I falter.

"I'm Guild now." He beams. "Or good as. Alex and the other Elders came to my study last night. There's going to be some kind of initiation—of course! I'd be disappointed if there wasn't!—and naturally, the rules have to be bent a little because everyone will know I'm not the Killer." He barely pauses for breath. Below us there are splashes and yells from the first swimmers entering the water. "But I can be Killed, so that's exciting!"

"I'm…pleased for you." It's all I can think of to say, and it's true at least.

His green eyes narrow. "But not pleased for you?"

I switch my gaze to the swimmers, because I can't look him in the face, and I certainly can't afford to look at any other part of him. Below me, almost everyone else is in the pool, swimming up and down in lanes. Only a few stragglers are still disrobing or talking to Mr. Churley, trying to distract him so they get a few more precious moments of dry.

"You don't want me to play with you, Cate?" Vaughan pouts, mock hurt. Then again, maybe not so mock. I feel a hot face coming on.

"No, I do…" I wonder if I'm brave enough to be honest with him. "It's just weird seeing you again. It's nice"—my face must be burning—"but weird. Mixing friends, past and present." I stutter, the words sounding so formal. "And the Game is a big deal, you know? Being chosen. I've kind of worked my way up to it…"

"And I waltz in, so easily?" He's looking at me intently, examining my every pore. "I can understand that."

I bite my lip. "I still don't know why you want to be in the Game so badly," I mutter. "I mean, let's face it, you haven't told me why you're here, how come you know all the stuff you know about the island and everyone here and the Game." He looks away, suddenly focused on the pool. "But even more than that, why do you care?"

He doesn't answer for a minute. Well, maybe it's thirty

seconds, but it seems like the full sixty. Clouds cover the sun. Any second now, Mr. Churley will upgrade his yelling to screaming at us standing up here on our own. Just as I think Vaughan isn't going to speak, and I might as well jump into the deep, he answers me.

"I like to be challenged, Cate. It's what I need." He's still not looking at me, and his voice is so quiet I have to lean in to catch his words. "The Game. Yes, the puzzle of whodunnit and all that, a problem to solve, a solution to find." He waves a hand dismissively. "But there's more to this. What really interests me is the social game. It's not about brains or algorithms or studying so hard you think your mind is calcifying." His shoulders rise around his ears, and he sighs, trying to force an ease of tension. "Social acceptance. That's everything, isn't it? It shouldn't matter, but it does because I've never had it. I just want to see if I can. The ultimate challenge for me." He glances at me and then back to the water. "And so this is my laboratory." His hand waves over the pool below. "This is my social experiment, my attempt to assimilate. If I can't make them love me here, in this school of freaks and geeks, where can I? You have to fake it till you make it." He turns to me again. "And the fact you're here, well..." His face crumples, and he suddenly pulls a silly expression, as if making light of everything he's just said. "It just seems right. You always were a good sidekick."

This is my cue to mock punch him, argue about who is the leader, who the follower. But I won't. "Thanks," I say, making myself look at him. His eyes shine with a sudden hope that pierces my heart. "For explaining. And for giving me, er, another chance."

He kind of coughs, looks away, and so do I. This is deep stuff. That was almost my apology. It's making me itchy. "We should go down there." I gesture vaguely to the swimmers, echoing Vaughan's own theatrical wave. It feels clumsy. I clamp my hand to my side to stop it from happening again.

Vaughan frowns. "What on earth is that?"

At first I think the comment is aimed at me, but then I realize he's also looking at the pool.

"There, in the corner." He answers my question before I've asked it, pointing to the far corner of the deep end. There's a kind of blur in the water, a dark patch in the pale blue.

"Nice," I say. "Is it oil or dirt or something?"

The clouds move, and the sun comes out again. The blur is vivid red.

"Or something," Vaughan says. I swear he licks his lips.

There's a swimmer in the corner. Cynthia, Elder of the Guild, in fact.

She doesn't seem to see the stuff behind her. She is treading water, skinny stick arms fiddling with her swimming cap, trying to push those enviable blond curls underneath the rubber. Then she swims to the edge of the pool, pushes off, and starts to head back the other way. A trail of red follows her.

"Is she bleeding?" Vaughan says loudly.

"Oh, please no." I cringe. My first thought: period. Every girl's total nightmare. Mother Nature shows up at the swimming pool and ruins the rest of your school life.

There's quite a trail of red. It's a slick behind her as she plows through the water, a red wake. And she is blissfully ignorant.

But others begin to notice. The small posse on the side of the pool have seen, and some of her fellow swimmers. There's shrieking, and *oh, gross*-ing, and before I know it, Vaughan and I are poolside. Mr. Churley is standing by, looking in with an expression of concern, irritation, and embarrassment. People are climbing out of the pool, pulling each other up, shivering with cold and adrenaline, as if Jaws has been let loose in the chlorine.

And still Cynthia swims on.

"Calm down, everyone!" Mr. Churley says, trotting up the side of the pool. "Cynthia! Cynthia, dear!"

Wow. First time he's ever called anyone *dear*.

A couple of Cynthia's friends follow. You can see they're debating whether to jump in and somehow "save" her, but let's face it, nobody wants to get in the water with all the red, and nobody wants to be the one to tell her.

She reaches the end of the pool, her head bobbing up for a quick breather.

"Cynthia!" Mr. Churley practically screams.

She stops and grasps the side, looking up at him and her friends and then the rest of us in puzzlement. She sees us looking in the water. And then she sees it. The red slick, the red swirling around her legs, trailing after her, pooling behind. Her face flashes alarm, then—oh the horror—full-on realization…

A small yellow thing pops up in the water beside her. She reaches for it and lifts it out of the water gingerly.

Pop! Pop! Pop!

More yellow things emerge across the pool. Cynthia thinks it's finally time to get out. She hauls herself up the ladder in the corner, red streaking her thin, pale legs. A friend wraps a towel around her, and the red leeches pink through the white toweling.

There's a splash beside me, and I turn to see a figure jumping clumsily into the shallows. Vaughan emerges, shaking the water off his hair, and reaches out for a yellow thing. He strides through the water, brings the yellow thing to the edge and throws it at my feet like a well-trained Labrador. I jump as it rolls against my flip-flop.

A rubber duck.

I bend slowly, picking it up between finger and thumb, as if it's contaminated—which it might be.

Someone has drawn big, fangy teeth on the duck's bill with black marker.

Back down at the deep-end poolside, Cynthia is fiddling with something on her lower back. She struggles for a few seconds, then holds whatever it is up in front of her. Difficult to see it exactly from here, but it drips red, like a giant, bloody teabag.

"Killed!" Vaughan shouts from the water. "Cynthia, you are Killed!" He runs down the side of the pool to her.

Not too far for me to see the look of disgust and anger on Cynthia's pretty face. She tosses the teabag into the water, striding up the poolside, the long, bloodied towel flying out behind her. Her chiseled features are set with anger, bony fists clenched. Everyone is laughing now; a couple more Killer Ducks are retrieved from the pool, and as Cynthia passes us en route to the locker room, someone starts quacking. She flashes them an angry look. Oh, blimey. Cynthia is going to be plagued with quacks forever, that's for sure. But I can see the relief in her eyes too; she may be the Duck Queen now, but at least she's not going to be Period Girl, because that would be utterly unbearable.

"Look around you. Who's here?" The whisper in my ear makes me jump.

Vaughan is beside me again, bare body glistening in the sunlight.

"Come on!" He grabs my arm, pulling me away from the throng and around the side of the grandstand. "Check out what I hooked with the pool net!" He holds up a sodden, very thin rectangle of material, about the size of a phone; the bloodied "tea bag" that was attached to Cynthia. It is still dripping red.

"Reasonably clever," he says. "Muslin, with an inner layer of polymer, I'd bet. Then probably the same dye as the Killer used in the showerhead."

"That little pouch caused all of that red in the water?"

Vaughan nods gleefully. "Along with Donald and Daisy." He holds up a couple of the ducks. "Look—this one's still got some of the polymer attached to the back."

"Er, poly-what?"

"Water-soluble polymer. You know, the stuff that covers dishwasher tabs? It melts off when it comes into contact with water." He chuckles. "Pretty ingenious."

"Who the hell has that lying around in their locker?" I'm shivering out of the sun.

"It's easy to come by. They wrap magazines in the stuff, eco-friendly, you know? Or you can buy it online." Vaughan shrugs. "Maybe they have some in one of the labs? Or the Killer came prepared just in case?" He looks around the corner to where I can hear Mr. Churley ordering everyone back into the locker rooms. "The important thing to know is that the Killer is here right now. Someone stuck this to Cynthia's back while she was swimming; she would have noticed it otherwise. And they planted the ducks at the bottom of the pool." His eyes narrow and he frowns. "I wonder how. Maybe they were weighted; maybe there was some kind of adhesive? But the Killer wouldn't have been able to place them there in advance because the plastic melts relatively quickly."

I pull a face. "OK...did you see anyone planting copious ducks at the bottom of the pool, Vaughan?"

"No." He shakes his head. "Oh, I wish I knew how it was done! Do you think Churley will notice if I jump back in and take a look?"

"I think he just might," I say. "Because you can bet that he's going to be furious that someone ruined his precious pool, and he's going to be thinking how in the name of Bloody Mary he's going to explain to Ezra why the thing needs cleaning." I grab

Vaughan's arm. He's surprisingly warm, given that he's wet and practically naked. "Besides, you always hated the water, didn't you? We need to go and get changed."

But in spite of playing mother hen, you can bet your life that I'm running through a mental list of who was here at the poolside this morning. I go into the girls' locker room. Everyone from the Guild was here, all except Marcia. I can probably cross her off my list of suspects. I sigh as I get my clothes out of my locker. But that would be a great way to fool us, wouldn't it?

The locker room is unusually quiet as we all get dressed. We're on edge, and no one more than me, fully expecting to find another note, a "you're next" in my shoe, or a "get ready!" in my bag, but there's nothing.

Clothes on, I feel the little black band around my wrist and get out of there—still alive, still in the Game. I loiter outside the locker rooms, waiting for Vaughan to appear, but he never does. As I'm about to give up, I notice something bright and familiar in the hedgerow that lines the path to the pool. I trot up to it and reach into the stinging nettles tentatively, grabbing a leather handle and pulling until the hedge gives up its prize.

Marcia's tote bag dangles from my hand. Unmistakable. How did it get here? I open it, but it's empty. Water drips off the material as if it's been sitting in a puddle, not stuffed into a hedge.

I run with it to the newspaper office, composing my questions for Marcia in my head as I go. The doorknob sticks in my hand; I give it a twist and a shove.

"Marcia!"

My voice sounds stern as it echoes around the room. The place is in darkness.

I dump the bag on the floor by her desk and go back to the door to leave, but it won't open. I turn the handle this way and that, pull it, and push it, but it's jammed again. Struggling, I feel my heart begin to pound. Just as I'm about to cry out in panic, the door opens and I fall outside and run the rest of the way back to Main House as if someone is chasing me.

CHAPTER 9

Saturday morning. Two dead, and I'm not one of them.

Alex thumps the yellow skull down on the breakfast table and a roar goes up. The Summoning is called for four o'clock; we are more than ready.

There's no bus to the mainland today, and after morning classes, the place is busy with people running around in the late-September sunshine. I don't like this; I want everyone not Guild to just clear out and leave Skola to us. After the high-profile Kills of this week, everyone is on high alert for interference from outside.

We all get IMs from Alex. We're under strict instructions to be as sly and quiet as possible, to travel individually, to double back and give any stalkers the slip. Of course, it strikes me that this is the perfect opportunity for the Killer to catch someone alone, and that could be deadly.

But before the fun and games, I have work to do. Daniel. The time has come. On the one hand I miss him; on the other I'm sick of the puppy-dog eyes I'm getting from across the crowded dining hall. Somehow, because the sun is shining, it makes what I have to do feel safer. Behind it all, everything between us is actually sunny and light and fine, and we will banish those silly dark clouds away before they block out the light completely.

I try the music studios first. I'm surprised he's not there, but not that surprised. He often goes to the cliffs to practice on weekends—a wandering minstrel serenading the seagulls. I think a little walk may be in order. I start to cross the library quad to swing by my study and pick up a scarf, because in spite of this startling autumn sun, I know it will be windy and cold by the sea. The quad is a natural sun trap, and this morning it is as busy as it gets—kids sitting on benches, a few on skateboards, messing around in a way only allowed on the weekends. The quad is enclosed by a continuous single-level building on three sides, which houses the upperclassmen's studies. Each study is tiny—just enough room for two desks and a small sofa, and all run off a narrow corridor which looks out onto the quad. On the fourth side is the library: a mock-Tudor, two-floor building with a clock tower. At Umfraville, this quad is the center of our world.

I duck into my study and grab the scarf. Marcia is so seldom here, but she must have been in earlier because she has shut the curtains, and only a chink of sunlight illuminates the tiny room. I sigh; Marcia's tote bag is a shadowy lump on the desk. After the pool, I'd tracked her down in the common room, told her

I'd found her bag in the hedge all wet, and asked how it had got there. But she was only half listening, laughing with Alex and Rick as they regaled her with the Cynthia Kill, and somehow she got it into her head that I was saying I'd borrowed her bag. She turned the questions around on me—why did I need it? How come it was wet? I gave up and left her to it. Some things kind of get lost in translation. Or maybe she was just being very, very clever.

I flick the light switch on in the room, and colors jump out at me—posters covering every inch of wall, a tasseled red-and-fuchsia scarf from Spain, and some of my more experimental acrylic paintings in bright primaries. Marcia's desk enjoys pole position on the opposite wall beside the window. There's a two-seater sofa on the other side, and there are two small bookshelves squeezed in here somehow. My desk is by the door...and on it is a steaming mug of what smells like hot chocolate.

"Ooh." My mouth waters. It smells so good.

There's a red card—a valentine's heart—propped up beside it. I pick it up and open the card. Typed words jump up at me:

LET'S BE FRIENDS AGAIN!

DRINK ME

I blush, fingering the heart, and I know immediately who it's from: Vaughan. Has to be. We used to have hot chocolate together when we were little kids; it was one of our things. We caused all kinds of chaos by melting down chocolate bars on the stove at his house—his parents let us do such things at eight mine never would have—and we'd make ourselves sick on the hot, sticky mess we produced.

And he always loved *Alice in Wonderland*, hence the "Drink Me" ref. *Oh, Vee,* I think to myself. This is full-on corny, but it's full-on lovely too.

I pick up the mug, hugging the warmth with both hands. The heart motif is continued in chocolate syrup resting in the foam. I imagine drinking deep from the mug, that foam caressing my upper lip, the warm liquid filling me up. Maybe it's not so awkward having Vaughan around after all. He's proving to be pretty popular with the female side of the senior class in any case.

I bring the mug up to my lips, taking in the sweet, creamy smell.

And then I stop, jerking the mug away sharply, so that the liquid spills down my hand and burns me. I cry out and drop it stupidly. The stuff splashes down my jeans and onto the floor, the mug rolling under my desk.

"What the hell were you thinking?" I clutch at my throat. "You stupid fool!"

We're in the midst of the Game, and I've just had my watch returned to me with a creepy note, and now someone leaves me a hot cocoa in my study with instructions to drink it?

I assume it's Vaughan? Get real. This was left by the Killer. Seriously, is this amateur hour? Sometimes I am so preoccupied and dense.

I sit down at my desk, breathing heavily. It was *Jabberwocky*

Vaughan used to like, not *Alice*. I wipe my hand on a dry bit of leg and look at the mug lying under the desk as if it's going to jump up and bite my throat. It's totally illegal within the Game now, but there could be laxatives involved. Not fun. On the other hand, hot sauce or just adding something bitter or gross-tasting but benign is completely allowed—and completely revolting. And if I was taken down by a Kill as ridiculous as this, I'd look pathetic!

I sniff at my hand. It doesn't smell hot sauce-y. That means nothing. I get down on my hands and knees and prepare to retrieve the mug, glancing behind me, up at the window. Is anyone watching? I scan the room for anything out of place, a camera, something? The other Kills were so public. This seems weirdly private—and wrong.

I lean forward and carefully pick up the mug. It's a standard white school one. Nothing special. I back out from underneath the desk and stand up slowly, looking inside the mug.

I'M WATCHING YOU

The same jagged red letters as the note with the watch scrawled inside. I nearly drop the flippin' mug again. Genuine terror rises up in me like white heat, crawling up my body and making my face hot and my head spin. Finding an insect in the bottom of your cup? This is worse, much, much worse. Thank God I didn't drink it.

A shadow passes in my peripheral vision, and my head whips

around to the window. I leap toward the curtains but stop short of opening them. What if the Killer is out there? What will I see? The sunshine and the background noise of kids screaming in the quad behind me give me courage. I pull back the curtains.

Nothing. A lawn, some trees. In the distance, a gardener is raking leaves. Beyond him is the walled rose garden. Nobody else around. I breathe.

I look down at the mug again, and as the fear dissipates, my heart sinks. Am I Killed? Am I out of the Game now? I didn't drink the chocolate though, and even if I did, it just says, "I'm watching you." Wouldn't it say something more like, er, "You're dead" or "Gotcha"? But no, he or she is just messing with my mind. Like with the watch. I put the mug back on my desk. Do I report this? Keep it to myself? I don't remember the protocol. It could be I'm not the only one getting these love notes from the Killer.

A knock on the door makes me jump out of my boots.

Shall I open it? Is this part of the Killer's plan?

I climb up onto my desk, grabbing my hockey stick and piling up some art textbooks to stand on. Leaning on the doorframe, I use the end of the stick to press the handle down and open the door slowly. I peek through the top of the door as it opens.

Daniel stands there, violin case in hand. Relief floods through me. Even Daniel is better than the Killer.

"Cate?" He's clearly freaked out by the door being answered by Ms. Invisible. And he's not holding anything. I decide to risk it.

"Hi!" I wave lamely from above. "Just thought you might be the Killer."

"Oh! Hello, up there." He smiles a little. "Killer? Maybe I am, but that's not why I'm here."

"No, it's not." I hop down, pushing the mug behind the art books so he can't see it. "Or at least if you are the Killer, I don't think you'd come knocking. You wouldn't be that ordinary."

He likes that, nods. Then we have that silence that I knew we'd have. At last, he breaks it. "I've been looking for you."

"Me too," I say, exiting the room past him. Something makes me not want to share the cup situation. I haven't figured out who to share Killer stuff with yet, apart from Vaughan.

Daniel follows me, and I shut the door, babbling nonsensically. "When I say 'me too,' I mean that I've been looking for you too, not looking for myself in some kind of existential soul-searching way or anything." I raise an eyebrow and sigh. "We need to talk, don't we?"

He gulps, blushes. Oops, too direct. Trust me to cut to the chase.

"Yes, we do," he says finally. "I know you've been avoiding me."

Hmm. I'll let that one pass. I lock my door behind us. We rarely lock our study doors around here, but normal takes a rest during the Game, so Daniel doesn't comment. We walk down the corridor and out into the quad where kids are still hanging out. Someone's kicking a ball, and I can see Alex in one corner, with some of his cronies and groupies around him. He's playing his guitar and pulling his best misunderstood-rock-star face. For a moment, I wish I was sitting there too, but I banish that thought.

"Shall we go for a walk?" I say. "Far from the madding crowd?"

"Absolutely." Daniel looks relieved. More than two people is a madding crowd for him.

We walk across the quad, dodging the skateboarders and ducking the football, and head for the archway. Then from behind us comes a scream. We both swing around.

Tesha, who had been sitting on the bench directly in front of the library, is standing, shaking her hands, and some kind of liquid is flying off them. Her friends, Whitney and Anvi, have also evacuated the bench, which is dripping with something gooey.

Splat! Splat!

Little explosions on the ground, and the goo splashes on concrete. Something is falling from the sky.

"Red," Daniel murmurs.

"Where are they coming from?" The sun is in my eyes, and I hold up a hand to shield my face.

"Up there." He points to the clock tower. Sure enough, another couple of missiles appear from a small window below the clockface.

"Killer!"

A shout from the archway—it's Vaughan. He runs to us, pointing to the crowd of Guild. "Quick, Cate, take it in. Who's here? Who's missing? The Killer must be in the tower. We'll catch him!"

And he takes off, sprinting across the quad toward the library. I follow, and Daniel—never given to sprinting usually—follows me. We run past the Three Witches—Tesha, Anvi, and Whitney—who are all now wearing varying degrees of blood splatter, and into the building. In the entrance hall, Vaughan pauses to look back and forth, but I'm way ahead of him.

"This way!" I beckon from a door in the corner. Vaughan doesn't know about the stairs that lead to the clock tower. It's usually out of bounds to kids, but a few of us art students were allowed up there last term to paint the view from the very window that the missiles appeared from. I race down a corridor through another door and then up the stairs. When my brain has time to catch up with my feet, I'll try to remember which Guild kids were included in that art class.

"This the only way in and out?" Vaughan bounds past me.

"I think so!"

Somewhere above us, a door slams.

"Quickly!" Vaughan leaps up the stairs, seemingly without effort. I'm close on his heels, Daniel somewhere behind.

I reach a door and stop—but Vaughan runs on.

"Here!" I hiss. "This is the room with the window!"

He jogs down the stairs again. "What's in there?"

I shrug. "Nothing much. It's a storeroom."

"And up there?" He points up the stairs. "Only the clock?"

"As far as I know."

Vaughan nods. "You." He points at Daniel, who has joined us, and is doubled over, panting. "Stay here. If the Killer comes down the stairs, yell."

Daniel looks up at him, raises his eyebrows. "Er, no."

"Please, Daniel," I whisper. "We'll just be a minute."

"I don't even know why I'm here to be honest."

Vaughan looks shocked, offended even. "You're Guild, aren't you? You want to find the Killer."

Daniel sighs but nods. "Go on, then. I'll play along. But if I get whacked standing here like an idiot, it's on you two."

Vaughan claps him on the back. "Understood. Good man."

I sense Daniel stiffen, but he says nothing, and Vaughan doesn't seem to notice. Vaughan nods at me and eyes the door. "After you."

Thanks. I give him a look, open the door slowly, and peek inside.

The first suspicious thing is that the light is on. Incongruous fluorescent strips, buzzing away in the exposed rafters of the sloped roof. Dust has been stirred up; I feel it in the air, scratching my throat and making my eyes water. I blink. The room is large and almost bare except for a few stacked library chairs, a couple folded trestle tables, and half a dozen boxes of books. There is nowhere much to hide.

I take a step in, and the bare, varnished boards creak spookily beneath my feet. There's a pillar a couple feet away from the door, and the view to the window is obscured. Vaughan and I tiptoe to the pillar and peer around it to the window.

Thock. Thock. Thock.

The window is open, and red, circular things are flying out of it. Below the window is a black box with what looks like a big bowl on top.

Thock. Thock.

The balls are flying out of some kind of machine.

Vaughan walks up to it. "It's a tennis ball machine."

I join him and pick a gooey, red tennis ball out of the large bowl at the top of the machine. I'm saving the ball from its fate. There's a hole in the bowl, and the balls fall down it to emerge a few seconds later out of the mouth of the machine at considerable speed. I squeeze the ball gently. There's a long slit in the ball that almost cuts it in two, and it oozes viscous red. It's gross—and highly effective.

"This Killer certainly likes blood." I shake my head. "I suppose it's nice to have a theme."

"He's reasonably inventive within the established tropes, I suppose," Vaughan says. "Some might say these are classic Kills—the shower, the clock tower."

"The pool one was just icky. And they're all so messy." I put the ball back in the bowl and wipe my fingers on the rim.

"Killer's a boy. Boys like mess. They're like dogs; they like to mark their territory," Vaughan says.

"Oh, yuck." I can't quite look him in the eye. "Don't go applying your own disgustingness to the entirety of the male sex."

"We're all the same, Cate." He takes a step closer, and this time I make myself look at him. He smiles when he sees the effort involved. "We're animals, I tell you."

There's a voice behind us.

"So?"

I spin around. Daniel. He walks up to us.

"I checked up the stairs. Door is locked, no way in. And nobody in here, I see." Daniel looks at the machine. There's only my oozy ball left; it drops into the hole and comes out with a final thock. "Clever. The Killer didn't have to stick around."

Vaughan is examining the machine. "The Killer didn't even need to be here to set it going. These things have remotes."

"Wouldn't you have to be in the line of sight?" I say.

He shakes his head, impatient. "RF remote, not IR." He sees my blank face. "These machines aren't infrared like your TV. They work by radio wave. Like a car key fob. They can go through walls, thirty-yard range easily." He gestures to the courtyard below. "The Killer was probably sunning himself with the rest of them." He grabs my arm. "Got any face powder on you?"

"You're in need of a touch-up?" I raise an eyebrow. "Best I can do is ChapStick."

"Ach!" Vaughan paces up and down. "I should have come prepared. It's an ideal opportunity to take some fingerprints off the machine."

"Hey, what's going on in here?"

"Were you throwing those things?"

Suddenly the room is filling up with the kids who all eventually had the same idea as us. The Triumvirate of Pretty—Tesha,

Anvi, and Whitney—are here, looking like roadkill and talking ten to the dozen.

"This is not a righteous Kill!" Tesha says. She's as red in the face as the stuff on her clothes. "We all three got splattered, but the balls could have landed near anyone!"

"The rules say no multiple Kills, and nothing that could affect any passersby." Whitney is calmer, but only just. "We are not accepting that we're Killed."

"Anyway," Anvi shouts, bleached ponytail waggling and brown skin flushed. "I hardly got any. It's just on my shoe. Tesha is covered!"

"Yeah, by accident!" Tesha's fighting for her life, globules of "blood" dangling off her curls. "The balls were falling nearer you but the first few bounced toward me. It was totally random!"

Everyone's monkeying with the machine now, and I can see Vaughan boiling at the lost opportunity to CSI the bejesus out of it. I'm actually a little surprised he doesn't carry some kind of kit on him for just this eventuality.

"Rick, Carl, take the machine away." Alex has appeared. "Apprentices, clear the quad. Let's do this before any teacher comes by."

"Alex!" Tesha squawks at him. "I'm not bloody dead, am I?"

He guffaws at her. "You're dead bloody." Everyone laughs. "Seriously, enough for now. Get cleaned up and we'll talk later at the Summoning."

I look around, and Vaughan has gone. I head down the stairs, Daniel following.

"If Alex thinks I'm cleaning fake blood from the flagstones, he's got another thing coming," he mutters.

"I suppose he doesn't want to give the school any more ammunition to close the Game down." We reach the ground floor. "The pool was an expensive prank." Outside, Martin has already got a bucket of water and is washing the blood away. I turn to Daniel. "Do you want to get out of here and talk still?"

He looks up into the sky, as if the answer is written in the clouds. "No need. Think we both know where we stand. I'll see you later." He makes a beeline for the archway without a backward glance.

"Oh that really helps, Daniel!" I shout after him. Martin looks up from his cleaning, but I don't care. And in that moment, I don't care about Daniel either. He's drama but not even in a fun way. He's just an energy sap. Even before the ill-conceived kiss, he was hard work. I'd put in endless hours of dealing with his moods and the frequent Eeyore-type nonsense he habitually threw, in return for what? An occasional wonderful, funny afternoon when he was doing manic, rather than depressive? And now I'm supposed to feel bad because I made a mistake and kissed him?

I close my eyes and groan. I do feel bad. I bounced into Daniel's arms on the rebound—meaning to stick the knife in Alex before he could stick it in me—but really the only person who got hurt in all of this is Daniel. And I think he's totally assuming I fancy Vaughan now. What a stupid mess. Daniel is my friend, and whatever bad romances are happening in my ridiculous life, I have to put this right somehow.

"Hey, stop!" I run after him.

"What's wrong?" To my surprise he does stop and turn, pale face alarmed.

"This!" I pant. "I don't want things to be weird between us, and I'm sick of your attitude. I know you're uncomfortable, and I know we, you know, kissed, but can't we get over it?"

He looks down at his feet, then up at me. I'm surprised by the fury in his dark eyes.

"Get over it? Just like that?" He looks down again. "You have no idea, do you?"

"What, that you 'like' me?" I flick my fingers in the air. "Can't we just be friends though? We were good at that." I take a deep breath. "I miss you, you know? I don't like it when you're not around."

"But I am around!" He says, ferocious. "You just don't see me! Especially when there are other people on the menu."

"On the menu...?" My jaw drops. "What does that mean? Who, for goodness sake, is on my menu?"

He turns and walks toward the music rooms again, refusing to answer me.

"You're not around!" I repeat. "When do you see me with all these people who are on my menu?"

He turns on his heel and stares me down. "Oh, I see you, Cate. You may not notice me, but I'm always there."

He turns and disappears into the music department

building. I groan, frustrated. What does he mean, he's always there? What kind of cryptic crap is that?

It's only when I'm dragging my heels back to my study that I remember the mug.

I'm watching you...

CHAPTER 10

Saturday afternoon and my heart is still beating. Just.

I'm early for the second Summoning, but when I arrive the cave is already over half-full. Daniel is there, sitting at the back next to Marcia, his head buried in some old, dusty book. I'm not even sure that there's enough light in here for him to read, but he's certainly giving his best impression of it. There's a golden oldie Evanescence song playing in the background, and the atmosphere is hyper, fueled no doubt by the morning's pseudo Killing. There was already so much to talk about, but now the chatter is threatening to spill over into the surrounding chambers of the caves and flow out on to the sand and to the sea.

"Were you followed?" Alex calls out to me as I enter. I shake my head. "Sure?" he presses.

"I'm sure!" Blimey. If we ever were on our guard, it's now. I find a crate to sit on and park myself. It's cold in here, maybe even colder than outside. The generator isn't on, and the cave is only lit by a single oil lamp and half of the candles. There's a sense of everything being rushed. I eye the electric heater with longing, but clearly Alex is saving the juice for when we really need it. I plunge my hands into my parka, and pull out gloves. Stuff clatters to the floor—my keys, my Guild rule book, tissues, lip balm. I scoop everything up and shove it back in.

The cave is filling up, slowly but surely. People arrive in twos and threes; maybe everyone had set off individually as requested by Alex but recklessly gave in to the herding instinct when close to the caves.

"Sit quickly," Alex says. "We have a lot to talk about." He casts around the room. "Are we all here?"

"Tesha almost didn't come," Carl says, a sly smile on his face. He's stirring the pot, but ever so casually, chin leaning on hands, his auburn hair looking startlingly red in the candle-light. "Tesha's in a huff at getting that crap all over her old-lady cardigan. Nice one, Killer."

"Shut up, Carl." Tesha sighs. "It's cashmere, and that paint won't come off."

"You'll get over it, Tesh." Alex can't quite suppress his own smile. With any of his ex-conquests, he's secretly a little delighted when they look foolish. "We are joined by the rest of the dead, and you don't hear them complaining." He looks over at Cynthia and Becky.

Tesha looks ready to explode. "We're not dead though—are we, Alex?" She glances at her friends for support, but Whit and Anvi sit tight, black and blond heads bent together, yin and yang, twins in negative. Their best bet could be to stay silent and hope that the victim is decreed to be Tesha. "It was a mass Kill, and that's not allowed—"

Alex holds up his hand. "Tesha, we'll get to that. Don't pee your pants." There's a tittering. "Now can we get started?"

"We're all here." Marcia has done a headcount.

"One missing," Rick says, jaw set.

"No," Marcia says, "Thirteen players, one Grand Master."

"You're forgetting our new recruit…" Rick growls.

"Hello, folks!" Vaughan is on cue at the doorway, waving like an over-animated clown. "Thought I'd give you all time to settle down before I landed on you." His entrance is not quite as crazy as last time, but it makes as much of an impression.

"New recruit?" Martin cries. "He's in for definite?"

"In like Flynn!" Vaughan grins, then looks at me. "Oh—no offense, I know how keen you are on your *mentor*."

I choke; I die and try not to look like I'm dying.

"We don't get to put it to the vote?" Daniel speaks up. Everyone looks at him, because it happens so rarely.

"Oh, you're still here, Daniel?" Vaughan says, all smiles. "Only this morning you didn't look like you were that keen. Not interested in getting to the bottom of anything, really. That being the case, the Killer would do well to spare you and keep you in the Game. Unless, of course, it's all an elaborate ruse and you're actually the Killer." Vaughan puts his head to one side, genuinely interested. "No, I don't think you are. All that blood, eh?" He tuts sympathetically. "Not sure that you have the stomach."

Daniel stands up, which in Daniel land is tantamount to throwing a punch.

"Settle down, boys." Marcia stands up too. "It's done. Vaughan presented a unique case for being included, and the Elders voted him in. Everything he said about his intranet looks like it's true, and Crypt will take this Game to new levels."

There's a murmur of discontent, mainly male discontent, and I understand why. People have waited years to make the team, and this new bloke just turns up and joins without any problems.

Alex hushes everyone. "Rules are this: Vaughan's obviously not the Killer. He can vote, and he can be Killed. That's it."

"I think it's a great idea." Whitney twinkles at Vaughan, peering at him coyly from underneath fronds of black hair. "Welcome."

"Good decision, Elders." Emily is smiling too, crossing and uncrossing those long, tanned legs.

"Don't worry. He will have his own special initiation," Rick says, practically licking his chops.

The boys laugh at that. You can bet they've already discussed what the initiation will be. Rick Musclehead is obviously relishing the chance to be cruel and unusual with someone new.

"So, to this week's Kills," Alex says. "We have much to talk about..."

Vaughan sits down on an empty crate beside me; I can feel

the girls' eyes on him, and I surprise myself with a tiny slither of pleasure at the fact he is beside me.

"Our Killer has been very busy," Alex says. "I can only commend them for that. I can't remember a year when there were three murders in the first week."

"Two!" Tesha says. "Only two!"

Alex closes his eyes and pauses for a moment. "The first Kill. We boys didn't get to see it in the flesh, but of course we have our spies everywhere, even the girls' shower room."

The boys laugh. Some of the girls tut and roll their eyes.

"You wouldn't dare put a camera in there!" Whitney says, loving the idea a little too much.

"Hey, Vaughan"—Carl grins, his freckled face lighting up—"can we post videos on this new intranet?"

Vaughan nods. "Oh, it's definitely possible." He cracks his knuckles. "But let's not go there."

"Enough!" Alex says. "As I was saying, the first Kill. We open with a classic: blood shower. Our Killer is kicking off to a great start with a nod to traditions past. Well done, whoever you are."

No one speaks. We all sit there, eyeing each other, wondering who the guilty one is.

"Second Kill, however, Killer goes big," Alex says. "And sadly, classy goes out the window."

"That doesn't even begin to cover it." Cynthia stutters out the words, pulling a blanket around her thin frame protectively.

"Yeah, well," Alex says. "Cynthia has a bloody wake, and the pool is out of action for the rest of the term." He sits up a little.

"Now that in itself may be no bad thing, but the Killer broke the cardinal rule on this one: don't incur the wrath of staff. Because while they will tolerate stupid stuff and the odd mess that can be wiped away, Ezra does not like pool clean-ups that cost him major dough."

Carl leans forward. "We removed the waterfowl, and the paint was all but diluted within minutes, but even so. The pool has to be drained. Ezra called Alex and me into his office to ask us what we knew about it. Obviously, we know nothing and told him it was a random prank, not part of the Game. He gave us the benefit—this time. But one more stunt like that, and the Game could be in jeopardy."

"And you wouldn't want that," says Roger, excitedly slapping his palms on to fat thighs as he sits. "Not while you've still got some more Kills in you, Carl."

Carl grins wolfishly and winks at him. I wonder if it is him. There's something unsettling about Carl. He's the real strategist of the Elders. Alex is the mouthpiece, and Marcia the obvious brains, but I suspect a lot of the ideas originate from Carl. He's like a man in boy's clothing, and he unnerves me a little.

"And that brings us to Kill three, or at least, attempt three." Alex finishes the sentence before Tesha can jump on in. "Now, I have nothing but awe for the concept. Nice creativity, but stupidly messy and stupidly random. Firstly, Killer, you need to remember that you're a serial psycho, not a mass murderer. One Kill at a time. You can Kill one victim, then do another five minutes later for all I care. But they have to be separate murders, not the result of raining blood-soaked tennis balls on the general populace. There were non-Guild there, and if you had hit them, you would be history. As it is, we all know you splattered three apprentices: Tesha, Whitney, Anvi. So who's dead?"

The three sit up, awaiting their fate.

"We Elders have voted on it," Marcia drawls.

"And it looks like you were targeted, Tesha," says Cynthia. Tesha's face drops. Even the curls droop a little.

"But," Alex says, "we can't be sure. It was too imprecise. And because of that, all three of you live to fight another day." He lets the girls have their noisy celebration and told-you-sos. "Be specific, Killer! This is your first and last warning; don't let it happen again or your reign is over. And"—he turns to the girls—"be on your guard! Chances are one of you was on the Killer's hit list. Don't make it easy for them."

Alex relaxes a little and cracks open a can of something. "Right, before we vote on who the Killer is, there's time for Zuckerberg here to show us around our new digital home. Fire up the generator."

Rick exits into the corridor, and the fairy lights flicker on. The generator hums as Marcia taps away on the laptop and then hands it to Alex. He swings the screen around to face us all.

"The Elders have discussed how this is going to work, and it's up to its creator to explain it all to the rest of you. Vaughan?"

Vaughan leaps up and takes the stage willingly. He taps on the keyboard, and the school's intranet home page comes up.

It's a photograph of the school with links to the instant messaging app, a school bulletin board, and the online version of the school newspaper. In the top right-hand corner is the school crest, a large red flower against a yellow shield, with a phoenix rising behind the shield. Vaughan smiles at us all.

"I'm aware that almost everyone here is dazzlingly clever, but for the sake of the athletes among us, I've kept the log-in process simple."

Rick mock laughs and swears under his breath. Vaughan is not winning himself many friends from that particular demographic.

"First time you log in, it must be from a laptop. All you need to do is this." Vaughan talks as if to a toddler and moves the cursor until it is centered on the eye of the phoenix. "Left click, while holding down Control and K, I, L simultaneously, like so."

"Oh yeah—like how many fingers do we need to do that, eh?" Rick scoffs.

"You do need two free hands, so you'll have to take one out of your pants," Vaughan says seriously. Rick glares at him. It's true he has a full-on pocket billiards habit. The girls—and Alex and Carl—reward Vaughan with a laugh.

Rick points at the screen. "And nothing has happened. Uh-oh, broken."

"I'd forgive you for thinking so, Rick," Vaughan says. "But guess what? You have to press the buttons again! Input that key combo twice in more than five seconds and less than ten. So just one-crocodile, two-crocodile up to six, press again, and you're in. Simple…provided you can count that high."

"Ha-ha," Rick says. "Tell another one, I'm wetting myself."

"Oh no." Vaughan looks at him, concerned. "How unfortunate for you." He presses the keys, his eyes on Rick all the time, and the screen with the William Blake picture comes up again. "And here we are. Now click on the owl, and when the password box pops up, enter 'Neanderthal Ricky'—"

"Are you kidding me?" Rick yells.

"Ah, so astute." Vaughan grins at him. "I am. Enter 'Live2playPlay2live' in the box." He grabs Marcia's pad and pen, tears off a piece of paper, and writes the password down. "Memorize this. Do not copy down. This note will self-destruct in ten seconds." He displays it as we all read and commit to memory, and then he crumples the paper, pops it in his mouth, and starts to chew.

"Nutter," Rick says.

Vaughan chews some more and some more, finally swallows, licks his lips, and hits Return. A second box pops up. "Now, it'll ask you to create a profile. Once everyone has done that, I'll Easter egg a prompt box on the school home page for easy access."

"Easter egg?" Rick snarls. "What are you, a fluffy bunny?"

"He means he'll hide it, Rick," Tesha says scornfully. "Do you know nothing?"

"Not everybody here speaks nerd," Rick shoots back.

"Thanks for proving my previous point." Vaughan smiles at

him sympathetically. "Don't worry. You'll all be told how to find it. Then you'll be able to access the network from any laptop, tablet, whatever." He types quickly and hits Return. "And we're off!" The page with the skull flashes up again. "Ladies and gentlemen, welcome to Crypt." Vaughan smiles at it lovingly.

"Everyone, even the recently deceased"—he nods at Cynthia and Becky—"everyone gets to create a profile. And here's the thing; it's up to you to decide if you want to give your real name. I suggest we all go incognito. More mystery that way, no?" Vaughan looks out at his rapt audience. "Once you've registered and created your own username and password, this little darling works like your common or garden social network. Here's the bulletin board, where all the official things get posted by Alex or Marcia or me, and then here's a rolling wall with everyone else's posts. You can post text, pictures, photos even." He smiles at us. "Not that anyone's got their phones, presumably. But if you're a traditionalist with an actual camera, go crazy."

"What if someone sees this page when you're looking at it?" Anvi asks. "It seems really risky."

"Well, you'll obviously do your best to prevent that from happening," Vaughan says. "We all have our designated World Wide Web time, so a teacher or nonplayer is not necessarily going to think anything is amiss if they catch a glimpse of the page. But if you're completely inactive on your machine for sixty seconds—no browsing, typing, scrolling—Crypt will redirect to the school home page. Emergency? Then hit Escape or End, and it's an instant kill switch back to Umfraville Central."

"Tell us about the messaging," Tesha says. "How does that work?"

"Thank you for asking." Vaughan clicks on a link and a box appears at the bottom of the screen. "This is your normal Umfraville intranet IM box. Crypt just cuckoos into this box. It drops your Killer IMs in here, both public and private messages." He looks at us. "Only difference is your public Killer messages are also available to view on Crypt, as part of your news feed. Got it? This way, when you're logged into Crypt, you can be working on something totally legit and still have one eye on the Game."

"You've really thought of everything," Rick snarks.

"Nice of you to notice," Vaughan says.

"Tell them about the tracking," Alex says quietly.

"Ooh, I will!" Vaughan claps his hands. "OK, folks—so if you click on this little map icon, you can see which users are online at which locations."

He clicks, and a map of the isle of Skola pops up. There are a couple giggles. It's been designed in a blocky, pseudo-medieval style, very Minecraft. There are even little people walking around, clutching books.

"So cute!" says Whitney, beaming at Vaughan. "And really clever. You built this all yourself?"

Vaughan nods, trying to look cool, but I know him well enough to guess that he's bursting with happiness.

The map is fun. There's Main House and then the various satellite buildings—the boys' dorms, the studios, classrooms and laboratories, the library quad and studies, the theater, rec center, and staff quarters—and then the pool, playing fields, and amphitheater.

"You can zoom in and out." Vaughan shows us. I lean in and see the caves marked and the causeway to the mainland. Vaughan has clearly spent time exploring the island—when did he have the chance? Every beach and wood is depicted, and the fields to the north of the island have little cube sheep and cows in them.

"Tracking. How does it work? Well…" Vaughan clears his throat. "As we are all painfully aware, there are only four reliable locations you can get on to the Umfraville intranet with Wi-Fi: the quad, the computer science lab and nearby classrooms, Marcia's newspaper office, and now here in the caves. But just for the extra frisson"—Vaughan's eyes light up—"on this map, I've included every workstation in the school."

"Meaning what, exactly?" I ask.

"Meaning…" Vaughan's eyes are twinkling in the candle-light. "Any hardwired machine that is connected to the school intranet is also fair game, potentially. The PC in Ezra's office, for example, or Mr. Flynn's Mac in his cottage"—he winks at me—"if you can access any of those to spice things up a little, by all means, do. You'll show up on the map as a little red skull, tagged with your username, and we'll all know where you are."

"I don't get it," Martin says, shaking his dark, spiky head. "Why would we want tracking anyway?"

"Because we get to know who is where and when," Marcia

answers for Vaughan. "If you know users A, B, and C were online in the library at the time of a Killing in the ballroom, you could potentially guess who those users are and eliminate them from your suspect list."

"That's only the beginning," Vaughan says, then nods to Alex. "Our Grand Master has made the decision not to activate tracking now, but when he does…" Vaughan lets out a low whistle. "Hold on to your hats…"

"OK." Alex slaps the table. "Everyone, you have twenty-four hours to log on and create your profile. Then look out for the first post from me."

He stands up and reaches for the velvet bag on the table. "Rick, kill the generator. It's time for our main event. We need to vote." He walks into the alcove and pulls back the curtain. There's an audible gasp from us apprentices as we see the altar for the first time. It's bigger than I expected. A dark wooden central pillar holds multilevel shelves, staggered at random like branches of a tree. Each shelf is lit with votive candles and is laden with photographs and trinkets from Games past. There are curly-cornered pictures of old Guild members: kids in masks with wicked smiles on their faces. There's a pewter goblet, its rim crusted with something terrible, a school tie fashioned into a hangman's noose, and a shiny, black "bomb" with a fuse sticking out of it. The yellow skull is on the uppermost shelf and around it are piles of bracelets, cut from the wrists of poor victims long ago.

Alex empties slips of paper from the velvet bag into a big

brassy bowl at the altar and turns around to us. "When it is your turn, take a slip, write a name, and place it in the velvet bag. If you don't know who the Killer is, write anything—Elvis, Mickey Mouse—but write something. If you know who the Killer is, write his or her name down. But be very sure, because if you guess wrong, you're out of the Game."

We take our turn, in order of when we were harvested. I'm last. I get to watch everyone walk into the alcove, kneel, and scribble something. Some people are really quick, some ridiculously slow. Finally, it's my go. I kneel on the dark cushion placed on the cold, sandy floor and take a slip of paper. I reach for the Pen of Doom—an oversized wooden stick with skulls carved into it. It is heavy and unbalanced in my hand, and as I clutch the end, my hands are slippery with cold sweat. I feel everyone's eyes on my back. Do I know who the Killer is?

I do not.

I write: Santa Claus

After I've scribbled it, I pause, mainly because I wish I could think of something wittier. But that's it. I fold the slip once, twice, three times.

I place the slip in the bag. It's half-open, with a few of the other pieces of paper visible. I try to make out writing, but everyone has been thorough with their origami.

Alex is standing, waiting for me to finish as I exit the alcove.

"I'll read the votes," he announces to all, then steps inside the alcove and pulls a curtain across.

We watch the curtain and listen. The sound of the sea in the background is very eerie—not so much waves hitting the shore, more a kind of low rumble, echoing through the caves. I strain my ears. Maybe I'm just imagining it, but I believe I can hear the sound of paper against paper, Alex unfolding, examining, discarding.

He laughs quietly. Clearly somebody's suggestion was wittier than mine. A minute later, there's another low guffaw. Then nothing. We wait. And wait some more. Then it gets a little ridiculous. Alex is taking more time to read everything than we took to write it all in the first place. Has he fallen asleep? Gone missing down a rabbit hole? I look at the bottom of the curtain, trying to see some movement of feet, a shadow, something.

Suddenly the curtain is drawn back, and I stifle a scream.

A cloaked figure, wearing a mask, holding a flaming bowl of fire in front of him.

"Ashes to ashes! Dust to dust!" Alex has his ceremonial voice on again. It's actually quite funny, but we apprentices jump a mile. The others get to smirk at us.

Alex lowers the bowl to the ground, then scoops up a pile of sand, extinguishing the flames. He stands, cloak and mask still in place. He extends his arms to his audience.

"There were no correct votes cast at this Summoning," he booms. "But I did appreciate 'Killer Kardashian' and 'your mum.'"

There's laughter, and Alex unmasks, de-robes, and chucks his stuff down on the table.

"The Killer lives to Kill again. And the rest of you are playing it safe so far. Class adjourned!" he says, normal voice back now. "Profile up, and I'll see you in cyberspace."

We leave gradually, on the lookout for any non-Guild who might spot us. Vaughan is one of the first to dash out. I'm slightly disappointed. I wanted to congratulate him on joining us, make up for my half-arsed reaction when he told me at the pool. I'm not the only female whose hope is blighted; Whitney and Emily in particular look grumpy.

I linger until Daniel has gone, until only Alex and Carl are left, and then I get the heck out. I get halfway up the cliff path, and I can't see a single soul around me, Guild or otherwise. The light is fading. I put my hands in my pockets and draw out my key ring. Sometimes it gives me courage to hold my study room key in my hand like a dagger. But it's not there. I stare at the key ring as if I'm suddenly going to locate the key on the ring. My two small gym locker keys are there but no room key. Damn. I've been meaning to replace the fob for a while now; it's not the first time the catch has come undone. Did the key come off in the cave when all that stuff dropped out of my pocket? Damn and double damn. It's nearly dark now. Marcia has a key, of course, but she's probably going to be more difficult to find than my key. Nothing for it. I retrace my steps, wishing I'd brought a flashlight to help in the twilight.

By the time I reach the caves, all is in darkness, and the salty air is muzzled by the smoke of recently blown-out candles. I didn't pass Alex and Carl on the cliff path. Where can they have gone? Maybe there's another route that I don't know about, but it's slightly spooky that they somehow slipped by me.

There's dim light in the outer chamber, but the inner cave is completely dark and silent. If it was gloomy outside, it's pitch-black in here. Panic begins like a gripping feeling in my chest. I want to get my key and get out. I feel my way along the wall past the generator, and once in the Place Most Holy, the only way to proceed is to get on my hands and knees and crawl until I get to where I was sitting. I find what I think is the right crate and feel in the sand. Metal, a jagged edge. There it is! Muttering a prayer of thanks, I turn and make for the exit to the first cave, where I can stand up and use the wall to get out.

And then I hear it. A banshee, keening desperately in the distance. I freeze, hands against the wall behind me.

The sound comes again—not a cry or a moan but more like a low, hopeless wail. I breathe. Come on, Cate, think logically. Is that a seal? There are sometimes gray seals on the rocks around here; they make ridiculously spooky noises. And then those stupid seabirds. Maybe it's one of them?

And again.

No, this is human—live, sad human. I gingerly edge along the wall toward the light of outside, and the noise gets louder. Oh crap. It's here, in the caves somewhere, back in another passageway or chamber, somewhere I've yet to discover—inside. I stop again and listen closer. There are sobs and snuffles and low, desperate wailing.

It's Vaughan.

I recognize that cry. Because crying, like laughter, doesn't really ever change. The voice gets deeper, older, but the cry is the same. I heard it when he fell off a wall and scraped his arm when he was seven. I heard it in my head when I left that day in my dad's ridiculous sports car.

I think about going to him, somewhere back there in the darkness. Why is he crying? Did he not just get everything he wanted? To be part of the Game? To launch Crypt and wow us all? I move off the wall in the direction of the sobs.

Then they stop. I stand still. Did he hear me coming?

I listen hard and wait. All I can hear is the sea. I take a step in the direction that the sobs were coming from, but something stops me again. A chill sweeps through me. Was that really Vaughan? I begin to doubt. I feel the hairs rise on the back of my neck. I want to call out, but suddenly I don't want the thing that was making those noises to know where I am. My breathing sounds horribly loud, and I'm sure that whoever or whatever is crouching in the darkness knows exactly where I am. Maybe it's the Killer. Maybe he or she saw me come back in here and is tempting me back into the cave to finish me off, like a siren in the waves. Maybe I only imagined it sounded like Vaughan because he's on my mind constantly at the moment.

Whatever, I'm not going to hang around. I turn and stride out of the cave toward the half light. And then when I hit the beach, I start to run, and it's only when I have sprinted three quarters of the way up the cliff path and have to stop to catch my breath that I turn around and look at where I have come from.

There's a shadowy figure on the beach below looking up at me. I watch, trying to make out the face, but it's an amorphous blob. And it doesn't move. Stupid, it's a rock.

I gulp in air, then take off on my burning legs again and don't slow down until I see the yellow lights of the school buildings pooling out into the darkness.

Later at tea, Vaughan is at a table, laughing and engrossed in conversation with Alex, Carl, and Marcia. Rick sits elsewhere with non-Guild.

I must have imagined it, I think as I see his beaming face. He's loving this. He's right there, in the thick of things with the most popular kids. Exactly what he wanted. It can't have been him crying in the cave.

So who was it?

CHAPTER 11

Early—very early—Sunday morning: unconscious but still in the land of the living.

Asleep, I know the hand is going to be placed on my arm before I feel it. Somehow, in dreamland, I sense him in the room with me. My body is dead to the world, but my head is flicking through lost images of us as kids—nettle stings, a burned hand from a sparkler on bonfire night, a trip to the beach, and a dead crab. And then suddenly, there's the hand on my arm, and I'm awake and in my dorm bed, and the clock is reading 1:23 a.m.

Vaughan gets into bed with me. Without asking, as if it's the most natural and innocent thing in the world. I shift over in the single bed, like this happens every night. The bed is small, and I feel the cold of the wall on my back as I press against it, away from him. His body radiates a ferocious heat, as if he has run all the way here. My arms are in front of me awkwardly, as if I'm protecting myself from him getting any closer. Our legs touch, briefly, before I draw mine back. He is fully clothed, jeans, sweater. Thank God.

"You found a way in, then," I whisper to him. I expect a smile, but I think his face is serious. His head is on the pillow beside mine, but I can't see his eyes properly, just the general contours of his face and the outline of hair against the dimness of the room behind.

He nods.

How different from when Alex was here on this bed with me. That felt thrilling, dangerous, but this…this is better. Vaughan feels like an equal. Vaughan feels like home.

"It's tonight, isn't it?" he whispers. "My initiation."

"Oh. I don't know," I croak. "No one's said anything."

He shakes his head slightly. "They wouldn't. Not to you. But it must be tonight, no reason to wait any longer." He lifts himself up slightly, whether to look at the clock or the door, I'm not sure. I realize the room is quieter than it should be. I sit up a little too and look across the room at the other bed.

"No Marcia," Vaughan says. "That's a sure sign. I should… go back and wait, I suppose." But he doesn't. We both relax down into the bed again, side by side. My eyes have adjusted now, and I can make out the worry on his face. I'm sure I can feel his heart beating through the mattress. Suddenly the years strip away, and it's like we're eight again. He's scared.

"I thought you wanted this," I whisper. It sounds weird and awkward to me, like I'm talking about us being here, together, in my bed.

"I do!" His eyes close, and he lets himself breathe. "But you know. I'm no masochist. I just want it over."

I want to hug him, hold him close, and tell him that it will be all right, but I can't because, obviously, we're not eight, and we're in bed. And also, because it might not be all right. I have no idea what Alex and the Elders have planned for him, but I do know that they will not make it easy.

His eyes open again. We wait for one of us to speak, for me to reassure him.

"I should go," he says finally. We listen to each other breathe, although I think I'm probably holding my breath. His eyes bore into mine, and I'm almost overtaken by the urge to put my mouth on his and kiss away his worries. It's terrifying.

I open my mouth to say something—anything—to break this moment, and suddenly he's moving again and out of the bed as quickly and silently as he got in, and he's leaving the room and leaving a huge empty space in my tiny bed. I exhale. I wish I could have said more, anything to help. Or just something to make him stay in bed with me, because it was nice. It strikes me that they'll come for me before they come for him; I hope he doesn't meet them on their way. Not long now.

I shift onto my back, one hand moving onto the warm place where he was lying. I like the warmth.

"Get up. It's time."

Marcia's standing over me with a flashlight. I can only have closed my eyes for a few minutes. I hope she didn't see Vaughan leaving. I should stall the Guild to give Vaughan time to get back to his dorm, but then my gaze moves to the clock and it is beaming out 3:02 a.m. I must have fallen asleep.

"Now, Cate!"

I dress quickly. "What are you going to do to him?"

Marcia doesn't answer me. I shiver, reaching up to the door hook for a coat and scarf. She pushes past me, opening the door, flicking the flashlight off, and looking both ways before padding down the corridor without a backward glance. She's wearing her Elder cloak and it billows out behind her as she moves. I follow, like she knows I will. She barely pauses all the way down the stairs, pulling her hood up and out into the night air, across the open, toward the woods. There's a half moon, enough light to see where we're stepping. I catch her, because I'm faster, and because my adrenaline is pumping.

"Where are we going?" I hiss.

"We need to hurry." She switches the flashlight back on and takes the left path toward the studios. We're heading to the cliff path—going to the cave? We clear the trees, the gorse our only cover now, following the path toward the sea. A startled seabird flies somewhere above and ahead, announcing our presence with alarm calls, leading us down to the beach. But then at the point where we should start our descent, Marcia continues left, along the cliff top. I slow down. The promontory. The cliff top.

"Come on!" Marcia urges. "They will have started already!"

I stop in my tracks. Because all at once I know what

they're going to do to him and why Marcia is bringing me late to the party.

"Marcia, he can't swim."

She stops too, looks back at me. "Sure he can. At the second Killing...everyone said he jumped into the pool."

I shake my head. "In the shallow end. He can't swim. He can't swim!" I grab the flashlight from her and set off, hurtling along the sandy path as fast as I dare, heading for the promontory. I can't see them yet, as there's a slight incline before the path dips down toward the part of the cliff that juts out into the sea, but I know where they are, exactly where they are.

A few years ago, there was an unusually hot summer, and a bunch of kids thought it would be fun to do some tombstoning. There's a place on the cliff promontory where you can climb down a yard or so and find a natural launchpad off into the sea below. It's maybe a thirty-foot drop, and below is a reassuring patch of lighter blue that indicates no rocks. A natural diving pool, you might say. Well, if you were totally off your rocker you might say that. But jumpers have to be careful, because there's only one spot that's safe to hit; too far left or right and you're fish food on the rocks below. I was just a new girl, too young to be included, but I saw them do it because it happened more than once that summer, and everyone got wind of it. And then of course, the staff heard, and it stopped happening. It was a phase, and not one that held much attraction when the sea temperature dropped several degrees back to deathly cold, and the penalty for jumping was expulsion.

And now, this is Vaughan's initiation. Alex is going to make him jump.

I reach the brow of the hill, and before I know it, I'm on them. Dots of light moving around the ground, a couple lanterns. The apprentices are huddled, watching, and the Elders and Journeymen stand around at the cliff edge, their cloaks blowing slightly in the breeze.

I can't see him.

"Vaughan?" I mutter. "Vaughan!" This time, it comes out as a shout. The Elders turn to look at me, and as they part, I see him there, in the middle of them. His bare skin stands out against the black of the cloaks, the black of the night, and the sea stretching out behind him. He is stark naked. Standing, hands tied in front of him, feet tied also. I scan the hooded figures, looking for Alex, but all is a blur. I find my breath, and my voice again. "Are you going to make him jump?"

Nobody answers me, and it's all the answer I need. Then I hear Rick's laugh.

"No!" I yell.

"Cate," Marcia is at my side. "It'll be OK."

"No it won't!" I say, striding up to the group. Rick steps forward and puts a meaty hand out to stop me. I strike it away with a strength that rarely presents itself. He yells at me, pumped up and ready to grab, but Alex pulls him back and walks toward me.

"Don't interfere, Cate," he warns me. "There has to be an initiation."

"But not one that will kill him!" I yell back.

Alex guffaws. "Don't be overdramatic, Cate."

Marcia is behind me again, her hands are on the top of my arms, squeezing them reassuringly. "Let it happen," she breathes in my ear. "He'll be fine."

"He won't be fine!" I shout at them all. "He can't swim!"

Alex frowns.

"Yeah, right. We saw him jump in the pool." Rick again.

"He wasn't out of his depth," I say. "You make him jump, he'll drown."

"Alex," Marcia says under her breath. "If it really is true he can't swim, we shouldn't make him jump."

Alex sighs and bites his cheek. This is not going according to plan, clearly.

"Come on, man!" Rick says to Alex. "We'll untie him." A knife blade flashes from his pocket, and Rick bends to cut Vaughan's feet free. "He can doggy-paddle back to shore!"

"It's not that far, and look, it's as flat as a millpond." Carl assumes the voice of calm. "Cut his hands too. He gets in trouble, we pull him out."

"Oh, 'course you will!" I cry. "Are you completely thick? He can't swim a stroke, and he'll drown!"

Vaughan just stands there, not meeting my eyes, staring at the ground. Rick cuts his hands free, reluctantly, and Vaughan doesn't move a muscle, doesn't even shiver.

"Ask him!" I try, desperately.

"Well..." Alex is irritated. Because it will be a big step down if he doesn't follow through. Not to mention a royal pain in the arse to think up something else. "Vaughan, can you swim?"

Vaughan raises his head and looks past them, right at me. "Like a fish."

"Ha!" Rick is jubilant. "In the drink! In the drink!"

"He's lying." I feel the panic rising in my chest. "Vaughan, don't be stupid. Tell them!"

Vaughan smiles at me, like he's just seeing me for the first time, then takes a step backward, toward the sea and oblivion, then another, until he is standing right at the edge, back to the sea. All the time he looks at me.

"Jump! Jump!" Rick shouts. A couple others join in.

"No!" My voice is choked, not loud enough. "Not from the top, no one jumps from the top!"

"Jump, you loser!" Rick calls again.

Vaughan smiles at him, lifts his arms out to the side, and gives Rick the one-fingered salute.

Rick runs into him and gives him an almighty shove. The force propels Vaughan in a straight line out over the edge, and for the weirdest split second, he just seems to hang midair, Wile E. Coyote with peddling legs, and then he's fallen out of sight, as if he was never there.

We all listen for the splash. There is none. Everyone runs to the edge, looks down, but there's no clear view straight down. Even with the flashlights dancing on the water below, we can't see anything.

"Where is he?" I gasp. And then I'm running, back the way

we came, and then cutting down the cliff toward the beach, not knowing if I'm on any actual path or if I'm forging my own and am going to be meeting my death on the rocks below. I'm aware of people around me, see Alex overtake me, feel his panic match mine. He doesn't want an actual death on his hands; he probably wasn't going to make Vaughan jump, just taunt, threaten, humiliate. Alex just puts things in motion and washes his hands of the consequences. That's more his style. We scramble down the cliff side and find the beach below, then sprint across the sand toward the sea, Rick and Carl hot on our heels.

There is no splashing, no cries for help, only the sound of the sea gently lapping the beach.

"Vaughan!" I cry.

"Shut it!" Rick spits at me. "Someone will hear you!"

I don't care. I throw off my coat, kick off my shoes, and wade into the water, the icy cold slashing me around the legs. "Vaughan!"

Everyone is on the beach now, and flashlights scan the water. One of them finds a pale shape, hunched over a rock at the bottom of the cliff face. It is not moving.

"There!" I shout, and more flashlights join the one on the shape. "Vaughan! Are you OK?" I can't see his face. The beams of light dance on the pale shape like fireflies, and I think I can make out the curve of his back, his feet, one arm flung out behind him awkwardly. I try to look for the red of blood or for the rise and fall of breath, but he's too far away and the flashlights are too weak.

And we all just stand there. Alex, Marcia, and Carl have joined me, knee deep in the lapping water. For all this talk of jumping in to rescue Vaughan, we are all just standing there, because there is no panicked drowning, and the water may well be flat, but it is very, very cold. What's done is done. He's on the rocks. Either he fell on them and is probably dead, or he scrambled onto them and he's probably all right. I hate myself for hesitating.

"Alex!" a voice hisses from behind us. "Someone's coming!"

That's enough to make us look around. Martin is standing halfway up the cliff.

"I saw a car's headlights, and somebody shouted!" Martin has everyone's attention. "We need to get out of here!"

As soon as he's said it, bodies get themselves moving. Cockroaches scurrying from the light. I grasp Alex's arm. "Help me get Vaughan."

Alex doesn't reply, but Carl is wading toward the shore. "Alex, we have to go before they come."

Marcia tugs at my hand. "Come on, Cate. We can't hang around."

I turn on her. "What are you talking about? Vaughan is hurt. We have to help him!"

Her eyes flash. "How? If someone's coming, they can help him." And then she's splashing back to solid ground, and I'm picking my jaw and my heart off the ground. I can't believe it. I search the fleeing figures for Daniel, without much hope, and I come up short. I'm not even sure he was here to begin with. Only Alex stands by, panting, eyes darting up at the cliff, looking for the mystery person that is surely going to end his career at Umfraville.

The flashlights have gone from Vaughan, but now I know where he is I can still make out the shape of him against the gray of the night sky. I remember how to move, and my brain kicks into action. I splosh toward the shore, ripping off my sweater and tossing it onto dry land, and then I make my way back to Alex, who is still frozen to the spot, watching the cliffs.

"Come on! Help me!" I grab at him, and he finally comes to life and shakes me off, but he's still transfixed by the cliffs.

"Stranger at the party," he murmurs.

I follow his eyes and see the flash of headlights on the cliff top. Martin was right. The cockroaches have disappeared, and now it's only us. I don't feel panic. I just feel relief. Here's help. Someone to help save Vaughan.

"Alex, we need to tell them. They can get an ambulance, someone to—"

Alex turns on me, furious. "Are you kidding me? We'll be expelled, probably charged with something. It'll be the end of everything for me!" He seizes my arm and makes for the shore, dragging me behind. "We have to hide; we have to go!" I try to free myself from his grasp, but adrenaline is making him too strong for me to fight. I dig my feet into the shale and seaweed below to try and gain traction, but he's too powerful. So I choose to buckle and flop into the water, the icy wetness covering my body and barely registering in the struggle. Alex is strong, but not strong enough to drag me all the way to shore quick enough to escape, so he drops my hand and sprints away into the dark.

On all fours, I shake wet hair out of my face, the salt stinging my eyes. The cold makes me pant, but it's OK. I'm wet through now. I spring to my feet, turn out to sea, and throw myself through the water toward the shape that is Vaughan. I neither know nor care who is in the car on the cliff top. All I care about is reaching Vaughan.

The swim is easy, even with my clothes dragging me down. I thank my lucky stars there are no waves. When I am a few feet away, I feel the brush of rock, sharp on my knees, and start the scramble up onto dry land. This is far more difficult than the swimming part, because it's slippery as hell and every splintered, chiseled edge of rock is like a tiny blade on my palms. But I make it, and when I'm up there and raise my head, I no longer see a body hunched on the ground, but a naked figure sitting up, head in hands, in parody of *The Thinker*.

"Vaughan!" I try to speak, but the word comes out more as a gulp for air.

He raises his head, and all at once I know he's OK. I rush to him, kneeling down, my hands on his face, my eyes searching for wounds oozing with blood, bones sticking out. There are none. No doubt scrapes and scratches, but no missing limbs or gushing arterial spray. I don't know how he got here, but he's in one piece. And he's trembling with cold and shock, and there's nothing I can do about it. I look around for anything that will help us or a path along the rocks to the beach or up the cliff, but there is nothing.

Up on the cliff top, the headlights have disappeared. I don't know whether to be pleased or devastated, but there'll be no rescue from the mystery driver. Which means we only have one option.

"We have to go back into the water," I say to Vaughan. He nods and starts to rise to his feet, shakily. "I'm a strong swimmer." I put an arm under his and around his back, helping him over the rocks. Shaking aside, he seems surprisingly steady on his feet. "You float on your back. I'll tow you in."

He nods again, apparently imbued with a faith in me that I'm not sure is justified.

We scramble down the rocks to the water, and as I ease myself in, it feels cold all over again. Vaughan slips a little and splashes in beside me, but I still have solid rock underfoot, so I can gather him up in my arms and begin to tow him to land. There's a moment when my foot leaves the rock and I'm swimming, kicking at the nothingness beneath me and trying not to panic, but Vaughan is perfectly calm, trusting me, lying so flat and relaxed in the water that I wonder for a moment if he's still conscious. I tow him textbook style, hand underneath tilted chin, just like Mr. Churley taught us in swimming lessons, just like I never thought I'd have reason to put into practice. After a minute, I feel shale underfoot, and we haul each other up onto the beach and collapse down on the sand by my discarded coat and sweater.

I catch my breath a minute, then wrap my parka around Vaughan, rubbing his arms and back to warm him. He puts his arms in and zips it up, and I'm thankful that I chose the oversized coat tonight rather than my girl-sized biker jacket. I peel my wet T-shirt over my head, hurrying to pick up my sweater and pulling it on quickly. Vaughan totally looks, by the way. All that time he was naked before me, and I didn't sneak a peek at him—because, you know, bigger things at stake here— but for a second I'm in a bra and it's like he can't stop his eyes from wandering. Bloody boys.

"Thank you for saving me." He shivers. "Thank you so much."

I kneel down by him. "Are you hurt?" I finally ask. "Did you hit the rocks when you fell?"

He shakes his head. "Only the water, but that was enough."

"How did you make it out?"

His hands move over his face, pushing back straggles of dripping hair. "I have no idea. Thrashed around. Swallowed some sea." His eyes crinkle shut, pushing back the memory. "Horrible. Then I got lucky and found a rock."

"Thank God," I say. "I can't believe you told them you could swim." I feel the anger pushing its way back, warming me. "Have you got some huge death wish? Self-destruct button?" I swear under my breath. "Rick is going to suffer for this, believe me."

"I couldn't show them weakness. They'd eat me alive." He's shaking so much, I struggle to hear the words. "Plus, now they're scared of me. They think I'm crazy."

"And that's going to make you popular?" I throw up my arms, exasperated.

"I'll be accepted." He ruffles his hair, spraying water everywhere. "Another lunatic at the asylum." Then he's raising a hand, pointing to something behind me. "Look."

I turn around, and there's a figure on the cliff path above us, winding its way down toward the beach. My heart leaps—Marcia, having a flash of conscience? No, it's male, I'm sure of it. Alex, perhaps? But why should it be? Much more likely it's the mystery driver. And I can only assume he's seen us, because why would he be coming down here otherwise?

"Can you move?" I ask Vaughan, and he nods. Suddenly, I'm not so sure I want us to be rescued. The difficult part is behind us, and although we probably both have hypothermia, it would be crap if we got caught now. There's also something really unnerving about just why someone is driving around Skola at ridiculous o'clock at night. I pull Vaughan up to standing, and together we hobble over the sand to the shadows of the cliff face. "Can you see him?" I lean out a little, looking for the figure.

"No." Vaughan shivers. "My feet...they smart, a little." He holds one up, picking sand off it. I reach across him for Marcia's flashlight, which is sticking out of the parka pocket, and shield it in my hand as I click it on. The sole of Vaughan's foot is ripped open, and blood drips from his heel and in between his toes. He gently places that foot down and picks up the other. It's not as bad but still grisly.

"Ow," I mutter. "Can you go on?"

"What's the alternative? To the caves?" He nods in the direction of the Guild's home, on the other side of the bay. It is probably our best bet, the nearest place to warm up and regroup.

"Good thinking, Batman." Cringe. How dorky do I sound? But it makes him giggle in spite of his shudders, so I take the hit.

We set off, hugging the cliff as best we can, while staying on the sand for the good of Vaughan's bare feet and speed of travel. We quickly reach the bottom of the gorse-lined steps that I came down the day of the first Summoning; the caves are just around the corner.

"I need...to stop...just for a second," Vaughan pants. He holds his worst foot again, leaning against the rail of the steps for support. "Maybe a sit down." He plants his bare behind on the bottom step.

"No, come on!" I urge him. "Almost there, let's keep moving."

But Vaughan shakes his head, and I know he's not only giving his feet a break, but also keeping himself together, keeping the tears at bay, gathering his strength. Because there's a chance that when we hit the caves, some of the Guild will have had the same idea. I would gamble that most would be running home to the dorms, but I wouldn't be surprised if Alex and his Elders are having a crisis meeting before heading back to school. And if I've had this thought, then so has Vaughan, and he needs to get it together before he faces them.

I sink down on the step beside him and look out to sea. All is deceptively still. "It's OK," I tell him, patting his knee chastely, like his maiden aunt. "You'll be OK. Let's take a moment, and then we'll get dry, find something to patch those feet with. Besides, we've lost that guy who was looking for us."

"No you haven't." The voice behind me makes my heart stop.

CHAPTER 12

I spin around so quickly I almost slither off the step.

Mr. Flynn is standing on the stairs. I don't need the flashlight to see that it's him, but I make the mistake of flicking the switch and shining it on his face anyway. I wish I hadn't; I've never seen such fury.

Vaughan turns and looks up at him, then sighs, like a resigned dog that has been kicked one too many times. Flynn glances at him, a flicker of surprise on his face, then puzzlement and anger as he clocks the bare legs sticking out from underneath my borrowed parka.

"Tell me that you're both OK." Mr. Flynn addresses me and me only. His hands are held out in front of him like he's pushing his anger away.

"We…are," I say, carefully, because I feel that we are probably very far from OK at the moment.

"What in merry hell are you doing out here?" Mr. Flynn says.

"What are you doing here, sneaking around? It's so dodgy of you." I can't imagine why I feel I can say this, and from his reaction, neither can Mr. Flynn. He leaps down from the step with a kind of yell and seizes my arm, pulling me to my feet.

"Cate, this is beyond stupid! I can't believe you'd do this to yourself. Breaking curfew? Why are you wet? Have you been swimming? What were you thinking?"

The gasp that is stretched across my face obviously helps to bring Mr. Flynn to his senses, and he drops my arm, but it's probably also something to do with the fact that Vaughan has leaped to his bloodied feet and is making a halfhearted attempt to wrestle Flynn off me.

"Stop!" Mr. Flynn cries out, throwing up his hands. "Enough!"

Vaughan backs off, with some relief.

"It was a dare," I invent. "We just had to dunk ourselves in the sea." Oh jeez, I sound so pathetic. "Sneak out, dunk, go back to school."

Mr. Flynn visibly takes a deep breath and counts to ten. "Where are the others?"

"There are no others." I'm not protecting them. I'm protecting the Game. "Just us."

"So how do the people who 'dared you' know that you did it?" Mr. Flynn has a point.

"Well, when we get back to school all wet and cold, they'd have to believe us." I also have a point.

"And his clothes?" Flynn turns around to point at Vaughan.

"Oh, they're just down by the sea." I gesture vaguely waterward.

"Yes? Where? Show me."

"Um, well, I can't remember exactly where we left them…" I wander down the beach a little, and Mr. Flynn is right behind me. "Down there?" I point the flashlight at a place I know the clothes won't be. But then again, who knows where the Guild stripped Vaughan? The way this night is going, I may well find the exact spot. But I don't. I up the shivering a little. "Er, maybe over there a bit." I flash the flashlight around, hoping Vaughan is going to chime in sometime this year and help me out. Although given the dynamic between those two, maybe it's better he doesn't contribute. I could do with some help, however.

Mr. Flynn clearly has a similar thought.

"You—Vaughan, is it?—show me where you put your clothes!" He swings around. We both turn around—to nothing. Vaughan has disappeared into a puff of smoke. Vanished. Melted into the ether or sucked into the sand, he has gone without a trace.

"Vaughan!" Mr. Flynn calls out. I think of joining in, then think better of it. Did he scale the steps? Nip around into the caves? We could probably follow the blood drips and find out, but I don't enlighten Mr. Flynn about that. We stand there as if waiting for Vaughan to materialize again.

Mr. Flynn swears. He does this quite a lot in class and even more when we're alone. I think he was so shaken by finding me wet and wild in the middle of the night that he had the swears chased out of him for a while, but he's clearly finding his equilibrium again. It's kind of reassuring.

"We need to get you back to school."

Instantly we're on our own, and he relaxes slightly.

"Yes." I start to really shake, the cold truly setting in for the first time. "I'm freezing."

"What do you expect?" He shoots me an exasperated look, then softens. He pulls off his jacket and puts it around my shoulders. "Come on."

I follow a few steps behind as he leads off back down the beach the way we came. He takes a path up the cliff that I never even knew existed, and I struggle to keep up. The climb warms me up though. At the top of the cliff, his bashed-up black hatchback is waiting. He climbs into the driver's seat without an invitation for me to get in.

I open the door and poke my head in. "I'm all wet." I rub my legs in an embarrassing way.

"I'll cope," he says. I get in and he pulls away, and although he turns the heat on, I notice he leaves the headlights off. We drive, slowly, over the rough ground until we reach a gravel road.

"Why were you in your car?" The question comes out before I can stop it.

"I think you're the one who owes me answers, not the other way around." He keeps his eyes dead ahead. "But if you must know, the causeway was open, and I was coming back from the mainland." No more details. I wonder if he was with a woman.

We travel along in silence. Is he going to take me to his cottage? No, more likely he'll just dump me at the dorm.

"What are you going to do about this?" I hardly dare ask, but I have to.

He lets me suffer in silence a full minute longer and then pulls over along by a tall hedge, with Main House on the other side.

"Cate, I'm not sure yet." He sighs and looks down, then across at me. "You tell me you're OK?"

I nod furiously.

"Then sneak back to your room whichever way you came out. Do not get caught."

"And?"

He shakes his head. "And I'll sleep on it."

I nod. I doubt I'll get much sleep.

"Do I need to go looking for that fool of a boy, or will he get some sense and make it back to his own bed?"

I flinch at the word "own." "He'll be OK." I think Vaughan will be OK. I mean, obviously his feet are a mess, but I don't think he's going to bleed out or anything. And him hopping back to his dorm through the woods is preferable to enduring five minutes of questioning in the car with Flynny.

Mr. Flynn nods curtly. "Go."

I go.

Marcia is in bed and apparently asleep when I get in. In the midst of it all, I'd forgotten the betrayal, but when I see her lying there, the anger kicks me up inside and I feel like tearing the bedclothes off her and pulling her onto the floor in a fit of rage.

I don't though. She can't be asleep, can she? She'll be waiting for me to do something. And I won't. I'll keep her on tenterhooks, just the way I am with Mr. Flynn; it seems only fitting.

Tomorrow, however, there will be hell to pay.

CHAPTER 13

It's Sunday. I'm definitely alive, but that's all I know.

I wake up and I have no idea where I am. That used to happen all the time when I first started at Umfraville, but I'm so assimilated to the cult of boarding school that I'm now used to being woken up by umpteen reluctant bodies trying to get dressed and down to breakfast in time to avoid a detention. This morning all is quiet, however, and this must be the reason I feel weird. The sun is shining in through a gap in the curtains.

Memories of last night suddenly slap me around the face. Did that really happen? Vaughan. I should have checked if he got back last night; for all I know he's lying naked in a ditch somewhere. Or maybe I imagined the whole thing.

Before I move, I glance over at Marcia's bed; it is unoccupied and made. So that means she got up and got out. Avoiding me, as well she might.

Sitting up, I glance at the clock. 11:13 a.m. Perfect. I've

missed breakfast, then. I swing legs out from under the duvet, and my feet touch a bunch of cold, wet clothes on the floor. Oh, it did all happen last night. A dip in the Irish Sea did that.

Among my soaked clothes is Mr. Flynn's jacket. I hope I can return it without anyone noticing; that would really fire up the rumor mill.

I dress quickly, because it's chilly in the room and I'm shivering. My throat feels scratchy; my head feels hot. But what about Vaughan? What kind of a state must he be in? I leave my dorm room, run to the stairs lightly, and make for outside. It's warm; there's a bright-blue sky against the orange and yellow of the autumn leaves. Someone, somewhere is having a bonfire. Not a soul is around, and that will work in my favor. I must search Vaughan out; we can regroup and think about where we go from here. I run across the Main House lawn, toward the quad—feeling a little ridiculous, because it's Sunday, and nobody over the age of twelve runs in this place, especially at the weekend. Will he be holed up in his study or hiding somewhere else? I duck into the main entrance to the studies, turning left to go down the corridor to Vaughan's room, which is on its own at the end of the hall. In the light of day, will he want to continue with the Game? Will he report Rick and Alex—everyone, really—because who would blame him if he did? I need to find out what's inside his head because he must be feeling lousy as hell—

There's a roar of laughter behind me. I stop in my tracks and spin around. The laughter comes again from the direction of the common room. I retrace my steps and continue toward the closed door. I hear Rick's voice—and Marcia's too. Oh, lovely. What are they all talking about? Are they actually laughing about last night? I feel the anger rising in me again. I grasp the door handle and enter the room.

The common room is large and airy. It has a battered sofa and a couple armchairs in front of a TV in the corner nearest the door. There are beanbags around a low coffee table, where the previous day's paper can normally be found, eviscerated for the crossword. And there is an oven, a long kitchen counter, and a sink on the left side of the room, where you can make toast and coffee if you need the kick to propel you to study harder, longer.

But nobody is making toast or watching TV or sprawled on a beanbag. Everyone—Rick, Alex, Marcia, Martin, and the Triumvirate of Pretty: Tesha, Whitney, Anvi—is grouped around one of the half dozen computer terminals in the far corner of the room. And Vaughan is right in the middle of them.

He's laughing the loudest of all.

"Some of these are so friggin' obvious!" Tesha is howling. "I mean, 'IceColdBlond'? Totally Cynthia. And "Banana Hammock" has got Roger written all over it!"

"Yes, well," Vaughan says, "I cannot be held responsible for the selection of usernames. And who knows? It could all be an elaborate facade."

"Roger doesn't do subtle," Anvi giggles. "Can you imagine him trying to type something else?" She puts out her hands in front of her. "Must. Not. Put. That." She groans like a mummy, arms outstretched. "Must. Not. Oh, sod it, Banana Hammock it is!"

Everyone laughs again, and then Vaughan looks up and winks at me. "Hi, Catey. Come and look at Crypt."

He knows I hate being called Catey. I walk up slowly. "Er, isn't this kind of risky?"

"Nothing to see here if the wrong person walks in." Vaughan smiles at me brightly.

"I could have been the wrong person," I reply.

"But you're not!" He gives me a wink.

"I followed the laughter. You should stop."

"Looking at Crypt or laughing?" His smile is fixed.

"Hey, we're just having a quick look. Chill the hell out," says Tesha, like I've suggested everyone does something totally unreasonable, like, oh, I dunno, jump off a cliff or something.

"You after your jacket, is that it?" Vaughan says. "I put it in your room."

Rick makes a suggestive whistle. Tesha laughs out loud. Whitney shoots me daggers.

I stiffen. Heaven only knows what he told them about what happened last night. I instinctively glance toward Alex, and he averts his gaze and drums his hands on the desk.

"Right! Let's break this up." Alex stands and gives Vaughan a clap on the shoulder. "Great job with Crypt, seriously, mate."

Vaughan gives Alex a dweeby thumbs-up as Alex strolls toward the door. Marcia, Rick, Tesha, Anvi, and Martin follow.

As Marcia passes me, she flashes me a quick smile. My heart sinks. No, friend, this is not all over just because Vaughan thinks it is. Not by a long way.

As Rick exits, he cocks invisible guns at Vaughan and shoots him with a fake-friendly wink. They all leave.

I quell the urge to puke and turn my attention back to Vaughan. Whitney is standing behind him, leaning over and pressing herself against his shoulder ever so accidentally-on-purpose as she points to something on the screen.

"Come on, Whit," Anvi calls to her.

Whitney whispers something to Vaughan and they both laugh. Anvi turns and looks at me, rolling her eyes, shouting behind her as she leaves, "Put the boy down, Whitney."

Whitney trots after her finally, with a slight pitying glance at me, and then Vaughan and I have the room to ourselves.

"You might want to wipe the drool off your chin," I say.

Vaughan raises his eyebrows at me, then reaches over to the computer next to his and types something. He pats the seat next to him. "Sit?"

"Why? Can't get up?" I reply. "Has she turned your legs to jelly?"

He huffs, shakes his head, and starts typing something.

I stay where I am. "I cannot believe you're best chums with them this morning."

"What's not to be chummy about? I'm part of the Game now."

"Rick pushed you off a cliff."

"I asked for it."

"Wow." I walk over to the chair he patted and sit in front of the screen. Crypt is displayed in full glory. "That sounds like victim-speak if ever I heard it."

Vaughan doesn't say anything, just tappy-taps away on his keyboard, typing something that I can't see from here.

I swivel away from the screen and face Vaughan. "So are we just conveniently forgetting what happened last night, or what?"

Vaughan speed types some more, punctuating whatever he is writing with a couple pronounced key strikes. "No, we are not forgetting." He stretches out his fingers. "But what we are doing is playing the Game. Because otherwise, my Peter Pan into the drink last night is for naught."

"And what about Mr. Flynn?"

Vaughan resumes typing. "What about him?"

"Aren't you worried about what he's going to do?"

"He's not going to do anything. If he was, he would have done it by now." He leans forward and stares intently at his screen. "You have a 'special relationship,' don't you?" Before I have time to respond, he plows on. "It's reasonable to assume that he'll give you a big talk about how you have to be careful to stay on the straight and narrow for the sake of your blessed exams and burgeoning art school career, but beyond that, I doubt we'll have any trouble with him." He stops suddenly, turns around to me. "Aren't you curious? About Crypt?" he whispers. When I don't respond, he leans over, takes my hand, and gently places it on the mouse. "Take a look."

"I cannot believe you're letting this slide." I move my hand away.

"What?" He's genuinely confused. "Oh, the initiation thing?" He tuts at me. "Cate, keep up. That was so twelve hours ago."

"Not even!" I shout back.

"OK, OK." He sighs. "Be assured, Cate, I forget nothing. But it doesn't serve me to get upset about it now. This is where my focus lies." He taps the screen.

I loll my head back and groan.

"I also haven't forgotten that you saved me," he says quietly. "I never will. Thank you."

OK. Well that's something. I give a kind of half grunt of acknowledgment, and we both sit there in uncomfortable silence for a second.

"Now, I ask you—beg you"—Vaughan points to the screen again—"make it all worthwhile and take a look...please?"

I turn around to the screen again, slowly, and read this time.

There, on the wall is a roll call of all the users who have signed up so far:

Grand Master

CharlotteCorday

DeadMcTavish

I_did_it

Banana Hammock

AllKillerNoFiller

13*is*my*lucky*number

IceColdBlond

Vaughan watches me. "So, this is the first time you're viewing this list. I can therefore deduce you're not any of those already signed up."

"That's overconfident of you. For all you know I was here logging on while you were showering off the salt water."

"Too true." He chuckles. "All I know is that you weren't in the shower with me. Other than that, I'm in the dark."

"Anyway," I say, running my fingertips along the edge of the desk. "Can't you tell who everyone is? You are the mighty webmaster or whatever."

He shakes his head. "Nope. I was telling the truth when I said it's all anonymous."

"But you said we can keep private notes on here, files we don't want to share?" I click through some of the posts. "What's to stop you from logging in as someone else and checking out all their ruminations?" I look at him. "Other than a sense of honor."

"That's the great part!" He leans forward, excited. "The hardest aspect of this was to keep the passwords secret, even from me. Because the system has to align a password with a username, but it also has to keep that hidden. I don't fully trust myself not to look."

"What do you think? Has the Killer signed up yet?"

Vaughan sits back, thinks. "No. Three attempted Kills in the first week? We know this Killer is eager to spill himself all over this—he's dying to, if you'll excuse the pun—but he wants to sit back and see what other people do first. He won't risk the deadline, but he'll leave it as long as he can to sign up."

The list refreshes. There's a new name:

General Disarray

Vaughan barks out a laugh. "Oh, nicely played!"

I lean in. "Someone is online somewhere else?"

"Yes!" He's thrilled. "Now if the tracking were in play, we could see which location. And I'm itching to switch it on. But Alex gets to decide when that kicks in, so I will restrain myself for now." He grins as he taps on the keyboard. "Soon as that happens, I'll have this Killer pegged, you'll see. I'll get him."

I sigh. "Tell me why you keep insisting the Killer is a boy."

He smiles to himself, shaking his head and staring at the ground as if he's astonished I can't see it. "I'm disappointed in you. You really don't know?"

Irritation flashes through me. "I really don't. Enlighten me with your wisdom."

He sits up, excited. He loves to explain, always has. "Look at the victims. All girls."

"So?" I think about it. "It's always the way. It's almost traditional." I reach into my pocket and flick through the little black Game book until I find the pages I need. There in the back of the book are the lists of Games past. The victims are listed in the order they were Killed. I read and think some more. "Actually, it's pathetic, but it is true. Girls are always picked off first. I think they're seen as easier Kills. The Guild used to be more of a boys' club, certainly, back in the day—and it was kind of seen as lacking respect to Kill the bigwigs first. Start with a few newbies, then move on to the real players." I scratch my head. "Ugh, that's so insulting."

Vaughan nods dismissively, as if this is hardly the point. "You could put it down to the pattern of 'Girls First,' but it's more than that. Look at who's been targeted. Becky, Cynthia, and then probably Tesha or Whit."

"Yeah?" I shrug, ignoring the fact he said Whit. "Cynthia's an Elder, so that doesn't exactly fit what I just said, but she's still female."

"They're being Killed in order of fit."

"What fit?" I say, exasperated. "I fail to see the pattern."

He laughs, and it comes out like a bark. "As in, how fit they are. Hot. *Bellisima*." He leans forward and touches my knee. "Are you familiar with any of these terms?"

"Urgh!" I pull back. "Stop it! Of course I am." I feel myself going red. "It's certainly a theory. And now I consider it, it's quite an insulting one."

"What?" It's Vaughan's turn to be confused, but that doesn't last long. "Oh lordy, how female. You're actually insulted that you're not sexy enough to have been Killed. You'd rather be dead and hot, than alive and mediocre."

"Mediocre?" I bellow at him.

"No! No!" He holds a hand up. "I don't think you're mediocre. I just mean that as far as the Killer is concerned, you're not top three." He tries to grasp my knee again, but I'm too quick for him. He sighs, gives up. "If it's any consolation, I think you'll be next."

"What?!" I am—I'll admit it—all at once terrified and pleased.

"Oh yes." Vaughan gets up, paces, muttering. "I mean, it's terribly subjective, of course, but by a popular standard, I'd expect you to be next in line. Arguably, you should have been before Tesha, but then we don't really know who those bloody balls were supposed to be aimed at. You were right with what you said in the clock tower. This Killer has a theme: blood." He fiddles with his mouse absentmindedly. "He likes to get messy. Remember what I said about marking his territory? It's like he's spraying his victims."

"Oh, bring me a new breakfast," I moan, not able to look at him. "Please do not elaborate on that train of thought." I don't give him the chance. "Well, if this 'hotness correlation' is correct, then maybe it's not a boy—it could be a jealous girl who's the Killer or, for that matter, a gay girl."

"No, no, no," he mutters. "Not the jealous girl, because—as I think I have explained, very well indeed—these kind of messy Kills are very male. Oh—and of course the Killer's not a gay girl, because otherwise you would have been Killed first."

My eyes widen, but I don't give him the satisfaction of responding.

He continues: "You'd be top of their list."

"Thank you," I say carefully. "You being the expert on these things."

"Oh, I have studied 'these things,' believe me." He's serious. He looks me dead in the eye.

"There are so many things wrong with what you just said." I don't let myself blush.

Instead, I think hard about telling him about the messages, the watch, the writing in the mug. If it is him leaving these little love notes, he'll be wondering why I haven't mentioned it. However, the more I think about it, the more I'm sure it wasn't him, because he takes this Game too seriously to joke around with it. And if the messages are not a joke, then "I'm watching you" is not a friendly thing to leave at the bottom of someone's coffee cup. It's an intimidation. Maybe it has nothing to do with the Game, maybe it's just someone's idea of putting the frighteners on me? Or maybe Vaughan's right, and I am next?

"Oh! We have a new post." Vaughan points to the screen.

INVOKE YOUR SAFETY!

THINK YOUR TIME IS NIGH? THIS WEEK ONLY, WIN THE CHANCE TO HAVE INVINCIBILITY. THIS HAS TO BE EARNED; PICK UP YOUR RED WRISTBAND BURIED IN THE SAND IN THE ENTRANCE TO THE CAVE. ARE THERE ENOUGH FOR EVERYONE? IF YOU FIND ONE, WEAR IT WITH PRIDE AND THE KNOWLEDGE THAT YOU ARE SAFE...FOR NOW.

YOUR VERY OWN GRAND MASTER XOXO

"Nice." Vaughan nods approvingly. "Safe all week? There will be a rush to grab the spoils. Shall we go digging?"

"No." Somehow I can't quite face going down to the beach yet. Or maybe I just can't face going down there with Vaughan. "I—I'll maybe leave it up to fate. I need to have a shower and do some work at the art studio."

His face twitches. "All righty." He closes down his workstation and pushes his chair back. "Be nice to me, Cate. I'm going down there, and if I find two wristbands, I might give you one."

I can't tell if he's being sarcastic. "Thanks," I say. Now he can't tell if I'm being sarcastic. I change the subject. "How are the feet?"

"Shredded." He shuffles to the door. "But I like a limp. Very Keyser Söze."

I smile at him. "You would like that film." I try to remember the exact line. "The greatest trick the devil ever pulled was convincing the world he didn't exist."

He smiles and nods, delighted with me. "And like that"— he blows on his fingertips—"he's gone." He vanishes through the doorway.

As I watch the empty space where Vaughan was standing, I decide that if he is OK with what happened last night, I have to be too. I have a hunch he's right about Flynny; I don't think there will be any repercussions beyond a lecture. And the Game is still on, and Vaughan is part of it. I look at the screen, click on Create New User. A box jumps up, and I begin to type in it. If

I'm honest with myself, I'm stoked to still be alive in the Game and excited about Crypt.

I type. Log in as the new me. The list of users refreshes again, two new users joining the bottom of the list:

Clouseau

Skulk

Ooh, somebody else has just registered at the same time as me. I scan the full list and spend a few minutes wondering who is who, reaching no particular conclusions beyond what the others were saying just before I broke up the party. Maybe it will become more obvious once everyone has signed up.

Some instant messages start to ping in response to Alex's announcement of the invincibility bands buried at the caves.

CharlotteCorday

Can we keep as many of the bands as we find?

Grand Master

Be my guest. Get digging, my pretties.

General Disarray

Grabbing my bucket and spade!

In spite of my earlier reservations, I feel an urge to run down to the caves right now. I finish what I'm doing. Just as I'm about to log off, a new message pops up.

Skulk

Watch out, watch out; the Skulk is about

I chuckle. This is going to be fun.

CHAPTER 14

I leave it as long as I can before venturing down to the caves. I really do not want to be there with Vaughan. But after an hour of hanging out in my study alone, thinking about working in the studio and then deciding I am too preoccupied to achieve anything, I can't hold back any longer.

Arriving at the caves, I thankfully find myself alone. The floor of the first cave is a total mess. It looks like a pack of dogs has gone crazy digging for bones, the sand in furrows and piles as far as my flashlight can see.

I kick at a few holes in the ground, with little hope that there will be any bands left. Looking at the cave in full daylight for the first time, I realize that it stretches back farther than I thought it did. I begin to walk the perimeter, looking for any patches of undisturbed sand, but it doesn't look like my fellow players have missed a single spot. I pass the entrance to the tunnel leading to the Place Most Holy, and then go farther around the rock, the bright arch of light to the outside world diminishing the more I walk. I pause by the unexplored passage that runs deeper under the cliff. Nope, I'm not going to venture there. Alex's post said the first cave only, and I'm happy to stick to it. That passageway was where I'd heard the weird crying noise coming from yesterday.

I continue to walk the perimeter, finding no more passages, and no patches of undisturbed sand. Whoever has been here before me has truly gone to town with the excavation. No doubt there had been a big gang of Guild members here all at once, and it was probably a whole lot of fun; I feel a pang of regret for the laughs I've missed.

Might as well leave. But there's an urge that's been itching away at me for the last few minutes: I have to check out the "crying" passageway. Could there be a band hidden just an inch or two in there? I walk to the back and flash the light into the passageway.

The diggers have taken Alex at his word; the sand in the passageway is completely smooth. But I know that Alex can be sneaky. Maybe it's his idea of a challenge. Should I go farther?

"Sod you, Alex."

I step in. The sand quickly gives way to rock, uneven and slippery. I walk on, carefully, the ceiling of the passageway suddenly lowering. I have to duck my head to continue forward, but as I flash the light up, it looks like the passage opens up a few feet ahead. I walk on. This is not just about immunity bands. It's about that noise. I need to see the spot where Vaughan—or whoever it was—was sobbing so wretchedly. I crouch low in the tunnel, and then after a couple feet, the roof falls away upward, and I am able to stand up again.

A huge cavern—I fling out my flashlight but the beam doesn't find any far walls. High too. Echoey, like walking into a church. I shiver in my parka. There is no natural light in here, and in spite of the feeling of space above and before me, it's claustrophobic, like being buried in a bubble, far below ground.

Noise comes from behind me somewhere, and I spin around, looking back through the passageway.

A shuffling? I click off the flashlight and hug the wall. The noise came from the first chamber—it is probably just another Guild member looking for a band, too late to the party like me. I strain my ears to hear footsteps, a voice, the sounds of digging, but there are none. And then something else: a laugh. Soft, high-pitched.

Fear presses on my shoulders, cold and heavy. Someone—or something—is between me and the sunlight, and that is not what I want. Suddenly I realize what a stupid move it was to come here alone. The Killer knew that everyone would head down here to try and get immunity. It's the perfect place to get someone on their own, make the Kill.

The cold fear starts to flush hot, adrenaline coursing up through my body, willing me to flee. Vaughan said I'd be next on the list, and I hadn't listened to him. I'd had those damn messages! Why the hell hadn't I come down here earlier with the crowd and got myself a band? Stupid, stupid, stupid. In front of me, someone is waiting in the shadows, and behind me, the despair of darkness and the unknown depths of the caves. No escape.

I'm buzzing, but I'm like a fly stuck to the wall. I wait. Breathe. Try to calm down.

No more sound. My ears are so attuned now that I think I can even hear the sea outside and the very distant cry of a seagull. Maybe that's all I heard before? Just another minute, got to be sure.

Finally, I can wait no longer. If nothing else, I need to pee so badly I'm beginning to think of digging my own hole in the sand and squatting right here, right now.

OK, I'll do this. Leg it. I'll switch the flashlight on, point it to the ground to find my footing through the low tunnel, then when I can see the archway of daylight at the other side of the first chamber, I'll sprint for home and never stop. I'm nimble, and I have the element of surprise on my side. Unless the Killer rugby tackles me to the ground, I'll make it past them and out of the hideous, dark cave. And if they get me in the open air, at least it won't be as horrible as being Killed in this tomb.

Or maybe there is nobody there after all.

I chuckle lightly to myself. Talk about spooking myself out.

I bend low, click the flashlight on by my feet, shielding the beam with my hand a little. I only have to get myself clear of these rocks in the tunnel, and then I can run like hell.

There by my left foot is a red snake.

I jerk back with a yell, dropping the flashlight on the rocks. It dies instantly, and the dark takes me, smothering my face, leaping down my throat, and pressing on my chest. How different it feels to be in darkness now I don't have a light in my hands. I fall forward onto the hard, cold rock, shooting out my hands for the flashlight. Please, please, come to me. I can't stand to be without you. I don't know which way is up. I need you.

My hand closes around the flashlight, and I turn it on, feeling foolish now that I have the luxury of light.

That cannot have been a snake. Skola probably doesn't have so much as a slowworm. I find my feet, and I find what I'm looking for. It's a red wristband, a double length of braided red plastic, with a snake's head on one end. In place of the snake's tongue is a catch; the snake's tail has a loop. I wind it around my wrist twice and fasten it.

Ha-ha, Alex. Bet you gave the sane members of the Guild a good old giggle when they dug these up.

I have no idea how this wristband got here, if someone put it here on purpose or by mistake, or if I dragged the thing in on my shoe somehow. I cannot get rid of the nagging feeling that Vaughan left it here for me. He said he'd try and get me an extra one. Maybe he knew that I'd heard him crying in this cave before and maybe he knew I'd come in here to check it out. It's a ridiculous notion, but it's wriggling away in my brain…like a snake in the sand.

I extinguish the flashlight, scrabble through the tunnel on hands and knees, and as the passageway opens up to the outer chamber, I rise up and run, taking huge, exaggerated leaps over the churned-up sand, my feet scrambling and ankles twisting on each landing, but I keep going, heading for the light. I'm nearly there. I can feel the fresh air on my face, and I'm nearly out when the Killer brings me down. I fall flat onto my stomach, the wind knocked out of me. I claw the sand, pulling for breath that isn't there, dread filling me, and regret that the Killer has got me, has won.

But then nothing happens. No stab with a rubber knife, no dousing with a grenade of blood. Breath rushes back in painfully, and I roll over, blinking.

I am alone.

Stupid piles of sand! I've just barreled through a huge one, and that's what felled me. No secret assassin, waiting in the shadows, just an almighty sand castle. I would laugh out loud if I had the breath to spare.

I get up, brush off the sand. My flashlight has died for good with the last clonk it received, but it doesn't matter now, now I'm back in the light.

"Are you OK?"

I shriek. A full-on, girlie one that embarrasses the hell out of me.

Martin is standing behind me, grinning and toothy. He has a trowel in his hand.

"Were you in the cave?" I snap at him.

"Yeah." He looks a little hurt. "I saw you running and trip on the sand. Are you all right?"

"Yes!" I bark back. "Thank you. I am." I look behind him, back into the darkness. "How long were you there?"

Martin shrugs, puzzled. "Four or five minutes. I was looking for a wristband, but I think they've all been taken already." He looks really disappointed. "You've got one though. Where did you find it?"

My hand flies to my wrist. "I—it was just on top of the sand. At the very back of the cave," I sputter.

Martin sighs. "Lucky you."

"Yeah." I want to go, but I have to ask him. "Martin, did you laugh?"

He looks blankly at me. "When?"

"Four, five minutes ago, when you first got here. Did you laugh at all?"

He looks at me as if I'm deranged. "I'm here alone. What would I laugh at?"

"I don't know," I say. "But you didn't?"

He shrugs again.

"So..." I'm confused. "You might have laughed? You don't know if you did?"

He laughs now. It's soft and a little high-pitched for a boy, but I have no clue if it's the same laugh that I heard before. He shakes his head. "There's nothing funny here, Cate."

The way he says it creeps me out. I realize that while we have been talking, he has edged around me, so that now he is between me and the outside. I sidestep, and he mirrors me. I frown at him, and he tilts his head to one side, questioningly.

I hold up a wrist in front of me, like I'm Wonder Woman with her bulletproof bracelet. "I have a red band."

"Yes, I know that. You told me," Martin blusters, suddenly losing his swagger. "I suppose I'll keep looking."

"You do that." I walk around him and out of the cave.

That afternoon, I hide in the art studio all alone. I plug my MP3 player into the music system, thumbing through my playlist until I find something cheery, and start work. For the first half hour, I'm watching the door for Flynny, certain he'll be coming to find me, but after a while I lose myself in my screen printing, and three hours pass before my stomach and the clock tells me I'm going to have to run to make it to high tea.

As I'm clearing away the final things, the door opens. It's Mr. Flynn.

I was sort of prepared for it and inclined to believe what Vaughan had said about Mr. Flynn not acting on what had happened the night before. But as soon as I see him, looking ridiculously handsome and disheveled in a Sunday way, and wearing the most thunderous look I've ever seen on him—apart from the one he wore last night—I'm immediately reduced to Pathetic, Quivering Schoolgirl.

Of course, I don't let him see this. I walk toward where he stands in the doorway.

"I'm going to be late for high tea," I say.

"Sit down."

I sigh. "Ms. Lasillo is on duty. She definitely will notice I'm not there and would just love to give me an absence mark."

"Lucky you, it's Mr. Churley tonight." He nods to the nearest table. "Find a chair."

I teen-shuffle to it, slugging my bag down and looking up at him.

"Vaughan is OK."

"I know he is," Mr. Flynn says. "I've just finished talking to him."

This makes me sit up a little. "You have?"

Flynn nods. "He assured me that nothing untoward was going on last night. Beyond kissing and skinny-dipping."

I can't help the sharp intake of breath. Oh, sweet cheeses. I have to fight the overwhelming urge to put him right, but of course I instantly realize that this is the best scenario by far. Flynny thinks we were having a bit of reasonably innocent tongue-tussling down on the shore, followed by a dare to jump in the sea? Perfect. The Game is safe. I stay silent.

"Vaughan tells me you used to know each other as kids?"

I nod.

Mr. Flynn nods too. "This is not like you. I couldn't smell anything on either of you last night, but if there was booze—or worse—involved, I suggest you do not do it again."

"There wasn't." Ah. At least that part is true.

"Fine." Mr. Flynn walks up to the table and sits down beside me. "Cate, I've seen it happen time and time again. Girl is ambitious, clever, focused. Girl meets boy, falls in love or lust or whatever—"

I blush and look down.

"—and loses ambition, loses focus. Becomes one half of a couple and little else. Lets it hold her back from jumping into all the other things she has to do with her life."

"That's a bit sexist, isn't it?" I mumble. "You saying it never happens the other way around?"

"Sometimes, it does," Mr. Flynn says. "But rarely, because most teenage boys don't let a silly thing like love hold them back."

I look up at him sharply. "Are you kidding me? That's so completely misogynistic."

"No, it's not," he says equally sharply. "Often in life, not thinking about anyone else but your own sweet self is a major flaw. But not when you're in your teens. Now is exactly the time when you should be thinking about you and you only."

I roll my eyes.

"I know this"—he leans forward—"because I lived it."

"What," I say sarcastically, "someone was so infatuated with you that they ceased to function?"

"No," he says simply. "I was the lovestruck one."

I look at him, shocked.

He nods. "It's true. I had an offer from an art school—Saint Martins, no less—and I didn't go because of a girl. Chose a part-time college instead to be near her and did a teaching degree. Started working to support her. She wanted to be a jewelry designer, and she was, for a while." He shifts his weight, and the chair creaks. "Now, I love being a teacher, but who knows what would have happened if I'd gone to Saint Martins instead

189

of dancing to her tune and doing everything for her at a time when I should have been focused on me? I don't want you to repeat my mistake."

I stay silent for a while and trace a pattern on the table with my finger. This is all rather bizarre, because despite our closeness, this is the first time Mr. Flynn has offered up any kind of personal history beyond insignificant fun facts. And also, it's not relevant. Vaughan and I were not kissing, and we are not in love or lust or in any danger of being...that way.

Even as I think this thought, I feel guilty, because I'm not sure that it's...one hundred percent accurate. And I cannot allow myself to pursue that thought, not at the moment. Mr. Flynn is right. I can't lose focus, and the Game is the thing threatening to do that, not some boy. Probably.

"Are you still with her?" I say finally.

"What?" Mr. Flynn says. "Oh, the girlfriend? No!" He laughs. "That was a million years ago. She's a police officer now, down south somewhere, I think. Wife to Rob someone, mother of three chubby boys, according to Facebook. But that's the point: when you're sixteen, you don't realize how you'll change and how the decisions you make now can alter the course of your life."

I nod sagely at the table. "Well," I say slowly. "I'm glad you did do the teacher thing, or you wouldn't be here at Umfraville now, would you?"

"Don't suck up to me, Cate," he says. "It won't work." But there's a note of humor in his voice. "You should be glad I'm here because nobody else would be letting you and that brass-balled boyfriend of yours off the hook so easily."

"Not my boyfriend," I say.

"Glad to hear it," he says. "Now get to tea and if Churley gives you any rubbish tell him I kept you back."

I get up. "Thanks." I point at the chair behind his desk. "Your jacket. Thanks for the lend. And by the way, nobody saw me wearing it."

"I should hope not. Now get lost." Mr. Flynn rises too and walks to his desk. "And, Cate? If your work drops off at all, remember, I'll be on you like a ton of bricks."

I let that one hang in the air as I skedaddle out of the door as fast as my lucky legs will carry me and race to tea.

Later, I hit the library for my scheduled hour of Internet study time.

Housed in the mock-Tudor clock tower that dominates the quad, the Umfraville library consists of one very large room filled with floor-to-ceiling book stacks and a couple long, oak reading tables in the middle. There's a mezzanine level above, with twenty or so small desks interspersed with shorter stacks on wheels. These desks are the best place to sit, because you don't have any pesky teachers or librarians looking over your shoulder unless they come right up behind you. The desks have outlets, and you can even push the stacks around you a little to give yourself a degree of privacy. I bag one of the last desks with my back to the stairs—not too private, but it gives me a good view of the room, including the reading tables on the main floor below. Firing up my laptop, I take a quick glance around me and log on to Crypt.

Ooh. Everyone has registered! There's a complete user list on the news feed:

Grand Master

CharlotteCorday

DeadMcTavish

I_did_it

Banana Hammock

AllKillerNoFiller

13*is*my*lucky*number

IceColdBlond

General Disarray

Clouseau

Skulk

Smee

Becky_is_Dead

RAW

sooperdooper

Nimrod

Hmm…this Game just got even more crazy—crazy good. I chew on a thumbnail and study my screen. Who's who? Grand Master is obviously Alex. I think sooperdooper is Anvi, because she's always saying "sooper"…unless it's a bluff. Becky_is_Dead is clearly a bluff; Becky herself would never do that in a million years. I suspect RAW is Becky, because it's her initials, and I doubt she would bother putting much effort into her username now she's dead and effectively out of the Game.

But other than those two, I haven't got a clue who everyone is. Apart from me, of course.

Wait—I count the names: sixteen of them. That's not right. Thirteen Guild members and one Grand Master, that's how it should be—oh no. There's Vaughan now too. But that still only makes fifteen in total. Somebody has registered twice. Is that allowed? Some kind of error? I make a mental note to ask Vaughan later.

Right, better get on with some actual homework.

I'm only minutes into researching art nouveau when Guild IMs begin to pop up.

Smee

Who got a wristband, then?

sooperdooper

Yeah, fess up!!!

Grand Master

No telling online, folks. Otherwise, we can connect usernames to Guild members and your covers will be blown.

sooperdooper

Oh yeah, never thought of that!! Or perhaps it was all part
of my plan...mwah—ha-ha-ha!!!

Yeah, sooperdooper is definitely Anvi; all those headache-
inducing exclamation marks. I read the messages as they come
in and write a couple. It feels totally decadent. Then Alex
messages us again.

Grand Master

Check out my new posting on Crypt for details on the lucky
winners.

Ack. I glance at the clock on my laptop and reluctantly log
out. I'm longing to read who my fellow invincibles are, but I've
only got forty minutes of Internet time remaining and a lot of
work to do. I was checking Guild members out at tea, looking
for another red snake, but I couldn't see anyone wearing one. I
had pushed mine up my sleeve because I didn't know if it was
wise to have it on display yet. After tea, I exited the hall and
Alex whispered in my ear—no, in fact, he hissed, nothing else,
just one long "hisssssss!" Just like a snake. I nodded at him, and
he left, grinning.

Damn. I have to log in to Crypt again. Just a peek. With a
quick glance to see that no one is looking my way, I type in
my password and go to the home page. Sure enough, there's
a new post:

INVINCIBILITY CLAIMED!

I AM ECSTATIC TO ANNOUNCE THAT ALL OF THE RED
WRISTBANDS HAVE NOW BEEN DUG UP FROM THEIR
SANDY GRAVES! THERE ARE THREE IN PLAY AND THREE
ONLY. THE LUCKY PLAYERS ARE:

ANVI

MARTIN

CATE

WEAR YOUR BANDS. WEAR THEM WITH PRIDE. YOU
HAVE THE WEEK TO RELAX...BUT USE THIS TIME TO
GATHER INTEL ON YOUR FELLOW PLAYERS FOR THE
VOTE NEXT WEEKEND.

AND REMEMBER...JUST BECAUSE THE PLAYERS ABOVE
HAVE BANDS, IT DOESN'T MEAN THEY'RE NOT THE
KILLER!!!

LOVE, YOUR GRAND MASTER XOXOX

Martin! The little weasel. Said he didn't have a band when I
met him at the caves. Was he telling the truth? Or is it possible
he found it afterward?

I go back to my art homework but keep logged in, and the
IMs ping every few seconds. Everyone is excited, chatting
about who found the bands and who didn't, but trying not to
reveal identities at the same time. It's really distracting, because
I want to study the chatter, try and guess who everyone is from

the personalities emerging. sooperdooper is excitable; Smee is a character of few words; General Disarray is sarcastic, superior. And of course, I'm checking out who is at the other computer terminals around me in the library, watching who is typing and when, and if anyone is giggling or making faces at the messages. All the Guild members are here—except Vaughan... I haven't seen him—but on another night, we could all be in our studies or elsewhere on the map, online. I see now how this tracking thing is going to be invaluable to guess who's who. As far as I can make out, all users are contributing to the conversation, including the extra user, whoever that might be. The only one who isn't posting is me. I write a couple quick IMs to avoid standing out.

Suddenly, I sense a pressure change in the room; a teacher has walked into the library.

A couple teachers are on duty every evening, and they do the rounds to check that everybody is actually working. It's Ms. Lasillo tonight. Head of computer studies. Damn. If anyone is going to notice something amiss with the IMs, it's her. A palpable wave of dread runs through the room. IMs ping out, like little birds warning each other of the arrival of a sparrow hawk. And that's a good description of Ms. Lasillo. Small, sharp, with quick eyes and a quicker brain. She does a lap of the main room, past the workers at the reading tables, barely seeming to look at everyone's screens, but you can bet that she's checking what everyone is looking at, and if anything extracurricular is going on, she will strike. I've seen it in action: someone pulls a hack and logs on to a social media site, and they are toast. It's Lasillo's job to police all of this; she puts the gatekeepers in place, and when someone finds a crack in her coding, she comes down hard on them.

Click-clack, click-clack.

Suddenly, Lasillo's heels are on the stairs behind me. I quickly log out of Crypt and return to my work.

"Arse!" Carl mutters under his breath. He's my nearest neighbor, at a desk to the left of me, but still a good three or four yards away.

I see him try to hit a few keys, but by the look on his face something has gone wrong. I can't see his screen from my seat, but Ms. Lasillo will be able to in a few seconds.

I get up, a book in hand. Then, as I pass the back of his desk, I fumble and drop it on the floor. As I duck down, Ms. Lasillo approaches from the top of the stairs. I quickly pull the cable out of the screen of the desktop. Ms. Lasillo is passing behind Carl. She stops in her tracks.

"Carl?" she says. "Is there something wrong with your machine?"

"What?" Carl looks up, as if disturbed from some deep thought. "Oh, sorry, Ms. Lasillo, no—I just switched the screen off to avoid the glare while I was reading."

Ms. Lasillo frowns. "Fine. Well, remember to switch it on again for the next person when you're finished, yes?"

Carl smiles. "Of course. Thank you."

Ms. Lasillo peers over at me, where I'm still crouching on the floor. "Have you fainted, Cate?"

"No, Ms. Lasillo." Something about her always makes me prickle. "Just dropped my book."

She tuts and shakes her head, like I'm the clumsiest oaf in the world. "I'm sure you have some work to be doing, Cate. Please get up and get back to it."

I'm sorely tempted to tell her to go jump out of the window, but there has been enough blood spilt in the quad...for now. Plus, she's pals with Mr. Flynn, and if he finds out I've given her lip, I won't hear the end of it from him.

I nod my head and straighten up, and she trots off to the next workstation.

"Thank you," mouths Carl. I wink at him, then return to my desk. Lasillo is still walking around, but I can't resist logging back in to Crypt.

Skulk

Nice work, Cate.

My hands hover over the keys, ready to shoot off a reply— argh! I stop myself in time. If I respond, everyone will know my username.

So, Skulk saw what went down with Carl? I fight the urge to look around the room but visualize where everyone is sitting. Who would have a good enough view of what just happened? Is Skulk Carl? He's the only one who could actually know what I did. I glance at him. He seems preoccupied with a book, not even looking at his screen. The cable I unplugged is still on the floor. He's not risking fiddling with it until Ms. Lasillo is out of the room. So that means Skulk can't be him, doesn't it? I suppose he could, in theory, write an IM with no working screen—the computer itself is still on, the keyboard connected—but it's a bit of a stretch.

Nobody is responding to Skulk's message, too afraid that whatever they write will identify them, in the very least as Not Carl and Not Cate.

Another message pops up:

Skulk

slow clap

I take a breath. He or she is trying to taunt me now, trying to make me say something. They're also running the risk that Ms. Lasillo will see an IM, because she's still here, although currently rummaging through some oversized books in the back corner. Any moment now and she'll probably be making her way back toward the stairs and past the workstations.

"What did I miss?"

Vaughan plops down on the seat beside me.

"God, I wish people would stop doing that," I mutter, hand on my heart.

"What, talking to you?" Vaughan whispers. "I'm sure it can be arranged."

I turn around in my seat and look at him. "When you said you can't tell who users are, were you telling me the truth?"

Vaughan looks surprised. "Of course. Why would I lie to you?"

I sigh. "Oh, to save me from myself, perhaps. Because you would know that at some point I'd start asking you who everyone was."

"Sorry, mate." He chuckles at me, leans over, and ruffles my hair. It's supremely annoying, just like it was when we were eight. "Other than using my excellent powers of deduction, I really can't tell who each user is." He nods at my screen. "Who do you want to know about?"

I shake my head, move my hand to the mouse, and close my IM down quickly. "Nobody. It doesn't matter."

Vaughan looks disappointed. "Aw. Don't want to share any more theories?" He bats his eyelashes at me. "I was so looking forward to you being Watson to my Holmes."

"Yeah, I can see that you would be." I hesitate. "You've noticed, of course, that there's one too many users."

He nods, green eyes smiling. "Adds an extra something, doesn't it?"

I frown. "People can do that? Make more than one profile?"

He pulls a face. "I didn't put any limit on it initially. Somebody took advantage, and now they have an alter ego." He runs his hands through his black curls. "But the Elders noticed and asked me to change things so that no one else can do that. Makes sense, I guess. After all, only one of us is living a double life in the Game."

"You think the person with two usernames is the Killer?"

He shrugs. "Would be a good move, wouldn't it?"

I don't answer, but inside I'm thinking: Skulk, Skulk… it has to be. I pack my bag, giving up any hope of achieving anything more on my computer. I'll work in my study and do the rest of the online stuff tomorrow. As I stand up, Vaughan grabs my hand.

"Relax. Enjoy. You're safe." He rubs his thumb up the inside of my wrist. The touch sends electricity up the inside of my arm. "You have the wristband after all." He snags it with his thumb, and I pull away, embarrassed.

"Yeah, safe." I throw my bag over my shoulder, unable to meet his eyes, and scuttle down the stairs and out of the library as fast as I can.

It's only when I'm back in my room, sitting at my desk, door locked, that I allow myself to breathe again.

CHAPTER 15

Monday morning, Tuesday morning, Wednesday morning...
and I'm breathing easy.

I love being safe. The little red snake around my wrist feels
wonderful. Guild members eye it, some with envy. One of them
is looking at it and mentally crossing me off their hit list—for
this week.

The Game is buzzing. I begin to live for screen time. Crypt
is the place to be. Players are posting stuff constantly—jokes,
theories, even pictures. Analyzing clues. Having fun. And part
of that fun is keeping in the loop while keeping your username
private and not letting any non-Guild in on the secret.

Suddenly, no Internet is no big deal. My personal devices
are connected to the school intranet and I can get on to Crypt
whenever I like, as long as I'm in range of the Umfraville Wi-Fi.
There's a mad increase of Guild members carrying around
tablets at all times, chuckling at them in lessons, lounging

around with open laptops in the quad, trying to pick up a signal in the pottery studio or in the toilets. The staff must think we've all become very industrious. We'll have to be careful.

But Vaughan is on point. By Tuesday afternoon, there's a post on Crypt from him.

Greetings, assassins. This is your webmaster.

Please click on the link below to download this simple yet highly addictive game onto your personal machines. Once downloaded, in the event of an emergency, this game can be toggled to hide any Game IMs or Crypt page you might be viewing.

Yours prophylactically, Vaughan

I have to smile. He's smart, that boy. I click on the link, and before long I'm playing a bright and obnoxious matching game called Kreepy Klowns.

The days pass with no Kills. Perhaps the Killer is too busy matching lines of clown faces and bantering online on Crypt. Perhaps one of us with immunity is next on their list, and they don't want to waver from the plan. Perhaps they're enjoying heightening the fun by lulling everyone into a false sense of security.

But then on Thursday, the fun starts to sour.

I don't see it coming at all; I've had a good day. Swimming

has been replaced by a choice of yoga or hockey, and I'm all about the om. I have double art, and art history winds up the day with the batty but charming Miss Biddulph. I'm coming out of class, chatting to Whitney and laughing about which Kreepy Klowns level we're on, when Anvi comes running up to us, peroxide blond hair bouncing in her usual ponytail.

"Where have you been?" Her brown cheeks are flushed scarlet, dark eyes wild beneath the long fringe.

"Art history." Whitney looks at her friend as if to say, er, duh.

"Not you. Her." Anvi nods at me. "Have you seen it yet, on Crypt? Everybody's talking."

My heart sinks. I have no idea what she's talking about, but I have a feeling I'm not going to like it.

"Spill the beans, you tease!" Whitney says.

Anvi doesn't answer, just grabs my arm painfully, looks from side to side and marches me around the corner of the main block of classrooms. She whips out a tablet.

"Should pick up the Wi-Fi here." She swipes away Kreepy Klowns and Crypt pops up. "Look!" she urges me. I do. Nothing untoward, just a news feed of various posts... She scrolls down. There's a box with an arrow.

"Cool." Whitney is looking over my shoulder. "Someone uploaded a video?"

Someone did. Anvi taps the arrow, and the video begins to play.

It's very dark. The picture is blurred. For a moment I think it's the caves, and I wonder why Anvi's showing it to me specifically. It's obviously something to do with the Game.

The cameraperson (female?) chuckles a little as the focus comes in and out. We're not in the cave, but that's water, isn't it? Then…stairs? Two blurred figures. Ah! It's the grandstand at the swimming pool.

Oh. Oh please, no.

This is nothing to do with the Game. But everything to do with me.

The camera zooms in, and in spite of the dim lighting, it's easy to see what the two figures are doing. Kissing. Arms wrapped around each other, one on top of the other. The one on top stops for a minute, throws back her head, and laughs. The one on the bottom laughs too.

Me and Daniel. Nope, nope, nope…

I'm vaguely aware of Whitney suppressing a gasp in my ear. Anvi's not so subtle. The tablet is shaking as she giggles. I snatch it.

"Hey!" Anvi grabs at it, trying to get it back, but I hug it to me.

"Who posted this?" I shout at her.

She shrugs, face passive. "Smee."

Great. Smee, one of the users who I have no clue about. I have little sense of whether they're friend or foe, male or female, Killer or not. One thing I do know about them now, however: I know they're not Daniel.

"Smee better damn well delete this!" I shove the tablet back at Anvi, poking her in the chest with it. "And if you know who they are, make sure they get the message from me!"

"Don't get your big girl pants in a twist," Anvi says. "Be thankful that this actually makes you interesting for a change. Momentarily."

"Really, Anvi?" I step up to her. "You find this interesting? Interesting enough to post?" I push her shoulders. She's half my size but hard as nails, and she doesn't budge.

"Stop!" Whitney steps in. "You need to calm down, Cate. You know Anvi had nothing to do with this." She looks at Anvi. "You didn't, did you?"

"No!" Anvi says, revolted.

"Great," Whitney says, turning to me. "Rise above it. Talk to Vaughan or Alex and get it taken down. After all, it's seriously Off-Topic when it comes to the Game. Nobody's going to care about old gossip after a day or two."

Nobody's going to care? Daniel will care. Daniel will care a lot.

"Fine." I turn tail and head off, not sure which direction I'm heading in. It's true—in the grand scheme of things, this will be five-minute news. I'll suffer for a few days, and there will be jokes forever, but it's nothing I can't handle. Daniel? A different matter. He will be devastated. He'll leave the Game for sure. He might leave school. He hates, hates this kind of thing. He cannot cope with it. Oh God, I hope he doesn't think I've got anything to do with it. Would he think that?

But instead of heading for his study or the music rooms, I run in a different direction.

When I burst in to the study, Vaughan is bent over his laptop, tapping away.

"Take it down."

He holds a hand up, still typing with the other. "Just a sec."

"Take it down!"

He looks at me, shocked. Hits Enter. His hands lower. "OK. What am I taking down?"

"The video, of course. Don't tell me you haven't seen it."

"Yeeeah." He nods, overly serious. "You and Daniel."

"Of course me and Daniel!"

"Of course." He tilts his head to one side. "I'm curious. Past or present?"

"What?" I say. "Past! Last-term party past!"

He nods understandingly. "One-off?"

"Look, not that it's any of your business." I step inside the room and shut the door, becoming aware that a few people are lingering at the other end of the corridor, attracted by the drama. "But yes, it was a one-off. A random, stupid mistake on my part. Not to be repeated. And definitely not to be broadcast."

"On your part." Vaughan taps the top of his laptop with a restless finger. "But not a mistake as far as Daniel was concerned?"

"Just take it down," I say. "Now."

I turn and am about to flounce out when I see a white school mug of hot chocolate sitting on the table next to Vaughan. Untouched.

"Did you make that?" I point to it. "Did it come with a note?"

"What?"

I don't wait for a proper reply, just grab the handle, lean forward, open the window, and chuck the drink out into the grass.

"Oi!" Vaughan protests. "What are you doing?"

I stare at the bottom of the mug. No writing. Just an ordinary mug. An ordinary hot chocolate. Ex-hot chocolate.

I fling it down, and the mug breaks. I leave.

By the time I reach my own study and log in, the video is down. I'm relieved but also slightly aggrieved. I wanted to view it again, in the privacy of my own room, and process how bad it really was. And also to look in that laughing girl's eyes and try and see what she saw that night.

Daniel's not at high tea, nor in the library that night. I drop by his study and the music rooms, but I can't find him anywhere. Last thing before curfew, I find myself at the Loathsome Toad office. I see Marcia working in the brightly lit room. She's on her own. I twist the temperamental doorknob and look in.

"Knock knock."

"Hi." She doesn't look at me but continues to type.

I sigh. Walk in, sit down. Put my feet up on the desk so she knows I'm not going anywhere.

"Want a smoke?" she says, still not meeting my eye.

"No," I say. "It's been ages since I've seen you. You sneak in to the dorm right before curfew. You avoid me at meals. You're never in the study."

Marcia keeps typing, shakes her head. "I'm not sneaking, and I'm not avoiding. I'm busy."

"Oh, I'm sure." I stretch my arms out, faking a relaxation I do not feel. "But you know, I'd have thought you'd make the time to apologize for ditching me at the beach the other night. And maybe check I was OK the next day. I'd have also thought you'd come and seek me out when some idiot posted that video on Crypt."

It's Marcia's turn to sigh. She leans back and snaps the lid of her laptop shut.

"I knew you were OK after the beach. I ran because I wanted you to run. I didn't want you to be caught."

"What about Vaughan?"

She shrugs. "I felt scared for him, but what's he to me, compared to you? I wanted you out of there."

My chest feels tight. "You should have known I wouldn't leave. I'm funny like that. I don't leave my friends when they're in trouble."

She holds her hands up. "We all do what we think is best."

I look at her, but now it's me who can't hold her gaze. I stare at the floor. "And you thought it was best not to tell me when that video was posted?" I tap my feet. "Posted first thing this morning, apparently. Don't tell me you didn't know about it."

"I did."

I look up at her, and she nods.

"But I thought it was more important to tell Daniel about it. You can deal with this; Daniel...may not."

She has a point. "You could have IMed me at least."

She stays silent. She's not one for saying sorry. She doesn't have the British way of overapologizing for everything, and sometimes that hurts.

"Did you find Daniel?" I sit up.

"Yes."

"I looked... I couldn't find him." When she doesn't enlighten me further, I go on. "How was he?"

"How do you expect?" She pushes her chair away from the desk and turns around to look at me, face on. "He's broken. He hates to look a fool. He didn't even realize that anyone else knew, so it's even worse for him."

Irritation rolls over me. "Most boys would be bragging and having a laugh about it."

Marcia frowns at me. "Daniel is not most boys. Or didn't you know that?" She begins to pack up her stuff into her big tote bag. "It's worse because he actually wants you, of course, and he knows you don't want him." She puts on her coat, clearly ready to get out of here and away from me as soon as possible.

I cringe at her words. But it's all true, of course. I change tack. "Do you know who Smee is?"

She pauses. "Even if I did, it wouldn't be in the spirit of the Game to discuss it with you."

"Oh, come on!" I stand up. "Posting make-out videos is hardly in the spirit of the Game, is it?"

She pushes her long hair out of her face. "Smee's female, I'm sure. I think I have some of the boys' usernames guessed, but Smee has a female voice, and I don't know who. Whitney, maybe?"

"Whitney was with me when Anvi showed me the video." I think about it. "If she is Smee, she's a great actress."

"Then Tesha? Or Emily?" She scratches her head. "To be honest with you, before this, I thought that Smee was you."

I blink at her. "But you don't think that now, do you? Nobody thinks that I'd post this myself, do they?"

Marcia doesn't say anything but grabs her bag and swings it over her shoulder, heading for the door. I stride after her, reaching for her arm.

"You don't think I posted it, do you?"

She turns around. "I said before this happened I thought you might be Smee. I don't think so now, no. But do others think that?" She nods. "Yes. Yes they might."

She turns and goes out of the door. I'm not going to run after her, partly because I'm finished with making a fool out of myself for one day and partly because I now feel weighted to the floor with the horror that the Guild members think I did this myself.

I move to a desk, to one of the PCs, turn it on, log in to Crypt. There's some chatter.

AllKillerNoFiller

Awwww...the skin flick is gone. Bring it back, Smee!

I_did_it

I think we've seen enough

AllKillerNoFiller

Is that you, Danny boy???

I_did_it

I'm not Daniel. That's why I think we've seen enough ;) You can bet D is staying far awaaaaay from here!

AllKillerNoFiller

No change there then

General Disarray

Question is, where's Smee?

AllKillerNoFiller

He's taken Smee out...KILLLLLLLLLED

I_did_it

Smee, nooo! We love you! Everyone forgives you!

General Disarray

Daniel doesn't

I_did_it

Hey, maybe Smee IS Daniel

General Disarray

Or Smee is Cate. That would be more like it

Skulk

Smee's not Cate.

I_did_it

How do you know?

Skulk

Because I know who Cate is.

Skulk

I'm watching her.

AllKillerNoFiller

Yeah we all were, before her gal-pal Vaughany took the vid down! :P

I log off, quickly. "Skulk" knows who I am, do they? They're watching me? As in, hot-chocolate-watching me?

I move to the window of the office, but outside is overcast and gloomy. Anyone out there can see me, but I can't see them. I draw the blinds, but that seems even worse. I move to put out the lights, but before I do, I find my keys in my pocket and hold them between my fingers like a knife. It feels ridiculous—what am I going to do, stab one of my classmates in the eye?—but it makes me feel better to step out into the dark. I part the blinds a little and peer out. Now the darkening sky has more definition, shapes of trees in the distance, the roof of the Main

House silhouetted against a scarlet-and-purple sky. I can't see anyone lurking out there, but that doesn't mean they're not hiding. There's Marcia's water bottle on the desk where she was sitting. It's almost full. I pocket my keys, take off the top of the bottle, and move back to the door. If Skulk—or anyone else—is messing with me, I'll drench them with water and run.

I make it back to my study and hide there, skipping high tea, doing little work, and watching the Crypt chatter. Around 7:00 p.m., Alex posts something:

Evening, assassins. This is your Grand Master.

Please remember that Crypt is to be used for the Game, and the Game only. All posts that contain anything outside the interests of the Game will be removed, and the user who has posted them will be banned from Crypt for the remainder of the Game. I would also like to take this opportunity to remind you that there should be absolutely no reference made to Crypt or anything posted on it to non-Guild members. Breaking this rule means instant and eternal excommunication from the Guild without negotiation!

Thank you, and have a pleasant evening.

Phew. With the latter half of that post, Alex has effectively prevented the rot from spreading to the rest of the school. Of course, he's just protecting the Game, but I'm grateful to him anyway.

I await reaction, and the IMs start. There is a little comeback from a couple users, mainly arguing that anything concerning the players of the Game is relevant to post on Crypt, but that is quickly knocked on the head by Alex. The fact is, gossip about the video is already on the wane. People move on quickly.

I watch the users come and go, and post a few comments so it's not obvious I'm hiding. Only two users don't join the discussion this evening: Skulk has disappeared, and just before curfew, the other absentee finally shows up online.

Smee

Sorry, everyone

Smee

I'll be a good Smee from now on

Smee

Only hope I haven't upset the wrong person...

I log off. My watch is telling me I have precisely five minutes to run up to my dorm and check in with my housemistress or else risk getting a late mark. I close my laptop, run out into the courtyard. There is no one around. The lights in the library are off, and the studies are dark too. I exit by the archway, turn right, and start to run toward the Main House dorms.

Something—a noise? Or just the feeling of being watched—makes me look around, back in the direction of the courtyard.

A hooded figure is standing there. I can't see the face, but the height, the posture…

I'm sure it's Daniel. He stands perfectly still, looking toward me. I realize I'm standing under one of the Victorian streetlamps that line the pathways between Umfraville's central buildings. I feel exposed; he can see me, but I can't properly see him. I step into the shadows. He takes a step toward me.

Is it Daniel? Doubt creeps in now. I feel for the band around my wrist. I'm immune! But somehow, this doesn't make me feel any better. The figure takes another step. I turn on my heel and sprint for the dorms, not feeling safe until I'm up the stairs and in the comforting light and bustle of the girls' corridor.

Marcia is in the dorm, reading. When she sees me come in, she gives me a quick smile. But this time, it's me who doesn't feel like talking. I return the smile, however, and reach for my pajamas, changing quickly. I visit the bathroom, clean my teeth, and the lights are out in our room by the time I return. Thank goodness. I feel my way into bed, and as I do, I feel the rustle of a little slip of paper someone has placed in my bed. My heart beats faster in spite of myself. Oh, Killer. Let me guess: You're watching me?

I hold the paper up to the digital clock to see what is written there.

Chin up!

V xx

Warmth spreads through me. I hold the paper in my hand, and lie there, wondering if Vaughan will sneak in here tonight. Wondering and hoping.

I lie there awake for ages. He doesn't show up.

CHAPTER 16

Friday, and the blood is still coursing through my veins.

I sit on a gray chair in the ballroom and play with the two bands around my wrist: the black one that denotes I'm still alive, and the red one that ensures I'll stay that way for another two days at least.

Morning Exchange is what other schools would call assembly, but Ezra had to be different. Once a week on a Monday, Ezra gets wheeled out of storage and talks, and we listen. Not so much of the "exchange," but it's vaguely interesting to see he's still with us—physically, if not so much mentally.

On Tuesdays, some poor teacher is roped in to get things going. Usually they read something moderately profound or educational and then ask a bunch of questions at the end. In normal schools, they'd probably be hit with a wall of silence, but at Umfraville there are nerds just itching to pick the teachers to bits. It can make for some entertainment.

And then, once a week, on Friday, an individual or group of students steps up. Everyone has to do it eventually. In my school career, I've faced it twice, and it was torturous. My first effort was a group presentation about graffiti. Marcia talked, and Daniel and I gassed everyone by spraying inexpertly on a canvas to demonstrate what Marcia was talking about. All was well until the "exchange" part of the talk, when some gnarly dweeb two years below me made the point that graffiti wasn't supposed to belong on canvas, but on the wall…the furniture… and he dared us to demonstrate "properly." Marcia talks a good game, but she couldn't find a convincing argument. Daniel and I went for it…and went down in the history books…and the detention books. I smile at the memory; what were we thinking?

The second time—when I was on my own—was a far more sober affair. I talked about the history of Skola and Umfraville and by extension, my family's history. Everyone was rapt. I think it's because they got some of the information that they'd always wanted to ask. Not so much about the horse rendering plant that was on the island in the nineteenth century or how Skola is an important breeding ground for the roseate tern or even why the school paper is called the Loathsome Toad. They were far more interested in how and why a "normal" like me was at the school. Who my family really are, and how we got so lucky.

Through death is the answer to that last question.

This week, however, I can relax. It's Emily's turn to speak. I don't have high hopes, because it's not her forte, but if she screws up, then at least it will give everyone something to talk about other than Daniel and me locking lips.

Emily's sitting at the back of the stage while we all pile in and take our seats, and for some reason that will no doubt become apparent soon, she's playing "These Boots Are Made for Walkin'" on her MP3 player through the school speakers.

I feel eyes on me. Marcia is on the other side of the room, and Daniel's not even here, thankfully. He probably has some kind of extracurricular fiddle scraping to do. The only good thing is that because of the Game, the kids who have seen the make-out vid are duty-bound not to gab about it with the rest of the school. I plonk myself a seat or two away from Alex, and then Vaughan sits next to me. I turn to him shyly.

"Thanks for the note," I whisper.

His eyes widen. "What note?"

"Comedian," I whisper back.

He winks at me, and his hand slinks over mine and squeezes it quickly.

The doors shut. The music cuts. We're all in, and we wait like hungry lions at the zoo, or in the gladiator stadium, more like.

Emily stands up.

Now, Emily technically had all summer to prepare. Her name was on the list way back in spring term. The pressure is on because, of late, these little student presentations have taken on the appearance of a TED talk or a lecture at the Royal Society. But in truth, I bet Emily was too busy being Emily over summer to write anything. There were track meets where she got to come first in a bunch of competitions of who can throw the pointy thing or the heavy thing the farthest, or who can jump over more sand than anyone else. I'm guessing that she also had a couple weeks tanning at her family's place in Barbados, which would be very time-consuming. And since she came back to school? Well, the Game, of course! She's a new apprentice. All of this excitement is not exactly conducive to prepping a school assembly talk.

Emily strolls easily over to the lectern. She's over six feet tall in her sneakered feet. It's warm in the ballroom with the morning sun beating in through the floor-to-ceiling windows, and Emily's wearing a tank top under a sheer silk-knit cardi, skinny capris, and that Barbados tan. Her long fingers touch the side of a tablet placed on the lectern, shaking ever so slightly, and as she flicks her eyes up to take in her audience, she licks her lips.

"Giants—are they really a myth?" she reads.

A flutter of laughter. Nothing like a bit of self-deprecation to get everyone on board. Beside me, Vaughan snorts. A few heads turn to look at him.

"Almost every culture has its tales of giants." She looks at us for encouragement. "Indeed, giants, or cewri, feature prominently in Welsh folklore. But what are their origins? Did they really exist? And are they still walking amongst us?" Another smattering of laughter. "As a person of size"—she chances a little flirt with her audience—"I was excited to find out."

Warming to her subject, she reads an essay that is clearly

pseudo-copied from the school encyclopedia or some Wiki. But as an athlete, Emily should be applauded for even finding the library. Her talk is lightly amusing, and for what I suspect was an eleventh-hour under-the-duvet piece of frantic composition, it's none too shaming. There's a decent amount of Welsh to keep her tripping over bundles of consonants and a slight element of us laughing at, not quite with, her. But that's OK. In many ways it's a sympathetic audience of preoccupied genii—and the rest of us, who are just very glad it is not our turn.

"Canthrig Bwt, a giantess and witch notorious in the folklore of Gwynedd, lived under a great stone in Nant Peris and killed and ate a number of the community's children," Emily enthuses.

Nice. Sometimes I think we could do with that kind of giant around here.

My mind begins to wander, regardless. Vaughan is bored too. He's shifting around in his chair and staring at various people around him, like he's trying out a remote Vulcan mind meld.

I'm wondering when I can talk to Daniel and what I'll say to him when I do, when I see something twitch in the corner of my vision. It's as though something was moving in the shadows of the velvet curtains, onstage to Emily's left. Vaughan thinks he sees it too; his head turns, and he squints. I rub at my eyes. No, nothing there. I need to start getting a little more sleep.

"Although, in most legends giants are not generally thought of as child killers. Indeed, in the story of Jack and the Beanstalk, it is actually an ogre and not a giant who is the villain of the piece."

Vaughan titters. "Fee! Fi! Foe! Fum!" he bellows. Oh no. I clap a hand over my own mouth, as if I'd done the shouting myself. Vaughan grins to himself. "A popular misconception, indeed."

Everyone is looking at him, including Emily, who clearly did not anticipate audience participation this early in proceedings. Down the line of seats, Alex leans forward and raises an eyebrow at me. I'm searching my database for a suitably resigned grimace, but before I can slap it on my face, the velvet curtains twitch again. I turn to look. Definitely something there. What is it? A mouse? I wouldn't be surprised; this place is old and Ezra is not big on pest extermination. Most nights I fall asleep to the sound of things scratching in the walls.

Something skitters forward on the stage. I sit up a little straighter. Not a mouse—it's the wrong sort of movement. I look around me. Does everybody else see it?

Most do, but Emily doesn't. She clears her throat, still red in the face with Vaughan's interjection. I don't think she's big on ad libs.

"Although typically attributed with prodigious strength and physical abilities..."

The skittering thing suddenly moves into her field of vision, and she does the classic double take. There's a ripple in the audience. Finally, we're all looking in the same direction.

It's a spider. A huge one. Tarantula-type huge. And it's heading for Emily.

"...prodigious strength and physical abilities." She takes

another run at the sentence, unable to stop glancing down at her feet. "Giants are frequently depicted as benevolent. And even if they have antagonistic tendencies, as with Goliath"— she glances again, and her voice wavers—"they can be swiftly brought down with something significantly smaller than them."

The spider rears up on its hind legs and jumps. It lands on Emily's trainer. She yells and hops around, shaking her leg in a frantic jive. It clings on.

"Get it off me!" Emily is pointing her foot out to the side, getting the spider as far away from the rest of her as possible. She flaps at it with her tablet. It's not a terribly effective deterrent.

The spider jumps again, this time onto her bare lower leg. Emily screams a full-throated scream and snags the spider with her hand, sending it up into the air.

Everyone stares, nobody moving. The spider falls to the ground a mere foot away from Emily and starts to skedaddle back into the shadows of the velvet curtains. Emily watches it, and then her head falls back, her eyes roll white, and she sinks to the ground.

And then suddenly the room is churning. Kids screaming, some laughing, everyone standing up, some pushing forward to see, some cowering back from the drama. Mr. Flynn dodges the melee, runs up to Emily, and takes the stage with a flying leap. He lifts a foot, which hovers over the spider for a moment—

"No!" cries Vaughan beside me.

Mr. Flynn's foot crunches down on the arachnid. "Argh!" he cries. That spider was a lot hardier than he was expecting.

He kicks it over the stage. Bits clink off it and bounce on to the floor.

"It's mechanical," Vaughan mutters. "A mechanical spider."

The staff starts herding, getting us all out of there, pronto. A couple teachers, plus Mr. Flynn, are bending over Emily, who has come around and is coughing and spluttering.

"Someone get the EpiPen!" Flynn roars. I try to catch a glimpse of Emily, but all I can see is one outstretched hand, reaching for something. The rest of her is obscured by staff.

"Right, upperclassmen, you're out!" Mr. Churley yells at us.

I make for the door.

"EpiPen?" says Vaughan excitedly in my ear. "Is she having an allergic reaction?"

Before I can answer him, the projector screen at the back of the stage starts to unfurl, remotely controlled from somewhere else. Something is written on it, in three-foot-high letters. I recognize the font before I fully take in the word:

Killed

I gasp. There are a couple screams and some laughter. Kids who exited the ballroom start to try and come back in to look, and there's a logjam. Teachers shout, telling everyone to leave, and I weave through the crowd and get the hell out.

No need to go looking for trouble. It usually finds me soon enough.

CHAPTER 17

Trouble finds me straight away.

The ballroom is evacuated swiftly and more efficiently than I ever thought possible. Kids are rushed into the corridor like cows on the way to slaughter.

A hand grips my upper arm. "We need to get a look at that robot spider," Vaughan says, pulling me aside under the stairwell. "What's left of it anyway. Before they sweep it up." He thinks fast. "You create a diversion; I'll sneak in and grab the pieces."

"A diversion?" I say. "Were you actually in the room just now? How do I divert from a robot spider biting a pupil who goes into anaphylactic shock?"

Vaughan shrugs. "Take off your clothes?"

"Isn't that your thing?" I begin to walk away but turn on him before I get swept into the crowd heading out of Main House. "Do you really think they'll let anyone in there? It's a crime scene now. Emily actually got hurt, and for all we know, she may die."

Vaughan looks amazed. "Do you think so?"

"Yes!" I splutter. "She collapsed, and Flynn was shouting about EpiPens, you heard him! She has some nut allergy or something. Everyone knows. She's even got a flippin' necklace on that tells you so. I would have thought you'd have noticed that with your amazing skills of observation."

He looks stricken. "The Rod of Asclepius?"

I raise my eyebrows at him. "If you say so. The snake and sword symbol thing that means medicine. On the back of it, it says she's allergic to stuff."

The hallway has cleared. In the distance, I think I can hear shouting from the ballroom. Vaughan does too. He edges out from under the stairs and starts to float toward the double doors.

"Vaughan!" I hiss at him, but he's not having it. I pad after him. "Look, if you must—come with me." I grab him and pull him right, along a short corridor and through another door into a second corridor. There's not much light in here, and I'm perfectly happy with that.

"Where are we going?"

"Backstage." I hang a left and we find the door. The ballroom isn't used for theatrical performances often, as we have the amphitheater and a barn that has been converted into a theater, but I happen to know there's a small backstage area to the ballroom stage that is stuffed with chairs and hymn books. Once Daniel was rehearsing in the ballroom for a recital, and we ducked back here for a look.

I open the door to backstage. A light is on, a reading light balanced on a pile of chairs at the far end of the room.

"Whoa." I put a hand on Vaughan's chest. "Someone's definitely been here."

Vaughan pushes past me, starts searching the floor. He whispers to me, "Oh—I see, there's a safety curtain between here and the stage. And here! A gap. Just enough for the spider to be launched."

I tiptoe over to him. The thing he's calling a safety curtain looks more like a sliding door that folds into itself when retracted. Normally it's locked into place, but someone has pulled it open a little to reveal the velvet curtain which hangs on the stage in front of it. On the other side, we can hear the voices of the people in the ballroom, muffled—and some kind of scrabbling noise.

"They must have moved her from the stage," Vaughan whispers. I nod. The voices aren't very near. We listen for a few seconds. I can recognize Mr. Flynn's voice and Ms. Lasillo's, and I think I hear Emily groaning, but it's hard to make out actual words.

Vaughan bends low. "It's so dusty in here you can see the marks where someone knelt to line the spider up properly."

"Yeah." I trace our steps back a little. "Shame we've probably scuffed away any footprints with our own."

"Cate, this isn't Nancy Drew," Vaughan snarks. "What were you going to do, trace a drawing of them?"

I fume at him, hand on hip. "At least we could see what size the Killer's feet are. Could determine girl or boy."

Vaughan sighs. "Boy. Do I need to repeat again? Another female victim. A mechanical spider, for heaven's sake."

"That's sexist. And pretty ignorant, given the robo girl-geeks we have at this school." I give him a look.

"Hmm. Still something very male about sinking your teeth into a girl's leg." He does vampire teeth at me, and I roll my eyes. He chuckles and continues. "So, the Killer places the spider here, and then he's free to operate it remotely." Vaughan moves away from the curtain, on hands and feet like a monkey, bobbing his head down to look beneath chairs and dusty boxes. "What are the chances?" He reaches under a low table. "Wake up, little spider, wake up." He retrieves something slowly, with a handkerchief. He looks at it, being careful not to touch it directly, and then holds it out on his palm to show me. Half a spider's face, with one googly eye and a little metal fang.

"Be careful!" I can't help but warn, even though the thing is pretty mashed.

Vaughan sniffs it, then places a gentle fingertip under the fang.

"What are you doing?" I say, alarmed. He rubs the fang, then sucks on his finger.

"Vaughan!" I say. "Are you insane?"

He mock chokes, then smiles at me. "Yum."

I shake my head. "So go on, tell me. It's peanut butter, isn't it?"

"Smooth, not crunchy." He nods. "The Killer knew about Emily's allergy."

"Jeez." I shudder. "That's not red paint in the shower. That's messing with someone's actual life."

Vaughan pushes his sleeves up and rubs his hands over his hair. "It doesn't make sense, does it? This Kill is completely different from the other three. No, this Killer has a completely different personality."

"Two Killers?" I pull a face. "Would Alex put two Killer cards in the mix?"

Vaughan looks at me. "You know him better than me. What do you think?"

"Maybe." I clear my throat. "It would certainly make this Game memorable. Alex would like that."

"Yeah, well." Vaughan wanders over to the gap in the curtain again. "Killer number two is maybe forgetting this is all just a game."

On the other side of the safety curtain, the noise suddenly ramps up. Vaughan beckons me over, and we crouch together, ears against the gap.

"They're not here yet?" It's Flynn, shouting. "Then what's their ETA?"

Whoever replies is too far away for us to hear.

"…causeway…emergency…" It's Ms. Lasillo, but her voice doesn't carry as far.

"Of course," Vaughan whispers to me, his face serious. "How does the ambulance get here if the tide is in?"

"Ssh!" I listen again.

"…the lifeboat, although if it wasn't under control…helicopter…" It's Mrs. James, the deputy head.

"By boat or by air." Vaughan shakes his head. "They're taking no chances."

There are some bumping sounds and murmurs of instruction and then everything goes quiet.

We do a quick scan of the rest of the room, but there's nothing else to find. Vaughan pockets the spider parts, and we leave.

The staff has succeeded in getting most students into classrooms, but when the helicopter flies over, there's little they can do to tear people away from the windows.

I'm in psychology, with Marcia, Tesha, Carl, Alex, and Daniel, plus a couple non-Guild. We're not close enough to Main House to see Emily being stretchered out, but we see the helicopter fly over on its way back to the mainland.

Our teacher, Ms. Carol, puts up no fight as we line the window.

"Don't worry," she says. "Emily's in expert hands now. I'm sure she'll be all right."

"She'd better be," says Carl grimly.

"Do any of you know if this was some kind of prank?" Ms. Carol says gently.

No one speaks. But really, Ms. Carol—what else could it be?

"I'm sure no one intended Emily to actually get hurt." The teacher fills the gap. "Anyway, let's begin the lesson now."

"Did they call the police?" Marcia asks Ms. Carol, but the teacher only shrugs.

"I know as little as you. It may be up to Emily's parents." She beckons us from her desk. "Let's all sit down now."

As the lesson begins, I'm willing Ms. Carol to tell us to do something on our laptops, because then I can surreptitiously log on to Crypt and see what the chatter is. But perhaps there won't be any—after all, every Guild member is in the same boat: stuck in a lesson, dying to talk about what's happened. Except Emily, of course. She could just be, well, dying.

The first half of the lesson is a discussion, but after a while, we're tasked to begin an essay and everyone breaks out the hardware. As soon as I can, I log on. I'm impressed by how much talk is already going on. I look down the thread from the last half hour; sooperdooper has been online, as has DeadMcTavish, AllKillerNoFiller, RAW, Banana Hammock, and General Disarray. As far as I can tell, those users can't be in this room, because nobody here has had the opportunity to get online until now.

Or have they? Daniel had his tablet out briefly. Carl was called up to look at something on Ms. Carol's machine, and she stepped away from her desk for a few minutes. But it would take balls of steel to log on and post in that short space of time, wouldn't it?

As more posts begin to pop up, I look around at my classmates. Laptops are being abused left, right, and center. Tesha is sitting with Ms. Carol at the teacher's desk, going through a worksheet. I can tell she's really frustrated not to get online. I watch users join the fray. 13*is*my*lucky*number appears. Becky_is_Dead starts posting, and IceColdBlond. Everyone is reaching out for more info on Emily, but no one knows anything.

Then Alex posts:

ATTENTION, all members, this is your GRAND MASTER.

Emergency Summoning today @ 6:30 p.m. SHOW UP to
high tea; we do not want to draw attention to ourselves.
Leave promptly when you have finished, and go directly to
the caves. Do not be late.

STRICTLY NO MORE POSTS OR MESSAGES FROM
ANYONE BUT ME ON CRYPT UNTIL FURTHER
NOTICE.

The bell rings for end of lesson. I'm just about to shut down
my machine, when:

Skulk
Death is a debt we all must pay

Skulk
(That was Euripides)

Skulk
Bitch asked for it

Skulk
(That last one I made up all on my own)

I shake my head and shut down my machine. Whoever

Skulk is, they're a moron. And what do they mean by that anyway? Is Skulk claiming responsibility?

As I leave the room, Daniel is standing outside, leaning against the wall, bag of books over his shoulder and the ever-present violin case. He looks at me, and just as I'm about to make some excuse about how I have to run, he leans in and hugs me. Right there and then. In public.

"I'm sorry for how I've behaved." He squeezes me, his hands rubbing up and down my back. "I've been a prat."

"Yeah, me too." I do the half-reciprocated back-pat thing because I'm completely blindsided by this. In the distance, I spy a group of our year heading for the studies. I really hope they don't see us.

"Let's just forget about it all, shall we?" He nuzzles his face into my neck.

"Um, yeah. I'd be happy to." I push him off me a little so that he's at arm's length, then try to cover it up by looking at him intensely, as if I needed to see him face to face or something. "Are you genuinely OK with it all?"

"Yes." He smiles at me. "I've been doing a lot of thinking, and well, with this morning's events, we're yesterday's news already."

I pull a face. "Not for the best reasons."

"No!" He drops my arms. "Of course not. But every cloud has a silver lining, and this is ours."

"Yeah. I suppose so." I look toward the group of kids, but they've gone now. "And you're OK with…us?" I can't help but blush at the word.

"Totally." He nods, picking up his violin case and pulling it in front of him like a shield, running his fingers a little nervously over the big, swirly cat sticker on it. "We're friends. It's...cool." He turns around, looking in the direction of where the kids were too, and starts to walk backward, long fingers drumming on the violin case. "Things to do..."

"Sure!" I shout, a little too loudly. I don't move until he's disappeared. I should be pleased that he's over our awkwardness, so why have I got a knot in my stomach?

CHAPTER 18

Later that day, in the precious gap between the end of classes and high tea, I'm in Vaughan's study. The only news on Emily is that she's in the hospital and that she's in a stable condition. There's a rumor that the police will be coming over to the island when the causeway's open, later this evening or tomorrow.

Vaughan's room is the tiniest of the tiny, but he has it all to himself. It has bare, pale-yellow walls and is mainly furnished with boxes of junk—oh, sorry, computer parts—that cover every square inch of floor and desk space. He has an oversized beanbag in place of the usual sofa, and in honor of my visit, he's thrown a pile of coffee-stained scatter cushions on top. We're lying on the resulting squishy nest, side by side, feet up on the radiator. Vaughan is balancing a tablet on his chest, alternating between reading old Crypt posts and coding something too dense and clever for me to even guess at what it might be. I'm staring out of the window at the sky. The sun shouldn't set for another couple of hours, but it's weirdly overcast, and there's an expectant, pinky twilight in the air.

"It's Tesha." Vaughan's face is lit only by the light from the tablet.

"What is?" I watch starlings streak across the sky in a huge swarm.

"Smee," Vaughan says. "Tesha is Smee. Tesha posted that video."

I sit up abruptly and look at him. "I thought you couldn't tell who is who from the usernames?"

He shakes his head. "This is not a techy thing." He snorts. "More of a de-techy thing. I was in the girls' bathroom an hour ago and I just overheard Anvi, Whitney, and Tesha talking. Tesha took the video at the party last term on her mini-video-cam. They all knew about it, Alex too, apparently. Tesha was denying she'd posted it, but the others weren't convinced, and neither was I."

"OK," I say. "Skimming over the part where you were in the girls' bathroom for now—just for now, mind—what makes you think Tesha definitely posted it?"

"Well"—he places the tablet on the floor—"after I heard that, I had a little search in her room."

"You did?" I lean on one elbow. "Naughty."

He shrugs. "She gave me reasonable cause. Anyway, I found the mini-cam with the video still on it."

"What did you do with it?"

"Nothing." He does some more typing, then turns around to look at me. "Oh. Should I have deleted it?"

"Yes, Vaughan, you should have deleted it," I say, exasperated. I say it, and yet what I truthfully would have wanted is for him to bring it to me so that I could delete it.

"She'll have a copy on her laptop from when she uploaded it anyway," Vaughan says. He stops typing and faces me. "Look, I'll go back later tonight and delete it. And it won't take much for me to get onto her machine and wipe it off there if you want?"

"You'd hack her laptop?"

He blinks at me. "The less you know, the better."

The equivalent of twelve long-stemmed roses from him. I smile.

"Thank you."

"You're very welcome."

I stretch out on the beanbag nest again. "Tesha as Smee makes sense. Smee didn't post this morning on Crypt. I was in psych with a bunch of Guild, and Tesha was the only one who didn't get on her computer all lesson."

Vaughan nods. "Smee was quiet. So was Clouseau and Nimrod, RAW and CharlotteCorday." He smiles at me. "And we can deduce that Tesha is one of them—probably Smee— and Emily, of course, has to be one of the others. We'll work it out when we see who doesn't start posting again."

I feel like testing him. "Think she might be Clouseau?"

"No. Clouseau…is you." He puts his tablet down on the ground and twists around to me.

"And why do you think that?"

He stares at me. "Hunch." I hold his gaze, daring him to look away, but he doesn't. His eyes widen. "Well?"

"I'm not telling."

He sighs, head to one side. "Even if I tell you who I am?"

"You don't need to. You're DeadMcTavish."

His eyebrows shoot up indignant. "How did you guess?"

"Because of 'Magic McTavish'!" I blurt. "When we were little—that made-up superhero you used to channel when the other kids were making your life hell. I'd forgotten all about him, but DeadMcTavish kept bothering me, and then it finally dawned."

"Bury me now for I am deaded." Vaughan flings his head back on the beanbag. "I thought that was all after you'd left!"

"Where on earth did you get McTavish from anyway, when you were a kid?" I laugh. "It's not your average superhero moniker."

"I had a Scottie dog toy when I was a toddler called McTavish. I lost it, cried for days, but then the name came back to me when I needed it." He half smiles, half cringes at the ceiling. "I am so busted…"

"Your secret's safe with me." I put a hand on his. "Why the 'Dead' bit though?"

He continues to look at the ceiling, but his hand squeezes mine, his thumb slowly stroking my knuckles. "I don't know. Given the Game, it seemed appropriate?"

We lie there, with him stroking my hand.

Eventually, I speak. "Speaking of alter egos, I'd like to know who Skulk is."

Vaughan nods at the ceiling.

"Crypt's very own troll. Every forum has to have one." He looks at me. "It's probably reasonable to assume that Skulk is somebody's evil twin, the extra username. Maybe they are the Killer."

"Or maybe they're Killer number two, the rogue," I say. "Skulk is certainly nasty enough."

"Perhaps," Vaughan says. "Although, the losers who get nasty online generally haven't got the guts to do it in real life. They're too cowardly."

I pull my hand away from his, because it suddenly feels all wrong to be talking about trolls and Killers while holding hands. I turn around a little to face him. "But this is cowardly. Whoever hurt Emily is pretending it's all part of the Game, aren't they?" When he doesn't agree, I turn away again. "I guess we'll know more after the Summoning."

He grunts, and we lie there in silence a while. I wish he'd hold my hand again. There's nothing stopping me from taking his hand. Except that, perhaps, I'm too...cowardly.

"Daniel is OK," I say finally.

"Oh?" Vaughan tries to sound casual. "You've spoken to him?"

"Yeah. He said that he's over the video. And he's fine with me and him just being friends." I frown a little. "At least, I think that's right."

"Good," Vaughan says. "I'm pleased for him. And you." He looks at me. "And I'm pleased for me too." He moves crunchily on the beanbag, toward me, eyes full of longing. He leans in.

I hold my breath. Is he going in for the kill? I know it, bloody hell, he's going to. He opens his mouth slightly, takes a breath. "And Alex?"

I sit up, startled. "What about Alex?"

"You and him." His face is unreadable, eyes searching mine. "That a thing?"

"No!" I splutter. "I… We… Just once. Look, how do you know this stuff anyway?" I'm bolt upright now. Vaughan sits back, ruffles his hair.

"Instinct."

"Rubbish!" I say, slapping the beanbag with both hands. "All your sneaky insider info! The way you know all the gossip and just about every inch of Skola. How? Tell me, now!"

Vaughan rolls his eyes back, shuts them, then takes a moment to examine his beloved ceiling. "The Alex thing? Again, I overheard Tesha talking; girl loves to talk. But to be honest, I kind of had a feeling. The way he looks at you, like you're chopped liver."

"Always such a nice expression," I mutter.

"And how come I know my way around Skola?" He pauses again. "I came here, beginning of summer. Walked the causeway, broke into school."

"You lunatic." I look at him sharply, but he's still staring at the ceiling. "Why?"

"Recce." He licks his lips. "Prep work for the Game. Tinkering with Crypt on the servers here. I camped out for a couple days in the dorms, explored the island. Apart from some gardener, there was no one about." He gives me a shy flash of the green eyes. "Turns out I slept on your bed."

"Oh my God!" I shriek at him. "You creep!" I grab one of the scatter cushions behind me and try to whack him with it.

"What?" He laughs, dodging the blows. "I didn't know it was yours then, did I? Besides, if I had, I wouldn't have chosen your bed. I would have chosen Whitney's—"

"Loser!" I hit him over the head with the cushion, and he wrangles it away from me, holding my hands so that I can't get it again, and my cries of indignation turn to hopeless giggles. I lose my balance and half fall on him, and the beanbag sags and our heads almost knock together, making us laugh all the harder until there is no laugh left.

And then I kiss him.

We both hold our breath. The kiss is gentle at first, and then I pull him closer, the beanbag sags once more and this time he almost topples onto me. We part slightly, stupid with giggles again, but then he kisses me back, and this time it's more confident, passionate. My arms slink around his back, and I hug him to me, not quite daring to believe this is happening, scared it will stop, but a little frightened about what will happen if it doesn't.

There's a banging on the door.

We both freeze.

The banging again. I suppress a snort.

"Oh God, perfect timing!" Vaughan struggles to sit up on the beanbag. "Yeah?" he shouts.

Whoever it is doesn't reply. Vaughan groans and staggers to his feet. I sit up a little on the cushions and wonder if it's completely obvious what we've just been doing. Vaughan gives me a quick look, checking that I'm ready to face the outside world, then flings the door open.

Nobody there.

"Hello?" Vaughan steps out into the corridor, looking in both directions. I get to my feet and look at my watch.

"Someone helpfully telling us it's time for high tea?" I say.

Vaughan comes back into the room.

"How nice of them." He smiles guiltily and raises an eyebrow. "After all, we don't want to be late…"

As he's speaking, something rolls into the room, coming to a stop between Vaughan's feet. A can with a white furl of smoke coming out of a hole in one end.

"What the—" Vaughan leaps toward me and pushes me into the farthest corner of the room, which, given the study's tiny dimensions, isn't too far. He stands in front of me protectively. The can continues to smoke, the smell of sulfur filling the room quickly.

"Vaughan," I whisper to him. "What the hell is that?"

He gulps. "I know what I really hope it isn't."

"Which is…?"

"White phosphorus." He shakes his head. "Mixed with carbon disulphide, hence the smell. Highly incendiary. Highly unstable. Check your *Anarchist's Cookbook*."

"Damn," I murmur. "Must have left my copy in the dorm."

I look to the window. "Can we climb out? I mean, is the thing going to explode?"

"Maybe not. Look." Vaughan nods toward the can; the smoke has stopped.

"Now what?" I say.

"We have to be very, very careful." He takes a baby step toward the can. "Just because it's not smoking, it doesn't mean it's completely safe."

"Hey, hurry up!" Alex appears in the doorway. "You two see my post?" He walks in, not seeing the can, not noticing we're petrified. "Don't want to be late for high tea. Get a move on." As he turns and walks away, his foot catches the edge of the can, skittering it across the carpet toward Vaughan and me. We gasp, transfixed as it rolls. It stops just short of us, bumping into the beanbag.

"What are you waiting for?" Alex pops his head back around the doorway. "Now!" He screws his face up. "Vaughan! This room stinks. Cut down on the eggs, bro!"

With that, he's gone. But I don't really watch him go because I'm too busy staring at the side of the can, the side I didn't see when it first rolled into the room. There's a plain white label on the aluminum, and it has red letters on it:

YOU'RE NEXT

Vaughan has read it too, but he leaps over the can to rush out to the corridor. He looks left and right, and I can tell by his reaction that there's no one else out there. I give the can the widest berth and join him. At the far end of the corridor, Alex is striding toward the exit, but apart from him, there's no one there.

Vaughan starts down the row of study rooms, opening doors. I run after him. He flings doors open, finding no one home. The last room in the wing, the door is locked. He rattles the handle. "Whose study is this?"

"Er." I rack my brains. "Non-Guild. Peter Glames. He's in my design class."

Vaughan thumps the door with his fist and shakes his head.

"You can't picture him?" I lower my voice. "Thin, geeky kid? With jam-jar glasses?"

"Yeah, that really narrows it down in this place." Vaughan is threatening to kick the lock in.

"Oh! And Martin," I remember. "Peter shares with Martin."

Vaughan lowers his foot. "Martin," he whispers. "He absolutely could be the Killer. He does chemistry and physics. This would be a breeze for him." He puts his ear up to the door and listens.

"Well?" I whisper.

"Ssh!"

I put my head to the door too. I hear nothing, only a low hum somewhere, the wood of the door carrying the sound to my ear. But it could be anywhere, not even necessarily in the room.

A door slams violently at the end of the corridor. Vaughan and I run flat-out toward it. It's still daylight outside, but the sun has slipped behind clouds, and on running out into the cool air I feel exposed, leaving the warm, safe light and bursting into the scary unknown.

"So who was that?" I pant, looking around. "Someone's messing with us. Are they crazy? Alex was right there. He must have missed them by seconds."

Vaughan nods. "I need to go back—pick up the can. It's evidence."

Before I can protest, he's gone. I stand, listening to the starlings chatter in the trees above. Even from here I can smell the food in the dining hall, beckoning us. But I have no appetite. In less than a minute, Vaughan is back.

"It's gone." He looks furious. "The can. That door slam must have been a distraction. Someone doubled back and took the thing right out of my room."

"But how?" I say.

"Through a window? Or the fire door at the other end of the corridor?" Vaughan drops his hands onto his knees and sighs. "I'm such an amateur. I don't know why I bother."

"You read what it said on the can."

"I did." Vaughan moans at the ground. "Guess I'm next."

"Vaughan." I'm stunned at his self-centeredness. "I was there too."

"The can was chucked into my room, Cate." He looks up at me. "Plus, you have immunity." He nods at my bracelet.

"Only until tomorrow!"

"I'm the target." His face is cloudy.

I roll my eyes. "Are we really fighting over who is going to be the victim? Besides, where do you rank, 'in order of fit'?" I pull at his arm. "Come on. We'll go to high tea. Then to the Summoning. There's a lot to think about here."

He straightens up. "Yeah, like if we should tell everyone about what just happened, for a start. It might be better to keep it to ourselves until we get a handle on it."

Well, yes. We jog to the dining room together. I still haven't told him about my messages. That's proof enough to me that I'm next on the list.

We're probably last to get to the dining hall. The lines for hot food are short, and most of the tables are full up.

"Ezra's here," I whisper to Vaughan.

It only happens once in a blue moon. Normally the teachers who are not on duty eat in their own quarters, but today there's a table filled with all the senior department heads. Ezra, Mrs. James the deputy, and a bunch of others. At one end of the table, Mr. Flynn catches my eye.

"Come on," Vaughan says.

We both skip the spaghetti and veggie lasagna and grab the end of a table that is partially filled with non-Guild kids a year below us. Anything to be sitting down and blending in. A few tables away, most of the Guild fills up three tables with no room to spare. The mood is somber. I think Alex must have decreed that no one gossip about Emily; he knows that the Game and the Guild are walking on the thinnest of ice.

The rest of the school is talking about it, however. It's

obvious—the looks that the Guild are getting, the hushed laughter and pseudo-concerned looks.

"Let's get something to eat and get out," I say.

"Toast," Vaughan says.

We go to one of the toasters by the wall, where there are still a few slices of brown bread left over. I feed a couple of them into the machine. It's the type that takes the bread for a little ride on a rack, achingly slowly, toasting on both sides and then dropping it out of the bottom. It always takes just too long to linger and wait for it to be done, but if you step away to grab some coffee or butter and jam, by the time you've come back, your toast has fallen off and been stolen by someone else. But today, we loiter, no place to go.

Already, people are finishing their meals. Guild members, anxious to slip away. The rest of the school wants to get away from the huddle of teachers. My first piece of toast is spat out by the machine. I unpeel a little silver pat of butter and leave it to melt. I'm reaching for a knife when there's a scraping of chairs and Alex, Carl, and Rick head out.

"Count to sixty, then Marcia, Cynthia, and Becky will be next," says Vaughan. "They're so predictable," he mutters.

We never get to find out. As the three boys get to the dining room's double doors, the doors open inward, there's a little scuffle, and the boys back off, giving the people entering right of way.

Everyone takes in the uniforms, and the room falls silent.

The real detectives have arrived.

CHAPTER 19

"There are dark forces at work here. But I am Grand Master, and everything is under control."

Alex barely waited for everyone to sit down in the cave. He's standing by the tables, arms spread, handsome face frowning with intensity, addressing his flock. It would be funny if the mood were different.

"Trust in me." He nods somberly. "I will protect us all. Whoever is doing this will feel the full force of the Guild upon them, I swear. I will find them, and I will stop them. You can be sure of that."

"Can we?" Marcia is standing too. "Sorry, Alex—I don't mean to doubt you—but this is crazy. The police are here. Whether we like it or not, we need to think about shutting the Game down."

"No!" Alex stamps petulantly, his messiah act slipping. "Guess what? I have spoken with the Killer, and they have assured me that the whole Emily business was nothing to do with them."

"And you believe them?" Marcia says.

Alex nods vigorously. "I do. I've good reason to trust them, absolutely."

Everyone lets that sink in. Alex trusts the Killer; so is it one of his close circle?

Finally, Cynthia speaks. "The way I see it, we have to have a hiatus," she says. "Let Emily come back to school. Let things cool down before we start playing again."

"Yes," says Roger. "That's probably the best way."

"That's stupid. Not feasible and supremely unintelligent." Alex is standing firm.

"Yeah, makes us look guilty," Rick chips in. "Emily was stuck by some Guild wannabe, someone who wants in on the Game. Or"—he gets more animated—"maybe it's revenge—someone we didn't pick for the Guild, and they want to shut us down. Don't give them the satisfaction!"

"More likely this is from within the ranks." Vaughan is sitting on a box beside me. "We have to face the fact we have a broken arrow."

"Someone here, right now, has, like, gone rogue?" Tesha says. "Why?"

Vaughan shrugs. "Maybe they're disappointed they didn't get to be Killer. Or maybe…they're just a psycho?"

Tesha does not like this at all. Her face reddens, and there's a glint of tears in her eyes. "Who made robo spider?" she shouts. "Come on! Fess up!"

There's a gulpy silence. We all look at one another. Anvi giggles, but no one joins in.

"OK, well I'm just going to come right out and say it," Tesha says, taking a breath. "Who is Skulk? Because he or she is clearly claiming to be some kind of big bad wolf, and if they are not the Killer in the Game, then presumably they are suspect number one when it comes to the attack on Emily."

More silence. Alex looks around. "Anyone want to come forward and claim to be Skulk? I mean, you'll ruin the Game, but you'll satisfy her curiosity." Nobody says anything, and Alex looks at Tesha. "You always did take things too literally, love. People say a lot of things online. Wise up and don't believe all of them."

"Nobody here would do that to Emily!" Whitney says. "She has no enemies. This isn't personal, and I agree, it's nothing to do with the Game. It's just some lower school loser who wants attention."

"Whatever, we should take a break at the very least, I think," Marcia says. "Just for a couple weeks, until things calm down!"

"Absolutely not!" Alex says.

"This is not just Ezra having a word in our ear," Carl says to Alex quietly. "It's the police, man."

"So?" Alex says. "Everyone here is under oath not to talk about anything!"

Carl rolls his eyes. "Alex, yeah. But nobody wants anything bad on their school record. Things will come out—the Game, initiations"—he glances at Vaughan—"the other Kills. Probably Crypt too. There'll be some mud flinging. And this kind of mud sticks."

There's a noise from the outer cave, and Martin appears in the archway. I hadn't even noticed he wasn't here before. He's holding a flashlight and panting.

"Good news is Emily's OK." He looks at Alex. "Bad news is her parents want a proper investigation." He collapses on the nearest cushion. "I ran all the way..."

"How do you know this?" Marcia asks him.

"Alex asked me to snoop." He nods at our Grand Master. "The cops were in Ezra's office, talking with him and Mrs. James. I listened in." He smiles a little. "They had to speak up, because Ezra's going deaf. I heard most of it."

"And?" Carl says.

"Rumors were right. Emily had an allergic reaction to some nut oil on the spider. Her parents flew in from Barbados. She's OK. She's left the hospital and is somewhere on the mainland with her folks." He takes a breath. "But, bad news is, the family wants to press charges."

Carl swears.

"However," Martin says. "The police were actually quite cool about it. Said they thought it was a practical joke gone wrong, no real malicious intent. They said that if the school takes the right actions, they think they can persuade Emily's parents to back off."

"Right actions," Carl says. "Find the joker, and kick them out. Great."

"So what, Carl?" Rick barks at him. "If it wasn't you, then what do you care?"

"Was the Game mentioned?" Marcia says.

Martin sighs. "Ezra didn't say anything, and I thought we were going to be OK, because the police said they didn't have much time tonight before the tide comes in. But then Mrs. James brought it up at the end. She said she had no doubt the Game was connected."

Rick swears loudly and kicks out at something. Luckily for him it's sand, not rock. Roger and Martin get sprayed, but they're smart and don't protest too much.

Alex's face is thunder. "What happens next?"

"The police said they'd be back early tomorrow when the causeway's passable again," Martin says. "To talk to everyone. All day, if necessary."

"What do we do?" Tesha says. "Everyone knows the Game is on. We can't lie to the police."

"Just answer truthfully," Cynthia says. "Yes, the Game is being played, but this wasn't part of it. Tell them that it's against the rules to actually hurt someone. None of us know who did this."

"Do not mention Crypt, people," Alex says. "There's no need."

"Well, I'm grateful for that," Vaughan says. "But, Alex, I think there's one thing we all want to know. Will you be telling the police the identity of the Killer?"

Alex doesn't hesitate. "The police don't know that I know, and there's no reason to enlighten them. I'm sure each one of us will be asked if we're the Killer, or if we know who he or she is, and it's up to you to make the decision as to how you answer."

Everyone thinks about this.

"Ezra is going to tell us to stop the Game," I say. "It's stupid to think he won't. If we continue to play, we'll have to act like we have stopped. Kills will have to be private, at least for a while."

"That has its perks." Vaughan smiles at me. "Some things are more thrilling when they're secret."

There are a couple giggles at this.

"All right." Alex grabs the velvet bag. "Like everything, we put it to the vote. We go to the altar, one by one, write one word on a slip of paper indicating what we want to do. Three choices: red, yellow, green." He looks over us. "If it's not completely obvious what those words mean, here it is: red for the Game to stop immediately and completely, yellow if you want to put a hold on things for now, or green to continue covertly. Agreed?" He looks over to Marcia, Cynthia, and Carl. They nod. Nobody argues. A vote is fair.

One by one, we go behind the velvet curtain in the order we were harvested. By the time I'm kneeling there with the Pen of Doom in my hand, I've gone back and forth in my mind so many times my head is spinning.

Eventually, I write:

Green

After all, you only live once.

After me, it's Vaughan's turn. I bet my life he'll vote green too. When he comes out, Alex is waiting to go in and read the votes, but Marcia stops him.

"We all need to see the votes this time, Alex."

He glares at her. "That's my decision. I'm Grand Master. What, don't you trust me?"

"I do. Completely," Marcia says. "But I don't want to give anyone here any doubt. Transparency."

"Fine," Alex says. He gets the bag and brings it back to the table, reaching a hand inside for the first slip of paper. He brings it out and reads it.

"Yellow." He exaggeratedly holds it up for us. He gives Marcia the paper then delves for a second. "Red," he says between gritted teeth and quickly goes for a third. "Green."

"Don't you love the democratic process?" Vaughan quips, relieving the tension a little.

Alex continues to read the slips. Fourteen of us are here to vote, and soon it begins to look like this Game is not ending. After thirteen slips have been opened, only four are red. Alex is looking happier, but he's not out of the woods yet. Five players are in favor of pausing the Game, and there are only four votes in favor of continuing.

He takes the final slip out of the bag. "Green."

"It's a tie!" Tesha says. "Split vote, hung parliament, whatever."

"As Grand Master, I get the deciding vote, and I say green for go," Alex says grimly.

"We did not decide that, Alex," says Cynthia.

"*We* don't have to!" Alex shouts. "I am Grand Master! This is my Game!"

"What about Emily?" Whitney says. "Shouldn't she have a vote? Should we email her or something?"

"Like she's going to care!" Rick spits.

"This is ridiculous." Marcia stands up. "We don't have time for it. The Game is on, Alex's decision seconded by me, and I actually voted yellow, so I've switched my vote. Done. As far as the rest of the school is concerned, we've stopped playing. Be mindful: Kills must be private. No throwing down skulls in the dining hall, no wristbands nailed to the bulletin board. No evidence of anything."

"If anyone has a problem with that, leave now," Alex says. "You four who wrote down red, if you're unhappy, leave now. And if it turns out one of you is the Killer, the Game is over anyway."

Everyone is silent. No one moves.

"Good," Alex says. "Now for heaven's sake, keep a level head out there. All of you. Let's get back to civilization before anything else happens."

Vaughan gets up first and offers me a hand. He pulls me up and I stand a little too close to him. Everyone is getting ready to ship out, nobody is paying us any attention. He slips a hand under my coat around my waist, and pulls me toward him slightly.

"Oh. One more thing. Vaughan," Alex says. Suddenly all eyes are on us. I step back awkwardly. "Tracking on Crypt is activated. All users can now be located on the map. If these Kills are going to happen privately, we have to give everyone else half a chance to guess who the Killer is. Make it happen, Vaughan."

Vaughan gives a little salute. As we leave, he whispers in my ear. "Now things get interesting. We have two Killers, the one playing within the rules of the Game and the rogue. Will either of them have the balls to strike with the police sniffing around?"

I look at him. "Again with the balls. Even now we have two Killers, you think both are male?"

He raises an eyebrow at me. "I guess all bets are off."

"Aren't they just?" I whisper back. "All we really know is that one of us is next."

When we leave the caves, it is dark, and we click on little flashlights to help with the walk back. Vaughan and I climb the cliff path, leaving a respectable distance between other Guild members. Vaughan is slightly ahead of me. When he gets to the top, he stops suddenly.

"Hey." I push his back gently. The path is too narrow and scratchy with gorse. He has to move or I can't get past him. He stands there with his back to me, stock-still, as if he's spotted something in the distance. "What's up?" I say.

"Hey! Was that...?" he mutters. "I thought I saw..." He looks at me, then back to whatever had caught his eye before, and sets off at a run.

"What?" I call to him.

"Come on!" He sprints back to me, grabs my hand. "Hurry!"

"Vaughan, what the hell?" I run after him, the beam from my flashlight bobbing on the ground. He heads up toward the studios, then makes a left toward the woods. "Where are we going?" I try to catch up, but by now he's too far ahead for me to grab. "Stop!"

"I just saw—you need to be quick!" He doesn't stop but plows on, the thicker grass under the trees not slowing him. I follow as fast as I can, but my legs are leaden, and I begin to lose him, flashing my light up and just catching glimpses as he darts around the next tree. I keep up as long as I can. "Vaughan!" My heart is slamming, my breath short and painful. The woods are thinning out again now, and I stop and drop hands to knees, panting. I should be able to see him. Even if he's quite a way ahead, I should be able to see his flashlight at least.

But I've lost him.

I catch my breath and straighten up. "Vaughan?" I mean to shout, but even spoken, the word sounds too loud in the quiet of the woods. I walk slowly toward what looks like the tree line, every hair on my head standing up, feeling the electricity that only comes from being watched. He's here, somewhere, just watching me. Or someone else is. Maybe the person we were running after.

I clear the woods, look down, and realize where I've come out. I'm at the top of the amphitheater, the semicircle of grass before the stone slabs start, the slabs that make up the rows of seats built into the side of the hill. Below me is the sandy stage, the scene of my initiation.

In the middle of the stage, still switched on, lies Vaughan's flashlight.

I plod slowly, carefully, down the steps toward the stage. "Vaughan?" I say again, almost under my breath, but the acoustics amplify my words. I reach the sand and walk over toward the flashlight, picking it up.

"Vee?" I whisper.

Hands touch my shoulders from behind. I gasp and spin around, dropping the flashlights, and feel his arms wrap around me, his lips kissing mine. I enjoy it for a moment, then push him off me.

"You weirdo!" I hiss at him. "What were we chasing anyway?"

He moves in again. "Only this moment."

"You are so unbelievably corny," I mumble through kisses.

Later that evening, alone in my study, I log on to Crypt and lightly stroke my lower face. Ow. Stubble rash. Vaughan was going to have to shave more often if we were going to be doing this regularly.

The intranet is quiet; I suppose no one wants to risk being caught doing anything against the rules now the stakes have suddenly been raised. Tracking is activated; when I log on, a little red skull appears, hovering over the quad on the map. I move my cursor over it. It reveals my username, Clouseau. Blimey. This does feel risky.

As I sit looking at it, another red skull pops up alongside mine. Another foolhardy soul is somewhere in the quad:

Skulk

If the blue meanies are going to get me they'd better get off their asses and do something. (So said the Zodiac Killer. He's never been caught.)

Then, a private IM pops up:

Skulk

Wipe that smile off your face, Cate. Need me to spell it out, bitch? You're next.

My hand drops away, and my head whips around; the curtains are drawn. Nobody can see me. But two things are sure: Skulk knows my username, and Skulk rolled that can into Vaughan's room.

CHAPTER 20

Saturday, and although my red snake bracelet has disappeared along with my confidence, my signs are still vital.

Ezra graces us with his presence in Morning Exchange. There are two police cars outside Main House, and Mrs. James is no doubt keeping the fuzz happy with weak cups of Umfraville tea while Ezra gives us the pep talk, or prep talk, as it will probably turn out to be.

He gives a thinly veiled reading about integrity, then updates us with what we already know: Emily is doing fine, and the police are here to try and get to the bottom of what happened to her. Class is canceled this morning, and we are to be confined to our studies and the common room to wait to be called in for an interview. He urges each of us to speak openly to the staff in the first instance if we know anything about the matter.

The subtext is: if you know anything, keep it in-house.

We hit the quad and our studies. Technically, it's supposed to be work time, but there are no teachers overseeing us—yet— and everyone's too hyper to open a book. Crypt is still nervously quiet; even Skulk's not posting this morning. Most of my class-mates are hanging out in the common room or in the studies closest to it, doors open, music on. There's a weird excitement in the air, and I find myself enjoying it, even though this is serious, and Emily was hurt. There's safety in numbers. And after all, it's not every day that something actually happens here, and it's not every day that you get interviewed by the police. I have nothing to be guilty about, do I?

I spot Vaughan lugging some kind of boxed hardware down the corridor to his study, spilling those funny little polystyrene peanuts as he goes.

"Hi." I walk up behind him. "Got a moment? I need to talk."

He puts the box down. "Uh-oh. Dumping me already?"

I smile. "Nooo." I lean on the wall, slightly self-conscious. "I didn't know you were mine to, er, dump."

He doesn't say anything, just affects a serious face. It's intended to make me giggle, but I am all business.

"I got a message from Skulk last night." I keep my voice low. "Telling me my time is nigh. And being kind of nasty about it."

The serious face is real this time. "And you believe it?"

I nod. "Truth is"—I lean toward him, lowering my voice— "I've had a couple real world messages before the smoking can in your room. Little notes telling me I'm being watched or I'm running out of time, all of that."

Vaughan looks puzzled and slightly angry. "And you're only telling me this now?"

"Yes." I shut up as a couple kids squeeze past us, stepping over Vaughan's box with some sighs and tutting. When they're gone I lean toward him again. "To be honest, before, I thought they might have been from you. Having a laugh. Or your idea of...affection. In a slightly scary way."

"Really?" Vaughan says. "But you don't think that now."

"No. Not unless your idea of affection is calling me a bitch."

"What?!"

"When in doubt, bake goodies!" Marcia shouts down the corridor. "Who's in?" There are whoops and hollers from the general direction of the common room.

"Listen," Vaughan whispers. "I need to get this box in my room. Then I'm up with the boys in blue over at Main House." He pulls a face at me. "The glories of having a last name at the beginning of the alphabet. I'll catch you later, and we'll talk more. Hang on in there."

I nod and let him go, watching him stagger off down the corridor before turning and following the noise into the common room.

Marcia is standing by the counter and the oven at the back of the room with a big mixing bowl. Most of the Guild is here, lounging, making coffee or toast, messing around. Notably, no one is touching the computers.

"So are you making brownies?" Rick shouts at Marcia. "What are you putting in them, eh?"

Much laughter at this.

"Only yummy stuff." Marcia smiles, mixing furiously with a spatula. "I think cupcakes are the order of the day." She reaches for a glass bowl of chocolate that she has melted over a pan on the cooktop and pours the thick stuff into her mixing bowl. As I watch the gloop, I have a flashback to my initiation. Marcia obviously doesn't. "Mmm," she says, dipping a finger in and licking it. "They're gonna be so good!"

"Didn't know they had cupcakes in Spain," Rick says, trying to lean over and dip a finger in too.

"Hands off!" Marcia smacks him on the behind with the spatula, and cake mix splatters.

"Oi!" Rick shouts, turning around to look at his bum. "Now what does that look like I've done?"

Everyone is howling. If I ever found Rick funny, I certainly don't now. Even if Vaughan forgives him for pushing him off the cliff, I'm not sure I can. I linger in the doorway, not wanting to join in and yet really not wanting to go and sit in my room by myself.

"How are you holding up?"

Daniel has joined me in the doorway. For the first time in recent history, I'm actually glad to see him.

"Yeah, great," I lie.

He gives me a look. "I'm exhausted. Just came out of my interview."

"You did?"

He nods. "Come to my study?"

"Yeah, of course!" I glance at Marcia, who is pouring mixture into little paper cupcake holders while trying to dodge Rick. He's got chocolatey hands and is creeping up behind her and trying to grab her white T-shirt. I have a feeling this is going to degenerate into an all-out chocolate battle—and soon. I'm pleased to escape.

Daniel's study is as far away from the common room as it is possible to be, and that's the way he likes it. We walk there in silence, his violin case our companion, as ever. He unlocks the door, and we walk in. The room is immaculately tidy; he shares with a kid in our year called Geoff—another musician, who's currently on tour with some youth orchestra and won't be back in school for another couple weeks.

"Nice having the place to yourself?" I sit down on the edge of his sofa.

He sets the violin down carefully on his desk. "Wonderful." He sits on the chair facing me. "Geoff's not bad, but he's always tapping out beats on his desk while we're trying to work. Drives me crazy."

I laugh. "Sounds like someone I know!"

Daniel frowns. "What, me? I don't do that."

"Daniel, you do," I say. "You *musos*, you're all the same."

"Cate, I don't think I have ever done that." He's serious and annoyed. "And don't class me with Geoff, please. We are not on the same level, at all."

"OK." I hold up a hand. "I only meant it as a joke."

Daniel stares at me. There's an awkward silence as I sit there and try and think of a way to change the subject. Nothing smooth comes to mind.

"So, how was the police interview?" I smile. "You're not in handcuffs, so that's good."

Luckily, this time he cracks a small smile.

"Yes, well. I hardly think they were interested in me." He rubs his hands together, as if trying to warm them. "I'm barely friends with Emily, and it's not like I'm up on making a robotic spider or whatever that thing was." He shakes his head. "They're not Scotland Yard either. I don't rate their chances of catching the culprit, particularly." He crosses his legs and puts his hands on his lap rather self-consciously. "But I really wanted to ask you how you are."

"Oh." I pull a face. "Why? I mean, I'm fine. A bit shaken up with all of this, of course, but totally fine."

"Good," Daniel looks at me. He uncrosses his legs, stands up suddenly, and moves to the window. "And are you in love with Vaughan?"

"What?" I look up at him sharply, totally blindsided. "Where did that come from?" I struggle to find words. "No!"

He laughs, strangely, shaking his head. "So it's just lust with Vaughan, is that what you'd say? And what about Alex? Because last term, around the same time that we, you know—well, I heard that he was flavor of the month with you."

"Bloody hell, Daniel!" I stand up. "Stop it. You're making a fool of yourself—and making me sound like some desperate flirt in the process!"

"Well, are you?"

"What?" I try to swallow my anger. "Even if I was, what of it? Guys like Alex, Rick, and Carl kiss their way through the school, and everyone thinks they're the big dogs, but if a girl does it? Different story." I shake my head. "Seriously, is this still the world we live in? Who I…kiss…that's my decision. Not even a friend—which is what you're supposed to be—gets to tell me what to do."

"Not even Mr. Flynn?" Daniel says, watching me. "Doesn't he get to tell you what to do? Whispering in your ear, sweetly?"

"Are you totally mad?" I feel like I'm about to choke. Daniel leans in, a hand snakes around my back, his breath hot in my ear.

"Teacher's little pet."

"Get off me!" I push him hard, heels of my hand jabbing into his collarbone. He laughs, as if in shock, and shoves me back with a surprising ferocity. As I topple onto the sofa, he falls on top of me, forcing a kiss, his lips smooshing up against my lips, teeth knocking teeth. I make a smothered noise—telling him no—but I just sound like an indignant elephant. Wriggling, I try to twist my head away, not feeling frightened exactly, more embarrassed for both of us. Finally I manage to free a leg and my foot kicks the edge of his desk, jolting his precious violin onto the floor. He looks up, for a second, and that's all I need.

I bring my right arm back, make a fist, and with as much force as I can muster, punch him on the nose.

He cries out, rolls off me and onto the floor by his violin.

I stagger to my feet, adrenaline pumping, waiting for him to come at me again.

But he doesn't. He curls into a ball, weeping. His nose is dripping blood through his long fingers, and he is wailing, and suddenly I know who it was in the caves that day. Not Vaughan, but Daniel. That's the cry I recognized. I don't know how I could have mixed them up before now. I suppose I must have been blinded by the guilt I felt for both of them.

He wails on, his power gone as quickly as it arrived; he's just a small, pathetic thing on the ground, howling and dripping blood. I give him a moment, and no more.

"Get up," I say to him quietly.

He looks up at me, almost shocked that I'm still there.

"Go and clean yourself up."

He nods, pulls himself up on the desk, then tries to bend over and retrieve his blessed violin case, which only produces a further stream of blood.

"Leave it. I'll pick it up."

He eyes me through his hands and staggers to the door.

As he shuts the door behind him, I start to shake—with relief and also with the urge to go another nine rounds with a punching bag. I breathe, the adrenaline trying to leave my body. It's OK, it'll be OK. I pull at my clothes and scrub at my mouth the same way I did after I was face down in cowpat. What just happened? How far would he have gone? The little voice in the back of my head is asking me lots of questions I don't want to answer... Why aren't you running the hell out of the study?

But I don't run.

I bend down to pick up the violin case. It has blood on it, running all over the stickers, and the catches have popped open. I try to shut the case, but the violin is wonky inside. I open the case to try and nestle it into its velvet so I can close the stupid thing.

I'm about to shut it all back up again, but then I see a little corner of black pushing its way out of the place where the purple velvet inner meets the hard edge of the case. I pull it out slowly.

It's a folded card, black on the outside, with red inside just visible. I unfold it slowly.

Killer

The word, written in black.

I read it again, because I might not be seeing straight. Daniel is the Killer? Daniel is the Killer. I'm flooded with the weirdest mixture of disbelief, disappointment, and relief.

I find my legs. I put the card back in the case, and I leave. As I shut the door, I hear a noise in the corridor.

The boys' toilet door opens. He's standing there, handkerchief up to nose. I turn and head the opposite way.

In the common room, they are clearing up after the messy fight I'd predicted. Alex is washing his hands over in the corner. My heart is still pumping fast. I go up to him.

"Are we having another Summoning this afternoon, as usual?"

He nods. "Soon as the interviews are over. I'll post something on Crypt. Lots to talk about."

"And we'll vote on the Killer?"

"Of course."

"Good." I turn on my heel and head to my study. No Marcia, as usual. I shut the curtains, log on to Crypt, but no one is online. I lock my door, lie down on the sofa, and shut my eyes, a plan forming.

If I make it alive to the Summoning, I'll have my revenge.

CHAPTER 21

I'm woken up with a knock.

I peel myself off the small sofa. How long have I been asleep? I stand carefully and pull my clothing into shape. I feel bedraggled and creased and kind of like I want to take a shower. Not all of that is due to Daniel, but some of it.

The knock comes again. I really hope it isn't him.

"Cate! Are you in there?"

Not Daniel. The voice is female and familiar, but in my haze I can't immediately peg it. I open the door, and Ms. Lasillo is standing there, looking impatient.

"There you are," she says, as if she's wasted all morning looking for me in far more sensible places. "It's your turn."

I frown, and then I see Rick lurking behind her, and I catch on. We both have last names at the end of the alphabet; it must be time for us to go and talk to the police.

"Come on!" Ms. Lasillo trots her little legs quickly down the corridor. "Everyone else is at lunch. The dining staff has been instructed to keep you each a plate warm for after your interview. It shouldn't take long."

"Ms. Lasillo?" Rick says. "I need to pee."

She sighs. "Quickly, Rick. I'll wait for both of you outside. Now, hurry!"

Rick goes off on his special excursion, and I follow slowly as Ms. Lasillo strides down the corridor, then pauses, looking into a study room. By the look of her face she likes what she sees there even less than us. "Marcia? Alex! You were told to proceed to the dining hall. Please go there immediately." She resumes walking at a clip.

I reach the doorway of the study, and as I do, I see Marcia and Alex both looking like they were disturbed deep in conversation. No doubt comparing notes on how the interviews have been going. I flash a smile at them. Only Marcia meets my eye. Alex looks like he's closing down his laptop.

"Quickly, everyone!" Ms. Lasillo is calling for us as she exits into the quad. Alex walks past me and out with her, giving her a winning smile. Marcia hangs back a moment.

"You OK? You look weird."

I nod. I need to tell her about the Daniel thing but not now. "Just woke up."

She pats me on the shoulder. "Left you a cupcake in the common room." She goes to follow Alex. "They turned out well. I had to fight to keep you one." She winks at me. "Most of one anyway. You know what they say: never go to a police interview on an empty stomach."

"Yeah." I rub my eyes. "Never heard that one before."

"Cupcake? Where's mine?" Rick appears again, pulling up his fly, but it's too late. Marcia is not turning back. He looks at me. "Race you for it!"

I let him run and fetch it, like I know he will, and as I reach the door to the outside, he's there by me, holding out a little chocolate cake that resembles a lopsided turd in a paper case.

"Don't you want it?" He waves it at me at arm's length. "It's got your name on it."

I squint. On the top of the turd there's a squiggle of icing, white letters barely spelling out "Cate."

Rick sniffs the cake. "Mmm!"

I make a grab for it, but he whips it away, laughing. As he does, I catch a glimpse of more letters on the crinkled side of the paper case, but I can't read them.

"What does it say on the side?" I ask him.

"Eh?" Rick says, then turns the cupcake over. "Ooh, 'Eat Me!'"

My arms feel suddenly drained of blood. "Let me see."

"Not. On. Your. Nelly." He slowly unwraps the cake from its papery dress.

"Seriously, Rick." I hold out my hand for the cake. "Give it to me."

"Nope!" He scrunches the paper case and chucks it at me. I smooth it out in my hand, my heart beating. There are the letters, in red, in that writing. Rick opens his giant maw, eyes glinting at me, the cake looking even smaller in his huge fingers.

He licks the side of it with a huge bovine tongue then begins to cram it into his mouth, all the while looking at me.

"Rick, what do you think you're doing?" I try to keep my voice even. "We are playing the Game, and something says 'Eat Me,' and you shove it in your mouth? Are you a complete amateur?"

He stops. Spits the cake out whole into his hand. Swears. Then he thinks about it a second. "Wait. This cake was meant for you, and Marcia made it. I even watched her ice it. If she is meaning to off you, she just did it in front of a whole common room full of witnesses. Plus"—he looks at me, victorious— "Marcia took a nibble. A bit fell off the top when she was icing it, and she gobbled it right up."

I shake my head. "No, look, it's been sitting there in the kitchen since then, and—"

"Come along, people!" Ms. Lasillo flings open the door, stormy faced.

"Yeah, come on, Cate!" Rick tuts, then flings the mashed cupcake into his mouth again, crumbs flying, jaw chomping.

I follow, out into the open, the paper cupcake wrapper still in my hands, struggling to keep up with him and Ms. Lasillo as they head to Main House. Rick's not allergic to anything, is he? But then...Marcia meant that cake for me. But Marcia's not the person who rigged that spider for Emily, is she? Marcia's not Skulk? My head hurts with the effort. Maybe Skulk got to the whole batch of cakes, maybe everyone's going to get a particularly nasty case of the runs.

Serves Rick right anyway. I shove the cupcake wrapper into my pocket.

We reach Main House and walk through the big oak door and into the foyer that leads to Ezra's office. Ms. Lasillo points to some chairs outside the room.

"Sit there. You'll be called in one at a time." She knocks on the door, opens it a crack, and leans inside. "The final two. Ready for you," she says to whoever is in there.

Rick sits, grinning at me, chocolate still around his lips like he's a toddler.

I sit carefully, watching Ms. Lasillo happily scuttle off, now that she's done her duty and deposited us.

Rick doesn't seem to be ailing at all. He manages a highly tuneful burp, then slumps back in his seat and scratches his groin, contemplatively. "You'll be first," he says to me unnecessarily. "Wish I had another cake to keep me going, yum-mee."

Actually, if Rick is Skulk, and the whole batch is yucky, wouldn't this be a great way to divert suspicion?

The door swings open. A gingery young man in a police uniform leans out. "Catherine?"

I stand up. "Cate."

"Cate." His Welsh accent makes my name sound much nicer. He gives me a slightly tired smile and disappears inside.

I take a last backward glance at Rick—who has slid so far down the chair his huge legs sticking out make him look like some kind of modern art chair-boy hybrid—and then follow the policeman inside.

I've only been in Ezra's office twice before: once during my interview for the school, and once when Marcia, Daniel, and I did the graffiti talk and got crazy with the spray cans. It's cozier than I remember, filled with bookshelves and a series of overlapping Turkish rugs. There's a high painted ceiling depicting some kind of holy war between fat, cherubic babies and six-winged seraphim. The ceiling was created by art students a couple decades back. Wish I'd gotten in on that gig, must have been fun to decorate Ez's ceiling with copious little willies. Although if it had been up to me, I would have opted for a flying spaghetti monster.

The room is dominated by a huge window, which has a spectacular view over the rolling lawn, down toward the cliffs and sea in the background. Two policemen are blocking the view today, however. They are both perched uncomfortably on wobbly wooden chairs. The younger one who came to the door is balancing a notebook. An older, very tall policeman looks me up and down as he clutches a tiny cup of tea on his knee. Mrs. James is beside them, and she gives me a brief smile.

"Hello, Cate. Come in."

Ezra sits to the left of the window, barely visible behind a large desk. He flaps a welcome with one papery hand.

"Ah, it's Catherine. Sit down."

He has glasses balanced on his thin nose, and static is making some of the long, fine gray hairs stand up on his head, floating in the air as if we were all sitting at the bottom of the sea. I fight the giggles.

"Here." A voice comes from behind me, and I turn around, mouth open.

It's Mr. Flynn, proffering a chair. Suddenly I lose all desire to laugh. Oh no. This makes me nervous. Lie in front of Ezra, Mrs. James, and two random cops? No problem. But Mr. Flynn is a different matter. Why is he here? It's not like he's particularly senior. Maybe it's because he dealt with Emily when it all went down? I really hope he's not going to throw me under the bus with the whole beach thing with Vaughan. But that has nothing to do with this, and if it were the case, then Vaughan would have given me the heads up. Surely.

Mr. Flynn shoots me a look I can't read as he places the chair down and retreats into the shadows to one side of me. I sit on the chair, not sure who I should be facing. I shift my gaze between them all, probably looking like the epitome of dodgy.

"We will keep this as quick and as painless as possible." The older policeman flashes a chunky watch. "There's no messing with these tides, and we're all a little peckish."

I nod, trying not to look too pleased.

"So, Cate, you were in the ballroom when the incident of Emily's assault occurred, were you not?"

I nod. Wow. Just like Clue.

He nods back and smiles. "And would you say you were a friend of Emily's?"

I nod again. The young policeman's pen is hovering over his pad expectantly. Oh—I'm expected to actually answer.

"Yes," I croak, then clear my throat. "I mean, a bit. We weren't—aren't—close or anything."

"But you would say she's in your circle?" he presses.

"Yes, I suppose."

"The Assassins' Guild, you call it?" he says. "And your friends have already told us that this term you were playing a Game." He leans forward slightly. "A Game called Killer."

I swallow. OK, are we going there already?

"Yeah." I glance at Ezra and try to think of something else to say. Ezra appears to be dozing; this morning must have been a long one for him. Outside the door, I can hear Rick coughing. I look at the door. He's coughing quite a lot; what did he do, light one up? I wouldn't put it past him, the idiot. The coughing stops; there's a thump.

"Cate?" The policeman looks at me questioningly.

"Inspector Yates asked you a question." Mrs. James looks pointedly at me. "Was this incident connected with the Game?"

"Um…" I can't help but look back to the door. "No. Definitely not. It's against the rules to actually hurt anyone."

"Can you think of anyone who would do this to Emily?" Inspector Yates says. "Had she had any arguments with anyone lately? Trouble over a boy?"

There's a sort of tapping out there now. What the hell is Rick doing? I look back at the teachers and the cops—aren't they hearing this?—and then the tapping becomes much louder, more of a thump, thump, thump, and I hear a low moan. I stand up.

"Cate?" Mrs. James frowns at me. "Sit down."

I glance at her and point at the door. There's a scratching, and that moan again. Suddenly, as ridiculous as this is, I'm frightened. Is that Rick out there? Or is it the thing that's eaten him?

Thump.

"Is that a knock?" Ezra squawks, suddenly awake.

I move over to the door, mesmerized.

Thump, thump, thump.

"Mr. Flynn?" Inspector Yates says. "Can you check that for us?"

Mr. Flynn is already at my side, and he moves past me and puts his hand on the doorknob, face grim. "Just give me a minute."

He opens the door, and Rick falls into the room and lies there, facedown on one of the Turkish rugs.

My first thought is, Rick you utter, utter prat. So what if you're bored out there? This is a stupid thing to pull with policemen in the room.

But then Rick rolls. Over onto his back he goes, trembling from head to toe. His eyes wide, face aghast. Mrs. James gasps, the policemen move forward as one, and Mr. Flynn puts a hand out to stop me getting any closer.

"What's going on?"

The thumping is now coming from Ezra, who is penned in behind his desk, trying to move his wheelchair out to get a better look.

Mrs. James has regained her composure. "Rick, get up off the floor, you fool!"

There's a slightly embarrassed second, when everyone else around Rick wonders how to break it to Mrs. James that this isn't a joke. But then Rick does it for us, the trembles turning to convulsions, his whole body jerking on the floor like he's wired to the mains.

The two policemen kneel to hold him.

"Eyes dilated, sir," the younger one says.

"Son!" Inspector Yates says. "What did you take? Answer me."

Rick can't answer, except to convulse some more, as if he's trying to kick off his shoes.

"I'll call the ambulance!" Mrs. James utters. But before she can move, Rick sits up, opens his mouth, and projectile vomits all over her lower half. She squeals as chocolatey bile drips off her tweed skirt and onto her patent court shoes.

Rick slumps down, gasps, and stops moving.

The edges of the room close in on me, and as I back away, I almost tumble over Ezra in his wheelchair. Mr. Flynn and the policemen are pumping Rick's chest and breathing into his sick-coated lips, but it looks like Rick has left the building. I see it in his eyes, his floppy hand, his already-gray skin. The men continue, regardless, pumping him. I want to tell them to stop. It's obscene.

"I think we've...lost him, sir," the young policeman says finally, with a catch in his voice.

"He's still breathing," mutters Mr. Flynn, but I think he's kidding himself.

"Give him a drink of water to bring him around!" Ezra says helpfully. "I've got one, somewhere."

"I've called the ambulance." Mrs. James is standing at Ezra's desk, dabbing at her dripping skirt; there are chunks of something on her legs and a blob of chocolate on one toe.

Inspector Yates looks up at me, sweat on his brow. "Does this lad do drugs? Tell us, Cate."

I shake my head slowly.

He turns back to Rick, and they make a few more halfhearted efforts to rouse him, but Rick's not interested. Right about now it looks to me like he's knocking on the Pearly Gates and annoying Saint Peter with a dirty joke.

Back here on earth, things are definitely not funny. Inspector Yates stands up, looks at his watch, and moves to Ezra's desk, picking up the phone. The younger policeman is trying not to sob.

Mr. Flynn sits back on his heels, finally, and leaves Rick alone. He looks up at me desperately.

"What did he take, Cate? What?"

"I don't know."

But I do know what he took. He took my cupcake.

My body flushes cold.

Marcia.

Before they can stop me, I sprint out of the office.

CHAPTER 22

I run to the dining room first, because it's nearest, and that's where Marcia was heading last time I saw her.

Rick said she had taken a bite or a piece had come off the top of the cake when she was icing it, and she had eaten it.

When I reach the dining room, only a few kids are still eating. I scan faces quickly. No Marcia. In fact, no Guild—except Daniel, eating in the corner on his own, scooping huge spoonfuls of something gooey into his mouth. He looks up and sees me and smiles sheepishly, midmouthful. My stomach flips, and I turn right around and head out of there.

I run down the corridor toward the door to the courtyard, and as I near it, I hear a shout.

"Cate! Come back!"

It's Mr. Flynn. I don't stop.

She won't be in her room. She'll be in the Loathsome Toad office, I bet. It's a more concealed getaway for me too. I cross the courtyard and dodge behind the large hedge, then make my way down the path that leads to the studios.

OK, she ate a small piece. She ate a crumb, that's what Rick said. She looked fine when I saw her, so whatever was in the cake, maybe it wasn't in the piece that she ate, or maybe it was in such small amounts that it won't harm her. I run faster, past the art studio and the photography studio, the kiln and the toilet block. Just a little farther down this path, and then I'll be there.

No lights on in the office. Hard to tell if there's anyone home, but I'm sure she'll be here. She almost always is.

I arrive, panting, at the door, and try to open it, and as I do, I see something in the corner of the room through the window. Marcia's legs on the floor, sticking out from behind a table.

"Marcia!" I twist the stiff doorknob, then push it with all my might. "Marcia!" I remember the trick, lift the doorknob up and push again, and I'm through, almost falling into the room not unlike poor Rick fell into Ezra's office. "Marcia!"

She's lying on the floor. Alex is half on top of her, as if trying to do mouth-to-mouth.

"My God! Is she OK?"

Alex looks around at me. Marcia sits up and looks too. Same guilty face on both of them.

"Oh," I say. "Sorry for interrupting."

"Cate, listen..." Marcia begins, getting to her feet. "I know this must look bad, and I know you probably hate me, but—"

"Are you all right?" I walk up to her. "Are you feeling OK?" I hold her face in my hands, looking at her eyes. Her pupils are dilated as hell, but it's hard to know if that's because she's been poisoned or because she's been smooching Alex.

"Am I feeling OK?" She moves my hands off her face but gently. "Of course!" She frowns. "Are you being sarcastic? Look, I never wanted you to see us like this, to find out this way, but—"

"Marcia"—I bite my lip—"shut up."

"I know you must be upset with me—"

"I don't care!" I shout. "Not about him." I fling out an arm in Alex's general direction. "Do whatever you want with him for all I care, goodness knows he's tried everyone else—"

"Cate…" Alex growls at me.

"You can shut up too!" I fling out a finger at him. "You're nothing to me and you never were, and that's pretty hard to take, isn't it, Alex? What is this anyway? Some kind of payback?"

"Cate!" Marcia says.

"Urgh!" I cry, turning back to Marcia. "It doesn't matter anyway. All I care about is are you feeling OK?" I hold Marcia's shoulders. "No dizziness? Nausea?"

"What?" Marcia is looking at me as if I'm totally crazy.

"You might have been poisoned!" I yell at her. And that shuts her up.

"No," Marcia says, trembling a little, backing off.

Alex walks up to me. "What is going on, Cate?"

I stumble backward, searching for a chair and dragging it up to meet me before I sink into it. "The cake. The cake you made me, Marcia. It was spiked with something, something bad."

Marcia shakes her head. "No! I didn't!"

"Not by you, by our rogue Killer," I say. "By Skulk."

"*Ay, ¡Dios mío!*" She looks at me concerned. "It made you sick? Are you OK now?"

I sigh, the tremors rising up in my body, all that has happened beginning to bubble and threatening to burst through me. "I didn't eat the cake."

Alex speaks. "Who did?"

I don't look at him. A single, uncontrollable tear itches its way down my cheek.

"Who ate the cake, Cate?" Alex says again.

"I'm so sorry, Alex. I really am." I turn to look at him. "Rick did. I think…I think he's dead."

"Cate!"

Marcia sounds so shocked, but as I turn to her, I see her frown and realize it's because she thinks this is a sick joke I'm pulling to get back at Alex. I shake my head.

"It's true, Marcia. Dear God, I wish that it weren't, but I swear." The tears start to flow freely now. "I saw the whole thing. He collapsed on the floor, right there in front of me, had some sort of spaced-out fit and threw up… The police and Mr. Flynn tried to help him, but then…he just stopped moving." I start to sob.

"Where?" Alex hisses in my ear. "Where, Cate?"

"Ezra's office."

He runs out of the room and the door slams and swings open again, the wind blowing a bunch of leaves in. Marcia hugs me, and the two of us cry, clinging to each other until the sobs run dry. I hear the distant siren of an ambulance through the open door. Time to move.

"Come on." I detach myself gently from Marcia's arms and stand up, shakily. "I fled the scene. They'll be looking for me."

Marcia nods. "I'll get my bag."

"I'll wait." I leave the studio and walk out into the cool air, letting it dry my tears and cool my face. The ambulance siren has stopped now, and I can hear nothing but the distant cries of seabirds. I'm not sure why they bothered with the siren anyway. It's not like there's any emergency if he's already dead.

I begin to walk slowly up the path away from the studio, breathing the sea air, seeing the colors of the leaves so vividly, shivering, but relishing every sensation, enjoying still being alive, and feeling bad that I'm enjoying it. I stop by the first tree and lean against it, shutting my eyes and resting my head against the rough, damp bark. I shove my hands in my pockets and feel a crinkle of paper there. It's the cupcake wrapper. I take it out carefully and unfold it, looking at the brown crumbs as if they're going to leap up and bite me. This is evidence. I should totally give it to the police.

I refold it, put it carefully back in my pocket, and wipe my fingers on my jeans.

I hear the slam of the studio door back down the path, and Marcia comes up behind me. She looks up at me with a pale face and big, scared eyes.

"We should hurry. I've just thrown up."

She throws up again before we get to the courtyard, and as we struggle across the gravel toward Main House, she's shaking, my arm around her, holding her up. The ambulance has already gone—presumably with Rick inside it—but luckily there are still plenty of responsible people who rush to us as they realize something's up. Nobody will tell us anything about Rick. Another ambulance is called for Marcia, but by the time it arrives, Marcia's sweating and gibbering in Spanish and won't go in the ambulance. From what little I understand, it's because she thinks Rick's ghost is in there.

Eventually, they get her in, and they get gone. I stand in the courtyard and watch the ambulance zoom off, biting at my nails, and then remembering touching the cupcake wrapper and spitting frantically into a herbaceous border.

The police talk to me in Mrs. James's office. I tell them about the cupcakes. I'm quickly ferried off to the sick bay for observation. They wanted me to go to the mainland hospital with Marcia, but I told them I didn't eat anything. So they stick me down here to keep me away from everyone else.

The nurse produces oversized pajamas and makes me get into bed, which is entirely unnecessary. She smiles as she gently places a couple gossip magazines down on the bed for me to read. I have my tablet with me, and I try in vain to get on to Crypt. We're not too far from the science labs, and I can see the wireless show up on my settings page, but there's no consistent signal here. My mind is too buzzy to do anything; I can't even play Kreepy Klowns. I try to lie back and close my eyes, but every time I do, eternal gifs of Rick play in my head. Rick throwing his guts up; Rick convulsing; Rick suddenly still. In desperation, I pick up the mags and try and disappear into them.

After a while, there's a knock, and Mr. Flynn pokes his head around the door. "Hi, Cate. Can I come in?"

I nod, pulling the blankets up, even though I'm fully clothed underneath them.

"Any news about Marcia and Rick?"

"Happily, Marcia's fine." He pulls up a chair and sits down. "They filled her full of activated charcoal and apparently she's sleeping it all off."

"Good." I breathe out heavily. "Thank God. And...Rick?"

"He was alive but unconscious when the ambulance left." Flynn strokes his five o'clock shadow with one hand. "But only just. From what I've heard it's not looking terribly good, Cate."

My throat feels tight. "Have they any idea what could have caused this?"

Flynn shakes his head. "Not yet. No doubt they'll run tests."

I hug myself. "And your guess?"

"Cate, I have no idea." He leans forward. "Look, this is the most ridiculous question after what you've been through, but how are you doing?"

"I'm fine," I say. "Nothing wrong...physically."

He puts a hand on my arm. "And the rest? That was the most terrible thing to witness, for all of us. But especially for you."

I take a breath, cast my eyes around the room. Outside, it's beginning to get dark. "I'm OK. I…I think it might get worse later, when I…calm down. The shock almost protects you, doesn't it?" I look at him. "Does that make sense?"

"Absolute sense." He rubs my arm. "You'll be OK. You know this place. In no time they'll have more therapists on the island than there are sheep."

"We'll stay here?" I say, sitting up a little. "Won't they, shut down school or something?"

He holds his hands up in the air. "Who knows? It could absolutely happen. Even if Ezra and the police say it's OK to stay, you can bet that plenty of parents are going to pull their kids out as soon as word gets around. Ezra and Mrs. James are making a lot of calls." He stands up and moves to the window. "All I know is nobody's going anywhere tonight. Tide is in and a storm is forecast, so that means no helicopters. We're all stuck here until first light tomorrow."

"Nice." I shiver under my blanket. "And everybody—all the kids—they know what happened now?"

"A version of." Mr. Flynn moves back to the bed. "Ezra wanted to make an announcement en masse, but the police advised him to get the staff to do it in the classrooms. To avoid hysteria, I suppose." He sits down. "If you were wondering why you haven't had any other visitors, everyone is confined to the library and classrooms at the moment. The police are searching studies and treating the common room as a crime scene. There was…something written on the kitchen table, in icing sugar."

I blink. "*Killed.*"

He nods. "Everyone is being watched tonight. And that's a good thing." He pauses a moment. "Cate, do you have any idea who could have done this?"

I shake my head.

"And the cake that Rick ate—that was supposed to be for you?"

"It had my name on it."

There's a knock on the door, and the nurse comes in, a phone in hand.

"It's your parents," she says.

"I'll go." Mr. Flynn gets up. "Don't worry, Cate. There's a police officer outside in the waiting room. You'll be perfectly safe here. I'll try and get back before curfew."

He pats my arm and gives me a smile, and the nurse hands me the phone. They both leave, and suddenly I'm listening to my mum having kittens down the phone and all the time I'm thinking, *That cake was for me.* I didn't think too much about it until Flynny mentioned it. Rick was poisoned, but I was the one who was supposed to die. The Killer wanted me dead, not him, and everybody knows it. I have a cop outside my door, for crap's sake.

I don't hear what my parents say. They just sound really cross. I'm not sure if it's aimed at me or Ezra or the police or Rick. I let them rant, make all the right noises at the right times, and then plead fatigue and hang up. At least they called. I wasn't that sure they would.

The nurse brings me food. I realize I haven't eaten all day and shovel it up, and she calls for seconds. While I'm waiting for it, I go to the window with my tablet, and to my joy, I find I can just pick up enough signal to get on to Crypt and see what's going down.

The feed is active, and the debate is on fire, posts and messages flying back and forth.

I_did_it

We have to stop the Game now. We have to tell the police about Crypt and about Skulk.

Grand Master

No. Do not say anything yet. Do you want to get expelled, have your life ruined by this? Just play it cool.

IceColdBlond

Alex, Rick might be dead. The time for games is over.

I_did_it

Don't you care?!

General Disarray

Of course he cares. Don't you dare say that. Rick is his friend. But he's right. We have to stay together, play this smart, otherwise we could all go down.

Grand Master

Thank you, General. And you're right. We have to be clever. Trust me. We'll catch this psycho. Now wait on my post.

CharlotteCorday

I can't believe this is happening. Poor Rick. I can't stop crying.

Grand Master

Believe me, I'm crying more than all of you put together. But we do this right. We protect ourselves, and we get whoever did this.

I_did_it

Vaughan, are you out there? Who is Skulk? Surely you know?! It's time to name names!

Grand Master

Vaughan DOESN'T know. And we don't know Skulk is definitely the one who did this.

Becky_is_Dead

Did you do this, Skulk? Show yourself! I dare you!

But Skulk is silent. It's frustrating as hell. My signal keeps dropping, I miss messages, and the timeline messes up. I click on some stuff and it takes forever to load. I want to see where Vaughan is, so I check the map for users.

I spot DeadMcTavish. His little red skull is hovering over the library, along with Banana Hammock, Grand Master, IceColdBlond, General Disarray, and Becky_is_Dead.

CharlotteCorday, I_did_it, RAW, and sooperdooper are coming up as in one of the labs, probably the computer science room. As am I, technically, as Clouseau in the sick bay.

Smee is offline, as are AllKillerNoFiller, 13*is*my*lucky*number, and Skulk. Suddenly the fun of guessing all these users has disappeared.

I continue to monitor the feed as best as I can. I long for Skulk to message me. Come on, you coward. But for now, Skulk is skulking, biding their time, playing it safe.

I hear the nurse with my food, and I scuttle back to bed. I eat quickly, then return to my spot by the window and log in again to Crypt. The signal seems even worse this time. The wind is battering the window, so maybe it's the storm that's making things more difficult. It's apparent from what chatter I can pick up that the teachers are beginning to herd everyone to dorms and bed.

Then Alex posts:

Summoning is called. Tonight, 4:00 a.m. I don't need to tell you there are police around and some loser psycho who is gunning for us. Be extra vigilant, but be there. Rick is relying on you.

Grand Master

Unbelievable. Alex is deluded. How many people are actually going to turn up for that? I'm not. I'm shutting my eyes and I'm not waking up until daylight.

I go to the bathroom and brush my teeth. When I return, there's a little plastic pot with green liquid in it by my bed. I sniff it. It smells familiar, but you never know. I open the door to the waiting room.

Both the nurse and a policeman turn around, alarmed.

"Are you all right, miss?" the man asks me.

"Yes, thanks." I look at the nurse. "Did you leave this for me, by my bed?"

She nods, a little embarrassed. "It's cold remedy, but it will help you sleep, if you want it."

I look at her. She doesn't look like a killer. The bottle of cold remedy is there on her table. "Thanks." I down the liquid in one.

"I'm off to bed in an hour, but I'm just in the adjacent room if you need me," she says. "And Sergeant Maddox is here all night." She shoots him a shy glance. "In the waiting room, I mean."

Oh blimey, they fancy each other. Heaven help me.

I pad back into my room and go to pick up my tablet from the window. Mr. Flynn never made it back for another visit then. I pull the curtains tight, having first checked the windows are securely locked. As I go to shut down my tablet, I take a final glance at Crypt, half expecting Skulk to post something at the last possible second. Because that's what Skulk does, isn't it? I decide right there that if they do, I'm telling. Never mind the Game, never mind Vaughan's intranet. If Skulk pops up now, I'm tracking that little psycho down and telling Sergeant Maddox, and they are catching his or her arse. I'm sick of the thrill.

But all is silent.

I get into bed, snuggle down, the muffled tones of nurse and policeman next door lullabying me to sleep with their flirting.

Next thing I know, it's dead of night, and there's someone in the room with me.

CHAPTER 23

"Don't scream."

Words guaranteed to make you scream. If I weren't under the cloud of cold remedy, I would, but instead my heart just stops.

"It's me, Vaughan."

He's crouched by the bed. He flicks on a flashlight held under his chin, and I get a flash of his face.

"Jeez, Vaughan!" I whisper at him. "Do you want me to die of shock? What are you doing here?" I sit up in bed and shift over a little so he can get in. He shakes his head.

"No, come on. It's time for the Summoning." He gets up and starts looking for something in the room. "We're late; I had to wait for the policeman to go to the bathroom."

"Are you insane?" I'm angry as much about Sergeant Crappy taking a pee and putting me at risk. "Nobody in their right mind is going to be at that Summoning."

Vaughan flings me my jeans. "Hurry up. They'll be there. And so must we."

"We'll never make it!" I get up and start putting the jeans on anyway. "There are police everywhere!"

"Two blokes, walking a perimeter. I've watched them." He flings a sweater at me. "They've obviously never done this before in their lives. And it's stormy as hell outside, so they're lingering in the sheltered places. It'll be easy."

"Right you are." I pull on the sweater and scoop my shoes up from under the bed. "Just how do we get out of the room in the first place? Wait for Hot Fuzz in there to have another slash? Or are we breaking our way out through the glass?"

"Neither." He flashes a little key at me. "Remember when my feet were all cut up from the rocks?"

"Er, no," I say. "I'd completely forgotten about that."

"I came down here for some bandages. Told the nurse I'd dropped a glass in the bathroom and stepped on it." He goes to the window and inserts the key into the lock. "It was a sunny day, and she opened the windows with this key. Keeps it on top of the doorframe in the waiting room. Actually asked me to get it down for her, because she's a short-arse."

"Great," I intone. "But, Vaughan, I'm not kidding. I'm not going anywhere."

He looks at me, one foot up on the windowsill. "So why are you holding your coat?" He opens the window and a rush of cold air blows in. Without a backward glance he shimmies out and drops down on to the grass on the other side.

And I follow. Of course I do, stepping out after him and hurriedly pulling the window shut behind me.

Thankfully, it's not raining, but the wind is gusting, almost threatening to knock me off my feet. Vaughan is running ahead, keeping low, in the direction of the labs. I pull my parka around me and run, looking around me, expecting a shout, or the flash of a light to stop me in my tracks. But I'm not even sure I could hear someone yelling with this gale. We weave in and out of the classrooms, and then Vaughan diverts us around the sports center. He sprints flat-out, until we reach the corner of the gym, where he stops, panting. I catch up and throw myself against his piece of wall.

"That's where the cops are circling." He nods in the direction of Main House. "We have to cut down the back way and head to the cliffs from the bottom of the lawn. It's longer, but we won't be spotted."

I nod, and we set off again. It hurts to run in this wind, but every shadow, every shaking branch makes me run faster. When we reach the cliff, the wind is frighteningly strong, and I keep as far back from the edge as I can to prevent a gust from picking me up and hurtling me to the rocks below. The path down is more sheltered, but as we run out onto the beach toward the cave entrance, the wind buffets me again, pushing me backward like a giant's hand denying me of my destination. I bend over, leaning into it, and suddenly we're there, my ears popping as I stagger inside the first chamber behind Vaughan. We drop to our hands and knees and recover, then it is me who rises first, pulling at Vaughan's jacket, and making the final part of our journey into the Place Most Holy.

We are late, but we're not the only ones. In the dim light of the oil lamps, Carl, Martin, and Whitney are pacing, fretting.

"Did anyone else come with you?" Carl says. Vaughan shakes his head. Carl passes me a bottle, but I wave it away.

"You'll excuse me if I don't eat or drink anything."

The others immediately look at their drinks with concern. Martin rushes up to me and gives me a hug.

"Thank God you're OK!" he says. "I've been so worried about you! They said you didn't eat any of the cake, but I wanted to see you with my own eyes, you know?"

"Yeah, thanks." I frown at him. "You look...guilty. Got something you need to tell me, Martin?"

"No!" he says. "I'm not Skulk—look, let's wait until everyone's here."

"Tesha and Anvi aren't coming, and I really doubt Cynthia will be here," Whitney says, smoking furiously. "Tesh and Anvi have had enough. They're scared. They told me that tomorrow they're going to the police, going to spill the beans about everything, regardless of what Alex decides tonight."

"Where is Alex?" I look around. "This was his call. Where is he?"

There's a noise behind me, and I turn around, but it's only Becky and Roger.

"Where's Alex?" Becky says. "Did we miss him?"

"Not here yet," Carl says. "Look, let's start. The whole point of us meeting here was to discuss what to do and get our stories straight, and frankly we can do that in two minutes because I'm pretty frigging sure we're all agreed." He looks around at us.

"Alex talked about catching whoever did this," I say. "Obviously, I kind of have a vested interest in that."

Carl nods. "Understandable. But let the police handle it. I'm sorry, Cate, but I've nearly lost one of my best friends here, and I'm not going to screw around playing detective."

He walks up to the altar alcove, pulls the beads and velvet curtains to one side, and throws the bottle down on the altar.

"The Game is finished!" He tugs the curtains down and kicks at the altar; candles, photos, and the yellow skull go flying. "No more Kills!" He jumps up and swings at the fairy lights, bringing them down too in a tangle on the sand. He turns to us, strangely calm.

"Crypt is deleted, like yesterday, Vaughan, that way we don't need to tell them about your hack."

Vaughan nods, and Carl continues.

"We're straight with the police. Tell them everything else, even about these caves. Yes, we'll get into hell for being here, but if we give them something solid, they'll think they have it all. We take anything incriminating away now." He moves around the cave, gathering a few things—cans, an ashtray, and a small tin box—and stuffing them into a bag.

"And finally"—he turns to face us again—"Killer, whoever you are—you're over. We know you're not Skulk, and we know you're not responsible for Emily, Marcia, and Rick. Speak up if you're here, and let's end this."

"No!" Alex appears at the door, dripping wet. "This is my Game, Carl. You don't get to end it."

Carl shakes his head, goes over to Alex, and puts a hand on his shoulder. "It's already ended, mate—"

"I said no!" Alex swings a punch. Carl clocks it and manages to dodge, but the blow still strikes him on the ear. He turns, furious, and charges into Alex, knocking him to the floor, his hands around his neck.

Nobody yells stop. We watch, glued to the spot, as Carl's fingers tighten around Alex's neck, his face squashed and purple against the pale sand. Alex's legs kick out, hopelessly, and suddenly I'm reminded of Rick on Ezra's floor.

"OK, Carl," I say quietly. "Stop." But Carl just squeezes harder. "OK, I said!" I grab his shoulders and try to pull him back, and then Vaughan and Roger are pitching in and together we've thrown Carl off Alex, who sits up, spluttering and choking.

"The decision is made, Alex," Carl grunts. "End of Days."

Alex shakes his head. "I never thought you'd be the one to betray me, Carl," he croaks.

"Betray you?" Carl is on his feet again. "I am protecting you, Alex!"

"Is that what you were doing with your hands around my throat?" Alex laughs. "Anyway, it's irrelevant. The reason I was late here is that they spotted me. Any minute now we're going to be joined by our friends from the constabulary."

"What?"

"They're coming here?"

"Christ, Alex!"

Rats deserting a sinking ship. Becky, Whitney, Roger make for the exit without delay. Carl gives Alex a look and then follows them, clutching the bag. Martin flings out a hand for Alex, but he's not moving from the floor. And then Martin leaves and there's no one here except me, Vaughan, and Alex.

"How far away are they, Alex?" I ask him as he finally stands and starts to move around the cave, picking up some of the photos from the altar and shaking the broken glass off them.

"Meh. Top of the cliff. They don't even know the cave is down here. As long as they don't see those lemmings running out of here screaming, we should have a couple minutes at least."

"Look, it's clear everyone wants to come clean," I say. "It's best."

"For you?" Alex stops and looks at me. "Seems it's your life at stake."

I shake my head. "Maybe. Or maybe it's nothing to do with the Game. For all we know, Skulk has hacked into Crypt and they're not even a player." I look at Vaughan. "It's possible?"

"It's possible," he says.

"So any trap we lay for Skulk may not work. Time to let the professionals deal with it, Alex."

"Moving on, Cate?" Alex straightens up, looks at me. "Yes. Yes, you're right. Let's hand this all over to the grown-ups." He walks past me, in his arms a bag full of things he's gathered from the cave. "Remember that, Cate, when you're at their mercy, won't you?" He pushes past me, shouting back at us. "This isn't over!"

We watch him fade into the darkness. Vaughan moves to one of the crates, sits down.

"Why does everything I play with always break?"

"Oh, this is all about you, is it?" I sit down next to him. "Good-oh. I'm really bored of it all centering around me."

We sit there, listening to the wind and the sea outside.

"Must be raining now," Vaughan says.

"Yeah."

"We staying here?"

I look at him. "We are. I meant to tell you, those windows at the sick bay only open one way. When I shut them behind me I locked us out."

Vaughan nods. "Makes sense."

"I'm exhausted." I lean over, grab the velvet curtain that Carl ripped down from the altar. "We can make ourselves at home. Wait for them to come and find us."

We make a nest—rugs, cushions, blankets. A single oil lamp. It's cozy. As I settle down underneath the velvet curtain and Vaughan wraps his arm around me, I keep expecting the police to burst in or Mr. Flynn or one of the other teachers, but no one comes. We lie there, side by side, watching the entrance, the lamp flickering and casting shadows up the sides of the cave.

"What was it like when you thought you were watching Rick die?" Vaughan whispers.

At first I don't answer him. I resist the memories, watching the shadows dance, breathing with them.

"Awkward," I say finally. "It felt…awkward. Five adults in

that room—and me. And none of us knew how to react. Oh, they knew what to do—Mr. Flynn and the police—the CPR or whatever. But when it seemed like he was gone...no one knew where to look. It was like we were intruding on this... really private thing, the moment as he slipped away." I feel a shudder move through me and try to stifle it, but Vaughan just holds me closer. "Hang on in there, Rick," I whisper. "You've always been a stubborn donkey." We lie there, breathing in time with each other, and I cry a little covertly. And then the tears slide away, and still Vaughan holds me, and I wish that life was just this. All the outside stuff can just go away, and I'll just stay here with my old friend, feeling safe and loved and understood. But there are always things that get in the way, like conversations that have to be had, and revelations that have to be made. I wipe away my tears. "I know who the Killer is, by the way."

Vaughan twists around to face me. "What?"

"Not the real one, the one in the Game. It's Daniel."

"No way!" Vaughan leans up on his elbow. "Are you sure?"

"Yep," I say. "Found the Killer card in his violin case."

"Strange." Vaughan lies down again. "I didn't think it was him. Although now, I can sort of see the psychology of it. Female victims, he's hopeless around girls; he bloodies them. I was right! It was a boy."

I frown into the gloom. "I was surprised, I'll admit. I didn't think he was so into the Game that he'd do all that preparation. But I suppose that's a good cover, the apparent lack of interest.

And he's certainly clever enough to have thought it all out. I just didn't think he was motivated."

"Hmm," Vaughan says.

"What, you don't believe it's him?"

"Well," Vaughan says. "And don't take this the wrong way, but...I did wonder if he was the real Killer or at least if he was Skulk." He turns to me. "You see, I found something out. Remember we thought Tesha posted that video of you two?"

I nod. "Of course."

"She didn't post it. I went to her room to delete the video off her mini-cam, like you asked me, and then I searched her laptop for the video, but it wasn't on there. That got me curious. I searched again, and eventually I did find it. But not on her machine. It was on her roommate's laptop."

"Emily," I say, sitting up. "Emily is her roommate."

Vaughan nods. "We already know Smee posted the video. I checked back through Crypt's feed. Smee has been inactive since Emily's accident, so..."

"Smee is Emily." I finish for him. "So, you think Daniel found out she was behind it, and he hurt her? As revenge?"

"It would make sense," he says.

"But then he poisoned a cake?" I shake my head. "Daniel is a little unhinged, it's true—he might be Skulk. He might be a troll who makes empty threats, sends me messages to give me a scare. But I just can't see the Emily thing or the poisoning... Look, he might do some other screwed-up stuff, but he'd never really hurt me."

Vaughan thinks about this for a moment. "What is 'some other screwed-up stuff'?"

I sigh. "OK, your turn not to freak out. When we were in his study yesterday, he kind of...forced himself on me, I suppose you'd say."

"What!" Vaughan is sitting bolt upright now. "What did he do?"

"It's OK," I say. "Nothing too bad—he didn't hurt me. He asked me about how I felt about you, and then he went all weird and kissed me. Pushed me down on the sofa, wouldn't let me go."

Vaughan gulps, his face reddening. "I'll kill him!"

"No you won't, Vaughan," I say sharply. "And you're not to say that in front of anyone else, do you hear me?" I sigh. "I'm fine. I punched him anyway, if that makes you feel better. Really hard."

"It does." Vaughan lies down again. "A little. But anyway, this isn't about me. It's about you—"

"Yes, it is," I say. "And I am going to do something about it, but I don't know what yet. I was going to humiliate him in public, but the events of the day took over, somewhat. And it's just as well. He needs help, and he needs to tell someone what he did." I take a breath. "I don't think he would have gone much further, but he has to know how to deal without ever doing that again to anyone else."

Vaughan is silent. It irks me slightly, mainly because I want him to agree with my plan of how to deal with this, but he obviously doesn't, and really, I shouldn't care less what Vaughan thinks. This is nothing to do with him. But we lie there, and I lay my head on his chest, and he puts his arm around me, and we can agree to disagree. Eventually, he breaks the silence.

"What did you say?"

"Eh? When?"

"When Daniel asked you how you feel about me?"

I pause. "He actually asked me if I was in love with you."

Vaughan takes a breath. "And you replied...?"

"I said no." I feel him hold his breath, his arm stiffening a little around my shoulders. Oh, what the hell. You only live once. "But I lied."

He laughs, softly, and relaxes against me again. "I don't love you too."

We lie there, lying to each other, happily. Eventually, I speak. "I don't think anyone is coming."

The wind has died down. I think I can hear the rain falling, and the waves splashing, but the storm is passing.

"What do you think?" I tilt my head up and look at him. He's sleeping. Head back, lips parted a little, dark-lashed eyes closed, and eyebrows slightly raised as if he's having a surprising dream. I shut my eyes too and let myself drift away on the retreating tide.

When I wake the next morning, he has gone.

I look at my watch; it's 7:15 a.m. I get up, shivering, and look around.

"Vaughan?"

He must have gone outside for a pee. I pick up the oil lamp, pulling the velvet curtain around me like a cape for warmth, and walk slowly through the caves until I'm screwing my eyes up in the daylight. The wind and rain has all but gone; there's a chilly breeze, but the sun is trying to pierce the gray. I look around me, behind the gorse bushes, expecting to catch him unawares, but he's not there. Did he go up the path a little? Along the beach? I scan around. Doesn't look like it.

Then I see a dark mound on the sand a way off, not far from where the waves are lapping. At first I think it's a rock or a seal, but then I spot what looks like a boot. Is that him lying there? The mound is moving a little. What the hell is he doing?

I drop the lamp and start to run, my velvet cape billowing out behind me.

"Vaughan!"

A few yards from the mound, I slow to a stop. It's a pile of clothes, blowing slightly in the breeze. His clothes. His boots. I spin around, looking farther along the beach, toward the cliffs, up at the promontory, and back toward the caves in case I've missed him. And then, inevitably, out to sea.

"Vaughan!" I hold my hands up to my mouth, bend my knees, and holler at the waves. "Vaughan!" The breeze whips my cloak away, and it falls to the sand at my feet, joining Vaughan's discarded clothes. I look for a head in the water, the curve of a thrashing arm, or the splash of a struggle. I run toward the rocks where he was beached after his fall from the promontory and look there. But he has gone. Vanished.

Slowly, I walk back to the clothes, my head aching with possibilities. Is this some joke? A ruse to fool the police? But why? I bend down to move the cloak and examine his clothes. Why, Vaughan? What are you playing at now?

My eye catches a line drawn in the sand by Vaughan's jacket. I follow it, then see the series of lines and curls to the left of it. I step back and read the word written in the sand:

KILLED

"No," I say emphatically, stepping back farther in case I'm missing something, but that's the only word written there. *Killed. Killed. Killed.*

"No!" I scream. "Vaughan, no!"

As I fall to my knees, I see men and women in uniform running across the beach toward me.

CHAPTER 24

"And so, Cate"—the superintendent clears his throat—"having found various incriminating items in his study and bedroom, we have very good reason to suspect that Vaughan was guilty of poisoning Rick Wallington and causing injury to Emily Mullins and Marcia Alvarez." He shifts in the chair slightly, and it squeaks inappropriately. He coughs again. "I'm sorry to say that we also have compelling evidence that leads us to believe Vaughan committed suicide by walking into the sea."

I rub my eyes and stare up at the pale-green ceiling of the sick bay.

The nurse has been giving me something much stronger than cold remedy for the last forty-eight hours. Little blue pills, two at a time. I resisted at first, mainly because I knew Vaughan was still out there, and I knew he needed help—help from me. This was him pulling a trick, couldn't they see? Either—and this was the part I wasn't too clear on—the Killer had him, somehow, somewhere, and was holding him against his will—or Vaughan was hiding until he could expose the Killer for who he or she really was. It was so simple! Or was it? I...couldn't entirely remember.

"No." I form the word carefully, deliberately. "Vaughan wouldn't do that. He wouldn't hurt anyone. Not even himself."

"Cate." The superintendent's voice sounds tired. He rustles some papers on his lap. "Did Vaughan ever tell you why he was at Umfraville?"

Duh. This superintendent is really not so super. "Vaughan's too clever for Cambridge. He was having a break from the robots. Very demanding, those robots." I start to giggle uncontrollably.

Not-so-superintendent sighs. "Cambridge asked him to leave. He got into a fight with another student there and broke their jaw." The papers rustle again. "Last spring, he drank so much he had to go to hospital to have his stomach pumped."

"No, wrong again," I say slowly. "Vaughan never drinks. He doesn't like it. You can ask him when you find him." I wish the room would stop moving. The walls are wobbling intermittently, and it's beginning to annoy me. "Anyway, I keep telling you." I sit up drunkenly. "Are you even supposed to be doing this without my parents here? I mean, am I not a minor or something? Don't you need them here to question me?"

"And as I keep telling you, Cate," he says, "your parents have given us permission to interview you, and they are on their way

here. It is apparently quite a long flight from the...Maldives."
He pronounces it "dives," not "deevs," the idiot.

"Nice of 'em to bother." I flop back onto my pillow again and
close my eyes.

I wake sometime later. The cloud has lifted, but it has been
replaced by the pain, and I don't like that. The pain is lodged
in my chest, like a cold steel wedge. It won't shift. Not until
Vaughan comes back.

I get up, check the time, and pull on the dressing gown that
has been brought from my dorm, shuffle slippers onto my feet.
I go to the door, open it.

"Yes, Cate?" It's the nurse. And another policeman, a better
one. The nurse doesn't look happy; he's not as good-looking as
the last.

"I'd like...some fresh air, please." I begin to shuffle out of
my room.

"Er." The nurse looks at the cop, and he back at her.

"It's OK," I say. "I'll just go into the garden." I lean toward
the policeman and wink. "You can even watch." Yuck. I sound
like I'm inviting him to visit me in the shower.

They let me, and I step outside. Ouch, it's chilly. Just as well
I don't care.

The sick bay has a small garden with a wooden bench and
a goldfish pond bordered by a low hedge. I sit gingerly on
one end of the bench, look down toward the science labs,
and wait.

Since Vaughan disappeared, things have been a blur to say

the least. They won't tell me what evidence they have against him or why they are so sure he waded out to sea. I do know that they haven't found a body, and of course they won't, because he's still out there. Alive. He has to be.

I also know that the police searched the island and interviewed all of the Guild members, and after twenty-four hours and some full-on pressure from parents, the police sent all of the lower years home. They can't keep the rest of the kids here indefinitely, but while they're winding up the investigation and still interviewing us, we are stuck on the island, and classes are supposed to be in session. Which means right about now, Martin should be emerging from that laboratory and making his way back toward his study.

And there he is. Hooray for the predictability and regularity of the scientist.

As he gets closer, I hiss at him.

"Martin!"

He looks up, alarmed, like I'm the frigging Killer. I beckon him over. He eyes the hedge like it's an impenetrable wall. I roll my eyes at him.

"Over there! There's a gap."

He reluctantly squeezes through and joins me on the bench, his face full of concern and—urgh—pity.

"How are you?"

"Fine," I say. "Listen, you have to get me my tablet, OK? It's in my study, so unless they've bagged it as evidence for some random reason, you'll see it on the table."

"Why do you need it?" he says. "They're discouraging emails and messaging."

"I need to get on Crypt!" I say. "Have you seen anything on there? Anything that might suggest Vaughan's on the mainland?"

Martin's eyes dart down. "Oh, Cate. Crypt is gone. Didn't they tell you?"

I blink. "What?"

He nods. "Someone told the police about it—not sure who, Tesha, probably—and they tried to log in but it has disappeared. Ms. Lasillo tried and everything. We all did. Apart from the initial password box, there was no evidence it was even there in the first place."

A huge fireball of hope moves through me. "Oh, yes!" I punch the sky.

"What is it?" Martin looks at me like I've farted.

I laugh with joy and relief. "Don't you see?" I yell at him; I can't believe he's being so thick. "If it's gone, that proves Vaughan's alive! Nobody else could have taken the site down! Nobody!"

Martin shakes his head. "Not true, Cate. I wish it were. Vaughan could have nixed it the night of the Summoning, before we went to the cave. The last time any of us saw it was earlier that evening. Or Crypt could have had a kill pill."

I frown. "What's that?"

His face screws up in self-disgust. "Oh, I'm sorry, Cate. Bad expression. A 'kill pill' is when a site has an inbuilt code which makes it automatically disappear under certain conditions. Say, if the webmaster doesn't log in for a period of time, enter a password, that kind of thing. Shazam! It's gone."

I nod my head, but I don't believe him. Vaughan is out there. It would absolutely make sense for him to get rid of Crypt for now.

"Get my tablet for me anyway?" I pull a sad face for Martin. "To take my mind off things." He looks reluctant but nods. "Thanks. And one more favor. Can you find Daniel for me? Get him to visit?" He nods again, and I smile sardonically. "I bet no one can believe that he was the Killer, eh?"

Martin shakes his head. "What do you mean?"

"Daniel," I say. "Was the Killer. In the Game."

Martin looks angry. "He was not! Who told you that? No way, I was the Killer!"

"What?"

He stands up. "I was going to tell you all in the cave, before it—you know—happened, but then Alex showed up and told us the police were coming, and I didn't get the chance. But it was me, all right." He puffs up his chest. "I had to tell the police, show them everything I'd used in the lab, the paint powder, show them how I'd climbed up the drainpipe and in through the attic in Main House to drop down to the girls' dorms."

I choke out a laugh. "You did that?"

"Absolutely." His face is proud; then he falters. "My parents have got a bill for the pool clean-up. They're pretty peeved about it."

"I found the Killer card though," I say. "In Daniel's violin case. How did it get there?"

"You have it?" Martin says, moving on to the bench beside me again. "I lost it! Dropped it somewhere, just after the first Summoning. Alex said he was going to kill me! Can I have it back, please? For a souvenir?"

"Gosh, Martin." I pat him on the hand. "I'm sorry, I don't have it anymore. But well done you. I never would have guessed." I have a sudden thought. "Did you plant Marcia's bag in the hedge, after the Cynthia Kill?"

He nods sadly. "I saw you find it. Meant it to be a red herring so that everyone would think it was her." He looks mad at me. "Why didn't you tell anyone you'd found it? What a waste."

"Well." I clear my throat and smother the urge to shove him off the bench. "Sorry that particular strategy didn't work out for you. But hey, Martin, kudos for the rest of it. How on earth did you manage to pull everything together so quickly?"

Martin leans in. "Well, look don't tell anyone, but I knew in advance that I was going to be the Killer. Alex fixed it. He, er, owed me a favor."

"What kind of favor?"

"I wrote up a couple of his papers last term. Stuff he couldn't do himself. No big deal, but between me and you, yes?" He stands up again, looks around. "And no harm done, eh? Won't be playing the Game again, ever." He looks at me closely.

"And just so we're clear, as I told the police, the whole Skulk business? Not me. I was General Disarray, I'll have you know."

He walks to the hedge. "I'll bring your tablet after dinner. We're only here another day anyway. Then they're sending us home. Early half term," he says. "Then after that, who knows? I suppose now that we know that Vaughan was the Killer, we're all safe here."

"No, you've got it all wrong." I spring up. "Vaughan is not the Killer!" I hear myself scream. I should really tone it down, but somehow I can't help myself. "He's not dead, and he's not the Killer! Are you stupid? Is everyone stupid? He's not the Killer! Not the Killer! Not the Killer!"

Martin looks at me, scared, and leaves hurriedly. The nurse and the policeman appear at my side and walk me back to my sickbed. The little blue pills are waiting for me.

I wake up later, and it's dark outside and raining. My bedside lamp is on, and there on the table is my tablet. Thank you, Martin. I groggily crawl out of bed, take it over to the window, and get on to the school intranet. I tap on the password box and put in my password for Crypt.

There! It springs up immediately.

Stupid Martin, what does he know?

There's nothing new on Crypt. No Skulk, no Vaughan-as-DeadMcTavish, no nobody. I look at the map; no users online, except me, at the sick bay. I click on the new IM box, and my fingers hover over the text box. I type @DeadMcTavish. And I write. And write.

I tell him I know he's out there. I tell him to be strong, that we've got this, we'll clear his name, find the real killer, and everything will be all right. He just needs to tell me what to do. I tell him that Martin was the Killer in the Game, and that I'm going to talk to Daniel because I've thought it all through, and I'm really doubting that he's Skulk and was involved in what happened to Emily, Marcia, and Rick. No, Daniel's just a sad and lonely boy. Skulk is the killer, Skulk is a monster, and he's still out there and wants to kill me—kill us both. We need to find him, need to trap him, and we don't have much time because the police think it's case closed, and everyone's leaving Skola soon and it will be too late.

And then I tell him that I love him.

And then I delete that bit, because it's too bloody sappy and there'll be time for all of that later.

And then I press Return.

The message pings out into the ether. I watch the screen intensely, like I've never watched anything in my life before. I will him to appear. He has to. I wait like that for five, ten minutes, and then fifteen, refreshing the screen over and over to stop Crypt from logging me out, terrified that if it bumps me off, I'll never get on again. And then I wake up with a jerk of my head and I realize that I've fallen asleep in the chair by the window, and I hold my breath as I log in, and my heart leaps as Crypt appears, but falls again as there's no new message from DeadMcTavish. I stare at the screen, settling myself in for the long haul, gripping my fingernails into my palms to keep myself from falling asleep again.

An hour passes. Nothing. Then an hour and a half. No word.

Dejected, I stumble back to bed. I wake once or twice in the night, and each time I check. Silence in the Crypt.

In the morning, I wake up with a clearer head.

I wake up my tablet, log in to Crypt.

Still nothing.

I get up, shower, put on my clothes, which have been thoughtfully laundered. Normal clothes make me feel more normal again. This is ridiculous; they can't keep me in the sick bay. I'm not sick! I pace up and down again, check in on Crypt occasionally, and just as I'm about to try and convince them to let me go out, there's a knock at the door.

I walk over and answer it.

Daniel's standing there, looking shocked.

"Hi!" He looks me up and down. "I was expecting you to be in bed!" He instantly flushes, realizing how that sounds. I resist the urge to roll my eyes, and beckon him in, where he stands, swinging his violin case against his legs gently.

"Grab that chair." I sit on the bottom of the bed.

Daniel stays where he is and holds out one hand.

"Cate, I just want you to know, I'm so, so sorry."

I nod. "What for?"

His head tilts, he's confused. "I'm sorry about Vaughan, of course."

"Don't worry about it." I dismiss him. "No, I thought you meant you were sorry about jumping on me the other day."

"What?" Daniel puts his violin case down by the chair with a thud. "Oh God." He shakes his head. "I would never, Cate, never hurt you, you know that—"

"Really?" I say. "Because it freaked me the hell out." I gesture to his arms. "You're strong, Daniel. Probably stronger than you realize."

He stares at me. "Well…I know I was a little out of control, but you didn't say no."

"Ha!" I cry out and jump up from the bed, walking toward where he's standing. "You really thought I was into it, did you, Daniel? Maybe I couldn't say no because your tongue was down my throat, did you ever think of that?"

He shakes his head. "No—I know, and, Cate, I am sorry. I'm so sorry. I'll never do that again. You pushed me, and then I was just so, I don't know, overcome with—"

"Sit down." I push his chest—gently but firmly—so that he backs into the chair and falls onto it. "And shut up." I look down at him. "This is what we're going to do. I don't think you're a bad person, Daniel, and I don't think you meant to frighten me, but you need help dealing with all your pent-up…stuff." I walk back to the bed and sit again. "I'm not going to tell anyone here what happened, as long as you do one thing: talk to a therapist. There's one here on the island—for post-traumatic Game-playing disorder or something—you've seen him around?"

Daniel nods quickly.

"Good. He seems OK. Came to see me but I was too zonked to talk. Anyway. Talk to him, tell him what happened. Get some help."

"Yes." He nods again. "I can. I can do that."

"You'd better," I agree. "And one more thing. I'm writing to your parents and telling them everything."

"No!" He leaps up from the chair. "You can't do that!"

I hold a hand out. "I can, Daniel. I have to. Now if you don't sit down, I'm screaming for the policeman outside that door." He looks at me, his eyes full of anger and fear, but sits down anyway. I take a breath. "You scared me, Daniel. Do you understand how that feels? Of course you do; you feel scared every day."

He deflates in front of me, bows his head. My voice softens.

"We're kids, Daniel. We like to think we're on top of it all, but living is really, really difficult sometimes. We can't be expected to deal with this all by ourselves." He starts to cry. "I don't want to ruin your life by telling anyone, but I've gone back and forth on what I should do, and I've decided that, actually, this is not my problem to solve."

He is sitting there, sobbing gently. In spite of it all, I feel sorry for him. "Your parents are OK, Daniel, you know? They'll freak out a bit, but they love you, and they'll help you."

I walk to the chair, pick up the violin case, and hand it to him. He snatches it from me, and as he does my nail catches on one of the stickers, his favorite one with the cat drawn in a red swirl.

"Oh!" I say. "Sorry, I didn't mean to—" The sticker rips and half hangs off the case in a curl.

Daniel looks at me, and this time his eyes are filled with nothing but hate.

"Die, Cate. Just go away and die." He rushes for the door, flings it open, and leaves.

The policeman comes in. "You OK, miss?"

"Fine, thank you." I nod. "Could I have a piece of paper and a pen, please? I need to write a letter."

It takes a while to write that letter. Firstly because my hand is shaking so much, and then it takes time to find the words. Halfway through, the nurse brings me lunch, and I have to start again because I get minestrone on the paper. Once it's done, I find Daniel's home address on my tablet. The nurse is kind and finds me an envelope and a stamp.

"Hmm, missed the collection today, I think." She looks at her watch and nods. "Do you want me to put it in the box for tomorrow?" she asks. The school's outgoing mailbox is in the courtyard at Main House. I nod and thank her and return to my room.

Exiting my contact list on my tablet, I give it one more go. I log in to Crypt, but I am the only one there again. On the map, one little red skull hovering over the sick bay. Clouseau. Yeah, that's about right. A rubbish detective, me. Laughable. As I stare at the skull, Crypt auto logs me off, and the tears come, tears of self-pity, tears of the stress of dealing with Daniel, and the creeping realization that maybe—just maybe—everyone else is right about Vaughan, and I am wrong. My whole body starts to shake, and I have to put the tablet down to hold on to the windowsill for support.

The nurse opens the door.

"It's time for your pills, but I was wondering if you want to ease off them now—oh." She sees my face, sees the tears falling, and my shoulders shaking. She comes to me, comforts me, wraps a blanket around me while I cry, and presses the small plastic cup of two blue pills into my hand. She watches me, nodding, while I swallow them with a sip of water.

"Let's get you into your bed," she soothes.

"I will." I nod. "Just shutting this down," I say, looking at the tablet.

"I'll check on you in a few minutes." She gives me a sympathetic smile and leaves.

I let out a sigh and reach over to close the tablet down. But it's like a sickness, an addiction even stronger than Kreepy Klowns. I log on to Crypt again.

Two red skulls.

The pills are making me see double. I blink, look again.

Clouseau is hovering over the sick bay. Me.

Another red skull at the caves.

I tap on the skull, and the username comes up.

DeadMcTavish

My mouth opens, gulping for air, I feel those walls start to wobble again, and this time I don't think it's the medication.

And then, a message appears.

DeadMcTavish

OK, darlin'. Let's do this. It's time to catch a killer.

CHAPTER 25

The first thing, the very first thing I do, is go to the bathroom and throw up those pills. They stare up at me from the toilet bowl; some of the blue has rubbed off, but they're intact. I grab a glass of water and down it in one.

And then I race back to my tablet and type furiously.

Clouseau
Vee?! Is that really you?

At first there's no reply, and I begin to think I'm going crazy, but then, a ping.

DeadMcTavish
It's me.

I gather my thoughts for a millisecond and then type.

Clouseau

Where the hell have you been? Are you OK??? Why did you disappear? What were you thinking? Where are you hiding—are you really in the cave? Are you OK??? Oh God, I can't believe this is happening!!!!

Nothing appears for a moment, then...

DeadMcTavish

Disappeared to protect you, to catch the killer. Only way.

I rub my face, frantically, then type again.

Clouseau

Who, Vaughan? Who is it?

DeadMcTavish

Just come. 6 p.m.

I pause, my heart beating so hard I think I'm having some kind of coronary event. But I can't listen to my heart here; I have to use my head. I type.

Clouseau

How do I know this is you?

I wait. And wait...

Ping.

DeadMcTavish

I love you.

A hot and cold wave flushes over me. I think I'm going to pass out. But I type again.

Clouseau

HOW DO I KNOW IT'S YOU???

I wait. Listen for the ping. And wait. And wait.

The little red skull over the caves disappears.

"Jesus Christ on a bike!" I shout at the tablet and then slap a hand over my mouth. I get up, look out the window. I look at the clock; it's just after 3 p.m. Nearly three hours to wait? Is Vaughan insane?

But I can't be angry with him—the relief, the sheer, wonderful relief that he is alive is so immense that I feel like I am exploding with joy and strength. I have the power of a hundred Cates, and I will get this done.

OK, OK, now…how do I get out of this joint? That's the first hurdle. You can bet that the nurse and my police guard aren't just going to let me go for a stroll. I stare out of the very locked window, and then it comes to me. I walk to the door and open it.

"Could you get the superintendent, please?" I say to the police officer. "I have some very important information."

He stands up, surprised. "What information?"

I take a breath. "I want to make a statement. To the superintendent. Could you get him?"

He nods, and as he reaches around to the front of his chest, my heart sinks. He grabs a walkie-talkie and clicks on a button.

Nope. Nope. Nope. I wanted him to actually leave, not call him!

He talks into the walkie-talkie, trying to raise the superintendent. But luck is on my side. Either the Skola wind is blowing in the wrong direction, or strange magnetic fields from whatever weird science our geeks are currently conducting in the nearby labs prevents the superintendent from answering. Eventually, some other police bod tells my cop that the super is at the sports center.

"Affirmative, mate," my cop says. "I'm nearer. I'll walk there. Over." He looks at me. "Sit tight in your room. I'll go and get him. Two minutes."

I nod and shut the door. Act One, done. Now for Act Two.

I reach for the half bowl of minestrone, still on the windowsill by my tablet, and I slosh my glass of water into it, the carrots and peas floating there ominously, alongside bloated pasta pieces. I pour a little of the mixture back into the glass, then pull the sheets back from my bed, and toss the contents of the bowl slap-bang in the middle of the mattress. Then it's back to the window, where I press my face against the glass to watch the policeman walk away.

Now, to leave it as long as I dare...I count up to ten,

slowly—one assassin, two assassin, three assassin—then duck into the bathroom, splash my face with water, and think sad thoughts.

I open the door to the waiting room. The nurse looks up at me.

"Hi—sorry—I'm, er—can you help?" I shudder and squeeze out a tear.

"What's happened, love?" She comes in, and I point in anguish at the bed. "Oh, don't you worry. I'll get this cleaned up in no time." She grabs some towels from the bathroom, mops up the worst of it, and begins to strip the bed.

I stand by the open door and wait until she has her arms full before letting out a moan. "Ugh, I think I'm going to—" I bend over, facing out of the door, and making a retching noise, I splash a concealed glass of the lovely minestrone blend onto the linoleum floor of the waiting room. Great sound effect. "I'm so sorry. I'll just grab another towel from your room." Before she can object, I've scooped my tablet and my coat from behind the door and am running out of the waiting room to blessed freedom, outside.

Eyes darting, I dig in and sprint. My legs scream with the sudden renewed activity, but I ignore them. I only have seconds to disappear, only seconds. I clear the hedge, make for the woods, run flat-out, and don't look back. If the nurse is yelling at me, I don't notice. If the police have spotted me, I'm not aware. I just run and run until I'm covered by trees and jumping over undergrowth and dodging around scrubby bushes.

But where to?

The urge to go to the caves now is extreme. But I mustn't. Vaughan said 6:00 p.m., and he has his reasons. He said we're going to catch the killer, and I have to trust he has a plan.

That's if I trust that the messages were from Vaughan.

Amid all the happy, I cannot help but have a little bit of doubt, a tiny little nugget of fear that those messages aren't from Vaughan. Guess what? It's called self-preservation. I may not be the cleverest kid at Umfraville, but I'm no fool. One thing keeps coming back to me, and that is this: I was numero uno. I was top of the hit list. The killer tried to poison me—not Rick—and he or she did not succeed. What's to say they're going to stop trying now?

I need backup, and I know what I have to do. It's not going to be a pretty scene. I head for the art studio.

It's time to cash in my chips with Mr. Flynn. If these messages are not from Vaughan, I'd be stupid to go to the caves alone. But I believe, strongly, that Vaughan will be there, and if I'm right, we're still going to need someone to help us convince the rest of the world of his innocence. I think—I hope and pray—that I can persuade Flynny just to give Vaughan a chance before he tells the police he's alive.

Breaking from the trees, I see that the lights are on in the art studio. I peep into the window in case there are any other kids in there, but it looks empty. Completely empty, no Mr. Flynn. OK—well, maybe he's rummaging in the store cupboard. I duck inside the studio, panting. If he's not here, I'll rest up for a minute if nothing else.

Nobody is home. I flop down at my table, dejected. Damn. Where could he be? Anywhere, potentially. Main House? On the mainland, for all I know. There's only one more place to safely search for him, and that's his quarters: a cottage on the southern tip of the island. A minute to catch my breath, and then I'll go.

I switch on my tablet and log on to Crypt. One skull on the map shows over the studios, me, Clouseau. No messages waiting for me. I'm about to log off when another skull appears hovering over the studios, right by mine. Vaughan! I tap my finger on it, to see the username.

Skulk

My chair makes a scraping sound as I jerk back in my seat. Skulk is here. Skulk is online, somewhere near me, right now.

Skulk's skull hovers ominously. I look around me, then grab my tablet and hit the floor, hiding under the table. How much do I wish the lights weren't on? Anyone looking in would have seen me in here, plain as day.

Skulk
Hello, Cate.

Damn! I move my finger over the log-off button, but I can't. Skulk knows I'm here already. If I log out, I'll be in the dark.

Skulk

Missed you.

I crawl over to one of the windows and peer outside. OK, think…this Wi-Fi signal originates from the newspaper office and covers the little area that makes up the art studio, photography studio, and the toilet block. He or she could be anywhere out there. Even skulking behind a frigging tree, for all I know.

Skulk

Aren't you going to say hi?

"No, you moron, I am not," I mutter as I crawl over to the other window and bob my head up quickly. Nothing out of that one either. No Skulk, no police chasing after me, no Mr. Flynn strolling down to his art studio, and no Vaughan to the rescue. Great. I crawl to the door and stand up, hand on doorknob. Before I open it, I glance down at the tablet again.

Skulk

Any final words?

I slump by the door, terror threatening to drill me to the spot. I press my back against the door and force air into my lungs, eyes scanning the room. There are some clay modeling knives sticking out of a pot on the counter. Get armed and get out of here. I scrabble to the counter, reach up, and snatch the longest, pointiest-looking one from the pot, the rest of them clattering to the ground.

Ping.

Skulk

I'm coming to get you.

No. No, you are not. I look at the door. Time to move. A third little red skull pops up alongside mine.

DeadMcTavish

Not if I get you first, Skulk.

Oh, jeez, Vaughan, thank you.

I open the door to the outside, my tablet under my arm, clutching my knife in my hand, head whipping from side to side. For the millionth time I curse the incessant screams of distant seabirds that make me jump out of my skin.

I press myself against the outside wall and glance at Crypt. Nobody is online. Everyone's suddenly logged off except me. Where did they go? I shut it down and get ready to run. As I do, I think I see a shadow move through the trees in the direction of the newspaper office. Every bone in my body is telling me to run in the opposite direction, but I can't. I can't leave Vaughan. If that's him, I have to see him, have to know he's there, he's safe. Against all my better judgment, I sneak down the path, sticking to the tree line as much as I can, and toward the Loathsome Toad office.

The door of the office is open, but the room is empty.

"Vaughan!" I whisper, looking around outside, gripping my knife. "Are you here?"

No one answers.

"Hey!" a voice shouts, and I jump out of my skin. "Cate?"

Back up the path toward the studios, Alex, Carl, and Cynthia are walking toward me. I meet them halfway.

"Are you OK, Cate?" Alex looks down at my knife. "Aren't you supposed to be in sick bay?"

"Yeah," I mutter. "Did you see anyone pass you up there?"

Carl shakes his head. "No. Why?"

I look at Alex. "What are you doing down here?"

He frowns at me. "Collecting some of Marcia's stuff from the office. What, you haven't been in touch with her? She says she's not coming back to school."

That hurts—the fact that she's gone for good, and the fact that she didn't tell me.

"Hey, were those policemen looking for you?" Cynthia says. "Up by Main House?"

"Yeah," I answer. "Probably. Do me a favor. If they ask, tell them you saw me running north, OK?"

The boys nod. Cynthia looks at me. "Where are you going?"

I start off up the path, past them. "To Mr. Flynn's cottage. To get his help. Before someone else gets hurt."

I don't bother looking back, and when I pass the studios, I disappear again into the woods and retrace my steps back toward the sick bay, only this time I keep on running past it, heading to Mr. Flynn's quarters, one of a cluster of staff cottages at the southeast tip of Skola. It's a trek on foot. The last few minutes I have to run across a field, out in the open, but I don't see anyone apart from a few sheep and the ever-present seabirds. When I reach Mr. Flynn's door, I bash on it with my fist.

No one comes. Oh, please be here! Please! I shove my modeling knife in my parka pocket hurriedly. Don't want him to think I've come to attack him.

I think I hear a thump from within, and so I bash the door again. "Mr. Flynn!"

The door opens a crack, and a disheveled head appears. The face frowns at me.

"Cate?" Mr. Flynn says. "What on earth—?"

"Let me in!" I push the door, and it swings open, and I hurry inside, making my way into the small sitting room on the left.

Ms. Lasillo is standing there. In an oversized, stripy dressing gown. A dressing gown presumably belonging to Mr. Flynn.

"Oh!" I gasp. "Oh!" I have literally never felt so embarrassed in all my life. My arms go sort of limp, my tablet falls, and the modeling knife tumbles its way out of my pocket and onto the floor in front of Ms. Lasillo, who makes a strangled yelp and jumps backward. "Oh God, oh God!" I say uselessly.

"Cate, now let's just be calm here." Mr. Flynn is coming toward me, hand outstretched. At least he's fully dressed. No socks, and he's sporting the messiest of bed heads, but at least he has on jeans and a T-shirt. "I'm sorry you walked in on this. It's really, very unfortunate." He's struggling for words, and at first

I think it's just because he's embarrassed, but then I realize…
he's scared. Of me.

"Call the police, James," Ms. Lasillo says quietly.

"What? No!" I shake my head. "I'm not here to do anything
bad. I'm here for help!"

"And we'll help you," Mr. Flynn says, nodding slowly. "But
I'm sure everyone is looking for you, and we should tell them
where you are."

"No! Please. Just hear me out…" I think for a couple seconds,
then roll my eyes. "OK, so I'm guessing that they're looking for
me because I said I had some information about the killer." I
grimace. "In retrospect, it might have sounded a little like I
was going to make some major confession, but I didn't mean it
that way. I just had to get rid of the stupid policeman who was
watching me in the sick bay."

"I see," Mr. Flynn says, nodding sympathetically. "And why
did you have to do that?"

"Because." I bend down slowly, to pick up the tablet, and Mr.
Flynn makes a dash for the knife, snatching it up from the floor.
"James, chill." I give him a look. "I am not going to stab you or
your girlfriend." I glance at Ms. Lasillo.

"Cate!" Mr. Flynn barks at me.

"Well, I'm not. Just crouching down, getting my tablet."
I wave it at him. "Anyway, to answer your question, I had to
escape the sick bay because I got a message from Vaughan."

Suddenly, they're listening.

"Explain," Mr. Flynn says.

"An instant message," I say. "And I came to you because I think I'm still in danger, and I was hoping that you can help us without instantly freaking out and calling the police on Vaughan."

Mr. Flynn nods. "Fair enough. Of course I'll help you, Cate." He puts the knife on a sideboard in some kind of show of trust. Well, out of my reach though, I note.

"And if it's anything to do with technology, I can help too," Ms. Lasillo says.

"Sure," I say evenly. "You can help me. Get your clothes on and make me a cup of tea."

"Cate!" Mr. Flynn roars.

"Sorry, I'm sorry. I couldn't resist. It's been a long day." I move to sit at the dining table, and they both follow slowly. I set up my tablet. "I took screenshots, because I knew no one would believe me. Vaughan is alive, and he's messaging me."

"What is this?" Mr. Flynn sits down beside me, looking at the screen.

"Crypt," says Ms. Lasillo, looking over my shoulder. "It is, isn't it? The social network connected to your assassin game? I've been looking for this for the last two days." She bends down to examine the screenshots more closely. It's slightly embarrassing, because of the whole "I love you" thing from Vaughan, but considering what I've just caught these two up to, I can live with them seeing my sappy messages. Ms. Lasillo frowns. "But the time stamp is from today. That's impossible."

I shake my head. "Yeah, that's the point. I can still log in. Let me show you."

Mr. Flynn gives me his Wi-Fi password, and I connect to the school intranet. I hover over the school crest, press the right buttons, and the prompt box comes up.

"Every player gave me their username and password, and none of them worked," Ms. Lasillo says. "We couldn't get any further than this."

"Vaughan left the door open for me." I type my password. Crypt springs up. I take them for a tour.

"This is incredible, the clever little toad." Ms. Lasillo shakes her head. "Excuse me!" she says, catching herself. "Totally inappropriate, especially given the fact Vaughan has, er, passed."

"Vaughan is a clever little toad, and guess what? He didn't croak," I say firmly. "I believe he blocked everyone from Crypt after he went missing, at least everyone apart from me, and another user called Skulk. Skulk has been making threats against me all through the Game." I rub my face. "Even twenty minutes ago. I was down at the art studio, looking for you"—I nod at Mr. Flynn—"and Skulk started messaging me, threatening me. At the last minute, Vaughan came online, and then they both disappeared."

"May I?" Ms. Lasillo gestures to the tablet.

"Kill it." I lean back and push it her way.

She gives me a look. "I'll be very careful."

I laugh. "No, k1ll1t is my password. All one word, lowercase, ones instead of *l*s. You'll need it. Crypt logs you out every sixty seconds if you're inactive."

Mr. Flynn puts his hand on my shoulder.

"Come into the kitchen. Let's have that cup of tea."

I nod and follow him. He fills a black kettle and flicks a switch on the side.

"Thing is, Cate." He gets three mugs out of the cupboard, and places a teabag in each. "The police seem very convinced of Vaughan's guilt. They discovered parts consistent with the construction of the spider robot in his study, hidden in the back of a piece of computer hardware, I believe."

"No!" I say. "We found those spider pieces together—after you stomped on it!"

"All right, you can certainly tell the police that." Flynn nods. "But you should know, Cate, there was also the poison; they found some kind of container in his study that had traces of belladonna in it."

"Belladonna?"

"'Beautiful woman,' quite literally." He adds sugar to his mug. "Heard of deadly nightshade? The plant?"

I nod. "But I thought it was made up, like a triffid."

Mr. Flynn puts sugar in Ms. Lasillo's mug; he obviously knows her well enough. He holds the sugar bowl up and looks at me. I shake my head. Hate that he never remembers that.

"Deadly nightshade is real and relatively common. Even grows here on the island. Every part of it is poisonous, apparently. A couple berries is enough to kill an adult. And they found some in Vaughan's room."

He waits until the water is boiled and pours it into each mug. "Milk?"

I nod and try to put poison out of my mind. The tea feels good—reassuringly hot in my hands and warming to drink.

"Vaughan wouldn't hurt anyone. Someone must have planted that evidence," I say. "The police told me he'd had some trouble at Cambridge, but there'll be a reason behind it, and it doesn't make him a killer."

"James!" Ms. Lasillo calls from the sitting room. "There's something here!"

Mr. Flynn puts his cup down and shoots me a look.

"Told you," I say, smiling. "He's out there."

CHAPTER 26

We go through to the living room. Ms. Lasillo is sitting in front of a laptop, my tablet beside her.

"I grabbed my machine from my bag," she says. "And now I'm inside the site I can unbutton a little of the code. Just a little—he's got it sewn up pretty tight. It's extremely early days, but I'd hazard a guess that Crypt has some kind of automatic system that drops messages when you log in."

I frown at her. "Meaning?"

"Sit down." She sighs. "Cate, my guess is that Vaughan planned all of this well in advance. I think that what you read as responses to your messages are actually things that he wrote some time ago." When I don't speak, she continues. "Vaughan isn't talking to you. Crypt is. He programmed it to respond to anything you say." She shakes her head, looking through lines of code on her laptop. "It's hard to specify at this point, but it's possible that he programmed Crypt to pick up certain key words in your messages and 'answer' you with prescripted responses." She scrolls through some of my screenshots on the tablet. "Most of these responses he's written are terribly vague. They would have to be, to make them fit a number of possible conversations."

I swallow. "When I was at the art studio, it wasn't just Vaughan who was online. Like I said, it was Skulk too. And Vaughan responded to Skulk. By name."

Ms. Lasillo purses her lips. "Cate, ever think that Skulk might be Vaughan?"

Mr. Flynn sits down beside me. "The police asked Sophia—er, I mean Ms. Lasillo—to go through a list of Guild members and try all of their passwords in the prompt box to see if anything would work. Most of the Guild members mentioned this whole Skulk business, and no one would come forward to admit to being Skulk. So perhaps Vaughan created Skulk to juice things up a little? To scare everyone. And now he's trying to carry that on—posthumously, I suppose, as crazy as it seems—to continue the deception."

I grip my fingers into my hands and say what I really never wanted to say out loud. "Daniel."

Mr. Flynn leans toward me. "What about him?"

"Daniel is Skulk. I think I've known it all along at the back of my mind, but I kept trying to deny it because he's supposed to be my friend. This morning I realized. I realized just how screwed up he is, and I ripped that big sticker he has on his precious violin case, the one with the red cat, and I realized for the first time that it's a fox, not a cat, and what's the—what do you call it again?—the collective noun, for a group of foxes?"

"A skulk," Ms. Lasillo says.

"Exactly." I slap the table. "It's him, I'm sure of it. The things he said...there were notes too. Creepy. And some other stuff." I look at Mr. Flynn. "I hate it, but it just makes sense."

"OK," Ms. Lasillo says. "Maybe you're right. Daniel was posting as Skulk. But it doesn't mean that's him posting now. This could still all be stuff that Vaughan has preprogrammed."

I rub my hands over my head and smooth down my hair. "All right. Let's try it, then."

"Huh?" Ms. Lasillo says.

"Let's talk to the ghost in the machine," I say. I look at the clock. "In a short while, I'm supposed to be meeting Vaughan at the caves. So let's send him a message about that. See what he says back."

Mr. Flynn nods. "OK. But, Cate, after that, I'm driving you back to the sick bay and we're letting the police know you're safe. We can't put it off forever."

"Fine." I move in front of Ms. Lasillo's laptop, and my fingers dangle over the keyboard. "Here goes." I type.

Clouseau

Vaughan, are you OK?

Come on, Vaughan. Come through. Show them you're real, not some computer program.

We wait. I refresh the screen after a minute to keep us logged in. And again, after another minute.

"Try something else," Mr. Flynn urges. I type again.

Clouseau

Vaughan, what happened with Skulk, at the studios?

We all sit there, watching. I refresh the page a few times, but nothing happens. I glance outside at the darkening skies, then look at the time in the corner of the screen.

Clouseau

Vee, I'm not going to make it to the cave by 6:00 p.m. And the police are looking for me. What shall I do?

I hold my breath.

And then, suddenly, a little red skull pops up on the map above the caves.

"There!" Ms. Lasillo cries, tapping on the screen lightly. I hardly dare move. Then it comes: the ping.

DeadMcTavish

Meet me at the causeway. Come now.

"You see?" I whisper, triumphant, turning to both of them. "It is him!"

Mr. Flynn shakes his head. "Not necessarily, Cate."

"It's vague. It's the program," Ms. Lasillo says.
I type some more.

Clouseau

They don't believe that you're alive, Vaughan. They think
that you're a machine, that you've programmed Crypt to
reply to me! How can I convince them?

We all wait. And then the ping comes.

DeadMcTavish

Come now.

My heart sinks. Ms. Lasillo holds her hands open as if to say,
I told you so. Mr. Flynn puts his hand on my arm.
"Sorry, Cate," he says.
Ping.

DeadMcTavish

Get Flynny to drive you in the car. And tell Ms. Lasillo that
if she gets her sticky fingers out of my code, when I've got
a second, I'll show her the back door in her intranet. Chop,
chop! Xxx

I laugh out loud. Long and hard. It's difficult to stop.
Mr. Flynn says, "Car's in the garage. I'll get the keys."
"We need to hurry!" I can't stop smiling.

Pacing up and down in the living room, I call to them again. Flynn is fetching his coat. Ms. Lasillo is upstairs getting dressed. Finally. Thank God. Don't want to think too much about that, because, you know, gross. But maybe she'll be a bit nicer to me now.

"The causeway." Mr. Flynn reappears and grabs a couple flashlights from a shelf. "Why on earth does he want to meet us there, do you know?" He opens a drawer and starts to rifle through things. "Tide timetable. Where is it?"

"On the intranet." I bring up the page on the Umfraville site. "Oh." I read down the list of times for early October. "Interesting. Tide comes in soon." I check the time. "Like, very soon."

"Of course it does," Mr. Flynn says. "Sophia, let's go!" He goes to the hall and shouts up the stairs, before turning to me again. "We'll get in the car. Come on." He leads the way out of the front door and around the cottage to the little alley that runs between the house and the garage. We enter the cramped garage by a side door. He opens the car and flings the flashlights into the backseat. "Get that, will you?" He gestures to the garage door, one of those big up-and-over types. I nod and move around the car as he starts the engine. I turn the handle on the middle of the garage door and try to lift it up. It won't budge.

"Stuck?" Mr. Flynn opens the car window and shouts over the engine noise.

I try it again, not wanting to seem completely hopeless, but it's like something is caught in the mechanism up on the roof.

Mr. Flynn swears. "It does this sometimes. Hang on." He cranks the window closed, gets out, the car still running, and starts to search around on the wall for something. "I keep a screwdriver handy to give the pulley a poke—can you see it anywhere?"

I shake my head, point to a crowbar. "This do it?"

"No, needs to be smaller. OK"—he smacks his forehead—"screwdriver's in the kitchen. Get in the car. I'll grab it and be right back."

I do as he asks, and he leaves the garage, shutting the side door behind him. The car's engine is running, keys in the ignition, and as I sit in the passenger seat, I toy with the idea of sliding over to the driver's side, flooring the pedal, breaking the door down, and driving to the causeway myself. But then I can wave bye-bye to any kind of support from Mr. Flynn. I look at my watch. How long since Vaughan messaged us? Ten minutes? Fifteen? That would be just enough time for him to get there if he ran all the way from the caves. I glance toward the side door leading to the house; Mr. Flynn and Ms. Lasillo are taking their time. I feel a surge of impatience. Come on! Time is a-wasting.

I check my tablet. No skulls, no messages. Another couple minutes go by. Right, I'm going to give them a shout.

When I open the car door, the fumes from the exhaust burn my throat on the first breath. Yuk. I skip quickly to the side door to the alleyway and turn the handle. It doesn't move. I give it a shove; did Mr. Flynn lock it for some reason? He doesn't want me skipping out on them? I feel a rush of panic, as the fumes from the car make me start to cough. Bloody stupid of him to leave the engine running. I pull my parka over my nose, give up on the door, and go back to the car, but to the driver's door this time. I'll just turn off the engine and hope this stuff dissipates quickly.

The driver's door is locked. I try it again, looking at it as if I'm doing something wrong. I cough, moving around to the passenger side, and then the two back doors, but the car will not let me back in. I feel the vomit begin to move in my stomach, sweep my arm across my face, trying somehow to shield the air that goes into my lungs. I stagger across to the garage door again, thump it, but it's not moving. I look around wildly—the crowbar! It feels heavy and unfamiliar in my hands, but I thrust it into the bottom of the garage door and lean on one side. A gap to the outside appears, big enough to get an arm through, big enough to put my face down there and gulp clean, cold air, but not big enough to squeeze through.

"Mr. Flynn!" I scream through the gap. "Help me!"

But he doesn't come. Why not? As I lie there trying to pry the gap open farther, a crazy thought pops into my head.

Maybe Mr. Flynn doesn't want me to make it out of here alive.

Could he be involved in all of this, somehow? Mr. Flynn, hanging around the cliffs at the dead of night during Vaughan's initiation. Mr. Flynn, first to the stage when Emily collapsed, right there on hand when Rick was poisoned. I don't want to believe it, but maybe he despises us, the privileged superkids, when he was denied his own chance to make his mark on the world?

Wooziness moves over me like a large hand clamped over my face. I suck in some more air, fighting it. Could it be Ms. Lasillo's the one? She's jealous of me, the attention I get from Flynny. She's clever; she could have easily made that robot. She was with us when Rick ate the cupcake. She could have poisoned it, intending it for me. She's as uptight and annoying as hell, but is she really a killer?

Maybe the two of them are in it together?

I breathe deep, trying to chase the fumes from my head. Whatever. It's up to me to help myself. I lie there, head wedging the garage door open, gulping air. This is not a sustainable situation. It's not an attractive prospect, to give up my fresh air and go back in, but it's the only way I'm going to free myself. I take, one, two, three gulps more, then wiggle back and let the door seal me in again. Grabbing the crowbar, I head for Mr. Flynn's car. He's not going to be very pleased. Funnily enough, I couldn't give a monkey's about that right now. Wielding the crowbar like a battering ram, I get angry and take it out on the driver's side window, hammering the sharp end of the crowbar into the glass. The first time I swing, the glass just frosts over into a thousand little sugary pieces, but the pane stays intact. I pull the crowbar back again and yell as I smash it again. This time the glass shatters and falls out of the window. My hand moves in to release the door lock, and I feel a swoon of fumes start to overtake my body again. It will not be enough to simply turn off the engine; I have to get out of here.

I launch myself into the driver's seat and grab the gear stick. I've never driven in my life, and unless I can figure this out now, I never will. I crank the stick to the number one, and there's a grinding sound—oh crap, clutch. My feet stomp around, first finding the accelerator, making the engine roar. I find the clutch and try the gear change again, and the car bunny-hops forward.

"Hand brake," I mutter, yanking the thing. It releases with a shudder. I press both pedals and the car makes an unholy screaming sound; this is a hell of a time to try and find the biting point. Oh holy greased lightning, please let me figure this out. I rev the engine again, easing off slowly, slowly, slowly…the wheels spin and the car leaps forward. I'm quick with stepping on the gas. No guts, no glory. Too late, I remember my seat belt. The front of the car smacks into the garage door and I jerk forward, my mouth smashing against the steering wheel. Despite the exploding pain and the taste of blood, I keep my foot down, and the car pushes the door, pushes, pushes…and stops.

But it's enough. Daylight—or what's left of it—is visible through the side of the door, enough for me to escape. On foot, but hey, I was never going to be able to drive this thing to the causeway. One hand carrying a flashlight and the other across my bloody mouth, I slide out of the car and stagger into the delicious cold air, my head spinning with carbon monoxide and the agony of smashed teeth. Once across the garden, I glance up at the cottage. What's going on in there? I'm not going to wait to find out. I don't know how that door got locked, but more fool me if it was Flynn or Lasillo who locked it.

As I set off across the field in the direction of the causeway, there's a high whine. Ducking behind a hedgerow, I see it: a police car, lights flashing, coming down the road. I haven't got much time. I run, keeping low and out of sight, and then I hit the woods, straighten up, and make a dash for it, leaping over undergrowth, swallowing blood and snot and tears and probably teeth too, but I don't care. I just have to get there. The woods give way to playing fields, and once I'm beyond the pavilion, there's nothing between me and the causeway except undulating dunes. Sometimes Mr. Churley makes us run up them, and it's ridiculously hard work, even on the days I'm not beaten-up and half-poisoned.

Reaching Vaughan is the strongest motivator. I can't see him yet, because the causeway is hidden by the rise of the dunes, but even if I had a clear view of the road, it's getting very dark, very quickly. This time the dark may be my friend; I cut across the dunes and risk the road.

Salt breezes blow my hair across my face. As my feet hit tarmac, I can hear the sea, somewhere out there in the darkness, and as my beam flashes into the gloom, it catches a large, yellow sign:

DANGER

DO NOT PROCEED WHEN WATER REACHES THE CAUSEWAY

I run up to the sign and lean on it, panting. Where is he?

There is a line of poles, maybe four, five yards high, on either side of the road, which itself is slightly raised out of the sand. When the tide is in, those poles disappear. The road across the seabed is a little over three miles long, and it dips in the middle because, you know, it's the seabed. There's a refuge—a tiny little shack on high stilts—about a third of the way across, for those crazy enough to attempt to cross when the waves are lapping at the roadside.

Which is what they are doing now.

"Oh, bloody hell, Vaughan!" I sigh, looking around at the dunes, and a small rocky outcrop along the waterline. There is nothing here, nowhere to hide, nowhere to skulk. "Where are you?"

It hurts to speak. I gingerly feel my broken lip and my front teeth for the first time. One is extremely wobbly, and I have a beard of crusty blood. I glance back up the road. I don't have much time before the police get here. I walk out onto the road. The tarmac is littered with sand and shingle deposited by the last tide. I can see a little way off along the causeway, and there is certainly no obvious place on the road that Vaughan could be hiding.

"Vaughan!" I risk the shout out across the causeway. I flash my light around—could he be in a boat?

Nothing. I click my flashlight off.

I've missed him. Or he was never here. He never made it down from the caves. Maybe the police caught him. Oh, no. I hunker down into a crouch. I'm so stupid. Mr. Flynn left me in the garage because he wanted to call the police, tell them Vaughan was online at the caves and would be making his way to the causeway. They've caught him, and they'll be coming after me next.

Or Skulk has him.

I have to go and look. Get to the caves. I straighten up, click my flashlight on again.

And then I see it. A flash out on the causeway. And another. And another. Someone is signaling with a flashlight, far out on the road, so far that the beam is just a little pinprick of light, dancing, feebly.

The light disappears.

I fumble my flashlight, suddenly heavy with importance in my hand. I wave it, then flick it on and off, on and off.

A pause. And then the dancing light flashes again, seemingly this time with more excitement, more urgency.

"Vaughan!" I shout, but it's way too far away for him to hear me and for him to answer me. Instead I flash my light back, and it takes me a moment to realize what I'm doing, but I'm running down the slippery causeway, away from the safety of dry land and out into the unknown. The light is still dancing ahead, pulling me to it. Myths of wreckers, evil souls luring boats to certain death on the rocks, jump into my head. Only this light is pulling me out to sea. The water is not over the road yet, but the farther I go, the more I risk being cut off. The tide turns suddenly here, and even in a car you can get stuck.

And it might not be him. Between the devil and the deep blue sea...

But still I keep running. Because otherwise, I'll never know.

I run and I run. The light is maybe a mile away, or at least it feels that way. I run on and on and it never gets closer. My face throbs with each thud of my feet on the road. The light disappears suddenly. I flash my light again as I run, shout some more, but there's nothing but the dull road ahead, the black sea on either side, threatening to spill over and consume me. Did I imagine the light? Did I imagine Vaughan? I stop suddenly, skidding to a halt, and look back the way I've come. Will I be stranded out here? I turn out to the causeway once more. My head spins, pain and light-headedness threatening to overtake me. Maybe I died back there in Mr. Flynn's garage, and all of this is my journey to the afterlife. Follow the light, follow the light...

It flashes again, and I cry out in relief, both at its reappearance and the fact that I'm almost there. I'm not sodding dead. I'm too achy and cold and miserable for that. I push myself on, running again, and as I get closer, I see exactly where the light is coming from. The refuge—the small hut, perched precariously high up on stilts. I can make out the shape of it now, painted white against the dark gray of the sky. The light is flicking on and off at the bottom of the stilts; that must be where he is. And as I run, I think I can see him, a shadow sheltered against the ladder that leads up to the hut. It makes me run faster, forgetting the flashlight, just pelting down that road as fast as I can, the cold salt air blurring my eyes with tears.

"Vaughan!"

Splash, splash, splash. There's suddenly water underfoot. The sea has started to swallow up the causeway. I don't care—he's there, he's sitting, the mop of curly hair shaking as he waves the flashlight. And he's shouting.

"...turn back!"

My lungs are burning, but I'm there. His face is crumpled, frightened—but his eyes shine and I fling myself at him, down there where he sits, throwing my arms around his neck and toppling over onto him.

"Oh God, Vaughan, they told me you were dead, you idiot!" I cry into his neck, hugging him, my hands moving over his back, his long, black wool coat, wet with salt water. "Are you OK? What are you doing here? Why are you sitting on the ground? Aren't you soaked?" I realize his arms are not reciprocating and back off. He holds his hands up in front of him; they're tied. I glance down and see his ankles are tied too.

"Did Skulk do this to you?" I crouch down, pulling at the plastic ties, but they are too tight and strong to undo. "Vaughan, it's Daniel isn't it?" I stand up. "I'm so sorry. I should have worked it out days ago. Did he hurt you? Where is he?"

Vaughan shakes his head. "What happened to you, Cate?"

"What?" I bend down and try to pull him to his feet. "Oh, the face? Little car accident, but no sweat, Dad can pay the dentist bills." I heave at him. "Can you get up?"

"Broken my ankle," he mutters. "So pathetic. Tried to climb the ladder, trussed up like this. Fell off."

"And your head?" I gasp, shining my flashlight at the matted blood at his hairline.

"I didn't think he was going to hit me," Vaughan groans, pulling himself up on the ladder, carefully.

"He hit you?" I help him to stand. "What with?"

"A plank? I dunno. It was kind of quick, so bloody quick I didn't see it coming," he groans. "So much for my plan to lure him out here and trap the sucker." He puts a hand on my arm. "But, Cate, it wasn't Daniel."

"What?" I search his eyes. "But he was sending me the messages. He was Skulk—the sticker on his violin case, the fox. He must have gone off the rails when he saw that we were, you know, together. Emily embarrassed him by posting the video, so he wanted to hurt her with that spider. I'm not sure he intended to actually kill anyone but probably just to lash out, humiliate!"

Vaughan lets me finish. "You're wonderful, Cate. But you're a rubbish detective. It wasn't Daniel that hit me over the head, and it wasn't Daniel who was Skulk, and it wasn't Daniel who tried to kill Emily and Rick." He looks behind me. "Oh no."

"What is it?" I twist around. There's a car moving toward us, down the causeway, spraying up the shallow water that is gathering on the road. It doesn't have its headlights on, and the front of it looks very strange, very beaten up. And very familiar. "Vaughan, it's Mr. Flynn. You know that car accident I mentioned?" I clutch at his arm. "I got locked in his garage, engine on, keys locked in the car. Nearly suffocated. Had to bash my way out. Thought I'd written off the car, but…apparently not."

"He's…here?" Vaughan sags against me.

"Is it Mr. Flynn?" I stare at Vaughan suddenly. "The killer?"

Vaughan blinks at me like he's going to faint as the car draws up to us. The one remaining headlight flicks on, dazzling. The door opens, and we watch as someone steps out.

"Hello, Alex," says Vaughan. His eyes roll back in his head, and he sways dangerously.

Alex stands there, in his Grand Master's cape, hood pulled up.

"Alex!" I feel a rush of relief run through me as I stagger, trying to support Vaughan's weight. I lose the battle and fall to my knees, the water soaking my legs, and Vaughan lolls on top of me. "Thank God you're here! Vaughan is tied up and he's injured. You've got to help us!"

Vaughan leans against me, his head flopping back. He's looking up at me, a strange expression on his face. "Alex."

"Yes, he's going to help us. It's going to be all right!" I reassure him.

"Cate." He looks at me, and suddenly we're eight again and he's breaking it to me gently that he dropped my Barbie doll down the gutter. "It's Alex."

I look up at Alex. We both look up at Alex. Alex moves an arm out from under his cloak; he's holding something.

"Hmm," Vaughan says. "And I was right. It was a plank."

Alex walks toward us slowly, through the shallow water, swinging the plank. A chill, more vicious than the freezing sea, moves through me. I stagger to my feet, pulling Vaughan up and half depositing him against the ladder, stepping between him and Alex.

Alex smiles at me. "Very sweet, Cate, very protective." He stops just in front of me. "But oh, nasty face you've got there. You could be ruined for life."

"What's going on, Alex?" I say, my eyes watering with the dazzle of the headlight.

"Come on, Cate." He takes a step toward me. "You know what's going on. Vaughan did an excellent job, luring you here. I think he wanted to use you as bait for me, but I turned it around a little and used him to bait you. That's the beauty of the Game." He holds one end of the plank and points it at me, dragging the other end down my body. I knock it away with my hand.

"Get off me!"

"Paging Dr. Freud," Vaughan mutters.

"You, quiet!" Alex points the plank at Vaughan.

"Oh, Alex," Vaughan says. "What an appropriate choice of weapon. You're such a plank."

"Alex." Fear drenches my body as I walk between the two of them again. "What are you doing? Is it you? Are you Skulk? Did you do those things?"

"God!" Vaughan groans at me. "Finally!"

"Cate, you're really into denial, aren't you?" Alex laughs nastily. "Denying what's right in front of your face. Denying you're anything other than *nouveau riche* trash. Denying what happened between us."

"Us?" I stare at him. "Is that what this is about?"

Alex sighs. "And I thought you were special, Cate. Special like me. But it turns out you're oh so very ordinary. Basic. Bland. Forgettable. And do you know what? Around here, that's the biggest crime of all."

I just stare at him for a moment, the undulating waves in my peripheral vision making me feel seasick. Am I hearing this? Is this real, or are the fumes I inhaled in Mr. Flynn's garage making me hallucinate? Alex is the one who hurt Emily. Alex is the one who nearly killed his best friend, and now he's come to get Vaughan and me? It makes no sense.

"Let me get this straight." My voice sounds slurred, even to me. "I didn't follow you around like a lovesick puppy after we got together," I splutter, "so now you want to kill me?"

"Nobody humiliates me that way, Cate." Alex juts his head forward and sways slightly from side to side, like a vulture eyeing a dead animal. "How dare you ignore me, reduce me to nothing." He spits. "No one says no to me, but you, you think you're so much better than me. And then you jump on sad old Daniel?" He throws his head back and swears. "You shamed yourself and me too. You're crazy!"

"Yep," Vaughan mutters. "She's absolutely the one who's crazy around here."

"Shut up!" Alex makes as if to swing the plank at Vaughan, then stops. He gathers himself, breathes, turns to me again. "Emily posted that video of you with Danny boy, twisting the knife in my side, so revolting I wanted to puke. Emily thought it was funny. Stupid girl; she actually came to me and apologized afterward. Thought that would be sufficient, but oh no. Not happening. Not during my Game." He shakes his head. "So Emily got the honor of being my first victim."

"That spider was something," Vaughan says. "Kudos to you—er, in spite of you being a sociopath, obviously—but there was some skill in making it." He narrows his eyes at Alex. "Oh. You didn't make it, did you? One of big brother's cast-offs. The genius engineer?" He shakes his head, tutting. "You even needed his help for that, didn't you?"

Alex ignores him, but he grips the plank tighter, and the veins in his neck are bulging.

"But you could have killed Emily," I say. "Just for posting some video?"

Alex shrugs. "I just set it up. What happens is not my fault. I don't Kill. I'm the facilitator, the Grand Master of the Game. And anyway, she didn't die. She just got punished."

"Like Rick?" I step up to him.

"Don't you dare say his name!" he yells, then forces himself to calm down again. "That was meant for you, and you know it. You were meant to eat the cake, suffer, puke your guts up. Or die, whatever. But you didn't even get that right. You just don't respect your Grand Master, do you, Cate? Don't know a good thing when it smacks you in the face." He lifts the plank and whomps it on to one of the legs of the hut three times. "In. The. Face."

"Put yer little stick away, Alex," Vaughan says. "It's embarrassing. Dead wood, just like you."

"No, you're the one who's dead!" Alex swings the plank over his head, aiming for Vaughan, who dodges, but the wood still catches his shoulder and he falls to the ground with a thud and a splash.

"Leave him alone!" I hurl myself at Alex, but he stands strong and pushes me aside with his free hand. I stumble, the rising water sloshing around my ankles.

"This is my Game!" Alex yells. "My Game is going to be the most talked about Game in all of Umfraville history, it's going to bury what came before! That's what it's all about, isn't it? Leaving your mark, making them remember you." He flourishes his cape. "No one tops my Game. I wrote this story, but you two, you helped me shape it, and you should be proud of that." He kicks out at Vaughan, who brings his feet up and shields the blow. "Vaughan? Misunderstood genius, gone off the rails." He winks at him. "I think the police must have found the belladonna powder in your room, Vaughan. Isn't it amazing what you can buy on the Internet these days?" He swings the plank out, pointing at me again. "And Cate? Crazy bitch. The two of you played Killer by your own rules. You made up a charming character called Skulk, you went on an attempted murder spree to take out your friends, and you almost pulled it off too, but luckily I managed to save the day and stop you. Do you see? I'm the hero in all of this. Oh yes—you both died, but it's collateral damage, and nothing that anyone will get too upset about once they know what you did."

"How?" I say. "Just how do we die, Alex?" I step up to him.

"You beat us to a bloodied pulp with that plank?" I shake my head. "Can't see you getting your hands that dirty. So please, share with us this amazing final scene you've written, because I don't remember you being able to write much more than your name. Unless you get Martin to do it for you."

His eyes flash with fury. "Oh, I'll share." He throws down the plank and drags me to the ladder. "Originally, Cate, it was going to be you tied and drowned by your boyfriend, Vaughan, who, filled with remorse at his brutality, climbs the ladder and makes the ultimate gesture of despair. Beautiful. But why don't we have a switcheroo?" He grabs me by the scruff of my neck and brings me up close. "Seems you like to do that, don't you?"

"Screw you."

"You had your chance." He spits at me.

I reach into my parka…and my hand pulls out nothing.

"Looking for this?" Alex holds up the modeling knife I'd dropped on the floor at Mr. Flynn's house. How did he get that? Flynny put it on the sideboard. Oh God, Alex must have been inside the house. He chuckles, flourishing the knife at me, and pushes me toward the ladder. "Now, up!"

"No!" I brace myself against the ladder, pushing back on him. Alex lets me go and leans down, holding the knife under Vaughan's chin. Vaughan is slumped, barely conscious, his eyes fluttering. "Want me to slice him up a little, for the fish?"

I scream, and Alex points with the knife, up at the ladder. Reluctantly, I start to climb, looking down at Vaughan.

"Don't worry, Cate," Alex says. "Your boyfriend isn't going anywhere. And I'll be right behind you."

"You better not touch him!" I yell down at him.

"Oh, I won't," Alex says. "I might catch something."

I reach the top of the ladder. There's a small platform with a rail around it, and the tiny shed-like refuge. I hurry into the hut, searching the inside for anything I can use as a weapon. There's little: a lifebelt tied to a rope, two life jackets, and a couple fusty-looking blankets on a bench.

"It's hopeless, Cate." Alex fills the doorway behind me, his singsong voice low and almost calm, his cape blowing in the breeze. "Hopeless. That's what you were thinking when you climbed up here." He walks over to the lifebelt and starts to unwind the rope. "You'd left Vaughan down in the rising water, trussed up, knowing the tide was coming in, knowing he couldn't swim, and it would just be a matter of time before the sea took him—for real this time." He chuckles and winks at me. "Third time unlucky, eh?" He unties the rope from the ring and sets the ring aside on the bench. "You wait until the tide is coming in, and Vaughan is flopping around, facedown, very sad. You stand—here"—he steps outside to the platform—"and watch his body jerk, his death throes, his last-ditch effort to survive. But it's futile." He walks outside and begins to tie one end of the rope to the railing that runs the length of the platform, then twists the other end and ties it into a loop. "Then, you see me—I've driven out as far as I dare, and the car is stuck in the water. I'm standing on the roof, and I'm shouting at you—'No, no, Cate! Don't do it!'" He giggles and walks toward me slowly, the loop of rope in his hands. I back into the hut again. "But I'm too late, and as usual, you won't listen to me. We know how stubborn you can be when you have your mind set." He follows me, dangling the loop in front of me: a noose. "And you have your mind set."

"No!" I push him away, dodge around him and out onto the platform, but as I break for the ladder he catches me easily around the waist and holds me in a horrible embrace as I thrash against him.

"Oh, Cate!" He laughs. "Give us a hug!"

"Get your hands off me!" I scream at him. I lift a leg and scrape the inside of my foot down his shin as hard as I can. He cries out in surprise, and as he releases me I take the heel of my hand and ram it up the underside of his chin, knocking his head back and making him stumble. Thanks for those boring self-defense lessons last term, Mr. Churley.

Something clatters onto the wooden floor. We both look down; Alex has dropped the modeling knife. We dive for it; I get there first, but the full weight of him falls on my head, making my ears ring. My hand is on the knife, but my arm is trapped under me, and I can't get it out. Alex pulls at me, grunting, and as I roll, I grab the knife and find my feet, and I'm backing away, brandishing my weapon in front of me.

Alex is on his feet too, panting, bent low, his arms holding out his cloak. He laughs.

"Thanks for putting your fingerprints all over that knife

again, Cate." He takes a step toward me. "I'd wiped it clean after using it on Ms. Lasillo. Now if they find it, they'll know it was you who jumped her."

I gasp.

He takes another step. "Oh, you should have seen her, Cate. I was hiding in the wardrobe, can you believe it?" He chuckles. "Always check the cupboard for monsters! She never saw what hit her."

I feel sick. "Is she dead?"

He beams at me. "I would think. Your dear Mr. Flynn certainly sounded like he thought so."

I step backward, steadying myself against the railing behind me. "You killed him too?"

For the first time, he seems a little crestfallen. "No. I didn't have time. Other places to be, you know?" He shakes his head. "Besides, I owed him one. He locked you in the garage, didn't he, with his dodgy motor? Priceless! Nearly finished you off for me."

Below, I can hear waves. That's not a good sign. Vaughan moans, and my eyes dart downward.

"Oh dear," Alex says. "The water is getting deeper." He grabs one of the life vests that has rolled out onto the platform and puts it on under his cloak. "I didn't want to have to make a swim for it, but I'm sure the police will be with us soon enough, thanks to Mr. Flynn." He picks up the noose again and smiles at me. "You'll excuse me if we get this over with, Cate?"

"You forget that I'm the one holding the knife!" I shout at him.

He laughs, shakes his head, whips off his cloak in a flourish, and holds it out in front of him, rushing at me with a roar. I dodge, holding the knife out to the side, trying to evade the cloak, but he is too quick for me, and he smothers it with the thick velvet, bundling it out of my hand and over the side of the platform. The momentum smashes him against the railing, and I spin around and try to push him over.

"Nah-ah-ah!" He ducks out of my way, waggling a finger in my face. "Don't you think I've seen that move a thousand times?" He laughs at me, reaches out a hand, and grabs my throat, pulling me in close. "You have a date, Cate." He puts the noose over my head, tightening it and holding my arms against me. I struggle, but he holds me fast, leaning in close and whispering in my ear. "Your last one. With death."

I turn my face to his, my mind racing. "It doesn't have to be this way, Alex." My cheek is against his, eyelashes gently fluttering against his skin. "Rewrite this. You save me, from Vaughan. It was all him, all along. I was the damsel in distress in the tower, and you came to my rescue. We wait until he drowns, we cut him free, push him out into the waves—they'll never know." I breathe into his ear. "Isn't that a better ending? That way you're really the hero." I laugh softly. "And bonus: this way, you don't have to get wet. We cuddle up together here until the police arrive."

He draws back from me, incredulous, chuckling. "I'm impressed. You really are the total package, Cate. Too bad I didn't realize that before the Game began. We could have worked together from the start." He leans in again. "Only one problem. I don't trust you."

"No." I see the movement from the corner of my eye. "No. You shouldn't."

Alex pulls back from me, crying out in pain, his hand moving down to his ankle, where the modeling knife has found a new home.

Vaughan lets go of the knife and hauls himself over the top of the ladder, his hands and feet free. "Push him!"

I don't need to be told. I hurl myself at Alex, who falls toward the gap in the railing where the ladder is and where Vaughan is trying to get out of his way. As I pick myself up, they tangle— Alex on top, Vaughan trying to shake him off. I aim a superhero kick at Alex's head, but even though I connect, his head snaps back, and he clings on still. It's enough for Vaughan to free an arm, and he swings a punch to the throat. Alex sits bolt upright, on top of him, a look of hurt surprise on his face.

"Go to hell!" I push him again, and this time he goes, falling backward down the ladder. But the fall is cut short. His legs get caught in the rungs, and he manages to throw out an arm and cling on.

I pull Vaughan back from the edge, and he hops up onto his good foot.

"Look!" he says, his eyes turned toward Skola. There on the island, lights are flashing. Headlights—two, three pairs. And a horn is beeping, cutting through the sound of the waves and the cry of the seabirds.

I go back to the edge of the platform and look down at Alex. He's still there, one arm hooked over a rung, the other reaching down to try and pull the knife out of his ankle. He frees the blade with a cry, but the knife slips through his finger and falls into the water below.

"Alex!" I shout at him. "They're coming!"

Alex looks in the direction I'm pointing. His face hardens, and then, unbelievably, he starts to pull himself back up the ladder toward us.

"What are you doing?" I shout. Vaughan appears at my side. Alex stops, threads his legs through the ladder, and sits there.

"I'm waiting this one out." He looks up at us. "Who are they going to believe? The nutso girl and the freaky new kid—with all that lovely evidence piled against them?—or me, golden boy?" He flashes his best smile. "Want to play?"

"Certainly." Vaughan kneels. "Because, Alex, if you should have learned anything about me, it's that I come prepared. Why did I go missing in the first place? Because I needed time to catch you. I've traced every keystroke Skulk made, back to you—your tablet, your laptop, the machines you logged into at school."

"You're full of it!" Alex snarls. "You told me you couldn't tell who any of the users were! If you had known, you would have told the police days ago!"

Vaughan shakes his head. "I needed time to access the code and lay a trap on Crypt. Why do you think I left the door open for Skulk?"

"So what?" Alex says. "Even if I was Skulk, that doesn't prove I Killed anyone, does it?"

Vaughan looks very serious. I feel my heart jump. "No," he says quietly. "It doesn't." He delves into his pocket. "But this does." He holds out Tesha's mini-cam. "Great little things, these. Waterproof, resilient." He shakes his head. "Good at recording stuff."

"Ha!" Alex snorts. "You expect me to believe—"

"This is my Game!" Alex is interrupted by his own voice, coming from the little camcorder. "My Game is going to be the most talked about Game in all of Umfraville history. It's going to bury what came before!"

"Alex?" Vaughan shrugs, turns it off. "You're Killed."

Alex shrieks at him, reaching up for the camera, but he's too far below. He looks toward Skola and the headlights, and then he makes his decision. He scrambles down the ladder, sploshing into the now waist-deep water, and wades toward Mr. Flynn's car, pulling at the door handle, but whether it's the water or the crappy locks again, it won't open. He reaches inside the smashed window, but nothing gives—instead, the alarm screams, and the headlight flashes on and off. Alex yells in frustration and, with a last glance at Skola, begins to wade down the causeway in the direction of the mainland.

We watch him, the orange of his life jacket visible for a minute or two, but eventually the darkness swallows him up, and he is gone.

"Bad decision," Vaughan says. "Two miles of water that way. Believe me, I thought about trying it."

The alarm on Mr. Flynn's car makes a funny, strangled, underwater noise, like it's drowning. Then it stops altogether. I lean against the refuge, Vaughan shuffles on his knees and flops down beside me, and together we look back to Skola. There's movement there, more lights. My guess is they're organizing a boat or two, probably phoning the coast guard. I wonder who they'll pick up first. I really hope we don't have to share a boat with Alex. That would just be awkward.

"Did you really trace Skulk to Alex?" I ask Vaughan. He laughs softly then sighs, leaning his head back on the wall of the hut.

"Nope. I've been sleeping in ditches for the last three nights. It's not exactly conducive to coding elaborate online traps. I only had time to hide Crypt from everyone but you and Skulk, so I could catch him online. Honestly? I wasn't totally sure it was Alex before he came out of the refuge and whacked me over the head."

"Really?" I sit up, shocked. "But you've got his confession on the mini cam," I say. "That was a genius move. You planned this, to record him like that?"

"Yeah," Vaughan says. "Good idea, don't you think?"

"The best," I say, leaning back again, shutting my eyes and breathing in the sea air.

"Thank you." He clears his throat. "Except the mini-cam shut off before he actually admitted anything."

"What?" I look at him. "How come?"

He looks sheepish. "I guess I couldn't figure out how the thing works."

CHAPTER 27

I pack up my art things and hand in my sketchbook to Mrs. Ellington. She's no eye candy like Flynny, but to be honest I'm very glad about that.

"Want to grab a coffee?" the girl with the blond-and-pink hair asks me. I shake my head.

"Can't today. Tomorrow, OK?"

She nods. "Totally. I'll text you later."

I pull on my coat and venture out, across the cracked tarmac of the playground, through the green iron gates, and onto the street. It's beginning to snow, but the flakes are feeble and dissolve as soon as they hit the damp London pavement. I check my phone.

4:15 p.m. Don't be late!

I grin as I pull my parka around my neck and hurry past the line of kids standing at the bus stop. I cross the street, threading through the rush-hour cars, and pass the tube station, where someone shoves a free newspaper into my hand. I take it without thinking, but then deposit it on a nearby bench. There will be something about him in there, and I don't want to read any more.

The movie theater is only a few bus stops up the road, but in spite of the weather, I choose to walk. The sense of freedom, the knowledge I could go anywhere—anywhere!—is the most powerful feeling I've known for a while. At first, it was almost too much. Now, all this walking heals, gives me time to think, to process what has happened, and that can only be a good thing.

That night on the causeway, Vaughan and I sat and waited to be rescued. We weren't in any hurry. When they finally picked us up, they took us to the mainland, to the hospital, under police guard, and tended our wounds, took our statements. My parents were there.

Ms. Lasillo was at the hospital too. I always knew she was tough. Mr. Flynn phoned the police and that's why they were so tardy in coming after me, because they had their hands full saving her, taking her to the mainland in the school speedboat. And happily, she made it.

Flynny came to visit me in the hospital one day after visiting her. He was full of apologies—for locking me in the garage to stop me from going without him, and for leaving the car running, and for being too busy saving Ms. Lasillo's life to come and save mine. I told him he didn't need to worry. I'd done a pretty good job of saving my own life.

I haven't seen him since. He sent my artwork on to my new school. Mrs. Ellington said there was a nice note.

Umfraville is closed. Ezra lost ninety percent of his pupils when it got out that there'd been a wannabe serial killer among the pupils. I'm interested to know who the other ten percent were.

And Alex? They picked him up, half-dead and floating, a couple miles out to sea. He'd tried to swim for it, but the tides had other ideas and started to carry him over to Ireland. I followed the news about him for a while, but I don't want to know anymore. There will be a trial. Until then, I'll shut him out.

After the recuperating, the police interviews, the dodging of the press—I had the weirdest Christmas ever, my family pretending everything was normal. And if there was any drama to be discussed, my parents managed to make it all about them. Apparently there's some terrible tax thing with Skola. They're moving to Spain and selling the island—to the RSPB, I think? The birds will be so noisily pleased. And now I'm living with my dad's cousin, two streets away from our old house in South London, and going to school at the comprehensive I would have gone to if the money had never happened. Some of the kids here are nice, and the rest judge me only by the brands I'm wearing and the bands I like, which I can live with. I even kind of like it.

I haven't heard much from any of my Umfraville friends, and for now, that's fine. I can't stop thinking of them as their usernames, and yes—we worked them all out in the end. Daniel was Nimrod, who posted about three messages in total. I should have guessed, just from that, but also because of "Nimrod." We googled it; it's a famous violin piece and slang for someone who's socially awkward.

Daniel sent me a letter just before Christmas. How old-school of him. It was long, apologetic, and from America. His parents also wrote to me and apologized. They told me they are trying to get him into Juilliard, and in the meantime, he's seeing a therapist. Which is good, I suppose.

I saw Marcia in London once. She was going back to Spain—not far from where my parents have landed, actually. I might visit sometime. I emailed her, but I haven't heard anything back yet. She must be feeling weird. We'll see.

Apparently Emily totally recovered from her spider attack; she's enjoying a long recuperation in Barbados, which is nice. And Rick? We shouldn't have been surprised; that boy is made from thick bricks and steel girders. He was in a coma for two weeks, I read in the paper...and then one day, he woke up. He's doing OK now. Not the muscleman he once was, but maybe that's no bad thing. At least he has his whole life ahead of him.

This snow is getting thicker now. The movie theater is a little farther up the road, the bright lights welcoming through the hurrying flakes. Someone's waiting for me in the doorway, holding popcorn.

"Get a move on, I told you!" he shouts at me.

"Vaughan, you didn't have to stand out in the cold, you dork." I stomp up the steps, smiling at him anyway. "And if you're working here, can't you start the film late?"

He gives me a look. "As ever, you overestimate my modest powers. Here." He shoves the popcorn at me. "It's getting cold."

We hurry inside. Vaughan takes me through the little foyer, nodding to the bloke collecting tickets, before leading me down the corridor and in through the heavy auditorium door. "Pick a seat. I'll be there in a few minutes."

He leaps up the stairs, and I follow slower. A trailer reel is playing; there are only a dozen people scattered throughout the auditorium. Hmm, where to sit? Is it really obvious if I pick the back row?

I settle for the second-from-last row. Behind me, in the projection box, I see his shadow moving. He says he likes it here. Zero future—projectionists are a dying breed—but fun for now. Not computers.

A few minutes later, the main feature begins. It's old, from the sixties? The titles start, and on the screen there's a little girl being presented with a big, pink diamond pendant necklace. What is this film? Then the animation starts, and that music with the tinkling triangle, and of course I immediately know. The title flashes up:

THE PINK PANTHER

I laugh. Inspector Clouseau. Very droll, Vaughan.

He jumps into the empty seat from behind me. "Good choice?"

I don't say anything but hog the popcorn and smile at the screen. Yeah, we're taking it slow. Vaughan doesn't know this yet, but we are.

The film is funny—old and a bit corny in places and a bit dull in others, with some crazy hairstyles. But it's nice to be here, with him, laughing, eating popcorn, just hanging out. A little while into it, he whispers in my ear.

"Got to go and change the reel. I'll be back in a sec."

I nod, and he climbs over the back of his seat, heading to the projection room. My mouth is all dry with that yucky coating of popcorn grease. I wish he'd got a drink too—no, wait, I've got my water bottle in my bag. I put the rest of the popcorn on the arm of the chair and bend down to get my bag, but as I do I knock the stupid carton off the chair, and popcorn is flung everywhere.

"Jeez!" I hiss, picking up the empty box. I hope Vaughan isn't going to be cross; he probably has to clear up all of this crap at the end of the movie. I set the box down and start shoveling popcorn, and as I deposit it back in the box, I spot something already in there. I hold the box up, scraping the popcorn away, but it's too dark to see properly. I empty the box on the floor again, my heart beating. Is that writing? I find my phone, and use the light to read what's on the inside:

WATCHING YOU

My heart jumps into my throat and I spring up from my seat, clinging to my bag, hunting for my keys to grip like knives in my hand, running to the end of the aisle, down the stairs and toward the door, the tears blinding me, half-stumbling, half-falling, toward the outside.

"Cate!" Vaughan is suddenly there, his hand on my shoulder. "What's wrong?"

"Get off me!" I burst through the door into the light.

"What is it?" He follows me as I run down the corridor, my hand feeling in my bag again for my phone, ready to dial. "Stop!" He grabs my shoulder.

"Let go!" I scream.

"You need to calm down," he says. "What is it? Tell me."

"The popcorn box," I stammer. "A message from him. *Watching you.* He's here, Vaughan. We have to call the police!"

Vaughan's face pales. "Oh no, I'm so sorry."

"What?" I say, looking around. "We need to go!"

"No!" He takes my hand. "I'm sorry, I didn't think—look." He drags me to a poster on the wall. "This."

I look up, the words and images dancing before me. Black, a pair of bloodshot eyes, long eyelashes. A streak of red behind them. And the title, of a movie, above them:

WATCHING YOU

"It's a new movie, and the popcorn box is a promotion." He runs to the concessions counter, leans over, and grabs an empty box. "Look, it's got it written in all of them."

I take the box. The same words, at the bottom, on the inside. I put a hand out and steady myself on the wall. "I thought..."

"I know," Vaughan says. "It's not him. He's locked up, Cate."

I look into his calm green eyes. "We never asked Alex if he sent those notes to me, did we? We thought it was Skulk who was writing them, but we never found out for sure..."

"Come on." Vaughan puts his arm around me. "Let's go back in, see the rest of the movie."

I nod, and he holds my hand and takes me back through the doors. Some of the people look up at us as we walk up the steps, back to our seats. I count them as we go. Eleven, and Vaughan and I make thirteen. Thirteen players, one Grand Master...

I sit down in the darkness with him, and the movie rolls on. His hand snakes into mine, and I grip it tightly, my breathing steady now, my heartbeat slowing.

This time, nobody runs away, and nobody gets left behind.

ACKNOWLEDGMENTS

I'm so happy to have a home at Sourcebooks Fire! Huge gratitude goes out to Aubrey Poole, Elizabeth Boyer, and all the team—I couldn't be more excited. Thanks as ever to all those who watch my back and kick my butt in the UK: Veronique Baxter, Laura West, Imogen Cooper, Barry Cunningham, and Laura Myers. And of course, how would I have done it without John Mawer, Didi McKay, the JP moms, and finally the Gripers (especially Sonia Miller for keeping me in fries and frappés)? Thank you so much to my readers; you're the best. No seriously, you are. You are.

ABOUT THE AUTHOR

Kirsty is a former actress and has written children's plays for commercial theatre. In 2008, she won SCBWI's competition to find new writers. She was born in the UK, but now lives in Boston, Massachusetts, with her husband and daughter.